by

Sibyl Dana Reynolds

Chandelles Press

While some of the locations and names included in *Ink and Honey* refer to actual places and persons, this is a work of fiction and the product of the author's imagination. All the characters, places, events, and names are used fictitiously. Any resemblance to actual persons, living or dead, events, or locales, is entirely coincidental.

Chandelles Press

ISBN: 0988349000
ISBN: 13:9780988349001

For Don
With love and gratitude for your generous heart and for our journey of a lifetime.

Contents

The Sisters of Belle Cœur

Beatrice, the cook and soothie
Cibylle, the waif
Comtesse, the needle worker
Gertrude, the carpenter
Goscelin, the scribe
Grace, the child
Helvide, the herbalist
Imene, the midwife
Mabille, the chanteuse
Marie, the helpmate
Petronilla, the prophetess
Ravenissa, healer for God's creatures
Sabine, the counselor

There are among us women whom we have no idea what to call, ordinary women or nuns, because they live neither in the world nor out of it.

—Franciscan Friar Gilbert of Tournai, thirteenth century

Prologue

4 May 1259
Le Monastère de la Visite

The Inquisitors are coming for us! No time for escape. We have loved and served God with our whole hearts. Our obedience has always been to our Creator, not to men who deem themselves holy. Their torture cannot pummel away our truth. Let them burn us...but let our accusers be warned. We will not be silenced forever! We will live again through our stories and relics, which must be hidden lest they too be burned. Know us! We were the sisters of Belle Cœur. Use our wisdom!

Book I
The Scribe

10 October 1258
Le Monastère de la Visite

I touch my quill to the parchment and search my thoughts for the starting place, for the way to tell the story. With dear Henriette, my faceless cloth companion, tucked safely in my apron pocket, I close my eyes to enter the honey hive of my heart. It is there where the sweetest memory is stored, the tender time when our sisterhood was born.

In the golden wheat fields of the French countryside near the town of Vézelay, home of Magdalene's cathedral, there is a simple frame house. Nailed to the weathered wall beside the door is a chased plaque of iron. At the center of the plaque is an equidistant cross within a rusted circle. Beneath, painted in blue, are the words "Belle Cœur."

The Belle Cœur cross is vivid to me still. It's as vivid and real as the parchment and ink upon the table where I now work. The long journey that brought me to this moment, to this page, with my blackened fingers and a river of prayers flowing through my soul, is as mysterious as the pathway that has brought this book into your hands.

I am Goscelin, the scribe. On these pages I will record the stories of our community, the sisters of Belle Cœur, and my observations of the formidable events that befell us. I begin my arduous task tonight as the first cold winds of autumn rattle the shutters, lending a shimmer to the candle flames and an airy chorus to the scratching of my quill.

Perhaps the change of weather is a blessing from God. Surely the chill in my bones keeps me from sleep so I might scribe what I am called to record for our manuscript, the stories of our way of life. From the vessel of remembrance will I draw forth the telling of our little community's round of days, our secret naming of things, our sacred tasks and burning prayers, and the call from God that drew us into the world.

We, sisters of Belle Cœur, once lived near the great church of Mary Magdalene. Dwelling under the protection of her spirit, we marked the hours with our prayers. Worship was woven into each day, the way the basket weaver turns the willow branch to create a strong and purposeful vessel.

In time, at our most shining hour, our community grew to include twelve women. We held our lives and practices close to ourselves, but our calling was to serve the people of Vézelay, the small village near Belle Cœur. In our infirmary, we tended all manner of brokenness and injury that afflicted those who lived nearby. We also cared for pilgrims on their journey and crusaders returning home, splintered in body and spirit. It was a life precious to us, meaningful and dear. In the most golden moments, we lived in harmony, joyfully greeting each day with grateful hearts and ready hands.

And then God called us. Rumor and suspicion of our ways forced our leave of beloved Belle Cœur, our home and sanctuary, to travel far, to seek safe haven elsewhere.

We arrived here at Le Monastère de la Visite, near the town of Chartres on the broad limestone plains surrounded by a thick forest. The sisters from the monastery offered us shelter in exchange for our assistance with their many tasks, and so we were able to continue to serve God's people in little ways.

Now once again we dwell in the light of a great cathedral. Though it was nearly destroyed by fire many years ago, Nôtre Dame de Chartres is being rebuilt to honor Our Lady and her holy relic, her veil, the

Sancta Camisia. A morning's walk from our quarters takes us there.

I warm my hands at the candle flame while I work late into the night in this small room with its gray stone walls. Nearby my sisters take their rest between the hours of communal prayer. Seated here on a wooden stool before the worn table with its slanted surface, I make my notations on stolen bits of parchment.

A raven feather quill is my instrument, my memory the wellspring for my words, and for inspiration… for inspiration the fire of Petronilla's prophecy. From Petronilla, the visionary of our sisterhood, came the luminous words that even now echo in my soul.

"You must write, Goscelin. Though an untold time of silence and darkness may pass, our story will be for the women to come. May they take heart from our love for them!

"Record this message in your manuscript so one distant day it may be discovered for those who will need our wisdom. Tell them this…

"*You are invited to make a sacred pilgrimage of remembrance. Our spirits arrive through these stories bearing flint and wood to kindle your creative fires. Sharing our stories unshackles us from our bondage as those who have been silenced and forgotten. We are longing to reach you, to know you, to teach you, and to guide you to remember your own true nature. We have been calling to you in your dreams.*"

Petronilla's deep blue eyes were wild with passion and pooled with tears. Her pale skin covered her tall, bony frame like a shroud. "Word for word, Goscelin.

You must write what I tell you. The ones who will find this book some future day will need our wisdom."

I dipped my pen into the ink and prayed to fulfill the task as my sister wished. Petronilla paced about the room muttering softly before she continued.

"Record these instructions for the ones who will come long after we have gone:

"*You must find the cathedral, the sanctuary, and the oratory hidden within you. We will meet you there, in spirit. We implore you to gather a circle of kin for shared study of this sacred manuscript. Read between the lines, and meditate upon the symbols offered here. Look for the allegories to reveal the hidden knowledge within these pages. Use what you discover as you would a map to help you find the way to your destination. You will learn through our stories how our sisterhood chose to live in beauty, with holy passion for God, how we transfigured our world in the time of the sword. The lessons for the art and craft of sacred living are offered here.*"

And then, after a long pause, Petronilla leaned close to me and whispered, "Dearest Goscelin, it is your charge to convey how we hold our sisters and brothers yet to come in our prayers. They will continue our legacy. Share with them our promise that our spirits will guide them as they search for the lost key to Eden. It will be their task to reclaim the Garden."

Petronilla's instructions weighed heavily. My prayer lives in me…a constant companion.

Beloved Jesus, guide my quill to complete the task I have been given. I long to do Your will. Amen.

Tonight I begin from the only place I know, the beginning of my story of how I came to be the scribe of Belle Cœur.

By the grace of God, Belle Cœur became my home. A home shared with my spiritual sisters, my chosen family. The family of my birth and beginnings were of a darker note and somber rhythm.

Before leaving the place where I was born and finding my way to Belle Cœur I lost the innocence of my girlhood to my father when the devil entered him through too much drink. To refuse him as a child was impossible. He was wickedly clever as he invented little games for us to play. Games to distract me while he did unspeakable things.

My child's heart felt sorry for poor Papa, and I wanted to please him, so I did as he asked. Although it felt terribly wrong no matter what he told me to the contrary. When my bosom began to grow and childhood was past, his games ceased, though he would often creep about to steal a look at my naked body when I was washing or dressing.

Miraculously, throughout his violations, my soul was protected. In those moments of horror, through God's grace, my spirit slipped from my body, the way the yolk slides free of the broken eggshell into the hand. In that place somewhere between heaven and earth, the golden living presence of love surrounded me.

I have always longed to touch God. Every time I attended Mass and heard the Kyrie chanted by the brothers in our village church, I felt I was in my true home. The smoky incense filled my nostrils. My eyes took in the sight of the orange blue flames of flickering candles while my ears tingled with the whispers of the villagers offering their prayers. Yet even the ringing of the sweet bells that called us to our knees could not surpass the moment the priest held the Host above the altar for all to see. In that instant I saw the face of Jesus, and my young spirit was stamped forever as belonging to Him and Him alone.

When I was small, Maman's prayer life was constant. Perhaps I fell in love with God because of my mother's fervent prayers while I was growing in her womb. When I grew older and my father's dreadful behavior silenced her in countless ways, I took her place as the one of our household who prayed. Longing filled my spirit to know God more deeply and to serve Jesus and His mother as I served my dear Maman.

Oh, but God was not only in that church! When I wasn't helping Maman bake the bread, or when at last my hands were still from household tasks, I fled to the out-of-doors. Free in the sunlight, with the wind that caught my breath away, I would stoop and collect into my apron the empty hummingbird's nest, a snail's shell, and every kind of feather on the path, blue, black, and speckled brown. These treasures of God's creation were gifts to me.

At day's end I carefully arranged my offerings on the little wooden bench beside my bed. I imagined I could become very small and climb atop the curled brown leaf so it would carry me to heaven on the wind.

The lacy, empty cocoon reminded me that one day I would become like the butterfly. On that glorious day, I would spread my wings wide and fly away into a new life, far from home, to a place that would better fit who I had become.

I imagined the small, round, gray stone that rested perfectly in the hollow of my hand to be a gift kissed by God, just for me. I hold that very stone tightly as I scribe these words with longing for God's merciful touch.

In my girlhood years, I prayed for a brother or a sister for companionship, but God, knowing best, sent me a friend, Comtesse. We delighted in one another's company. Comtesse's mother had taught her to use needle and wool to stitch flowers and chains of color on linen while I received Maman's wisdom for baking bread.

In spring Comtesse and I went to the meadow where we wove crowns from daisies and clover. Carefully we tied the stems, flower to flower, offering a prayer to the Blessed Mother with the twist of each pithy knot. When our creations were complete, we stood beneath the winding branches of the oak tree on the highest hill near Benuit stream. There we crowned one another as ladies-in-waiting to the Queen of Heaven and promised to be sisters forever, dancing 'round and 'round until our spinning dropped us to our knees on the soft, green earth.

We vowed to be sisters, but to the eye, we certainly didn't ressemble one another. Comtesse was petite and plump. My legs have always been quite long, giving me a lean appearance. I was taller than my friend though she was nearly two years older. Her curly, copper colored, hair fell to her waist. My long flaxen hair was straight and fine. Maman braided it in one long braid every morning. Both of us shared fair skin, though mine appeared speckled with little brown spots every summer. Comtesse's complexion was creamy and pure. Maman once told me, before a lasting deep silence fell upon her and robbed her of her voice, "*When you were born, dear Goscelin, the sight of your bright blue eyes, full pouty lips, and rosy cheeks made my mothering heart cry out with joy.*"

When I was ten I imagined I would one day go to the nunnery, to take the veil. My father forbade it. He said one as "comely" as his daughter, would never be right for the habit of a nun. He was a man who had cast aside his faith in exchange for drinking and whoring. I longed for a sacred life, far away from his ominous presence and my mother's pitiful silence, a life without danger or the threat of the devil's sickness that turned faces black and stole the future from so many in the neighboring valley. I sought peace and stillness and most of all a safe place. I imagined a life of prayer with others who felt the same as I.

To my horror, in my fourteenth year it was arranged by Papa that I was to marry. I was to become wife and property of a man some twenty years older. Monsieur Gerard was a widower in need of cooking, cleaning, and favors of the flesh. He would pay Papa handsomely to bed me and make me his servant and mother to his three rowdy boys.

Fear overpowered me. There was no love between us, and there was certainly no desire in me to service him and bring more of his babies into the world.

My heart belonged to God, and it was true I wanted to be a nun; but Bennot, the village baker's son, caused me to question my desire for cloistered life. We had never talked of love because we'd never spoken to one another. I was afraid to let him know of my affections. There was a certain quality of kindness in his eyes and crooked smile. My breath caught in my throat whenever I saw him pass by on the road or at Mass. I knew if ever I were to marry, my husband could not be a dreadful, old man.

I held tight to the foolish hope Bennot would choose me as the one who could love him best. Then he would surely claim me. But soon I learned a young girl's fantasy rarely becomes real. My lovely dream faded and became a nightmare.

It was agreed for certain between my father and Monsieur Gerard that I would be passed to him before summer's end. I wailed and went to the woods where no one could hear me scream aloud to Jesus.

Save me! Don't let him take me! I'm afraid! Don't let it be so!

Maman, caught in the web of her pitiful existence, grew ever more mute. There was no comfort from her empty, silent presence. I turned to my only true friend, who recently had sadly become more a nuisance than a companion.

At fourteen, Comtesse and I were no longer children. The little girl who was my playmate had now grown to challenge my every thought with her wild ideas. I became annoyed by her insistent ways, yet I envied her daring and wished to be brave like her. With the summer, wanderlust descended upon my one, true friend like a strange fever. We had always shared a certain easy, quiet way together before a sudden change of nature and newly discovered bravery led her on her way.

"Come with me, Goscelin!" She spun 'round in circles as she spoke, and her long, red hair fell down her lean, tall torso. It flowed on the breeze like the flag of an unknown country. "We will be Christ's heart and hands in the world. I heard my mother's friend, Madame Vergene, talk of a place called Belle Cœur where she received healing from the sisters who live and work there. It's a house and infirmary near Magdalene's cathedral, in the countryside not far from Vézelay. Madame Vergene calls it a sanctuary. I'm going to Belle Cœur, Goscelin. Come with me. We could leave tomorrow if you call up your courage."

Comtesse's deep green eyes flashed sparks of amber as if a raging fire were burning somewhere within her. "Belle Cœur is special. The prayerful women who live there have made a special place, a home they share together…"

"I can't go, Comtesse. Papa would surely find me. That would be the end of my little life before it's barely begun." Gall, the taste of my fear, rose in my gullet and burned like fire. I swallowed hard and felt the spew settle deep in my belly.

"So stay! You can become Madame Frog, because you will certainly have to marry that old frog of a man, Monsieur Gerard. Truly, he looks like a great toad with his bulging eyes and belly. What will your life become if you remain a cowardly mouse of a girl and stay?"

"God has a plan for me. He won't betray me. I'll wait for a sign."

"Yes, but perhaps you must make some effort to find the sign. To just sit and wait…that's what any simple sort would do. You're not simple-minded. Be daring, Goscelin! Please come with me. We'll share the adventure! "

But I did not. Emptiness chilled my body in those days after Comtesse went away. The prospect of marrying Monsieur Gerard loomed over me like a storm cloud. I searched my heart for courage and found it to be empty as my purse. My prayers flowed like a river all the day long, a young girl's petition to know her calling as clearly as Comtesse did. I longed to be uprooted by God, to be planted in a holy place far from my empty world. Guidance and answered prayer arrived as I slept.

On the night before Monsieur Gerard was coming to claim me, I clutched Henriette tight under my pillow and cried until my tears ran dry. No hope remained that Bennot would suddenly appear to rescue me and make me his wife. Exhausted, I fell into a deep sleep and was visited by a dream.

Comtesse sweeps the dust from the front doorway of a small house. She wears a white veil on her head, and there are several faceless women around her. They busy themselves in a garden. The sun is bright, and as I walk toward the house, my eye catches hold of a plaque hanging next to the door: a rusted cross enclosed by a blue painted circle at the center. In my dream a bright golden light shines around the circle's rim.

Comtesse turns about, already smiling in recognition. She waves and calls to me, "Welcome, Sister!"

The morning after when I awakened from my deep sleep, it felt as though someone other than myself guided my every move and calmly ordered my thoughts. Everything around me appeared sharp and clear.

A strange, unfamiliar peace came upon me when I took my father's hunting knife from its sheath. Carefully I scratched the circle and cross symbols from my dream onto a stone from the hearth in our kitchen. I dropped the stone into my apron pocket to offer certain protection for my journey. I was caught in the current of an unfamiliar river that was sweeping me toward my new life.

Maman's small green glass vessel she used sometimes for storing lavender seeds caught my eye. It was empty. I wrapped it in a scrap of cloth and put it in my satchel.

Henriette waited patiently on my pillow, tattered and stained from holding too many secrets. She was patched and shabby, the way a thing that is cherished becomes worn from long affection, or ragged from carrying too many fallen tears and lost hopes.

Maman had stuffed her small soft body with wool from our ewe. Henriette wore no smile. She had no eyes, ears, nose, or hair, but she always appeared beautiful to me. She was no bigger than my hand and was my best comforter.

"Where are we going, Goscelin? What will become of us?" I heard her whisper while I tucked her into my apron pocket with the stone in preparation for our great adventure.

"This is not a time for answers!" I startled myself with my firm reply.

I tore a piece of warm bread from the day's loaf and took two carrots from the basket near the door. I wrapped these in cloth and put them into the satchel. The thought sparked in my head that the bread might be the last food that I would ever taste made by my mother's hands. My courage began to waver like the loose wheel on our old wagon. Sweat ran down my back and under my arm while a strong, musky smell came from down below.

I wonder even now if the inspiration that found me in the following moment came from God or the devil. I went to the hearth and pulled away the stone where I had seen my father hide his small leather pouch. It held nine coins. I took three. My face burned hot. I put them into my shoe. He owed me at least as much. I became a thief for the first time in my life and surprised myself with my wickedness and such sweet irony. Papa was paying for my freedom.

Forgive my sinfulness. Don't let him catch me. Amen

Outside, Maman was heating water in an iron pot over the fire, preparing to wash the clothes. Frail and weary, she stood over the steaming water in the hot summer sun, like a faded lily, parched and thirsty. I contemplated what would become of her.

If only she had come with me. If only she, too, had run away!

Finally she stirred the lye into the water. Her body was without spirit and barren as her life.

Tears fall onto the parchment as I scribe these words. My memories of that time are alive tonight, an unwelcomed presence. They flood my heart and quill with their melancholy.

I kissed Maman quickly on her damp cheek, fearing I would begin to cry, thus giving away my plan for my escape. My lie caught in my throat before courage made me speak.

"I'm going to the meadow to gather flowers for my hair before Monsieur Gerard arrives, Maman."

She continued stirring the pot without a word.

At that moment smoke from the fire began to encircle us. Like a devil's rope, it began to coil around us, as though to bind me to my mother as her protector, her keeper, her fellow prisoner.

Maman never looked up, nor did she speak a word to me. For an instant I nearly fell into the devil's grasp. I ached to steal her away, but in my heart I knew she would not come. And if she had known I was leaving—oh, she would never have let me go!

Something within her had died long ago, and its rotting corpse had spoiled what remained of her passionate spirit. Even her song was gone. She used to sing so sweetly. He had suffocated her life's song with his abominable appetite and betrayals.

In the deepest part of her being, my mother knew my father's treachery. His power over her was merciless. It was as if she'd been given a strange potion that put her to sleep. She appeared to walk among the living but as one who had already died.

A fierce, hot wind suddenly blew from the south to tear the smoking devil's rope in two. I turned quickly away from the only place and life I had ever known.

"*Adieu, Maman. Je t'aime. Veuillez me pardoner,*" I whispered—while I ran toward the open meadow.

My tears were hot, and again searing gall made its way up my throat. I could not contain the nasty gush this time. I was sick beside the gatepost. This was how I left my home and all that was familiar.

My vision was clouded through the river of tears that coursed hot and salty to my lips. I ran to the meadow without looking back. The cicadas' song grew louder and louder in the heat of the early morning sun. My thirst was terrible.

I was at last on my way, and my earlier courage began to wane in the face of my fears of becoming lost, even though I knew the way to Vézelay. I kept repeating out loud to myself over and over again, "Welcome, Sister," just as I had heard Comtesse in my dream.

For hours I walked to the side of the narrow road where the tall summer grasses and weeds hid me. Finally, as the sun was descending from its highest place in the sky, I stopped to cool myself in the shade. Lying on my belly on the damp bank, I cupped my hands to drink from a tiny stream. I reached into the satchel for Henriette. The touch of her delivered a familiar comfort.

My legs began to ache while I walked alongside the road, hidden by tall, prickly broom. I heard a sound. It came closer. Faster it came. Horse and wagon!

I lay down and stretched my whole body flat into the dry earth, nestling deep into the brambly shrubs. My breath caught near my heart, and sweat streamed between my breasts like butter melting on warm bread. My trembling body became one with the weeds.

Just as the wagon rumbled past, I peered up to see Monsieur Gerard atop the wagon whistling a merry tune! The dust settled, and I waited for a long time, too terrified to move. The sun coursed through the sky until it was just above the hills; the cicadas were silent. Lying still, I pondered how surely Papa and the old frog would come looking for me—but thankfully it was going to be dark soon. They would not begin their search until morning.

I had left my home and escaped being caught. I prayed I would find Belle Cœur, or surely I would be cursed to wander forever, far away from Maman and even farther from God. I began to hum my own merry tune as if to fool my mind away from fear, but I hummed softly lest someone out of sight hear me. I knew two things: I had escaped, and I had to find Belle Cœur—but I had not planned how!

The sun was about to kiss the hills, though the air was still hot and my cheeks burned. With my next breath, I was filled with a new appreciation for my freedom, and before I realized what I had done, I stepped out of the weeds onto the dusty road. I became my best companion as I whispered to myself, *Think, Goscelin, think! Where will you rest tonight?* In the moment of that utterance, memory, or perhaps an angel, delivered a blessed gift.

Saint Catherine's Abbey! Yes! I recalled it would be just over the approaching rise. It was a place I had visited once with Maman when I was small. We had walked to the abbey on this very road, a day's walk. I could be there soon.

When Papa was away for three days one autumn, Maman had made her plan for our pilgrimage to

Saint Catherine's, the bravest thing she ever did. She wished to see the paintings of the Blessed Mother and the infant Jesus in the abbey church.

I remembered so clearly how after our steep climb to the crest of the rise, we looked down on the broad road winding toward us from the east. It appeared to my young eyes as a stream of living flesh: men, women, and children. Old, young, and many sick people carried on litters poured toward the abbey the way ants form a procession to feast on fallen crumbs.

"Who are they, Maman?" I asked as a flock of geese flew overhead. Their honking cries seemed to call to us: "*Allez! Allez*! Hurry on!"

"They are pilgrims, my love," Maman replied, hugging me close. "Journeyers seeking God in the holy places. Traveling far to see the paintings and to touch the relics of a saint. We will share a meal in sweet company tonight. Pilgrims are welcomed at the abbey. Today, we too are pilgrims, Goscelin, my girl."

Maman had never looked more beautiful. Her body was strong, and I felt safe and loved as she wrapped her arms around me. Where had that strong, capable woman gone?

Our two-day journey was our special secret. It was the only journey from our home that we would take together.

Stinging tears surprised my eyes while the recollection of that happy time squeezed my heart. I dried my sunburned cheeks with my apron, reaching into my pocket to touch my stone and Henriette for assurance. It was not the time for tears. I knew I must be quick and certain as I made my way. As I scribe this story I see it all so clearly, as if I am suddenly there once again.

I climb up and over a gently sloping hillside just as the sun drops behind the hills, leaving a glow on the Abbey of Saint Catherine. It appears like a holy city on the landscape. I remember this well. The path down the other side of the hill is worn, and once again at the place where it merges with the eastern road, there is a solemn band of pilgrims singing their prayers. Now I am very hungry and thirsty and just as dusty as the pilgrims. I run down the hill to join the end of their procession. I follow them past two monks in brown robes collecting a large basket from the vegetable garden. Together with the band of weary, dirty pilgrims, I pass through the iron gate to safe haven.

Thank you, God, for this sanctuary. Angels, stay near me. Amen

I feel as if I've a entered a small city, for such is Saint Catherine's. Forgotten memories of my time in this place with Maman return like a flock of birds to roost in my heart. Through arched stone passageways, I glimpse many wooden buildings. Smooth columns support the arches, and birds of all kinds flutter noisily high above in the rafters. Their droppings make a thick, gray carpet on the ground. The monks who live here come out to take charge of the throng of pilgrims. The sick are escorted to the infirmary, and the rest of us are directed to a large, open room where other pilgrims and monks have gathered.

Three of the brothers lead us through a garden and down a long corridor to the refectory, an enormous room with stone walls. There are many long, wooden tables with benches on either side. It is cool and refreshing here despite the crowds of sweaty pilgrims. I sit between an elderly man with one arm and a woman with a large belly full of child. Neither one speaks my language. We eat in silence. Other tongues all around me confuse my ears.

After supper, a small portion of hot soup, a cup of goat's milk, and a piece of bread, one of the monks silently leads us to the sanctuary for prayers. The first night of my new life, I sleep with the other women journeyers on the cool stone floor of a granary near the church. My satchel is my pillow. Henriette is safe in my apron pocket with my stone for company.

I close my eyes, and soon a dream begins. In the dream, I'm standing among a circle of women. We are watching a fire burn in the middle of an unknown town. Many of the women around me are crying. One holds a long pole with a cross toward the raging inferno. The flames leap high like a great, hungry beast about to devour its prey. There are screams... and faces... women's faces... within the fire.

21 October 1258
Le Monastère de la Visite

Petronilla's charge to write our stories is ever present, and I'm grateful to be finished with the daily tasks in the monastery infirmary, to return to telling my story of how I learned to read and write. Writing our stories at day's end, or often in the middle of the night, assures me I won't forget my learned craft, the sacred art of scribing.

My hem is damp and heavy with mud. The cold rain poured from dawn to dusk today. Comtesse asked to join me tonight while I add this entry to our manuscript. She sits on a stool near the lamplight, mending Ravenissa's cape, and she's promised to be still.

Yet, I'm doubtful silence will be my companion with Comtesse so near. Even now she is mumbling softly to herself as her needle goes in and out of the soft, gray wool. I dare not enter into her strange conversation. To do so would surely unleash a story centered on Comtesse herself as an endless tale that would go on and on until dawn.

For now, I will spill out my recall of that fretful time when I first arrived as a pilgrim at the Abbey of Saint Catherine on my journey to find Belle Cœur.

Guilt burdened my heart for leaving Maman behind, yet an eager anticipation for my future kept me alert to the sights and sounds that surrounded me at the beginning of my great adventure. I was awakened with the other pilgrims in the night and again at dawn by the sound of the abbey bells. The monks of Saint Catherine's chanted their prayers for Vigils in the depth of the darkness and again when they sang Lauds as praise to God in early morning. Their singing caught my heart, and I began to weep at the thought of Maman's anguish when she realized I had gone. Papa must surely have been enraged by my disappearance.

I rose quietly in the small outbuilding where the women pilgrims had been told to sleep, and found my way on aching, tender feet to a path, a place in the meadow near the sanctuary to relieve myself. Squatting in the weeds, steam rose from the damp earth as the warm golden water poured from between my legs.

When I stood to straighten my skirts, I caught sight of a tall, narrow stone tower standing alone in the meadow. Facing me was a narrow door...open, mysterious, and beckoning. No one was in sight, save a baby rabbit nibbling clover near the faint pathway worn through the summer grasses. I crossed the threshold to discover a small stairway curving round and upward like the inside of a snail's shell.

Suddenly, as if a trusted friend had taken hold of my hand, I felt invited to explore this strange, new world. I began to climb the stairs, step by careful step, pausing every now and then to take in the beauty of the countryside visible through tiny, open spaces as I coiled my way upward. Dizziness overcame me in a sudden rush, and I fell back against the cold stone wall to catch my bearings.

When I reached the last step I saw another door ajar before me. Once again the invisible hand tugged me forward. In an instant I was peering into a room, into another world, the likes of which I could never have imagined.

Jars of colored powders were arranged on a long, wooden table like so many jewels scattered by a queen in a fit of playfulness. The room exhaled strange smells, pungent as pepper, musty as mushrooms on the forest floor accompanied by woodnotes of something ancient.

However magical the sights and smells were, it was the mysterious sound that drew me to the room. It was a square room warmly lit by tall candles the color of milk, standing like guardians on wooden blocks. The amber light of early morning poured in through the small windows near the ceiling, casting shadows on the dark wood floor.

The sound, a curious, rhythmic scratching, was faint, yet somehow profoundly important. It captivated me, like a haunting tune played on a foreign instrument.

Fear, my nagging companion, was swallowed in a great gulp by my desire to learn the source of the music. Tiptoeing through the doorway, I was startled by the unexpected presence of a monk. He was bent over a slanted table, his humped back rounded like a stone under his brown cloak. The sound seemed to be coming from him.

My curiosity and the invisible hand that led me up the spiral stairs pulled me further. Fear returned, scorching my gullet with gall while the voice in my head screamed in desperation.

Run, foolish girl! You don't belong here!

Yet, my feet carried me closer and closer still to the source of the music until I was standing just behind the monk. I was guided by something much more powerful than my mind.

Baskets of rolled material stood in neat, straight rows on the floor near his sandaled feet. I tried to remember what this was called. Then it came to me… parchment!

To my left was a long and narrow wooden table covered with more parchments. These were painted with pictures of strange, colorful birds in flight and what appeared to be delicate flowers, vines, and other designs. I longed to see them more closely. Rows of shelves wrapped around three sides of the room. Shelf above shelf was filled with books rising from the wood floor to a blackened ceiling where cobwebs glistened in the light of the new day.

I had only seen one book in my lifetime. It belonged to a fine lady in our town, so small it fit into her gloved hand. Comtesse, being fearless, had asked her about it while we stood together outside the church one winter's morning.

Madame Plumette was dressed in fur and brown velvet. Her husband was a miller and important in the village. Madame had a friendly smile, and she spoke softly as she opened the book for us to see.

"This book holds prayers and stories about the Mother of God. See, my dears, here, written and painted on the parchment pages, is the story of Our Lady when she was told by the angel that she would give birth to Jesus."

There before our eyes was a tiny painting of Jesus's mother wearing a blue gown. She was looking at an angel with golden wings. Delicately colored crimson roses had been painted around her. I remember that the sight of such beauty had set my mind to longing to have my own book full of wondrous pictures and symbols holding knowledge and wisdom.

Now I was in a room full of books. Some were fat and small, others tall and narrow. Cupboards with iron grate doors lined one wall. Each cupboard was full of books. There were open shelves on another wall, also filled with books of varying sizes. The smell was intoxicating. If prayers hold a fragrance, that was what I was breathing in.

All within me longed for the brief chance to open just one book to see if God's face was painted there. My belly suddenly churned from hunger, or perhaps it was signaling a warning. I grabbed hold of my skirt to keep my eager fingers from reaching out to touch the parchments afire with living colors and edged in shimmering gold.

Pounding began in my head in tune with the wild thumping of my heart, as my whole being took in the nature of the hidden room. Colors I could not name filled my eyes and rekindled the longing I had felt since my first glimpse of the lady's Book of Hours.

Pictures thronged my imagining. They scurried forth like playful children rushing out of doors on a warm summer's day. Golden crosses and snowy-winged angels, a blazing sun and flowering trees, spirals and circles, all these things tumbled and played upon my mind like a dream.

I peered around the old man to catch sight of the instrument he had mastered so well.

Suddenly the delicate music stopped.

The giddiness of a moment before disappeared, I knew I should have fled, but my feet were heavy as stones. What had possessed me to trespass into such a sacred chamber? Surely I would pay for my transgression!

The monk slowly turned 'round on his stool. The top of his head was bald and shiny like the dome of a cathedral. A half halo of curly, gray hair rounded his skull from ear to ear. Gray eyes squinted up at me. Stale, putrid breath steamed through his broken, brown teeth.

Silence fell upon the room like a great cat paw. My ears roared with my terror, my breathing turned to panting, and I feared I might wet myself.

The monk grasped the tabletop and pushed himself up slowly. With his humped back, he was a turtle emerging from its shell. His crooked finger did not point with accusation, but instead beckoned!

"Come closer."

Terrified, I didn't move. "Forgive me, Brother," I croaked. "I heard music..." I was about to run for the door, certain the old man would not be able to catch me.

"Music? What music? Speak up, girl." His voice gurgled as though something were caught in his throat.

"Yes. Well, a kind of music like a scratching sound, sometimes fast, then slow…and the smells of this place and the colors…" I backed carefully toward the door and my escape.

"So you think I was making music." His laugh unleashed the smell of his horrible breath, tainting the same air that had been so intoxicating moments before.

"Brother, I have never heard the likes of such a sound."

The monk's laughter ceased, and he fell silent. Had I offended him? A particular heaviness came upon the room—the way the summer fog creeps into the woods and wraps itself around rock and tree. The old man's eyes opened wider. One eye was clear gray and bright, the other very clouded. He took hold of my chin in his hands and pulled my face close to his as if to stare into my soul. Only then did I feel hot tears flowing down my cheeks. They washed away what little power I was trying desperately to claim.

"I'm sorry, for trespassing." I sobbed. "Please may I go now? I only meant…"

He pressed a gnarled, stained finger against my lips. "Shhh. Don't you want to hear the—music, as you call it?" he whispered.

Then in a moment that is written on my memory, the monk took hold of my hand and motioned toward his stool, inviting me to sit. My insides tumbled and rolled, and my head felt light as dandelion fluff caught by the wind. Wetness dripped from under my arms. Never had I been in a place that stirred my body and spirit into such delight and trepidation all at once.

The monk pulled a long, slender, brown feather from a small crockery vessel on the table.

"Show me the hand you use for eating."

I offered him my trembling hand. With the gentleness of a woman, he pressed the feather between my thumb and two fingers; then he guided my hand, dipping the point of the feather into a small pot of black liquid. Together we tapped it once against the edge.

"Quill into ink will make you think!" His laugh became a rumbling cough from deep inside while brown spittle ran down the corner of his dry, cracked lips to the sparse, gray stubble of beard.

His spotted hand led mine until the point of the feather descended onto the creamy parchment. He whispered into my ear as he leaned over my shoulder, "Put your soul into your hand, my child. It will guide the quill."

I didn't understand his curious directions. Shaking his head, he curled his bony fingers over mine.

"Very well. *Quel est vôtre nom?*"

"Goscelin."

"Gah-sel-inn? Not Gah-se-leen" He asked.

"My father wanted a son. He chose my name." My face grew hot.

"Very well, Goscelin."

The sound of my own name caught my mind and turned it inside out. He began to gently move my hand. Black marks flowed out of the pointed end of the feather onto the parchment. It was the first time I had ever seen my name in writing.

G O S C E L I N

One by one the marks formed upon the parchment. They shimmered like stars appearing in the sky when dusk turns toward night.

"Your name is your first assignment, daughter. You will copy what I have written until this parchment is full with your name. Then I will teach you how to rule the page and how to begin to scribe."

Assignment? He would teach me? Daughter? What was he saying? I couldn't grasp his words and their intention—rather, I was captured in the midst of the miracle of what was happening before my eyes.

He slowly removed his hand from mine. I examined the mark.

"G, this is the first letter of your name."

I could feel him smiling. My lessons had begun.

I dipped the quill into the ink. Oh, I cannot find language to describe the first moment when I made marks upon the parchment! The scratching sound came from the quill. It was the instrument that played the music that became the song of my life.

I looked into my teacher's face. Surely he was the angel I had been fervently praying for.

"May I know your name?"

"I'm Brother Paul. Is this the music you speak of?" He pointed to the quill.

"Yes! Oh, yes! It's music to me. It's the most beautiful sound I've ever heard."

"Then you must play, my pretty girl. Make music that is pleasing to God."

I *would* learn to play my music for God. For our Creator had surely led me that blessed morning to Brother Paul.

In time I discovered he was the Armarius of the abbey's scriptorium. He provided over one hundred scribes with their materials and oversaw the copying of the texts.

"But, Brother, I am not privy to such knowledge. Girls are not allowed..."

"Are you not a child of God?" Little hoods of flesh fell over his eyes as he bent toward me. He was the oldest man I had ever seen.

"Yes...I believe so. Maman once told me this."

"We must trust that our good Creator has called you here for a purpose. Clearly the saints and angels led you to find my secret library. No one but a very few know of my hidden room. I can see how your body and spirit are in tune with the nature of the craft, in the same way the hummingbird knows the most succulent flowers.

"Perhaps you're the..." He paused and stared ever deeper into my eyes. "I would be denying God if I were not to teach you these things. One should never deny what God delivers...what seemingly falls from the sky, or what comes through the door as an unexpected guest. Our beloved Jesus offered healing to those in need on the Sabbath. If He could break the rules of His day, why not I?"

His words held certainty and caring. I could scarcely believe this turn in my journey. To this day I am certain Brother Paul was an angel sent by God to usher me into the world of words and wisdom.

Brother Paul knew my heart. He understood without asking that I was a pilgrim journeying into the unknown. Like all pilgrims, I had left home carrying very little, fasting, praying, and seeking the mystery of the journey to grow my soul, to claim a new way of being. With his gentle presence rather than words, he invited me to stay and become his student.

Thus began my apprenticeship.

The old monk's place of study became my new home. During the early morning hours, before Brother Paul went to the scriptorium, he brought me bread and milk and my daily assignment. On feast days he often shared a portion of *ragoût de legumes* made with carrots and turnips from the monks' garden.

Each month, late at night guided by the pale light of the waning moon, when the abbey was still, I went to the horses' water trough near the meadow to bathe. When the weather was too cold for outdoor bathing, Brother Paul brought a bowl of water for my washing up. On feast days he brought me the Sacraments after the Mass, offering prayers to nourish my soul...and my soul was filled.

I worked long hours, not because Brother Paul commanded me, but because I was consumed with the desire to scribe the letters perfectly, as my teacher did. I practiced night and day. As I bent, paying homage to the parchment hour after hour, I thought neither of the past nor what was to come, but rather I entered into a luminous stillness, save for the scratching music that I now played on my own. I had learned to call these feelings purpose and passion for learning my craft. I longed to become worthy to be called a scribe.

Brother Paul patiently taught me the sound of each letter, how they all connected together to form words, and then that the words fell into order to create language. Slowly at first, and then with increasing ease, I learned to read.

The abilities of reading and writing were gifts more precious than gold. The careful, slow savoring of the Psalms as I copied each sacred word to the parchment revealed unexplored terrain in my heart and spirit. The landscape of my memory was a blessed, wild, and uncharted field. My ability to remember the greater portion of what I wrote each day created a kind of inner manuscript in my mind where I captured what I was studying.

At night before sleep, I played a game with myself. Doing my best to retrieve word for word what I had scribed during the day, I lay on my palette recalling, then reciting a portion of the day's Psalm. This practice imbued my nightly prayers with meaning.

In you, I take refuge, let me never be put to shame. In your justice deliver me; incline your ear to me; make haste to rescue me! Be my rock of refuge, a stronghold to save me. You are my rock and my fortress; for your name's sake lead and guide me. Free me from the net they have set for me, for you are my refuge. Into your hands I commend my spirit…

The comfort and solace of reciting the day's Psalm each night became a stronghold I relied upon. My dreams—how they became alive with images of angels and acorns, honeybees and crosses!

Again, I dreamed of Comtesse. Her arms opened wide as she welcomed me to Belle Cœur. When I awoke after this vision of my spiritual sister and the sight of the house with the blue sign, my longing to find my way there was renewed. However, I knew God wanted me to learn from Brother Paul so I would know the holy Scriptures and the Psalms. It seemed I was being prepared to serve in ways that would later be revealed to me.

Outside the tall stone tower, the seasons fell one upon another. Scorching summer became radiant autumn that soon gave way to barren winter. All the while, Brother Paul provided for my needs. When the weather turned cold, he gave me monk's clothing for warmth: a brown woolen robe, a linen apron with a large front pocket at the waist, thick black stockings, and leather boots stuffed with wool to make them fit. The garments were heavy and too large. The monk's robe held a smoky, musky scent like our church at home.

Like the sacred texts on Brother Paul's shelves, I too was hidden. I was sheltered and absorbed in how my hands forged beauty.The old monk had grown to be my protector, my teacher, and the loving father I had never known. Life outside the tower moved along according to God's rhythm of the traverse of sun, then wheeling arcs of moon and stars. From the edge of the tower windows, I could glimpse the pilgrims coming and going. When the breeze blew from the north, it carried the faint sound of the monks chanting their prayers in the sanctuary to the west.

Our tower with its secret room was across the meadow from the monastery buildings that housed the large scriptorium. My eyes would never gaze on the wonders of that place where some hundred or more scribes sat at their tables, copying Scripture and Psalms onto parchment. For it was dangerous enough that I was in residence in a place full of men. Brother Paul was at risk himself.

"We must be careful, Goscelin," he had told me. "You should be safe here in my private study, as long as you are cautious when you go out of doors. This is my domain. As the armarius of the monastery's scriptorium, I oversee everything that happens there. I am also the guardian of this library, and only I am apprised to come and go from here. No one is allowed to visit this room without my prior permission." His smile as he told me this held a hint of holy mischief.

He was guardian of many secrets, it seemed. There were special texts he kept locked away, but without doubt I was his greatest secret.

"If you were discovered, surely the Church authorities would bring both of us before the inquisitors. Harboring a young woman and filling her with sacred wisdom would no doubt mean the stake for me, and you, dear Goscelin—I dread to think of what might happen to you."

Brother Paul spoke his warning frequently, lest I become careless when emptying my chamber pot in the early morning or while taking comfort from a bath in the pond near the meadow in moonlight.

My body and soul melded into the room. My hair and even my tongue collected the dust from the pigments. Ink-black stained my fingers from month upon month of practicing the fascinating forms of letters and mysterious sigils. Over time I grew even thinner than when I'd first arrived at the abbey, while my breasts grew larger.

Each month when the moon was full, I let my long braid fall loose and free. I suffered fits of crying and my belly swelled. During my monthly curse my fingers were clumsy and my scribing became awkward and messy. Pains grabbed my belly, and my back ached, distracting me from my studies. I bled down below for several days. Maman had done this as well. When I was but twelve years and my bleeding began, she had told me it was the fate of all women, and she taught me how to care for such a time.

Clever Maman took linen and rubbed herbs into it, then tore the cloth into fine strips. She rolled the fragrant concoction until it was the size of her finger. Next she coated the slender roll with goose grease and wound thread about it, leaving a length of thread at one end.

The first time I bled she taught me how to gently push this *l'eponge* into my winny and tie the thread about my upper leg. Later that same day I untied the thread and pulled it out. It was soaked with blood. I thought I would faint. I dreaded the onset of my monthly bleeding each time the moon began to grow.

At Saint Catherine's there were no herbs and no women to turn to for counsel or comfort for my monthly needs. I could only make do with small pads of linen, folded scraps found tucked away in a large basket in the cupboard. It was a task to keep clean from the stench of those days. I dug a place in the weeds near the pond, where I buried the bloody evidence of my womanhood. Caution always accompanied me lest I should be discovered.

In the late afternoon each day, save the Sabbath, Brother Paul went to the scriptorium and then the monks' quarters until the next morning. However, he always brought a slice of bread and pungent goat's cheese, milk, and sometimes a portion of soup after Vespers before he locked me in his secret place of study. There I stayed with only Henriette and the manuscripts for company.

Henriette's body became blackened like my fingers from my touch. Maman's green glass vessel rested on a small corner table near my bed, a straw-filled pallet on the lower shelf of a large, deep cupboard where I slept beneath a shelf of alchemical texts.

Brother Paul called me his protégée. He taught me to read and scribe; he directed me in the grinding of the pigments…lapis lazuli, ochre, and the most precious, gold. I learned how to space the text, and he instructed me in the many ways to give life and form to the words by adding colorful borders and patterns.

Because of my eagerness, I became a student of all subjects concerning the creation of illuminated manuscripts. Together we cut the parchment, crafted by the parchmenter from the fine skin of goat and sheep with the sharp, curved novacula and a regula, the fine, brass straightedge. Then we folded the cut parchments inside one another. Much later, after the parchments had been scribed and the illuminations were complete, the leaves were carefully folded into gatherings called quires, then stitched together and bound in leather hide.

I learned the strange names for books pertaining to the wisdom gathered in the sacred room. Antiphonarium, Kalendarium, and Ordinale…these volumes were filled with prayers, the order of Feast Days and the seasons, and the rules of the Church. The Antiphonarium was the largest book being scribed. When completed, it was to be used in the sanctuary by the monks as they sang their prayers.

The palate of my mind was awakened to new tastes, and hungrily I feasted on knowledge.

More, however, than teaching the required skill the crafting of the manuscripts, Brother Paul was my guide. He led me to discover how to read and form words, pictures, and patterns to express what was longing for voice within my soul. Soon seraphim and cherubim, crimson-colored roses in full bloom, coiled, speckled serpents, and all manner of fruit trees found their way onto the pages. I was lost in a world of holy wonder.

"These are the symbols used by our Hebrew brothers and sisters; these are from the Greek," Brother Paul instructed as he spread open text upon sacred text for me to study. Each symbol, letter, or illumination inspired questions, and my teacher encouraged me through our discussions to discover my own answers.

One afternoon in my first month of schooling, the old monk had brought Brother Jean, the illuminator and Brother Paul's trusted friend, to meet me. I had been startled by the visit.

The giant man who was capable of creating colorful designs and picture stories and all manner of glorious illuminations on parchment appeared hideous to me. He was certainly the most imperfect human being I had ever seen. His dark eyes were tiny and too close to his crooked nose, which was flattened wide upon his face like a great piece of pressed dough.

The silent monk was so tall he had to bend down to enter the room. His hands were square and thick, and he smelled of urine. Worst of all was his mouth. Large, wet lips protruded like two fat fish from his long, thin face. I wondered how God could have created such a pathetic creature. Where was the Creator's mercy the day he fashioned Brother Jean in his mother's womb?

When we first met, Brother Paul pulled the monster's sleeve to bring him closer to me. I stepped away toward the corner.

"You and I know the danger of your being discovered, Goscelin. Brother Jean is the only monk I trust with the knowledge of your presence. The seasons have turned, and with God's help no one has seen you. We must continue to be diligent, lest you be found. Such a find would surely mean torture and death for us both."

Brother Jean had been listening attentively to everything Brother Paul was saying. He nodded in agreement. His tonsured head was spotted with little crusted sores.

"I admire your work, Brother Jean." I swallowed the gall in my throat. My hands trembled in my apron pocket, where I fumbled for Henriette. She had gone into hiding. I continued haltingly, "Your scribing and illuminations are an inspiration to me. I'm grateful, for I've studied your parchments and learned much from you." The words flew out of my throat like birds set free from a cage. I dared not take my eyes away from his. He frightened me.

Brother Paul nodded to Brother Jean then pointed to the parchments I had copied. Brother Jean continued to stare at me in silence.

He held his gaze while he wiped away drool from his lips with the back of his hairy hand. I looked at

Brother Paul for assurance I was safe in the presence of the strange creature, his friend.

Finally Brother Jean noticed my puzzled expression. To my horror, he opened his mouth wide and made a sawing motion above the gaping hole where his tongue should have been. My frightful look caused him to laugh a horrible sound, more animal than human.

"Didn't I tell you he cannot speak?" Brother Paul leaned toward me. "His father cut out his tongue when he was but ten years. An unholy punishment inflicted because the boy dared to protect his mother from the wretched man's drunken outrage. Soon after his father's wrath, Brother Jean began having visions of Saint Michael. The Archangel directed him that one day he would use his quill as his sword. He was shown through his dreams how to make beauty his weapon against darkness! And here you see it in his illuminations. Eventually he ran away from his sorry life and came to our abbey to study and become a scribe. His days and nights are dedicated to God as he carefully crafts the illuminated Word."

Brother Jean's eyes filled with tears, and he nodded affirmation of the sad telling of his story. His face was unwrinkled, though I sensed he was aged. He bowed his head and moaned quietly from somewhere deep inside, as though his battered heart were speaking without words.

Tears came to me as well, tears of shame for my awful judgment of this poor man. Our loving God must have given Brother Jean the grace to want to live. He had surely blessed him with skill and craft. I cannot imagine the horror of being silenced in such a brutal way. It seemed we shared a common story as well. Perhaps Brother Paul was also loving father to Brother Jean.

I realized that unsettling day that not only Brother Jean had been silenced. I, too, was silenced in another way, hidden away with neither family nor friend save the two monks whom over time I grew to cling to. I wonder as I scribe this tale what my life would be if I had not stopped at the Abbey. If Maman had never taken me there, I would not have known of it. How would my life had been different? What if I had gone directly to Belle Cœur to be with Comtesse? What if I had never left my home and dear Maman?

I looked at Brother Jean's face and dared to imagine him as the terrified child he surely must have been. I turned away as tears ran down my cheeks and splashed onto my apron. The two scribes and their student were still for a time before the quills and parchments summoned us back to our daily work.

Brother Jean worked in the scriptorium by day. It was his task to add ornate initials and decorative flourishes to the pages. He was masterful with pigments for the colors, and sometimes he worked alongside Brother Paul and me, a collaborator in our secret. I watched him as he ground the saffron to make ochre. Red mercury became cinnabar and vermilion. Verdigris and malachite yielded green. There were other colors too plentiful to mention. Strangely, they were sometimes mixed with the wax from Brother Jean's ears or stirred with the golden urine he poured from a small vial. They were to my mind the strangest of ingredients, but it was these human substances that gave a special quality to the color that could not be created in another way. Such was the wonder lived each day in the hidden room.

Brother Paul's first instruction to me as an earnest apprentice was to copy the Psalms of Ascent. Later I also scribed copies of various sacred mystery texts. The original pages were encoded with emblems and alchemical formulas, illuminations of exotic birds, kings and queens, the sun and the moon, eagles and salamanders. I copied them carefully, honing the virtue of patience, understanding that I would have to wait to feel worthy of my craft until I was deemed a scribe. Only then would I begin to have a gleaning of their significance. In time I would come to learn how the combinations of these things were meant to penetrate the secrets of nature, unity, eternity, infinity, life, and death.

What was I being shaped to become? How was God using my life?

The angels had surely led me to Brother Paul. My mind was being fed knowledge and skill, and my heart was yearning to share what I was beginning to embody. Why was I being filled with such sacred gifts of the Spirit? Only God knew, and I trusted my Creator to reveal the answers to my questions.

My heart is stirred with this sweet melody; I serenade you with my verse, my leader:

my tongue is like the pen of a skilled writer. Psalm 45:1

26 October 1258
Le Monastère de la Visite

Brother Paul's words come to me tonight here in this cold, dark monastery as I continue to scribe my story. Earlier, while I prepared for tonight's writing, Comtesse once again took her place near my table and began her mending. Thankfully, she became bored by my silence. I looked up just now to find her gone without so much as a "*Bonne nuit.*"

I hear my dear teacher's voice clearly as if he were standing beside me. "Learn the gift of writing, Goscelin, and one day you will create language and pictures to tell the stories born of your daily life. And those more secret stories growing within you," Brother Paul said as he cut and shared an apple with me one warm afternoon in the tower. "Just as the manuscript made of parchment and hide is the container for the Psalms and sacred texts, so another kind of manuscript, the journal, will be the record of what lives in your heart."

Tonight I scribe on parchment that which will become our journal, a manuscript filled with our sisterhood's stories. Here I record my memory of the second year of an extraordinary apprenticeship with my tutor and his peculiar friend, Brother Jean, in the hidden room at Saint Catherine's. After years of practice, my fingers now scribe with ease. Gratitude flows through my quill as I recall the gifts, responsibilities, and vocation that were passed to me by the humpbacked holy man with foul breath and one clear eye.

Time passed swiftly in the hidden room at the abbey. The changing seasons and the caravan of saints' Feast Days marked my two-year stay. Brother Paul and Brother Jean continued to fill me with instruction and wisdom, the way Maman used to carefully ladle milk from the bucket into the pitcher until it was full.

Brother Jean showed me, in silence with his eloquent gestures of the quill, many different hands for scribing and ways to refine my illuminations. I stitched a little pillow to fit in my hand. It was made from a scrap of linen and stuffed full with dried lavender. When I worked beside Brother Jean, I held it to my nose to cover his stench.

One day I glanced up from my work to find the friendly giant picking up Maman's green glass vessel from the table. He held it up to the light of the candle flame, the way the priest elevates the chalice. In simple, sweet pleasure, he smiled widely while he studied the reflections in the glass. I could not help but stare at the dark hole where his tongue should have been. Though his speech was silenced by his father's abuse, all else about him now spoke to me from his gentle spirit.

I left the room to leave Brother Jean to his innocent delight, to stretch limbs stiff from sitting. Standing on my toes, I peered out one of the small, round openings in the stone wall where the tower stairs spiraled sharply 'round a turn. At once I was swept into the full glory of autumn. Billowing clouds illumined with royal purple and bright amber passed quickly cross the late afternoon sky. A gust of chilly wind caught my breath away, a swiftly passing harbinger of the frigid weather that would soon come creeping through the forest. I thought of Maman, took Henriette from my apron pocket, and clutched her to my heart.

In the earliest days of learning to scribe, my fingers trembled and I was unsure of how to form the letters. Those beginner's parchments caused me to cry and bite my fingernails from disappointment. Longing to scribe as Brother Paul, longing for perfection of the skill, I sometimes grew anxious at his diligence in tutoring me, and I confess I was glad when he left me alone. Then I would practice and practice, sometimes well into the night.

Over time the quill came to feel as if it were part of my hand. I learned to clean and trim goose feathers to form writing instruments. The point had to be dipped into the black ink after every three or four strokes. Long hours of practice yielded a comfortable rhythm, and I began to discover a confidence of certainty as each mark found its way to the parchment.

Only my thumb and two fingers held the quill, but strangely, after hours of scribing, my whole body ached. Though I felt I was inhabited with the life and meaning of the Psalms that I copied, perhaps they did not so readily commune with a girlish soul that was still being fashioned by God.

"You must offer prayers of gratitude, Goscelin, for you have been graced with a natural skill for scribing. You're doing very well. Soon you will be ready for a special assignment." Brother Paul had no way of knowing how much his words meant to me. He collected my completed parchments and assured me they would be put to good use, but we never spoke of what particular use they would serve.

One early morning in autumn of my second year at Saint Catherine's, as the light began to part night's velvet curtain, Brother Paul came to the room, startling me from a dream. He carried a bulging satchel over his shoulder.

"Get dressed, Goscelin. I will wait for you downstairs, just outside near the path."

"Where are we—?" He was gone before I could ask.

Once outside in the cold morning air that announced the turn from autumn to winter, hunchbacked Brother Paul looked this way and that before telling me to stay close and follow him. The sound of the monks chanting Lauds drifted on the chill wind from the sanctuary. We went ahead with caution as our companion.

We walked for a distance to a place where the path became faint. It was strange to be so far from the safety of the tower and its secret room upstairs. My senses feasted on the strange, peppery smells and the sight of plump, red berries on gnarled vines along the ground.

Ahead of us, beyond a thicket of dense bramble bushes, was the forest, dark and wide. A very large raven atop a pine tree swaying in the wind bobbed up and down, cawing out a warning to signal our arrival as we entered the domain of the birds and animals.

Where were we going? I knew I must stay silent and simply follow. As I trailed Brother Paul's vigorous gait, I realized I had grown since my arrival at the abbey. I was nearly a head taller than he. Surrounded by the towering trees, my teacher appeared curiously small to my eyes, as though he were an odd woodland creature that had emerged magically from leaf and bark.

At last, some distance into the woods we arrived at a small clearing. The light was dim on this gray morning. The north wind rustled the branches above, blessing us with a shower of brown pine needles falling gently, catching in my unbraided hair. Brother Paul knelt on the damp, mossy ground and with a simple glance instructed me to do the same. He opened the satchel and removed a bundle wrapped in a crimson cloth.

He carefully laid the bundle on the ground and unfolded the wrapping, placing before me four small volumes covered in rich brown hide. They were not much larger than my hand and not as thick as other small books I had seen.

Burned into the soft cover of each manuscript were unfamiliar markings brushed with gold, sigils perhaps, or merely decoration. They were strange and beautiful to my eye.

"You're wondering why I've brought you here?" Brother Paul's tone was gentle but serious.

"Yes, Brother."

"Because *you* are the one, Goscelin. You are the next one to grow the wisdom in these texts."

My heart leaped with his words. "*Grow* the wisdom?"

"You see, dear girl, the knowledge contained within these manuscripts is ancient. The scribe who first recorded all that lies before you is unknown. How these volumes came to be is lost to us. We have no history to explain how the holy wisdom contained here was seeded, then fertilized and grown. And yet..."

Brother Paul paused to reach into his satchel. He lifted out a small, round box made of black wood. Bowing his head, he presented it to me with both hands.

"Open it."

I trembled as I carefully removed the lid. Resting on a bed of dried lavender was a large honeybee. Perfectly formed, her wings slightly splayed. Her dark golden body was long and tapered.

"The queen," he whispered.

"I'm sorry. I don't understand. The queen?"

"The largest of the bees. She is most important to the other bees, the one they serve, and she in turn serves the hive."

I felt ignorant.

"Creation, Goscelin. The queen bee is a symbol for Creation herself. She represents the Blessed Mother, and her honey is the Christ."

"I don't understand."

He let out a deep sigh, pushed back his hood, and scratched the top of his shiny head. Then he took the box from my hands and set it beside the manuscripts.

"Look around you, Goscelin. Look around you. What do you see?"

My eyes searched for the right answer while the wind came up and acorns fell from above.

"I see trees. Mushrooms. Moss. A broken snail shell. Acorns. Pine needles and wrinkled brown leaves. Small stones..."

"Exactly. Now look again, and this time behold with reverence what God has made. Behold, Goscelin. Behold what is all around you. Illuminate your sacred faculty of vision with prayer. Now what do you feel? What do your senses tell you?"

I closed my eyes and drew a deep breath. When I opened them, I looked around me with the prayer and hope of new understanding.

"I behold...I behold...I behold God's Creation in the colors of the leaves. I hear God's presence in the sound of water rushing in the stream nearby. I smell tree bark, dampness, and smoke from perhaps a nearby chimney. I feel the wind caressing my hair. I taste the woody forest if I breathe it in deeply enough. Oh, and I touch the earth, the cool, moist earth here where I sit. Am I right? Are these the answers you're seeking?"

Brother Paul closed his eyes and bided in silence. I had never felt so tested.

"Exactly. Creation. Feel her. Taste her. Touch her. Hear her. BEHOLD HER!"

I wanted to laugh aloud with holy joy, but I held it in.

"Her? Creation is likened to a woman?" This idea astounded me.

"Yes. Yes! The generative power of life, birth, rebirth...these are expressions of the feminine nature of all things. Holy Wisdom is she."

Brother Paul grabbed a nearby branch and slowly pulled himself to his feet. The brown woolen robe hung loosely on his thin, bony frame. He appeared dwarfed by the tall sycamores guarding the glade. Yet when he raised his arms some majesty transformed him. In the morning light his poor fringe of hair glowed; his face grew bright. He spread his arms wide. "She was present at the dawn of all this. God, our God of Creation, is both Father and Mother."

"I'm—I'm trying to understand..."

Brother Paul lowered his arms and sighed. "There is so much I must share with you. It will take time, years perhaps, for the knowledge to finally live in your bones."

I was studying the queen bee on her bed of lavender as my teacher continued his lesson. A sudden gust of wind blew over my precious gift, fluttering her fragile wings ever so slightly, so that for a moment I thought she might reawaken to life and take flight in search of her hive.

"Creation, my girl. Creation. Earth, air, fire, water—the Dominions, the very elements of Creation, *la substance de la vie.* Why, even you, dear Goscelin, you yourself are made of earth, air, fire, and water. But it is God's breath that set these elements into motion at the very beginning of all that is or will ever be. Each dominion is alive with a unique purpose and intention. Do you understand?"

"I'm trying to follow you."

My lively teacher forced himself to sit against the deformity of his back. He looked upward and opened his arms over all that was spread out on the crimson cloth.

"Well, you may not be grasping everything I'm saying in this first lesson, Goscelin, but listen very carefully to what I am about to tell you. Put your gift away and look at me."

I closed the lid of the round box and sat up straight to signal my attention.

He was serious and still, then he leaned toward me and folded his bony hands in a prayerful way. "Today you are being entrusted with the living knowledge in the volumes of Dominions and Graces. Set your hand to copying these sacred texts, and you will harvest your own wisdom from them. These books will most certainly awaken in you understanding and knowing, both old and new. Your quill, your eye, your covenant with these pages will bring them to renewed life, and they will work in you and through you. But mind this! Until you have made the sacred knowledge your own, you must never speak of it."

We sat silently for a time. Brother Paul closed his eyes. When he opened them, he spoke urgently.

"When you feel your spirit rising within you, this will be the sign that you have begun to glean the Graces. The Graces are the scribe's reflective understanding cultivated through prayerful awareness and fervent study of the Dominions. You will write what you harvest into your copies of the texts, into the margins. Are you following? Tell me, girl."

"I believe I understand. The Dominions are the workings of creation, the ingredients, as it were: earth, air, fire, and water. Each working has a quality that reflects its purpose and deeper meaning like a sound, a color, and a season." I spoke slowly and took a deep breath as I tried to find a way to express my thoughts.

"Yes! Yes! You do understand, now…"

Rustling came from the thicket nearby startling us with the sound of squeaks and more rustling. Out of the thicket ran a red fox. Hanging from his mouth was a small rabbit that struggled to break free. The fox halted, lifted a front paw, and looked at us. Then he turned and ran back into the thicket with his suddenly limp and lifeless prey. The rustling ceased, and the forest became very still once again.

"Now what about the Graces?" Brother Paul asked as he thoughtfully pulled the hood of his robe over his shiny head.

"Ummmm. The Graces…let me see…as I study to understand the workings of Creation and Nature in all her forms, thoughts will arise…my thoughts. I will experience the wisdom in the texts through my senses, through prayer and communion with God. I imagine, from what you say, that studying the Dominions will inspire me. My inspirations will grow the Graces within me."

Brother Paul nodded and smiled.

"Then, I'll add my reflections and gleanings, the Graces that God gleans in me, to the margins of my copies. In this way my wisdom will join the wisdom, the Graces, of other scribes who have been the keepers of the ancient knowledge." I let out a deep breath and felt relief that I could at least remember the letter of my dear monk's instruction, if not yet the depth of his teaching.

"Very good, very good indeed. You are a bright girl…an intelligent woman. I knew you were the one to carry on the tradition."

Thoughts and questions tumbled together like newborn pups in search of their mother's teats. His compliment made me hungry for more instruction. My body tingled with joy—surely this was how I would have felt if Papa had ever praised me.

Brother Paul waved his hand slowly over the texts. "These are ancient teachings to be revered and grown for those who will come after us. I know I am not the one called to this work. I'm an old man. Others worthy of such trust must be taught to carry on the secret work and tradition. As one chosen by God for this holy task, you are bound to agree to protect these teachings for all our sakes, and one day you will pass on the wisdom to the next scribe, who will serve as guardian of the Dominions and Graces." Brother Paul spoke with a firmness I'd never heard before.

He took an apple and small knife from his satchel then cut it in two. We sat quietly eating our breakfast while two red squirrels chased one another 'round and 'round the trunk of a nearby tree.

A question burned within me until I could no longer hold the heat of it. "Does God bless these works, Brother?"

He wiped his mouth with his sleeve and scratched his head. "I believe so, Daughter, because God blesses the human imagination. Therefore God sanctifies human imagining when it's intended for good. Divine inspiration lives and breathes in our imaginations. Imagination is the place where Holy Wisdom comes to meet us, in a field, a vast fertile meadow in the mind. When we respond to our longing to know God and go in search of the One who waits within us with unending patience, we are gifted with wonders to behold."

"What kind of wonders?" I asked.

"Mystical wonders. Inspired dreams and visions of dragons that bite their own tails, flying horses, or trees that bend to catch us up and send us flying to the stars. Poetry that flows from quill to page in a torrent of beauty. Poetry so exquisite it's capable of either breaking a heart or mending it. The gift of song may be suddenly born in one's throat as though an angel sings from somewhere deep inside. Some feel a fever for dance or painting or building a cathedral. These responses happen when God feeds the soul through the human imagination. Divine inspiration is holy food, a Sacrament, true nourishment for the soul born from sweet communion with the Beloved."

Brother Paul opened one of the books. His swollen, spotted hand came to rest on the first page at an illumination of a two-headed angel with vermillion-colored wings. My teacher's fingers were stained so deeply they seemed to become one with the illumination. His foul breath was still foul, but I was now accustomed to what was once repulsive.

Together we regarded the strange angelic creature on the page. "I see such things in my mind and in my dreams, Brother."

"I know, my child. That's why I trust you to copy and study the four volumes of Dominions and Graces. You will be called to pass on the wisdom to others as you follow the invisible map God has drawn for you to follow.

"Study well, my girl. The imagination is a blessing and gift God wants us to share. Take in the symbols, the languages as yet strange to you, and the beauty of the illuminations. Sadly, there are many who believe it's the devil or witchcraft that inspires such pictures and knowledge. This is why this particular knowledge must remain secret and carefully hidden for now."

A shiver of unsettling understanding went down my back as I realized the great weight of responsibility being passed to me. The charge, the quickening, melded with my passion for scribing and learning. I was both eager and confused. My body tightened, and sudden thirst caused me to swallow hard. I thought I felt Henriette leap inside my apron pocket.

"I understand, Brother Paul."

"I know you speak with God and the angels, Goscelin. That's why I have sheltered you from the first day you arrived as God's sweet surprise for my aging spirit. When you spoke of the 'beautiful music,' I knew you had the gift of a quickened sacred imagination. It's why I risk my life and yours to entrust the ancient and new wisdom to you, the next scribe and guardian of Dominions and Graces."

I wanted to speak, but there were no words to mark such a moment. In truth, I began to tremble fearfully. How could I, only a girl from a humble and even tainted provenance, accept this task? Why was I blessed to be privy to such knowledge and a true vocation when only men were allowed to scribe and study?

Was I truly worthy of such work? What was God really asking of me?

Brother Paul coughed and pulled his robe tightly to his chest. A flock of crows called out as they took flight overhead. Droppings fell from above onto one of the volumes. Brother Paul laughed. "A crow blessing. Smart bird, the crow, he recognizes wisdom when he sees it."

I wiped the mess clean from Volume II, *Air,* with my apron.

"Another important facet of your task is that of the gatherer. Someday when it's time for you to return to the world, you will journey into the womb of nature. You will reap samples of all that catches your eye, shell and stone, bark and fern." The wind rustled the trees as if to echo Brother Paul's words. "Then you will press your holy cache reverently between the parchments where you will label them carefully and add your notations and illuminations. When the time comes, guidance will be found in '*Les Psaumes des Choses Sauvage,*' 'Psalms of the Wild Things,' recorded in Volume III. These teachings will instruct you how to behold the stories locked within the eye of the deer, the feather of the hawk, or the vein of an oak leaf. You will learn how to read the poetry scribed by God on the bee's wing."

I was dizzy with thoughts of being free to wander the countryside. I imagined filling my basket with nature's gifts while searching for the stories and poems fixed in the fur, feather, and fin of God's creatures.

Brother Paul's instructions poured over my concerns. I closed my eyes to capture all he described, for

I needed to cling to my teacher's wisdom until I found my own. New glimmerings of understanding stirred from an unfamiliar place deep within me—not unlike how I imagine it feels when an unborn child moves about in a mother's womb.

"You must hold these things in confidence and prayer. This is the code of conduct for the scribe. Goscelin, do you agree to serve God as scribe and guardian of the Dominions and Graces?"

Thus, with these words he recognized me as scribe! Oh, blessed day! I was sealed in a profession, a true vocation. I couldn't hold in the giddy laughter that suddenly befell me. Tears gushed. I laughed and cried as my whole being resounded, "Yes!" My excitement overcame me. "Yes! I agree to this service. I have much to learn. Please pray I am worthy to complete all you are asking of me. I will pray that God's inspiration will bring forth new wisdom to be added to the texts. May the angels help me so I might scribe my copies of the holy volumes as pure illuminations of God's truth." I wiped my eyes and caught my breath.

Brother Paul didn't join in my exultation. His lined face spoke of worry.

I ceased laughing.

"Your enthusiasm is both blessing and hazard. Certainly there is freedom in knowledge, Goscelin, but working with ancient wisdom is not a child's game. There's also danger in knowing what you'll learn. Especially for you, a girl...more rightly, a woman. Guard the power, your power, well. Protect what you record at all cost, lest it be discovered—and you and it be burned."

His tone haunts me even now, tonight here at Le Monastère de la Visite, so far away from that long-ago morning in Saint Catherine's glade. On that blessed and disturbing day, the weight of his words fell upon me like shovels of dirt being thrown onto one alive in a grave. My wild abandon for learning and knowledge was tamed by Brother Paul's tone beneath his message, as he conveyed to me a new understanding of the power, and peril, of wisdom. Caution became my constant companion while I prayed aloud:

"Jesus, the weight of my assignment is heavy and new. You have called me to task. Give me courage. Make me strong. Amen."

5 November 1258
Le Monastère de la Visite

It is midmorning. Our quarters here on the grounds of the monastery are quiet, as my sisters, save Petronilla and Mabille, have left for their various duties. I worked late into the night at the infirmary, and my assigned drudgery will begin again soon. I should be resting, but I must finish scribing the story of my time with Brother Paul. The awaiting stories grow impatient and clamor in my mind, like hungry villagers at the baker's stall on market day.

I am happy when I find a bit of time for my quill to make music on the parchment. Then my daimon delivers inspiration from the heavens to fuel my scrbing. I feel her presence calling for my attention. My invisible friend is *mon conteur bénie,* and I rely on her to help me find the words to tell our stories. To my mind she is part angel and part human.

The nuns also call for my attention, to scrub soiled linens and stuff mattresses with fresh straw. My hands are scratched and raw from my chores, but my fingers find comfort this morning as they pick up the quill to follow the thread of my story.

The seasons' ever-changing cycles circled round, one following the next. I rarely left the hidden room at St. Catherine's except to empty my chamber pot every morning in the field near the cemetery when the monks were at prayer.

Winter was long and the frozen ground hid all signs of the oncoming spring. Soon after my initiation in the woods, I sat at my table with the four small, leather-bound volumes before me. Candlelight flickered on the vibrant illuminations and the meticulous lettering, and my mind wandered as if I were dreaming.

What appeared upon the pages was both dazzling and confusing. The Dominions were full of unfamiliar symbols exquisitely rendered. The text itself was complicated, full of details of the natural world. There were new words to learn...Akasha, known as quinta essentia, which is actually the fifth element, Spirit, the quintessence.

With a new quill, a pot of fresh ink, and the finest parchment from our stock, I began to copy. In the margins of the texts were the scribings of the last guardian of the ancient books. His signature was a brown horse's head adorned with a crown of golden leaves. Wherever the previous scribe recorded his Graces, in the tiniest of script, I found his mark. Soon the poetic tone of his reflections became familiar. In the silent room, I believed I could hear his voice.

I put down my quill and imagined... *a young man, handsome, with a strong square jaw and deep green eyes. His thick, acorn-colored hair smelled of leather and salt. He was dressed in fine velvet, and together we rode through the meadow of my imagination astride his powerful steed donned with a golden laurel crown. My arms wrapped snug around him from behind as his horse galloped beneath us. Laurent's strong back pressed into my breasts while the wind caught my hair streaming behind me. Faster and faster we rode into the...*

"Stop dreaming!" Brother Paul's voice chased away my lovely vision the way Maman shooed away flies that assumed they were about to feast on our daily bread. I rubbed my eyes before I retrieved my quill.

"How many scribes have there been, Brother Paul? How many guardians of Dominions and Graces?"

"It's hard to say. Each guardian of the Dominions recorded his Graces in the margins of the manuscripts, but then they were passed to the next guardian to copy." Brother Paul rubbed his head and explained, "Each scribe copied his predecessor's wisdom from the margins into the body of the writings. The copying and merging has been repeated for centuries.

I'm certain you are the first woman to scribe copies of Dominions and Graces because these texts have been passed from scriptorium to scriptorium. Only the monks would be privy to such wisdom. You will copy the most recent Graces recorded by the one you were no doubt dreaming about a moment ago. You will copy these into the main portion of each page, and *your* Graces will go in the margins."

How could he have known my fanciful dreaming? Brother Paul's gifts included far more than fine abilities as a scribe.

"Some day, long from now, you will recognize the one who will follow you as the keeper of the Dominions and Graces." He continued. "At that time you will entrust him—or her—" he smiled his most mischievous smile, "with your copies of the texts. In this way the sacred knowledge will continue to grow over the years, scribe by scribe, line by line within the pages, the way nature draws rings inside the trunk of a tree to mark the passage of time."

Day upon day, I became more comfortable while I carefully copied the works and blended the previous scribe's Graces with the existing wisdom. Brother Paul gifted me with a special swan feather quill. I was eager to scribe my own revelations, my Graces. One afternoon I struggled to bring forth something of my own, a bit of wisdom to record. I began to scribe what I was thinking alongside an illumination of the Tree of Life abundant with round vermilion-colored fruit. The illumination depicted a portion of the fruit with many seeds inside. Pomegranates, I learned.

"It will take time, perhaps years, Goscelin, my girl, before you receive your first revelation." Brother Paul's voice came from over my shoulder. He gently removed the parchment I had been scribing and replaced it with a clean one.

Patience was my most difficult lesson. The task loomed large, and I pushed sleep away until my eyes could no longer bear the weight of exhaustion. Brother Paul began to spend more hours each day in the scriptorium. Brother Jean's visits were fewer. I was alone with God and my quest to bring my first work as a scribe and guardian of Dominions and Graces to fruition.

Each volume was dedicated to the study of an element of creation. The four volumes of the Dominions—*Earth, Air, Fire,* and *Water*—were uniquely individual. Brother Paul taught me that there were specific traits for each.

"Imagine the dominions, earth, air, fire, and water as branches on the tree of Creation. Each branch, each element as it where, is capable of producing a variety of fruit. The fruit represent a particular season and plant life. Each dominion embodies a creature, a sound, a smell, or a color to reflect its sensual nature.

"What of the Dominion of Spirit? I recall learning there is a fifth dominion." I asked.

"You're correct. The Graces, the wisdom gleaned by the scribes who have studied these texts—and now by you, Goscelin—represent the Dominion of Spirit."

"I don't understand."

"Again, Daughter, I'm referring to human imagination. This is how God speaks to us, through the realm of imagination. Spirit becomes visible by way of human creativity. When we invent something new or bake a loaf of bread or craft an illumination to represent the sun or the moon, we express the Dominion of Spirit."

Brother Paul continued his lesson while the light in the hidden room grew dim. He told me how the inclusion of Scripture, Psalms, and prayers supported the history of imaginative Graces woven over the centuries into the texts, by the lineage of scribes.

I did my best to honor the scribe who had copied the texts before me. I created a fanciful name for my predecessor, Monsieur Laurent. His Graces were copied from the margins and woven into my copies as part of the continuous story pertaining to the earth.

In my imagination I could hear his deep, mellow voice reading aloud to me as I reverently scribed each word exactly as he had scribed.

Water is God's elixir teeming with all manner of life. Leviathan, terrapin, pisces, and polypus live within the great vessel that is the sea. Yet, the waters where they so freely swim afford the human no relief from thirst. This is but one of God's great mysteries of creation. Brine and brill inhabit the great, black, foaming waters. We beings who walk about the earth, human and beast, must look to the rain for relief. The body thirsts and is quenched by the stream. The soul thirsts and is refreshed by the living waters of God's love.

I was careful to leave generous margins, known as limbo, in my fresh copy for the Graces I would soon add in my own hand. My mind searched for some glimmer of understanding half as wise as my predecessor. *Someday,* I thought. *Someday, I will capture an inspired thought to add as my own.* Meanwhile, I continued to copy what lay before me.

The Dominions of Creation and Their Properties
Volume I: EARTH
Bone ~ Autumn ~ Dusk ~ Harvest ~ Bear ~ Acorn ~ The Body ~ Stone ~ Footfall on Fallen Leaves ~ Musk ~ Vermillion
Volume II: AIR
Breath ~ Spring ~ Dawn ~ Seeding ~ Honeybee ~ Thistle ~ The Mind ~ Feather ~ Wind Moving through the Trees ~ Roses ~ Silver
Volume III: FIRE
Heart ~ Winter ~ Night ~ Gestation ~ Spider ~ Hawthorne ~ Transformation ~ Ashes ~ Burning Logs ~ Smoke ~ Gold
Volume IV: WATER
Blood ~ Summer ~ Day ~ Tending ~ Fish ~ Clover ~ The Emotions ~ Shell ~ Thunder ~ Rain ~ Green

Word by word I recorded the ancient knowledge onto fresh parchment. I breathed the sacred teachings into my mind. All the while, my heart silently offered Jesus's name with each mark of my quill, a constant prayer.

I felt as if God's hand was etching knowledge from the vault of heaven upon my soul. My bones ached. I was certain this meant my body was being stretched to "grow the wisdom," as Brother Paul had instructed.

At times I felt I was being refashioned from the inside with new purpose.

The stack of parchments grew slowly in the beginning, sheet upon sheet, to create a set of identical manuscripts. When the copying of each text was achieved, I sewed the pages into their leather cradle. My work built toward completion, the way stones are laid atop one another as stonemasons construct a great cathedral. I wished my task to be no less a statement to the glory of God.

I studied the texts, closed my eyes in prayer, and waited for the stirrings of my heart to become language, for my spirit to rise within me. One morning as I scribed from Volume I: *Earth*, I copied the description of autumn…

Autumn, the waning season of shedding corresponds to dusk. The purpose is the gathering and harvest of nature's bounty. All that has grown to fruition must now be collected and shared with the community. The earth gives of herself, and in return she is tended by those she so generously serves.

I closed my eyes and pondered the words prayerfully. My heart rather than my mind was flooded with impressions. I was carried deep into the golden fire that is autumn. On the following parchment, in the margin next to my small illumination of a brown squirrel surrounded by a cascade of crimson leaves, I wrote my first Grace…

Observe the creatures as they prepare for winter. Notice their frantic running about as they gather acorn and leaf. Dens and nests are warmed and fortified, and then all of nature grows still. God invites all of creation to rest and replenish what has been spent. Autumn is a Sabbath season.

Gratitude is the prayer. Take stock of the blessings received, and succumb to tranquility. It is the dusk of the year, and the darkest months approach, heralded by the North Wind as she takes the remaining leaves from the trees. It is a time for sweet reverie, appreciation, and preparation as all the earth approaches the season of silence and gestation.

With great care I illuminated a bee with splayed wings as my signature. The sunlight spilled through the windows, casting an amber hue over the page. I took Henriette from my apron pocket and laid her beside what I had just written. There on the parchment were the words of my first Grace, my inspired revelation, a gift from God.

I went to the door in hopes Brother Paul might be coming up the stairs. I was eager to tell him that at last I understood what he had so carefully explained. The landing was empty, but on the stone flagging sat my bowl of bread and milk. Nothing had ever tasted so delicious.

The very next day, a second Grace arrived to be added to the Dominions. In my copy of the Dominion of air, I scribed in the margin of the third parchment:

Surely as the seasons follow one into the next, and the plants follow a cycle from seed to sprout to blossom to fruit to seed, we mortals circle life's journey from heaven to birth to infant to child to adult to elder to heaven. We breathe in and out. Air is our connection to all that is. Each breath makes us one with nature and the circle of life. God is at the center. Creation is the Mother of all change.

Again I illuminated the bee as my mark.

And so from day unto sweet day, I joined my hand and spirit to the work of unknown scribes who surely must have realized the same tender ecstasy of discovery. My mind and spirit were nourished and sustained while I was locked away, a prisoner held captive by God in a sanctuary dedicated to beauty and knowledge. I could have taken my leave at any time, but the Holy One held me in the creative fire, to be forged for what would come.

As the months passed, Brother Paul read my Graces one by one. "You are growing the wisdom, dear girl." His assurance blessed me in ways he would never know.

By the second spring of my time in the secret room, I had copied all but the last portion of Volume IV. Hour upon hour while scribing, I imagined the bittersweet day when I would celebrate the completion of copying the texts.

One early morning I was sitting below the open shutters studying a bee that appeared to be dancing on my writing table. In the bright sunlight, every detail of her was uncommonly clear: her dark color and tiny golden striping, the shine of delicate wings, and the preciousness of her little round purses bulging with pollen. Suddenly she took flight before I could capture a glimpse of the poetry etched on her wings.

I heard heavy footsteps running up the stairs. They were not the daily, shuffling footfall heralding Brother Paul's welcomed arrival with my bread and milk. I ran to my pallet and clutched Henriette to my bosom, pulling the blanket over us. Without warning the tattered cover was pulled from my trembling body. I dared not open my eyes. A strong hand grabbed my arm, pulling me to my feet. Tears ran like a river from Brother Jean's eyes, spilling over and down his sunken cheeks through his sparse beard. I knew from his countenance before he could gesture with his hands that Brother Paul was dead.

A hole tore in the fabric of my life. Without blessed Brother Paul's teachings and loving guidance, a light in my world was extinguished, and it would never shine again.

Brother Jean left me with my tears. Throughout the day I paced and wept. Doors to my memory flung wide as I recalled the many shimmering, risk-filled moments the old monk had given to me so freely, so tenderly.

Late that night, before his burial the next morning and before the brothers had wrapped my teacher's body, Brother Jean took me in secret to see him one more time. I was happy to witness his furrowed brow at last smooth, finally freed from the constant strained squint of failing vision. Only his body was resting there, covered by a white cloth on the wooden platform where he would soon be wound tightly in scrim and dusted with lime. His form was strangely vacant, not unlike a snail's shell found on the garden path. One bends to pick it up in hopes of seeing the tiny creature living safe inside, only to find it empty.

I had brought his favorite quill and a small rolled parchment with my illuminated signature, the bee. Brother Jean held out his hand.

"You'll find a way to leave it with him? It's important to me. I didn't get to say good-bye. I didn't get to thank him."

Brother Jean nodded and grunted his sound for yes. I handed him my gift and stretched to softly kiss the beloved assistant on his forehead. We stood together gazing at Brother Paul, locked in place by our shared grief.

When the bells of the abbey rang on the morning of his burial, I placed my stool upon the pigment table in the hidden room. Carefully I climbed atop the makeshift ladder. Standing on my toes, I peeked through the open shutters down into the cemetery below. Four monks lowered Brother Paul's body into the dark hole in the earth while prayers were offered.

Late that afternoon Brother Jean came to give me a scribed message, the sad announcement that the new Armarius would arrive in five days. He also brought me a gift: a blue dress left behind by a pilgrim. He delivered his present with a wide smile, and I was happy to wear it after wearing men's clothing for so long. The dress was a bit too large but comfortable, and it made me feel girlish again.

I worked feverishly the next three days and nights to copy the fourth and final manuscript of Dominions and Graces. A sense of urgency came over me, banishing any need for food or drink. I barely slept.

On the last night when I turned the hourglass and stood to stretch my weary body, I noticed a small wooden box with intricate carvings perched on a corner shelf. "*This is a little treasure given to me by a scribe who was passing through,*" Brother Paul had told me. "*A souvenir purchased while on pilgrimage in Jerusalem. The wood is from an olive tree. Perhaps a tree near a place where Jesus walked. Touch it, child. It's the closest we shall ever come to where Christ lived and breathed on this earth.*"

I pulled the box from the dusty shelf and lifted the lid. It was empty save for a bit of scrim lining the bottom of the sturdy container. I sniffed inside. The odor was faint, like the smell of water in moonlight. Carved into the lid were the strange symbols I recognized as Hebrew letters, though I didn't know their meaning.

What other treasures called to me? I collected four small, round, glass containers filled with colored pigments: lapis lazuli, ochre, vermillion, and aubergine. After I placed them in the box with my quill and three small parchments, there was just enough room for a pot of ink. Quickly, I sealed the opening of the little, round vessel with wax. I took Brother Paul's empty satchel hanging near the door and carefully tucked my treasures inside. I wrapped the round box, home to the queen bee, in a piece of cloth. There were ten pages of the final volume of Dominions and Graces yet to copy.

Weariness overpowered me. I lay my head on the open manuscript of Volume IV and fell fast asleep. When I awoke, the sun was rising. I went outside to the pond near the woods behind the stone wall to empty the chamber pot and relieve myself. In the still water I saw my reflection. To my amazement my cheek was imprinted with crimson symbols from the sacred text. I rubbed and scrubbed with pond water to no avail.

In spite of my worry for the future, I found myself overcome by laughter. My work had overflowed into my flesh. I myself was becoming a book!

Later that morning all manner of conversation and commotion could be heard through the west windows; no doubt the new Armarius had arrived. He would soon be brought to the hidden room, to explore what was now *his* library. I thought him to be a trespasser in Brother Paul's world and in what had become my home!

Fear drove gall from my belly up my throat like a fountain of fire. I hadn't felt so wretched since I'd emptied my gullet at the gatepost when I'd left Maman. Maman. Maman! Not a time to think of her. Tears spilled, splashing on my apron. I was unable to catch my breath. My legs were limp, the way it feels when being chased by monsters in a dream. I held onto the tabletop to steady myself.

You are my rock and my fortress; for your name's sake lead and guide me. Free me from the net they have set for me, for you are my refuge. Into your hands I commend my spirit…

Panting like a dog, I gathered my copies of the four sacred manuscripts and stuffed them into a satchel. The final pages of Volume IV were not yet completed. I must have those last parchments—I went to tear them from the original issue.

"These texts must be preserved for the years to come, Goscelin."

I heard Brother Paul's voice in my memory. I would have to seek my own wisdom to complete the last manuscript.

The bells began to ring, calling the monks to prayer. I knew I must go at once! Swiftly, carefully, I returned the original volumes of Dominions and Graces to the secret shelf. So I would never feel far from my saving place no matter the great distance I might travel, I pulled three hairs from my head, one for each year of my studies, and tucked them into the fourth text—at the place where my copying ended.

I closed the cupboard door one last time and concealed it with the hinged shelf that held colorful pots of pigment. Quickly I claimed my final copy from the table and put it into the bag with the others. Henriette went into the deep pocket of my new frock.

I would never know what remained in the final ten pages of Volume IV. Time had run out! I seized Maman's green glass vessel on the table, kissed it, then put it back in its place with my prayer.

Please, God, let Brother Jean find this gift. Let him know he will always be fondly remembered. Amen.

I dared to pause for a moment in the center of the room. The now-familiar smell of pigments and tallow, parchment and ink, unleashed sweet memories. The first moments of my creative passion's awakening, when I was led to this holy place…the sight of rows and rows of manuscripts imprinting on my heart… Brother Paul when he placed the quill into my hand so long ago. Oh, sweet initiation! Oh, blessed teacher! Oh, holy room! Thus I was granted sustenance for my soul as I resumed my journey to find Belle Cœur.

I crossed the threshold to the hidden room for the last time, closed the door behind me and hastened down the spiral staircase. When I reached the doorway of the tower at the bottom of the stairs, I heard men's voices nearby. I peeked around the corner of the entrance to the tower as the Armarius was being escorted there. There was no place to hide!

Brother Jean led the way and the others were a little distance behind. I caught his eye for an instant then stepped back inside the tower. Without a moment's hesitation, he began to moan and fell to the ground. The Armarius and the other monks gathered round him, certain he was in distress. I made my escape and ran toward the meadow while my friendly giant and protector distracted certain danger.

Scribing this story fills my quill with remembrance of those sacred years at the abbey. I had become more than Brother Paul's student. In the end, I was his spiritual daughter and he my spiritual father. Even now, here in the darkest corner of this monastery, my body quickens as I relive the story of those blessed days. Such is the curious nature of memory.

I am dedicated to the protection of the wisdom contained within the pages of Dominions and Graces. One day I will share the knowledge according to God's guidance. I sense the time will soon arrive for the four secret manuscripts to be revealed and broken open for my sisters.

I am Goscelin, the scribe, keeper and guardian of sacred wisdom. Know me. Follow me in the search for the lost key to the Garden.

Book II Sisterhood

10 November 1258
Le Monastère de la Visite

The hour is late. The stories I carry continue to pull my mind the way a needful child tugs on her mother's skirts for attention. My aching fingers tighten on the quill. I bundle a blanket to cover the threshold under the door. There will be no cold draught tonight.

This tiny, dusty room smells of something I cannot name. Spider webs in the corner above me glisten in the candlelight. Their complicated patterns hang in midair like a lost language awaiting translation.

My mind is full to overflowing with stories of our journey. But how our sisterhood came to live *here*, within the enclosure of this monastery, is a tale to be shared at a later time.

I light more candles as if the flames will provide extra warmth. A fat brown mouse scurries up the stone wall. Distraction, be gone! Grasping at the thread of memory, I follow it back in time to the place where my travels continued after I made my hasty departure from the hidden room at the abbey. The veil of recollection parts to welcome me into sweet reverie and recall of my journey following Brother Paul's death. It was early spring when I resumed my trek at long last to Belle Cœur…

The dark gray morning sky on that first day's walk promised cold rain. By afternoon the clouds burst open with a brief shower, soaking not only my clothing but my spirit as well. The hem of my skirt and my shoes became heavy with mud from the road. Tender, watery sores appeared on my heels. Brother Paul's wisdom of flora and fauna played in my mind, but nowhere did I spy the aquilegia canadensis plant that would have brought comfort for my feet.

As I trudged along, I prayed the long country road would lead me to Belle Cœur. Curiously, I found the vast, open landscape surrounding me to be troublesome. Being out and about in the world after so long a time in the hidden room with only Brother Paul and Brother Jean for company made me wary of strangers.

My legs ached from hours of walking, and I felt dizzy as I breathed in the fresh air.

The first day of my journey was weighted by the pull of the heavy leather satchel on my shoulder and a loathsome burden of worry on my head. Step by step, my deepest concerns for a safe peaceful journey pressed on my body and spirit.

Maman's face appeared in my mind. *Are you still alive, my sweet mother? Did you look for me after I ran away, or are you perhaps still standing frozen from melancholy where I left you so long ago?*

By the time the cold, damp twilight descended, hunger burned in my belly, and bone-deep weariness plagued me like a demon. My quill and parchment were tucked into my satchel with the sacred texts. I longed to scribe my thoughts to purge my grief of losing Brother Paul, but fatigue wouldn't allow it.

My longing to return to the safety of the room at Saint Catherine's turned to obsession. I yearned to reenter the sacred world of illuminated manuscripts, to touch quill to parchment. These thoughts circled my mind like a wheel on a cart going 'round and 'round.

Mercifully, in the blue gloaming a blessing appeared. I discovered shelter for the night in a rounded hollow under a small wooden bridge. An old blanket, stained but dry, a gift left by another pilgrim, would provide a bit of warmth against the night's chill. There was nothing to eat. If only I had thought to pack a bit of bread as I rushed about. The growling in my stomach began to dance with the unwelcome fear that loomed in my mind like a dark angel come to torment me.

What would become of me if I were unable to find Belle Cœur? Perhaps it no longer existed. If I did find Belle Cœur and Comtesse was no longer there, would I be allowed to stay? Where else could I go? God's plan was not visible to me.

I reached in the satchel to touch the manuscripts and my few belongings for comfort. If I'd remembered to pack a candle for light, I would have dared to rally my tired bones to fill the hours that long and dreadful night with scribing. Sleep was fitful. The rain returned, and I was grateful for the dirty old blanket. Henriette stayed close, in between my breasts as a faithful guardian for my troubled heart.

Quiet my clamoring mind, Beloved. Lift the demon of fear from me. Replenish my faith. Amen.

Waking just before sunrise, I stood to shake out my limbs and to relieve myself. Cattle in the nearby field joined their lowing to the dawn chorus of myriad birds. Rose-colored clouds moved swiftly across the sky. *Earth and air.*

"*Everything in creation carries a message, Goscelin.*" Brother Paul's teaching returned to me as I stretched my arms above my head, observing the clouds. I bent to touch the damp grass with my fingertips and brought the sweet dew to my lips.

"*You must use your senses to retrieve what God has coded in the sky, placed within the turn of the seasons, and hidden within the acorn and the bark of the tree.*" He had spoken these things while he slowly turned the pages of Volume I.

What were the clouds showing me? They changed before my eyes. A slight wisp became a long, golden wing above me, only to vanish like smoke a moment later.

"Everything is constantly changing!" The sound of my own voice surprised me as I stood alone near the bridge that had sheltered me through the long night.

Bone-deep loneliness crept into my being like a sudden illness. As I stood in the early morning light in the presence of Creation Herself, hot tears fell onto my filthy apron. My sobbing was horrible enough to startle the cows and make them run a good distance. They were too far to be worthy of a chase for the milk they could provide. There was no strength within me to waste. I pulled Henriette from between my breasts and clutched her tight.

I don't know if it was sudden grace or my own determination that flooded me with the sheer willingness to continue. I gathered the dirty blanket, the satchel, and my wits. Belle Cœur. Belle Cœur. There I would surely find comfort.

Straw and mud dwellings with sod roofs were scattered about the countryside. One footfall followed the next while I played a game with myself, counting my steps between the trees that lined the muddy path. The greater the number of steps, the stronger I became.

Grass was the only food that appeared safe to eat. Maman had instructed me to be wary of *les champignons.* My hunger was so fierce that oddly I became accustomed to tearing up tender green blades and slowly chewing them, imagining myself one with the cows. Thankfully, water was plentiful for drinking because the streams and ponds were brimming.

I saw few people as I traveled, except for a small band of Templar Knights. They paid no attention to me as they thundered by on the narrow road. The uniform signifying their call—a white mantle emblazoned by a large crimson cross—made them appear grand. Their galloping steeds threw mud from huge hooves onto my skirt and arms, snorting and breathing out steamy clouds as they passed. They rushed by like a host of archangels on their way to crush the devil and his unholy works.

It began to rain again. As mud collected on my poor, worn sandals and weighed down my skirt, I thought that the wretched torrent was surely an evil curse for this journey. In the next moment, writings from Dominions and Graces echoed in my head.

All of the elements are sacred, as intended by God. Earth, air, fire, water.

The words returned to remind me of the hallowed properties of water and to contemplate the meaning of the rain that returned once again to plague me.

The elements are sacred because they come from Creation. But it's important to remember they may bring blessing or destruction. The authority within the elements is God's doing, yet there are times when humankind abuses that authority to use the earth, air, fire, or water for evil.

I recalled my studies as I waded through the puddles and mud along the road. But what was the authority in the relentless rain as it chilled my bones and soaked my clothing? How was I to discover the meaning of such a deluge?

Oh, if only Brother Paul and I had had more time together. There were so many questions to live into... What possible wisdom could I imbue into the texts when all I carried, to my mind, were questions?

On the third day, the sun shone his face from behind the clouds. An arc of brilliant colors grew across the dark sky on the eastern horizon. I stopped to drink in its glories and saw beneath the great blazing bow an angel in human form ahead of me. A tiny old woman bent under a crimson-colored cloak waited as I approached a row of huts where the road curved along the foot of the low, rolling hillside.

She held out a quivering, gnarled hand to present a silent offering, a handful of deep purple berries from her basket. Sweet sustenance! I devoured the berries in one gulp. Purple juice dripped onto my apron, adding to my filthy appearance. My belly rumbled its longing for more.

Then she reached into her pocket and retrieved a sprig of rosemary.

"For protection." Her voice trembled like her hand as she gave it to me. Her clear eyes belied her years.

"Please tell me, Madame, am I nearing Vézelay?"

A crooked finger pointed to the north.

"Follow the path, child. Stay true to the path, and you shall find an open meadow. You will know your way when you arrive there."

"I am looking for Belle—"

"God's blessings be with you." She pulled the hood of her garment over the sparse white hairs on her head and turned quickly away, like an apparition returning through the veil that separates this world from the next. Or perhaps hunger was making me fancy strange things.

"Follow the path…stay true to the path," she called back as she wobbled in the opposite direction.

Oh, why couldn't she have just led me to the meadow? My doubts about finding the way hung upon me like a leech to a sore. Thomas doubted Jesus, who stood before him showing His wounds. Pitiful girl. No better than the doubting disciple. My faith seemed to have been drowned by the rain.

The path indeed led me to the edge of a vast meadow glowing with green fire under the midday sun. In a month's time, God's hand of Creation would strew wildflowers of every color here. The fragrance of pregnant earth wet with the birthing waters of spring and resurrection filled my being.

The sight and scents of that place carried me back to the fields of home and to spring's sweet surprise of lavendula angustifolia and rosa gallica, wood-vine and flowering tree. A tender memory of Maman appeared. I imagined the sight of her setting off with her gathering basket, her bare feet creating a path for me to follow through the cool, wet grass.

"*Prenez garde des abeilles,* Goscelin," she warned me as the sunlight shone through her red hair, making her appear as a fiery angel to my childish way of seeing.

The bees were busy that time of year, and their sting on a bare foot was a reminder that the flowers were their domain. The memory of *les abeilles* and Maman making a path for me wrung my heart. Surely if I could have gazed inside myself, I would have discovered a bruise in the place where my mother's memory now lived.

Waist-high meadow grasses stretched before me. I stopped and closed my eyes to think, aware that my mud-laden feet were swiftly sinking into the soft moist earth.

Which way was I to go?

Guide me. Lead me. Amen.

With my next breath, a teaching from Brother Paul returned to me.

"*Genesis, Goscelin, the story is told here in the illuminations.*" Brother Paul pointed to the carefully drawn crimson, lapis, and golden scene of a woman with anvil and hammer shaping horse and hound, bird and fish. She was the symbol of Nature herself. He instructed me to close my eyes as he read aloud from Dominions and Graces…Volume I: *EARTH* .

"Then God said, 'Let the earth bring forth living creatures after their kind: cattle and creeping things and beasts of the earth after their kind;' and it was so. And God made the beasts of the earth after their kind, and the cattle after their kind, and everything that creeps on the ground after its kind; and God saw that it was good."

I leaned my head on Brother Paul's shoulder and we sat silently contemplating the Scripture, a rare moment of closeness in this way. I wanted to reach into my satchel for my copy of Volume I to study the wisdom. Instead, I chose to sink more deeply into the earth, to breathe in Creation's scent of seed and stem. There was also the faint odor of a decomposing snail. The scent of crushed shell, which had been his home, mixed with earth to create something new. I opened my eyes and tried to see what was being born beneath the soil, out of sight under my mud-encrusted sandals.

Then, with the clarity that accompanies God's grace, it came to me. I was to forge a path through the meadow. I needed a song to keep me company.

Step by step I make my way.
Step by step, night and day.
Creation leads me. Guidance feeds me.
Belle Cœur is near. My path is clear!

Courage came alive with my little tune. I pushed on across the meadow toward a long stand of trees. Just before the grove, I found another path marked by a small, wooden cross. Was I to continue along the wall or travel the way marked by the cross?

Unexpected tears began to flow. I moved the heavy bag to my other shoulder and wiped my eyes. "Ridiculous creature! So little trust. So little faith!" A red squirrel on a nearby branch stopped his playful skirting about to stare at the exhausted dirty girl who was chastising herself aloud as she passed beneath his tree.

The late morning sun broke again through the clouds. Now I was hurrying along the path bound on either side by bright green grass that shimmered and waved in the freshening breeze. I paused at a low rise.

A shiver ran up my back like a snake slithering upward from a well. My tired and hungry body quaked.

The picture before me was a vision to be hung for the rest of my days in a place deep within my heart where the most precious memories live forever. The vision in my dream was true. I was looking at it. Belle Cœur was real!

Embraced by thick, vine-covered stone walls, the frame dwelling with a sod roof hosted a large crow perched above the door. Near a grove of tall trees in a fenced meadow were three brown milk cows, flop-eared goats, and six fat, wooly sheep.

An early garden at the front of the house boasted tiny green shoots, and to the south a small orchard of bare fruit trees displayed the first buds of new life. A vast forest wrapped around on three sides of this setting like the loving arms of Creation Herself. This was surely a scene to be illuminated one day in the margins of the sacred texts! The closer my feet carried me, the more beauty I beheld.

Then she emerged from the doorway, broom in hand. My heart leapt. The girl from my childhood no longer existed. While I was in the hidden room she, too, had become a woman. She was round at the hip, and she swung the broom to and fro with sure strong hands.

Her dress was blue, and she wore a plain linen apron that covered her from collar to hem. The hem fell softly atop her brown leather slippers. Curls of red hair poked out from under a white cap too small for her head. This lovely creature had replaced the plump restless girl who was once my friend and companion.

Unaware of my advance, Comtesse continued her sweeping.

A large crow spread shiny black wings and bobbed up and down from his perch above the door, his cries signaling my arrival.

Comtesse quickly turned to gaze up at the bird. She chortled as he spread and flapped his wings and lifted each foot in a dance known only to crows. Playfully she swatted at the huge bird with her broom.

I echoed from where I stood near the garden: "Caw. Caw. Caw." Comtesse spun round and squinted.

"If you go that way, Madame," she instructed, pointing behind the house, "you'll find our infirmary. Someone there will help…"

"Comtesse, it's me, Goscelin! Here at last!"

She was silent. Her eyes and her smile grew wide, and in an instant all my black fears of the past days fled, the way demons scatter in the light cast by prayers and the presence of angels.

She came running and pulled me to her. I breathed her into me. Her scent was salty and musky with sweat yet, clean like clothes that have been dried in the sun.

In the fleeting time that followed, it was as if God had presented me the gift of proof within the long journey. There for my viewing, over Comtesse's shoulder, was a worn sign hanging next to the door. It bore a rusted cross enclosed by a blue painted circle—a sweet portent given me in my dream years ago, now made complete.

"Oh, Goscelin, look at you. Where have you come from? I gave up on you long ago. Are you not Mrs.

Frog after all? I'm so happy...so very, very happy to see you again. You must be exhausted. You look a fright!"

Her whole being broke into a smile as she pressed two fingers to her lips and then into the center of my chest, tracing a cross, enclosing it within a circle, the sign of Belle Cœur. In that moment, her simple, silent blessing became part of my life forever.

This portion of my story is scribed to the parchment with the blessed recall of the joy that spilled out that afternoon, as a sacrament of reunion. The thread that had been severed years before was rejoined in our renewed friendship.

Comtesse swung the door wide and drew me into the house. "Welcome, beloved of God. Oh, Goscelin, I've secretly hoped for this day."

Belle Cœur! My head felt light, and trembling overtook me with the realization that at long last I had arrived.

The house named Belle Cœur was a spacious, one-room dwelling with whitewashed walls and a low-beamed ceiling. The dirt floor was packed tight and swept clean. The entire south wall was made of stone with an open hearth. Before the hearth was a long, alder wood table with wooden benches on either side.

The northern side of the large room was the sleeping chamber. There were rows of cots, each neatly covered with a woolen blanket. The afternoon light poured through the open shutters. How I longed to lie down in comfort in the warmth of the sun! My stomach growled, reminding me that a meal would be even more welcomed.

"Goscelin! Come, sit, and still your rumbling belly." Comtesse brought a bowl of *pain du lait,* and I devoured my first meal in days.

As the goodness of simple, fresh food eased me, I looked around. A pot of rosemary near the fire yielded a pungent fragrance throughout. Clean linen aprons hung on wooden pegs along the wall adjacent to the hearth. The ceiling beams displayed bound sprays of plants hung there to dry. There were stachys officinalus, lavendula angustifolia, and other herbs. Comtesse saw me studying them. She chopped carrots while we talked.

"Helvide is our herbalist. She and Imene, who is a midwife, work together to create medicines for those we care for in our infirmary."

The home, the heart of Belle Cœur, was simple and clean. There was also another quality contained there. Sacredness.

Near the hearth a nook in the stones held the small, carved wooden statue of a woman in a flowing robe. In her hands was a lidded jar. A burning taper melted into the stone niche. It illuminated the tiny altar with flickering light.

"You're happy, Comtesse? It's a good life you've found?" I asked.

"You'll be happy here, Goscelin, I know it. You'll see. I'm so grateful to be with you again. It's a good life, but…" Comtesse frowned for an instant, then looked at me earnestly. "You'll soon see the suffering at the infirmary. It's hard work. But we're serving God and God's people! There are blessed moments of peace and joy when we are able to ease pain and offer hope. It will take time for the sisters to know you. You'll learn how we do things, how we pray, how we live."

"Where are the others?"

"Each of us has our work. In the infirmary, the garden, caring for the animals. Each of us must be useful. Let me show you to the pond where we bathe. You'll want this," and she handed me a soft blanket.

I soon found myself shivering in the cold water, but grateful to wash away the grime of the muddy roads. I wrapped up in the blanket for the walk back to the house, where Comtesse took a clean, blue dress from a peg by the door and slipped it over my head. She scraped the mud from my old, worn shoes and put them near the fire. The red, open wounds on my heels were gently covered with violet salve. Then she gave me a pair of woolen socks to warm my feet. Comtesse tenderly untangled and combed my damp, waist-length hair as we sat together on the wooden bench near the hearth.

"Tell me everything. I want to know what you do here! Comtesse, I have waited so long…"

"Slow down, Goscelin. It will take time for you to see and understand our ways. You mustn't appear too impatient. That will get you into trouble! Believe me. You must wait to be invited to become one of us. There are things to learn, and the community and you will decide together if our way of life is the right choice for you." My friend spoke her warning while she pulled my hair tightly into a long braid.

"I envy your beautiful hair," she continued. "See—mine is very short now except for the few curls I've managed to keep around my ears." Comtesse pulled back her cap; her fiery red hair was closely cropped in a manly fashion save for a few curls around her face.

I was shocked. "Why have you cut your hair that way?"

"It's our sisterhood's custom. Didn't I tell you that you have much to learn?"

Yes, I had much to learn, and I didn't know for certain if I'd be welcomed to stay, to make my home in the beautiful house. Suddenly, without warning, my remaining little strength left me. I had never been so tired.

"Pray with me, Comtesse. Please pray with me."

Comtesse nodded, and then she added wood to the coals; the flames cast our shadows on the wall. We sat together near the hearth.

"Loving God, You have delivered me safely at last to this sanctuary. I praise You for the blessing of shelter, for reunion with Comtesse, for a full belly, and for the beauty of this place. You called me here, Beloved. May my service in Your name begin anew. Bless Comtesse and our friendship. Make me worthy of these gifts. Amen."

The words made me tremble as I spoke my prayer aloud. Comtesse took my hand. After a time she made the sign of Belle Cœur over her heart, inspiring me to do the same. Tears of gratitude ran down my cheeks, anointing the corners of my mouth with their salty blessing.

As dusk approached, I helped my friend light the candles, now feeling nervous about meeting the other sisters. The house felt strangely alive with their prayers.

Comtesse introduced me to the placement of things. There was a small cooking space next to the hearth with shelves on either side that held wooden bowls and crockery and a bucket of water for washing up. She went to a door at the back of the room near the hearth, and opened it to show a stone pathway leading to a long mud-and-straw building with a dried grass roof.

"Our infirmary, Goscelin. You will learn how to care for the sick and wounded. There is so much suffering…and death."

My dismay showed, for she paused. "Well, you'll see the infirmary soon enough. You're tired, and it's getting late. Here, let me show you where you will sleep." She took my satchel and set it on the cot in the farthest corner.

I thanked her, but in fact it was not comfort but rather dread that came upon me. The thought of having to go inside the infirmary, to go to a place holding so much pain and illness, was terrifying. How would I do that? Was this the way I was to serve God? Tending the sick did not feel like my calling.

My sad thoughts were banished in an instant when the back door flew open and the sisters poured into the room. They were as lively and graceful as tall birds, all in the long blue dresses and linen aprons sewn by Comtesse. I have never witnessed such a goodly company of women. Comtesse rushed to my cot, pulling along one of her sisters.

"Beatrice, this is Goscelin! You two will…."

"Comtesse has spoken of you often these past years, my dear girl! We were sure you were long since married with lots of children. But now you're here. Thanks be to God!"

Beatrice was shorter than I, and round and soft like the bread dough I imagined she kneaded each day. Her bosom was large, and so was her belly. I wanted to lean against her sweet, motherly breast, but instead sat in the warmth that radiated from her like a welcoming fire.

She pulled me to the table and said to the others, "Sisters, meet Goscelin!" The women gathered round me with an outpouring of welcome and blessings. They were each full of questions about my life and journey. Their attention was genuine but daunting.

I was shown a place at their table, and Sabine said grace.

"We give thanks for this evening meal and for Goscelin's safe arrival. Bless this food, and as we take this nourishment may someone with an empty belly be filled tonight through Your grace. Together we say may it be so and amen."

I had not heard the words before, but they stirred in me a glimpse of understanding of the depth of heart and purpose of the sisterhood. A sudden, bitter-sweet memory of Brother Paul came to mind. Yes, he would have loved this blessing of the warm bread and the hearty *potage du pommes de terre et legumes.*

Sabine, the soft-spoken woman seated next to me, put a gentle hand on my shoulder. "Welcome, Goscelin. I am eager to hear about your journey."

"Thank you. I'm happy to share my story with you. I am so happy to be here. What is your work at Belle Cœur, Sabine?"

"I'm custodian of our little community. I look after our provisions and household tasks and of course our funds, which are few but sufficient for our needs. I also work in the infirmary, as we all do. There are many to care for. Too many sometimes."

Her small, gray eyes were widely set above her long, narrow nose. She was very thin, and she constantly twisted this way and that as she spoke.

"You will surely be a blessing for us, Gah-se-*line*?"

"Gah-se-*lin*. My father wished for a son. I think he would be surprised to know I can read and write better than most men." Bragging was something I'd never done before. I surprised myself with my boldness.

"You read and write?! Oh my, how I can put you to work. My skills as a scribe are poor, and besides I am far too busy sorting our tasks. We've no one to make a proper record for our household. You know, a list of our property, livestock, infirmary needs, our monies. Perhaps you'll keep our various reports to help manage things."

"Oh, yes! I can do that. I didn't mean to brag. You should know that I..."

"Don't be foolish. God has provided you a gift. You must own it and use it. Yes! You will definitely be a blessing for us all."

I nearly wept with relief at Sabine's words. Her excitement made me feel that I could be useful at Belle Cœur, and perhaps if I were busy scribing I would be excused from duties at the infirmary.

Numb with exhaustion but feeling the pleasure of a full belly, I helped clear the table.

"No. This will not do. You must rest after your travels. Go now and get some well-earned sleep. We'll put you to work tomorrow." Beatrice gave me a hug.

I made my way to the waiting cot. Comtesse followed. I slipped out of my clothes into the linen gown someone had placed on my blanket, and Comtesse hung my dress on a nearby peg.

"Sabine may depend on you to scribe the record of our life here, but I wonder how everyone would manage without my mending and stitching. Perhaps you should pray to God to discover how your hands might be of *real* use to our sisterhood, Goscelin. I could certainly use some help because much is required of me." Abruptly, she turned away.

Comtesse's sharp tone stung after her earlier tender welcome, but I forgave her hurtful words. And in any event I was at the end of a long journey.

I retrieved Henriette from my satchel and found the sprig of rosemary the old woman had given me "for protection." Well, here at Belle Cœur I wouldn't need protection! I laid my weary body on the cot and pulled the warm blanket to my chin. Watching the sisters finish their tasks by candlelight, I breathed the aromatic herbs, listened to the gentle voices…sleep came quickly. I succumbed to her warm embrace.

I woke with a start just before daybreak. Maman's face faded as a remnant from a fleeting dream. I was confused in my new surroundings. Then the wonderful truth came to me. I was safe. I was with kind people, and there was meaningful work for me to offer.

I stayed curled under my blanket for a few more moments, banking the delicious sense of peace like hot embers that would be needed later to stoke the fire.

The other sisters must have risen earlier in utter quiet, for I saw only Beatrice. She bustled to and fro from the hearth to the herb garden between the house and infirmary. I remembered that Comtesse had mentioned she was affectionately called "Sister Grand-mère" because she was the oldest of the community and grandmother to the youngest, Marie. I was puzzled because Comtesse had also called her their *soothie.* I soon learned that "soothie" was the Belle Cœur term for wet-nurse.

Comtesse appeared as I was putting on my blue dress and apron. She busied herself gathering her distaff and hanks of flax for spinning. "Bonjour, Goscelin. I hope you rested well. You'll meet some of the sisters who will be coming soon from the infirmary. Helvide and Ravenissa have been working through the night."

"Bonjour, Comtesse!"

She turned and beamed her old, familiar smile on me.

I was eager to be at peace with her. "I'm called here, Comtesse. I know it—and I know…I know I have something to bring." I thought it best not to suggest it might be my skill as a scribe.

"That's why you've come so far. I know your journey was not without effort, but it must be said again… this life is not easy. Courage is required for us to be exposed to so many who come and go, the pilgrims, villagers, and others we care for. You must be patient, Goscelin. It took me some time to understand the ways of Belle Cœur and the many ways of being with God that are held here within our prayers, and our silences. If you pay attention to what I tell you, you'll be accepted."

Suddenly I remembered the times when Comtesse and I were girls and she'd insisted I play her game rather than a game of my making. She hadn't changed so very much.

"You're telling me to become your student?" I asked in a tone that hoped for a compassionate reply.

Instead, she snickered at my question and retrieved her spinning implements, then strode through the back door.

My first days at Belle Cœur, I was overcome by so much conversation. Life in the hidden room at the abbey had been mostly spent alone or only in the company of Brother Paul and silent Brother Jean. Suddenly I was surrounded by women who seemed to all want to know me at once.

There were new names to learn, and with each name came a story. Serious Imene had the responsibilities of midwife and nurse in the infirmary. Gertrude, with her strange accent and manly build, was the gardener and carpenter.

Elderly Beatrice and quick-witted Sabine shared most with me those early days, telling me about the others. The first time I was introduced to Ravenissa and Helvide, I learned they were sisters. This was curious, because to my eye there was no resemblance at all. Ravenissa had dark eyes and hair, and she was timid and quiet. She tended the many pets and the livestock. Helvide, with fair hair, creamy skin and piercing blue eyes, grew the herbs and prepared many of the medicines used in the infirmary.

Beautiful but wan Petronilla, Beatrice's daughter, was said to carry prophetic wisdom, but she appeared very fragile to me. Young, playful Marie was Beatrice's granddaughter. Sadly, Marie's mother—Petronilla's sister—had recently died giving birth to a stillborn infant. There was a palpable familial connection between Beatrice, Petronilla, and Marie as mother, daughter, and granddaughter. Their united presence was certain blessing for the women of Belle Cœur.

I met Mabille last. She was plump, with a smile that caused her cheeks to puff up. Her ample body concealed her shyness. We spoke briefly, but not once did she look me in the eye. She helped in the infirmary, but her true gift, I learned from Petronilla, was her love of music and song.

After the evening meal, Beatrice sat at table between Comtesse and me. She suggested I should begin working in the infirmary the next day.

"You'd better learn right away, Goscelin, that Imene is very particular about how things are done in the infirmary. If you know what's best, you'll stay away from her when she's tending the sick. But if she calls on you to help"— Beatrice leaned close—"then you'd better move quickly."

"But…I know nothing about caring for sick people! The thought of it scares me, blood and wounds and suffering…" I dropped my head to the table in defeat.

"Nonsense!" Beatrice slammed the table with her wooden spoon. I quickly lifted my head. "Look here! God expects no less of you than to care for the hungry and the sick. You won't last long at Belle Cœur if you don't mop up the vomit and hold the hand of one who is dying. Just what do you intend to contribute if you wish to be a part of this sisterhood? Eh?" Again she pounded the table with the spoon, demanding an answer.

"I can write, Sister."

"Write! Write, she says!" Beatrice said, waving her arms about her head and laughing. "And what will you write?" Her frown deepened as she wrinkled her fat nose with seeming displeasure. "And how, please tell me, has a woman like you learned the craft of scribing?"

I wanted to run across the room and retrieve my work from my satchel to amaze Beatrice and Comtesse. Temptation plied me, but Brother Paul's warning to keep my texts secret, that I would know when to share what was recorded, overtook the devil's urging…except for the boasting that came out of my mouth without warning, like bats taking flight into the evening sky.

"I studied with a monk, with the Armarius of Saint Catherine's Abbey. He taught me—"

Comtesse gripped my arm tightly. "Goscelin has many stories to share, Sister. But you'll have to wait until morning to hear them. It's late. She's new to our ways. Tomorrow...there's time for more talk tomorrow."

Beatrice gave me a stern look before she began to clear the table.

Later, other women followed the stone path leading from the infirmary to the house. I would soon learn that the sisters were so devoted and their patients so desperate that the women often worked from dawn to past dinner. Now I saw that silence was the usual practice of the evening. I relished the quiet and found it soothing. Exhaustion took hold while we prepared for sleep that called us to our cots and to our prayers.

We began with praises to God for the tender mercies we had experienced that day. Then we prayed for the sick in the infirmary by name. Prayers for one another followed, and then came prayers for the blessing of the work of our hands. When our prayers were complete, after the last candle had been extinguished, we wished one another a blessed *bonne nuit.*

When all was still and Beatrice began snoring, I reached beneath my pillow for the familiar softness of the rag form. Henriette was weary, too. It had been an arduous journey from our starting place on that long-ago hot summer morning when we left Maman and home.

Home. Maman. Je t'aime, Maman. S-il vous plait, pardonnez-moi. As I pressed Henriette to my heart, my prayers carried me into a safe and dreamless sleep.

As I scribe these words, I am vexed with the paradox that life's blessings are often bittersweet.

My life truly began that first spring at Belle Cœur. How I long to shelter again in those first precious days of grace! All the Dominions—earth, air, fire, and water—came alive so that I knew them as the dark loam beneath the emerald fields, the soft breezes laden with the fragrance of flowers, the embers of our homely hearth, and the gift of gentle rain.

Yet it is true what Brother Paul said of the elements "*...remember they may bring blessing or destruction.*" At Belle Cœur and in the events that followed our eventual departure from our beloved home, I would come to know both.

I will put quill to parchment to record the story of Belle Cœur. I will write of both the enchantment and the sacrifices that grew certain wisdom to be shared.

14 November 1258
Le Monastère de la Visite

This monastery is a cold and unforgiving place. Here in my writing room, the door rattles and the candle flame flickers while outside the wind moans about the walls of our quarters. A familiar companion, the small, fat, brown mouse that has taken up residence somewhere nearby, squeaks in the corner. Henriette, of course, is at home in my apron pocket. I pinch my cheeks to keep sleep at bay. I must continue the scribing of my story and find a renewing vigor as I recall again my sisters' courage.

My hands are chapped from scrubbing bed linens today. The nuns of this monastery are grateful for our presence, but they require much of us. Most are reserved and silent, as is the way of their order.

Sabine answers to Sister Marguerite, the overseer of the monastery's infirmary. A severe matron, she is tall and slender as a crane. Truly, she observes everything from her bird's eye view. She is at least a head above the rest of us, and fortunately she's visible from a distance. Her pale, red-rimmed eyes rove the infirmary, commanding order. Her long, bony fingers are never still. Everything about Sister Marguerite is long, including her list of demands for our sisterhood. Each morning we receive assignments for the day's tasks from Sabine according to Sister Marguerite's instructions.

The infirmary has one hundred seventy beds. It is housed in a sprawling, one-story stone building next to the cloisters. Linen curtains separate the wards according to the nature and severity of illness. Four large open hearths provide warmth and fire for cooking the meals for patients.

Much is required of us…such drudgery as emptying chamber pots, scrubbing and laundry, bed-making, cooking, and so on. We are also expected to provide care for the patients. We help the nuns tend wounds, and often we sit in prayerful vigil with the dying.

When we first arrived at the immense monastery, it was Sabine who spoke with the nuns on behalf of our sisterhood. Though we were warmly welcomed and given a place to stay, we felt a need to protect our practices and our ways.

Our first night, as we made our circle in the former granary that soon became our home, Sabine stood before us, earnest and urgent.

"Imene is the only one of us they will trust to administer medicines, Sisters. Her understanding of midwifery makes her acceptable in this way. I sense that Sister Marguerite will view the rest of us as less than knowledgeable, perhaps even as country simpletons. Stay out of her way. Always busy yourself when she's about. We're capable of offering more, but we must be grateful for the roof over our heads."

Petronilla, who sat quietly folding linens, spoke softly. "With each fold a prayer is offered for one of you. Let us put prayer at the center of each task, and soon it will be finished! And the prayers will deliver blessing according to God's will. Even the harshest duties will become light if we breathe prayer into all that we do. Prayer is our true work, Sisters."

I have remembered this in the days to come.

Our prayers for the soldiers are fervent. We treat wounded crusaders making their way home to their beloveds. No word comes of Guy, Petronilla's husband and a crusader; perhaps even now he is traversing the Holy Lands. Guy has been away for over one year, but Petronilla's dreams promise her that he is safe as battles ensue.

When Guy and Petronilla began their life together, he heard of the call for Crusaders to fight the Mussulman in Egypt. The priest in their village, not far from Belle Cœur, announced the need for men to join with the king and journey on the Crusade. Guy and other men who responded to the call pronounced a solemn vow to become soldiers of the Church. Each soldier received a wooden cross from churchmen sent by the Pope for the occasion.

Petronilla and Beatrice took small comfort in Guy's absence, for they knew that as a soldier of the Church, he had been granted indulgences. These were special privileges vouchsafed by the Church in exchange for service, insuring his place in heaven. Petronilla prays he will return to her rather than follow the devil into trouble, knowing all his sins are forever absolved.

War is of man's making. It is not the way of women, and it certainly is not the way that Jesus gave us to follow. We are weary of the stories of killing and maiming. We are weary of men crying from the pain of suppurating wounds, raving at the memory of carnage, or silent before the final death rattle. Exhaustion is a way of life here at Le Monastère de la Visite.

Yesterday in the infirmary Sister Agathe, who is exceedingly thin, fell and gashed her forehead while she was tending a patient. Several of her sisters came running to carry her away. Many of the nuns appear to be very frail. I have witnessed several refuse food. When I asked Sister Marguerite about this, her reply was curt and direct.

"For some of us, the grace of the Sacrament of Christ's body and blood is all the nourishment required. We believe that depriving ourselves unites us with the suffering of Jesus." Her eyes shone with an avid light as she shared her community's ways. "Wearing the hair shirt, continual fasting, and self-scourging, bring us joy and fortification of the spirit."

The nuns' ways are different from our sisterhood, yet all of us love God with similar passion, although our forms expressing our love are not the same. Our understanding of God's love for all is expressed through our subtle changes of common words. Rather than referring to God's Kingdom, we say Kin-dom. We are all kin under heaven. Kin-dom speaks of family, of all life.

Jesus came to unite us rather than to rule over us. Kingdom speaks of power and special privilege. Jesus in His gentle way taught us to live as one community in God's love. The Kin-dom is the eternal circle of all Creation…embraced by the Creator. God's Kin-dom is here on earth, now, in this very moment. This is what we sisters of Belle Cœur believe. But how are we to share our beliefs when so many are fearful of change?

Sadly, there is a suspicious nature among the nuns here. They are wary of us, and it seems they are also wary of one another. Sometimes I feel as though I'm being watched. And if I guess correctly, the townspeople, too, are often suspicious of our ways. They thank us for our care but turn their faces to avoid our eyes.

Madame Muret appeared as one of God's messengers. She had come to the infirmary seeking a remedy for her infant son who would not nurse. She was strangely talkative and direct. Clutching Imene's sleeve before leaving, when no one was near, she whispered, "Be careful, Sister, guard your medicines. A healer who lives on the edge of the woods was put to the fire last week for making her potions."

Imene tried to ask Madame Muret for details about this horrid event, but the woman nestled her babe tight to her bosom and without answering turned and hurried away. Imene shared her story with Sabine, Beatrice, and myself after prayers the next morning. She urged us to take extra caution to do nothing out of the ordinary when the churchmen and priests were nearby.

We have heard many of the women villagers who have come for healing tell the nuns of the burning and raping of women when they dared to follow their heart's longing. The faces of the women as they share these stories reveal their fears and their choked spirits.

We cared for a pregnant woman who came to us with black and purple bruises all over her body. Imene asked her what had happened.

"It was the drink, Sister. He wouldn't have struck me except for the drink. The devil takes him over. The devil is in those putrid spirits he guzzles most nights."

"But what would cause him to beat you so?"

"I told him I was fearful. Fearful of the pain of birthing this poor child I'm carrying."

"I don't understand." Imene frowned.

"The devil came upon him, and he raised his arm and gave me such a blow I feared I'd drop the baby right there and then."

"But why would your fear of pain anger your husband so?" Imene began shouting in her desperation to understand.

"Because it's my punishment...You know, Sister, because Eve ate the apple when she had been told not to eat anything in the Garden. The birth pain is every woman's punishment because Eve went against God's command. My husband...well, he hit me again and said, 'Wretched woman, the child is better off dead than to have a mother who refuses her punishment from God.'

"I'm running away now. I fear for my child's safety as well. God help us."

Stories like this are regrettably frequent. Men capable of such horror use not only their hands to batter their wives, but their tongues as well.

We offer the broken spirits of the women who arrive at this infirmary a safe place to heal their wounds. We pray for those who are unable to find their way to us, who suffer and die alone in their silence.

Yet many choose to die from their illnesses and wounds rather than come to the infirmary for comforting and medicine.

"She who can cure can kill." This is what many say about us.

Fear is a disease for which we have no remedy. Healers outside these walls, like the woman near the forest, live dangerously close to the stake.

One young village woman, Madame Norbette, walked north for two days to see a healer named Odine. Madame Norbette told her husband she was in need of care for welts on her legs. In truth, she was making her trek to receive help for her stale marriage to the aged man.

Odine prepared an herbal bath of chamomile and powders Madame Norbette could not name. She was given a green potion to drink that smelled of mugwort root. Her condition improved, but her husband's hands and feet turned black and he died of the fever—no fault of Odine's.

Soon after his death, Madame shared the story of her visit to Odine with a woman she thought to be her friend. The woman told her priest, and within weeks Madame Norbette was charged with cavorting with a witch. "*Les sorcières*!" Madame Norbette and Odine were burned at the stake not far from this monastery.

It is said men, dressed in long black hooded capes, collected the women's worldly possessions soon after they were taken away. Where did they take their belongings? Who makes use of the women's clothing, pots, pans, and secret treasures now? Where do they hide these things?

We pray for the women's souls, and for the souls of those we never hear tell of, who are judged so unmercifully. Prayers for the betrayers and executioners stick in the throat, but we must also pray for the accusers and the ones who set the flames.

Thankfully we have also encountered good men in our midst. We pray their choices and example of how to live righteously will awaken the men who succumb to the devil's seduction.

Dare I write next what comes to mind? It must be recorded here that we cannot trust the priests and bishop who come to the infirmary to oversee our ways. We are careful to keep our herbal healing practices from the eyes of the clergy, the barber, and other men who visit the infirmary. They frown on our ways, and

I sense they are watching us closely for invented and imagined signs of the evil one working through us.

Our sisterhood's guardedness and secrecy, and the protection provided us as helpers to the nuns of this monastery, are all that separate our little community from the severest examination by the Church. The nuns would surely report any behavior they believe to be inspired by the devil. They are obliged to do so according to the bishop's rule, and to insure they don't fall into disfavor and suspicion themselves.

We long to share our healing and wisdom freely in the spirit of Christian charity. Will the time ever come when it will be safe to openly offer the love of our hearts and the knowledge of our minds?

The ominous and chaotic mood here calls our sisterhood to pray for God's protection. We rely on one another and God's grace for the strength to endure the daily hardships so far from our beloved home.

Now I understand ever more clearly the profound courage it took to bring the sisterhood of Belle Cœur to life. My quill returns me to a gentler time, to the beginnings of our sisterhood.

Before the others began arriving one by one to the house with the blue sign, Gertrude, Imene, and Sabine founded their created and covenanted order of Belle Cœur. It was their desire as the sisterhood grew in numbers to remain free, independent of the Church's rule, neither taking vows nor donning the veil of the nuns, free of vows of obedience to the bishop.

As the founders of our sisterhood, the three were inspired to live in a community of women, young and old, married and unmarried. Women called by God and dedicated to caring for the sick, the hungry, and the spiritually lost.

The dwelling that became Belle Cœur first belonged to Gertrude and Imene, who had lived there together before Sabine arrived. Like most who found their way to the little home with the welcoming spirit, Sabine was a pilgrim.

With her arrival came the seed that would grow to establish the sisterhood. Belle Cœur, meaning "beautiful heart," was chosen as the name for the house and surrounding land that Imene took on after the death of her brother.

Jesus's Sacred Heart represented the Belle Cœur of their existence. They chose to live anchored, like moss to a life-giving tree in the loving heart of Christ. Hence, the placard by the door and the sisters' sign of blessing were created...a circle to symbolize their community connected to all of creation, a circle of life embracing the cross at the center, the presence of Jesus.

One by one, Beatrice, Marie, Petronilla, Comtesse, Mabille, Helvide, and Ravenissa were guided by disparate circumstances to go in search of the house with the blue sign. As their community grew, each woman's gifts bloomed into loving action, an offering to God and the sisterhood. In the way the potter works bits of clay together to form a bowl, God melded the sisters' spirits and personalities into form. Ten women living together in full dedication of service to God and God's flock.

To my way of thinking, they were akin to the volumes of Dominions and Graces. Each woman was like a human book of holy wisdom, unique, a carrier of knowledge reflecting her personality and temperament.

~

The small barn with its stalls, troughs, and cot as an extra sleeping place provided shelter in foul weather for the cows, goats, and chickens. This humble structure, not unlike where Jesus was born, suddenly became the infirmary through an unexpected turn of events.

Their first patient was an infant. His young mother held the tiny child close to her bosom. The woman's sister was traveling with her as they made their way on pilgrimage to pay homage to the relics of Mary Magdalene. They appeared at the door of Belle Cœur looking for shelter because the baby had fever.

"I need help! Please help me!" She was frantic when Gertrude opened the door to the house. "Please, my baby. Please…he's sick." She was very young. Her long, black hair fell across her tear-stained face as she stood at the doorway. Her sister tried to comfort her.

"Vee vill help you," Gertrude told the woman. The frightened mother frowned as she tried to understand Gertrude through her heavy accent.

"I take dem to de barn and you fetch Imene from de meadow," Gertrude directed Sabine while she helped the woman and her sister inside.

The woman's infant son did not survive. Imene came quickly and gave of her highest arts to end his fever, but the angels did their bidding and later that same night carried his tiny soul to paradise.

Sabine prayed silently with the woman and her sister in their inconsolable grief. Tending the hearts and spirits of the sick would come to hold equal importance as tending the healing of their bodies. Prayer was present in all that took place at Belle Cœur.

The baby's illness and death became a strange christening on that day as the barn became the infirmary at Belle Cœur. The infant was buried at the edge of the forest, and that is how our cemetery came to exist. That sacred wooded ground would become the final resting place for the men, women, and children who died from all manner of causes while in our care. Many were healed as well, and they continued their travels and pilgrimages or returned to their homes in nearby villages.

Belle Cœur's infirmary grew board by board—and its graveyard stone by stone. The gardens were planted. Vegetables and herbs were harvested, and Helvide and Imene worked together to create medicines for use in the infirmary.

When Comtesse arrived with her stitchery craft and needle and thread, the sisters began the tradition of wearing blue toile dresses in the warm months and gray *toile et laines* when it was cold. A simple linen apron tied at the back of the neck and the waist protected the dress.

It was the founders' desire for any sister of Belle Cœur to be free to marry if she felt called to do so, although when I arrived, all the women were either widowed or unmarried save Petronilla. To become a wife or not; this question didn't worry the sisters of Belle Cœur. They would not be bound by the vows of the Church for women religious; vows of chastity or stability, a vow to stay in one place for the whole of their lives. They believed these vows required a specific call and could not be the way for *all* women who followed the Way of Jesus and felt called to live in community.

Rather, a sister of Belle Cœur was called to freedom. She could choose to move about wherever God beckoned her to serve the sick, the poor, and the forgotten.

Rarely did a woman dare to choose to live alone, without a husband or family to provide for her needs. Often families grew large, and daughters were sent as very young girls to the local monastery or convent to become brides of Christ.

I was eager to know the story of the sisterhood's beginnings and the stories of my sisters. How they had come to find the courage to choose a way of life that was beyond the accepted boundaries for women of our day. For most of us had been taught we had but two choices: to become a wife or a nun.

Sabine told me her story of her difficult choice soon after I arrived at Belle Cœur. I scribe it tonight to the best of my recollection because I'm certain that without Sabine, the spirit of our sisterhood would not be so fiercely blessed.

It was on a Sabbath afternoon in late spring that Sabine and I sat by the pond in the meadow not far from the house. I remember the intoxicating perfume of the clover that tickled my bare feet. The bees were humming their working song, and the sun was warm. Perhaps the moment of perfection opened a door within my mind where my question for Sabine had been waiting.

"I know you are the third sister of Belle Cœur. The journey that brought me here was long and winding. What of yours, Sabine? How did you come to the sisterhood?"

My afternoon companion drew a long breath while together we fastened clover to clover as Comtesse and I had so long ago.

"Are you certain you want to know so much of me?" Sabine asked, pausing to polish a plum she took from her apron pocket.

"Oh, yes, Sister. Our stories are gifts we offer to one another. Please share what you can. I can't imagine a better way to spend the Sabbath afternoon."

Sabine took a bite of the black, juicy fruit. The red juice ran down her chin. She wiped it away with the back of her hand. I search for words to scribe a portrait of Sabine. Grace-filled teacher. Yes, this is what I would say about her. Most striking to me are her deep gray eyes. Eyes so keen they can discern another's true spirit and intention. Her body, thin but soft fleshed, bosomy and agile. Her narrow nose and long, slender fingers appear like arrows pointing out the directions she spills forth to us throughout the day.

I lay back on the grass and watched the clouds change shape moment by moment. In spite of the soft spring air caressing us, Sabine's expression suddenly appeared fretful. She tossed the plum aside and began to nibble her fingernails while she fidgeted about. At a rustling in nearby bushes, she jumped to her feet and shook out her skirt. Finally, when she once again settled on the grass, she unfurled her tale the way Maman used to unfurl freshly scrubbed bed sheets on the grass to dry.

I was born in the season of the acorns, the eldest of three daughters, to a wealthy landowner. My early life was blessed with the uncommon advantages of comfort and wealth. My father insisted that my sisters and I attend plays, festivals, and study crafts such as basketmaking and tapestry weaving. All these pastimes were preparation for our certain, soon-to-be-arranged marriages to wealthy men.

I grew to be a determinedly willful young girl. So willful, in fact, that at the age of eleven I was delivered to a nearby monastery, much against my wishes and the wishes of my mother and sisters. My father was fatigued by my precociousness. He presented a large dowry to the abbess as payment for my entrance into the world of rule and discipline.

The self-denial required by the nuns was in sharp contrast to the spoiled, comfortable life I had led. I despised the abbess' strict schedule, the early rising, the menial tasks I was assigned, and I questioned every rule. Yet there was blessing, as I learned to read and write a little.

In truth, my mind was voracious and became pleasantly stuffed with learning. To my surprise, my heart began to open to God, but only ever so slowly. I felt angry and betrayed by my earthly father. How was I to trust God as my Father in heaven?

Soon after the beginning of my sixteenth year, tragic news arrived at the monastery, news that abruptly ended the slow awakening of my spirit. The abbess called me to her study. She grasped my hands tight and told me how a horrible fire had raged through our family home. My entire family—my mother, father, sisters, and our house servant—perished while they were sleeping.

One day became the next. I was utterly inconsolable. Endless wailing left me without a voice. My jaws ached from gritting my teeth. All the while, the nuns spoke of the death of my family as "a tragic event but clearly God's will," until at last my grief and rage thrust me into the darkness of certain abandonment by such a God. My vision of the spiritual realm was blinded by my grief.

I loved my sisters, Margot and Anne, who were near to me in age. The realization that we would never again ride our ponies through the rolling hills or share the secret desires of our hearts shattered my spirit. My closest companions were gone forever. Faith left me in a rush, the way breath leaves the body at the moment of death.

I was restless and prone to outbursts. I blatantly disobeyed every rule of the order, much to the dismay and disgust of the abbess. She saw me as resistant, a troublemaker, as if I intentionally knew what I was doing in my cave of grief. I can hear her scolding voice still.

"It will take time for your spirit to succumb to God's call for your life, Sabine. If you allow your free will to refuse

God's desire for your soul, the devil will surely step in. And when your life is over, you will burn in the fires of hell for all eternity."

The abbess spoke of the inferno of hell by day, and at night my bed was a place of torment with dreams of raging fire and smoldering blackened bodies. The cloistered life suffocated me the way my family had smothered in the flames. All the while my heart longed to return to the world beyond the monastery walls. Thoughts of carnal pleasures, fine clothes, and all manner of luxury enticed me like an impatient lover.

When I was nearly seventeen, the time approached for the final vows that would bind me to cloistered life. I was lost as I traversed the desert landscape of my soul without Christ's peace to comfort me.

One steamy summer's afternoon when the last of my wits were about to abandon my tortured mind, the way birds scatter to the winds when a cat enters the garden, God took pity on me at long last.

I was walking from the refectory to the cloister garden when my eye caught sight of the feed master's wagon outside the monastery gate. It was laden with a vast mound of hay. Without thought, I rushed swiftly and unseen to that golden mound and quickly dug myself in to become one with the prickly cargo.

The wagon belonged to a man from the village near my family's home. I remember I felt exceedingly pleased with myself at my impromptu escape.

When the feed master returned to the wagon and the journey home was underway, I began to devise a plan for my future. My newly claimed depth of courage was intoxicating. I prepared to do what I must do. Bump by bump along that dusty road, I discovered how truly devious I had become.

Uncle Gerome, my father's brother, held the key to my future. He was wealthy and the patriarch of our family. Gerome favored me. His penchant for young girls was insatiable. His uninvited and improper shows of affection for my sisters and me had been tolerated because of his position and power. My sisters suffered his groping and drunken banter as well, but I was his favorite, an unsavory honor to be sure.

"Come sit on my lap, Sabine. Look how those bobbins of yours are growing. Let me see what you have under your chemise."

His beard was coarse, and the memory of his wet, liquor-soaked kisses and prodding hands stain my soul with unending shame. Throughout childhood, my uncle's behavior toward my sisters and me became worse. My mother, in her fear of losing the source of our money, looked the other way. We pleaded with her to no avail.

"Mother, can't you make him stop? We hate his kissing and cooing!" My sisters and I went to her for help after a particularly disgusting encounter with Gerome. She was deaf to our pleas.

"Oh, my dears, you'll learn soon enough that men will want to have their way with you again and again. It will help if you think about another place and time. You are my creative girls, n'est-ce-pas? Make up a game in your sweet heads and while whomever does whatever...you play your game, and soon before you know it he'll be done." Her hands danced about in midair as if chasing away flies while she continued her pitiful counsel. "You'll be no worse off, and quite the contrary, you could do very well if you use your beauty to entice a wealthy man to enjoy your hidden treasures."

Many times I had reflected on the comfortless motherly wisdom I'd received as a girl. Yet while I was buried under hay in that rickety wagon, I contemplated my mother's long-ago advice with new understanding. My mother was wickedly cunning after all. In that wagon on the bumpy road to my future, I made the decision to do as I was told.

The wagon turned onto the road that would take me home. Red dust rose in a cloud under the wooden wheels, filling my nose and eyes while I peeked from beneath the hay. I recognized the east bridge as we crossed over into the rich, fertile land that had been my father's true love.

My heart beat faster when we approached the bend in the road. The shadows from the archway of trees cooled the hay and played upon our course. I longed to stand up tall to watch for the first glimpse of our gray timbered house and the stables where father kept the army's horses. I imagined Margot and Anne running across the field to meet me.

Suddenly the driver turned south toward the village. Soon the wagon stopped at the Vaschon farm. When he went to the door to announce his arrival, I leaped from the wagon and ran to the road leading to my home.

It was a hot afternoon. There was no breeze and no sound save the cicadas' drill and the cawing of a distant crow. I slipped off my sandals and pulled off my outer habit. My chemise clung to my sweaty body. I tugged the veil and wimple from my head and hung them from a tree branch. Perhaps some needy creature would drag them away to add comfort to her nest or burrow.

The earth proved too hot for bare feet, and I bent to tighten the strap of my sandals. In that ordinary moment my nose took in a disturbing smell. It was faint at first, like the scent of charred wood and ash when it's swept from the hearth. I began to run, and as I came through the stand of trees to the rise in the hill and looked down to the valley below, I was forced to my knees by grief.

There in the place where our beautiful home had once stood was nothing but blackened earth and ash. The trees encircling the property stood naked and dark, like sentries at the entrance to hell.

"No! No! You can't be gone forever…Maman! Papa! Anne! Margot!"

Great sobs of grief wracked my body. After what seemed a long time, I rose up and began to walk slowly down the hill. Soon I was running, carrying the thought that I might find something of them there in the ashes among the burned stones and wood.

Sweat poured down my back as I searched the ash for anything of my family that had survived, until I was blackened like the trees. Nothing. And then a flash of light caught my eye. The sinking sun showed me the treasure I'd been seeking. My hands reached into the black soot and retrieved it. A wide golden band encrusted with rubies, one of mother's rings.

Tears ran down my cheeks. I searched for more. As the daylight dimmed and the air began to cool, I put the ring on the middle finger of my right hand and bent to gently scoop two handfuls of the grainy black ash into my pocket. Grief grabbed my thoughts.

Why, God? Why would You allow this to happen to them…to me? I'm an orphan now. What did they do to deserve wrath such as this? Where are You, God? I cannot feel You. I cannot hear You. Why have You abandoned me? Why did You abandon them?

I found shelter that night in the charred hollow of the tree. The moon rose above the hills, and I was comforted by my mother's ring, a reminder of her last words to me as I left for the monastery.

"Remember, Sabine, try as they will, they cannot tame your wild, free spirit. Don't let them—for it's certain you will need it one day." My mother had never spoken to me with such feeling. I was living into her prophecy.

My mind completed the plan for what I would do.

When at long last daylight returned, I walked the short distance to the next town where I would claim my new life. I knew I had something that would equal a sizable trade for my fortune. I would give my uncle my virginity for a high price. My rage with God for taking my family fed my desire to disobey the One whom I believed had stolen everyone dear from me. I was intoxicated with the feeling of at last seizing control of my own destiny through outright rebellion of my soul.

Feigning innocence, I arrived at my uncle's house. He was shocked but pleased to see me and welcomed me as the child he thought I was. His servant, Chloe, drew a bath and offered me clean clothes then left me alone to dress. I took a glass vessel from the cabinet and carefully emptied the ashes from my pocket into it.

Then I pinched my cheeks till they were rosy pink and untied the strings of the chemise to reveal my breasts, which had grown much larger since my uncle last fondled them. It took little effort to interest him. This time, I didn't have the luxury to be afraid. I believed I had to do what was necessary to survive.

He was a dreadful man, my uncle, stupid and easily seduced. So I cooed to him, "I know you have always favored me, dear Uncle. I also know you have a taste for the harlots of this town and that you pay them a mighty price for their favors."

"Oh, but so worth it, Sabine. Oh, so worth it." His piggishness was despicable.

"I've come to offer you a proposal, one I'm certain you'll find irresistible. One that I have never offered to another."

"Well, come and sit on my lap, girl, and let me hear what you're thinking. You seem serious, and I'm intrigued by your little mystery. You know you've always been my favorite niece. The fiery one, the difficult one, eh? What's running wild like a mare in heat in that little head of yours?" He patted his knee invitingly.

Like a hawk circling over her prey, I recognized his vulnerability and went in for the kill. I held his gaze, moved toward him, and straddled his lap. When we were face to face, I took hold of his chin and looked straight into his clouded, blood-rimmed eyes. My anger chose my words.

"Uncle, it's not my head that has an offer for you; it's my body. But like your harlots down the road, I too have a price. I offer you the pearl that all men crave, my untouched self, but only on my terms."

"Tell me more, dear niece. Oh, do tell me more!" He tried to focus his gaze through his stupor.

"First we must drink together and feast in preparation for my deflowering. Then you may be the first to have me, dear Uncle. All I ask of you is a portion of gold in exchange for my gift. I ask this so that I might remember your generosity and this favor you have done for me as my first customer."

"First customer? Surely you're teasing me. Continue!" He laughed and coughed a loose, phlegm-filled cough before he squeezed me against his fat belly. I could feel his excitement push against me beneath my skirt. I wanted to flee, but my rage coerced me further into total rebellion. I wanted to kick

him and run. But it was too late. The game was underway. I was about to become a whore.

My mind worked fast to justify my actions. God had forsaken me, and I was forsaking God. I had given myself to God, and I believed He had betrayed me. Now I would betray God and answer the call of my flesh. I drew a deep breath and stepped off the cliff.

"Do you accept my special invitation, Uncle?"

He summoned Chloe. She brought food and more wine to his bed. That night I knew I had to keep my wits about me. I sipped the wine and craved more but resisted. My father's brother drank enough for us both. We laughed and made lewd conversation. The harlot was about to be born.

When at last his fat, naked body lay upon me, I closed my eyes tight and entered a darkness I'd never known as I embarked upon what I believed would be my life's vocation. I remember thinking how the abbess had been right after all and the devil had at last claimed me. Then, as quickly as my mind had been filled with that unsettling thought, I was spared by God's intervention through what I can only name as holy grace and a miracle.

Just before my uncle was about to enter me, my spirit lifted from my body. I left my flesh and hovered above the bed while below me I saw my legs and arms spread wide beneath the dead weight of Uncle's sweaty body.

From my precipice of certain damnation, I heard a voice in the depths of my soul clearly tell me:

You cannot punish God. You will only punish yourself. Forgiveness is yours. Begin anew.

When my spirit reentered my body I realized that mercifully my uncle had not entered me! He had fallen into drunken sleep. I was spared! It was truly a miracle of grace.

In that moment when I was saved from a life of desperation and decay, I lay under the weight of the old man's foul, heavy body and wept great, heaving sobs of gratitude and grief.

I quickly dressed and collected my dusty habit. I went to the nightstand and grabbed the pouch of gold coins my uncle had planned to reward me for my service.

I hurried to get away. I took bread and cheese from the larder and stuffed them into a cloth sack I found hanging on a nearby peg. I took two gold coins from the pouch and placed them in the breadbasket where Chloe would find them—and with utmost haste I fled and made my way to Uncle's barn.

To my surprise, and as if an affirmation of my mission, I found Mirabelle, the gentle dappled mare I had once ridden some years before. I climbed onto her broad back and rode away in the moonlight with prayers of thanksgiving in my heart...but not before spitting on the gatepost to my uncle's property. I rode to the ruins of my family's home. I took my habit from the bag and stood in the middle of the ashes, where I spread the tired garment on the ground before me. My covenant with the spirits of my beloveds poured out from my converted heart.

"I will carry all of you in my bones forever. I leave my old life here and go in search of the new. Pray for me from where you are, and I shall pray for you until our reunion at heaven's gate. Be at peace. Amen."

As I rode deeper into the night, a strange mixture of grief and gratitude overtook me like a fever. Once again I struggled with God in spite of the mercy I had received and the sacred commission to "begin anew." Tears of shame burned my cheeks. The weight of my own heart outweighed the coin-filled pouch.

I knew where I must go. Riding east, I began to encounter great numbers of pilgrims journeying on foot. I realized, the closer I came to my destination, that I too was a pilgrim.

At daybreak, when I was still a distance from where I was going, I climbed down from Mirabelle with my sack of provisions. With a hard slap to her rump, initiating freedom for both of us, I sent her galloping across the open meadow. I took the small vessel of ashes from my pocket and pressed it to my heart.

Give me your strength, women of my family!

I tucked the pouch of coins between my breasts, picked up the cloth sack, and joined the silent procession of seekers on their way to pay homage to Mary Magdalene at her cathedral in Vézelay.

As I walked the crowd grew and grew. Many of the men were stripped bare to the waist. They publicly scourged and flagellated themselves into a frenzy of grief as penance for their sins. I had learned from the nuns that self-mortification—starvation, wearing a shirt made of camel's hair, sleeping on boards, and even whipping oneself—were means to unite oneself with the suffering Christ. But these groaning men covered in bloody stripes frightened me.

The crippled, blind, and sick were eased into the crowds along the road. They too were making their way to Vézelay with hopes for miracles and healings. Some wore coquille shells sewn to their clothing, the emblem of the pilgrim. Many, no doubt, were sent on pilgrimage by their priests to serve penance for sins. I was plagued by my own transgressions, and my sobs soon melted into the pilgrims' chorus of repentance. I pulled off my sandals and walked the dusty road, weaving in and out among the crippled, the elderly, and the sainted.

Exhausted, but strangely content, I began to contemplate Mary Magdalene, sinner turned penitent. I recalled the pieces of her story from what I learned at the monastery. The Gospels of Matthew and Luke both spoke of her.

Magdalene was the one who anointed Jesus's feet with oils. His helpmate and companion, Magdalene was ever close to Jesus even unto His death. She was the first one He appeared to after His resurrection. He appeared to her, a woman, even before He showed himself to His disciples.

Now I was answering the call to Christ's discipleship. I would follow Magdalene's example of devotion to the Way of Jesus. My mind ran in all directions, pondering the mysteries of what was unfolding.

We weren't really all that different from one another, Sabine and Magdalene. After all, I had nearly sold my body to my uncle for money, the same as a prostitute; I had welcomed that life into my heart—yet God didn't abandon me. Now I was turning my life toward God step by dusty step.

Perhaps Mary Magdalene was no more a prostitute than me. Perhaps she was wise as a serpent and gentle as a dove and knew how to survive the dangers of her day. If one like Magdalene could end up favored by Christ, then perhaps I, too, was worthy of His love.

She loved Jesus with her whole heart. What did this mean? What became of her after the crucifixion? How did she live out her days?

With the ears of my heart, I heard Magdalene's spirit speak to me:

It was God's grace that changed me. I loved Jesus with my entire being. I walked beside Him and looked into His eyes, eyes that revealed His unfathomable depth of love. I held His hand and listened to His teachings. I witnessed His grief for the suffering souls who came to Him in search of healing. I observed His compassion for the broken and desperate. My days and nights were spent in His company. I was there when the nails fastened His blessed body to the cross. I was there at the final moment when His last breath was finished and all fell silent. I washed and kissed His wounds with his mother, and we put His flesh and bones into the grave. Oh, holy morning when I arrived at his tomb with my oils! It was Him ALIVE! Illuminated with love! Oh, blessed recognition when He spoke my name: "Mary…" He lives on, dear penitent woman, in you, in your brokenness, in your willful nature, in your wisdom, and forever in your soul. He is Jesus the Christ, who calls you to Him. Love Him as I loved Him. Follow Him as I did, and you and others like you will reclaim the key to the Garden.

Here I could not help but interrupt Sabine's story. "Sabine! What did you hear Magdalene say to you… the last of it ?" My heart was pounding.

"Do you mean 'Do as I did, and you and others like you will reclaim the key to the Garden'?"

I couldn't speak.

Sabine leaned toward me and touched my arm. "Goscelin, what is it? You've gone pale!"

"She meant the key to the Garden of Eden, didn't she?"

"Yes. That's how I understood her message..."

"Oh, Sister, I have so much to share with you. There is wisdom to pass on, but it's too sacred to spill out in this moment. We will make the right time and I will show you things too wonderful to speak of."

"Now you have me curious, Goscelin. Please don't wait too long."

"I will tell you and show you soon very soon. But please! What happened next? After you heard Magdalene's message."

Sabine stretched her neck and folded her hands as if in prayer.

By the time I could see the town of Vézelay up ahead, I felt I had been accompanied by a friend and teacher. Magdalene had spoken to me in the language of the heart. I came to understand she loved Jesus as her Beloved and He loved her and He also loved me...Christi Delectrix. On my pilgrimage I realized for certain I had come home to Him...through Magdalene.

The tired stream of pilgrims wound along the road, dusty and hot as the sun began to set. I could see my journey's end across the plains. Ahead was the hill where Magdalene's cathedral rose from the earth, surrounded by wheat fields like a huge breast. The cathedral devoted to Magdalene was the erect holy nipple ready to feed the hungry crowds of pilgrims a spiritual feast.

Trudging into the town, I joined the throng that was frantic with religious fervor. Old and young prayed in the streets. Many lay prostrate on the ground outside the heavy, carved doors begging forgiveness for their sins before entering the holy place.

To be a pilgrim approaching the cathedral and monastery where her relics awaited…to kneel and pay homage to the remains of Jesus's most beloved apostle…these acts of devotion were believed to surely deliver answered prayers. I became one with the body of seekers caught in the tide of the crowd until exhaustion and longing for comfort overcame me.

I used the first of my coins to secure lodging at an inn just beneath the stone path leading up the steep hill to the basilica. There I stuffed myself on cassoulet and barley cakes. My belly rumbled rebellion, unaccustomed to such a feast.

I relished the comforts of soft bedding so very different from the straw mat where I had slept at the monastery. Blessed sleep soothed my aching limbs.

With the morning light, I stretched under the cool sheet and squeezed the delicious weight of my coin purse under the pillow. My mind awakened with a thought surely captured from my waking dream. Clothes! I will buy new clothes today. *Oh, how long it had been since I had worn new clothes. I giggled out loud.*

Marthe, the innkeeper's wife, directed me to a small shop not far from the inn where Madame Laroque was sweeping the doorway to her husband's place of business. She greeted me with a most enthusiastic "Bonjour*!*"

Her hair in the morning sunlight was bright as a pagan bonfire; red and amber caterpillar curls cascaded around her round face. Woven into her hair were tiny, colored-glass beads. Two long, brown, speckled feathers swung over one ear.

Time fled in the presence of giddy Madame Laroque. She danced about amid a most sensual feast of color and beauty while she spread an array of fabrics before me as choices for my apron. "Verte ou bleue?" *she sang out as she unfurled ribbons to compliment the yellow linen I had chosen for my dress.*

"Bleue! Oui, le plus certainement, bleue! S'il vous plaît."

She assured me that in two days time she would make a dress the color of butter. The long sleeves would be fashioned to fall softly at my wrist. There would be a blue apron to slip over my head. The merry dressmaker provided me long stockings that wrinkled softly down my legs. From the cobbler I purchased comfortable shoes made of brown hide fastened at the ankles with long strips of leather.

I was grateful for the coins that weighed heavy in my purse. I shared them with beggars on the road and servants at the inn while I continued my penance for what those same coins had nearly cost me. Each time I gave from my heart, I merged with the longing I had nearly forsaken—but that had never forsaken me. Magdalene's spirit led me deeper into the contemplation of my calling to God's service.

I attended Mass with the throngs of pilgrims. When I stepped across the threshold into the basilica dedicated to Magdalene, my soul was lifted from the light that filled the vault high above. It was so different from the sanctuary at the monastery where I had lived, a place that was dark, heavy, oppressive. The ivory-colored stone walls and the soaring ceiling of Magdalene's cathedral bid my soul heavenwards. The golden sunlight of summer streamed in through the clerestory windows.

I prayed to receive the guidance to find others who were searching like me. All day I stayed in Magdalene's earthly shrine, prostrate on the cold stone floor.

The very next day I fell ill with fever. My stomach burned, and I retched all afternoon. Earlier in the day, Marthe had knocked at the door to see if the room was to my liking. Finding me sick, she promised to fetch me a tincture. In early evening she returned with an elixir. I was told to drink it down in one gulp with assurance I would be cured by the following morning. Within hours I was miraculously improved.

Marthe told me she had secured the powerful remedy from two women healers in the next village. They could be found at the house with the blue plaque called Belle Cœur.

Two days later, I felt well again. Better than well—I was seized with a vibrant sense of gratitude that called me to my feet. Determined, I set out to find the healers of Belle Cœur and thank them. The morning streets of Vézelay were still wet from a spring shower. Light glanced off the cobblestones. Madame Laroque waved good-bye as I set out after stopping in for my new clothes. The yellow dress I wore that day was as bright as my spirit.

I passed a woodcarver's stall. On a high shelf was a small, wooden statue of Magdalene holding her precious, lidded jar of spikenard, the costly oil she used to anoint Jesus. Instantly my purse was out—this would be my gift to the women of Belle Cœur.

The walk through the blooming countryside transported my spirit. I followed Marthe's directions, and with each turn of the road the surroundings seemed almost familiar. At last I arrived at the modest dwelling with the blue plaque by the door, Belle Cœur. A robust woman of determinable strength came out of the door carrying a large round basket on her hip.

"Velcome, Madame. De infirmary ist behind de hause. Just follow de path." These were Gertrude's first words to me. Just follow the path... *her first teaching.*

We made our introductions. I explained I was there in gratitude for her miraculous cure. I assured her I had no need to go to the infirmary.

At first I had a bit of difficulty understanding Gertrude because of her heavy accent, but soon we settled into an effortless exchange back and forth. She invited me to help her harvest shallots and fennel from the plentiful garden. When we had finished, she welcomed me to follow her inside the humble but enchanting house. Expecting only to present my small gift and return to town, I was surprised by her generous invitation.

Sabine's story came to a pause when a cool breeze rustled the bushes near where we were sitting. Sabine stood and gracefully stretched her arms toward the remaining sunlight. She shook her skirt and folded her hands at her heart before returning to her place on the grass. "Remember, Goscelin, how you felt when you stepped through the door to Belle Cœur for the first time?"

"Oh, yes! It was like stepping into another world. As if the house were an anteroom to heaven. The candles and little altars in every nook and cranny. And the fragrance—lemongrass and rosemary, like the first breeze of spring. Sacredness was...is all around us. I believe Belle Cœur is a holy place as holy as any church. Don't you believe this is so, Sabine?"

"Yes. Yes, I agree. You describe it beautifully. We are blessed to live here. We are sitting on holy ground."

Sabine continued her story.

When I first entered the sweet comfort of the house, grief stung my heart. Belle Cœur's order and beauty brought to mind the memory of my home and the joy of my childhood days. The magnificence of my family's home, the gardens, the beautiful horses, appeared suddenly to my mind. But Gertrude interrupted my reverie. She told me the story of how the little house that had become Belle Cœur had been owned by the brother of her beloved friend, Imene. Imene had cared for him till his death two years before.

Gertrude told me in her heavy accent, "Imene ist a nurse und midvife. Ven her brudder died, she und I moved into dis hause. I know how to build tings—I learnt by vatching mein fatder."

"Do many come here for healing?"

"In de beginnink vee offered our herbal medicins und teas to nearby villagers. Zoon, many hear stories of de healing powers of de two vomen of Belle Cœur. Dey come now from time to time."

When it grew dark, Gertrude lit more candles. I first met Imene when she returned home after delivering a baby at a nearby farm. A petite woman with delicate hands and pointed nose, she appeared weary.

Gertrude was friendly and talkative but in a rather brusque way. Imene was more refined, reserved but graceful in her movements, folding linens for the infirmary and tidying here and there. Just being near her made me feel calm.

I was filled with the desire to know them better. Belle Cœur was weaving its spell. Time seemed to slow. I felt like a painted figure in a work of art, a captive figure in a painting.

Gertrude and Imene moved together in harmony. There was a certain quality and rhythm to their life, women's rhythm. They shared a common language of gestures and phrases that were peculiarly their own. Their graceful motions as they prepared the meal and readied the table were like a dance. There was a flavor of gentleness to their shared life that I felt privileged to taste.

Soon I found myself telling my story, how I had been "banished" to the monastery, and how I ran away. I was surprised as the words began slipping out of my mouth like beads falling from a string. Testimony, I would later realize, to the safety and camaraderie I felt with Gertrude and Imene.

I surprised myself by speaking with great fondness of some rituals and rites that the nuns had celebrated together when I was a novitiate. Because I was no longer confined by cloistered life, the pearls of my monastic experience were set free to be fashioned into a rosary of remembrance.

After we finished Gertrude's supper, warm bread and barley soup, I told the women I needed to return to town.

"You have no place to stay?" Gertrude asked.

"Oh, I have my room at the inn."

"No, dis vill not do. You vill take de cot in de corner. You stay wid us. Vee could use extra hands for de many tasks of de day. Vee need someone to help us. Stay, Sabine. Stay at Belle Cœur for now. You can fetch your tings in de mornink und return to us." Gertrude was firm. This was less an invitation than an order!

"Yes!" Imene was convincing. "Oh, how wonderful it would be to have you join us! Your spirit would be a blessing to the sick. Your wisdom of the world and the cloister would be

a gift. Many who arrive at our door are in need of spiritual counsel that no doubt you could offer."

Silence came over us. I reached into my apron pocket and drew out the carving I had purchased earlier.

"Thank you. I accept your invitation. This little statue of Mary Magdalene is an offering of blessing for you and your work and in thanksgiving for the healing you have given... you are giving me."

They each kissed me on both cheeks with prayers of gratitude for our new friendship. Then Imene placed the little statue with reverence in a niche in the stones near the kitchen hearth. Gertrude lit a taper from the fire, dripped hot wax near the statue, and then set the taper in the waxy pool upon the stone.

Magdalene glowed as she claimed her place at Belle Cœur.

Excitement coursed up my spine. And to my eyes there was a bright flash of light from the niche, just the way my mother's ring had caught the sun from its place in the ashes. Magdalene's spirit was alive. I was certain she had led me to my new home.

Later, when I was settled on my cot I reflected on the guidance I had received that dreadful night with my uncle: Forgiveness is yours. Begin anew. *God's plan was in motion.*

While my eyes grew heavy, I pondered... Gertrude, Imene, Sabine... are there others who will join us? This was my waning thought my first night at Belle Cœur. Then I closed my eyes and dreamed of fire.

My hand is cramped but I have scribed all I recall of blessed Sabine's story from when she shared it with me that golden afternoon. Not long after leaving Belle Coeur, when we had been invited to stay and work here at Le Monastère de la Visite, I found Sabine crying in the garden outside our quarters.

"Are you all right, Sister?" I asked.

"Oh, Goscelin, I feel trapped! This monastery! Here! Where I am once again a prisoner to rules! I must forever and always in my heart remain free. Free to obey God and God only. I cannot be ordered to follow rules made by men and enforced by women who take vows to obey them. It is God and only God who guides my way and calls me to use my own wits to know what to do. Oh, Sister, I pray one day we will leave here to begin again. Perhaps the time will come when it will be safe to return to Belle Cœur."

Sabine pressed her hands against her face to rub her tears away. "For now, unending responsibilities fill my days and nights. I often feel like an exhausted mother surrounded by needful children. It seems there's always someone tugging at my sleeve or heart. I am forever called upon for answers to our sisters' questions, for direction, for instruction. I long for replenishment."

Silence fell over us. We watched a fat robin pull a long, curly worm from the muddy earth. I reached for Sabine's hand. She grasped it the way someone drowning grabs hold of a rope. Then we walked together to the infirmary where the sick and dying lay waiting.

19 November 1258
Le Monastère de la Visite

The day began with another deluge. The cold rain continues to pelt the shutters. I take Henriette from my pocket and place her on my writing table for company.

My eyes are heavy from too little sleep. Last night after all had gone to their cots, I fetched my copy of Volume II, *Air*, from it's hiding place deep in Brother Paul's old satchel. I keep the satchel stowed away behind the cupboard here in this little room. Dominions and Graces sustain my spirit, and I pray for more time to contemplate the teachings and grow the wisdom. I only read a little for fear of being seen and questioned about the text. The passage is now locked in my memory for safekeeping. I contemplate the message and await grace to come to me to add to the margins.

God breathes the earth to wakefulness after winter's sleep. Spring winds blow the trees, and the season of seeding sets Creation in motion. Clouds caught on the breeze fill and pour onto the ready ground, and feathers fall from above as raven and sparrow fly high and far in search of nesting places.

I have been assigned to the hard task of scrubbing the stone floors in the refectory. Today the mud from the monks' sandals will surely have dried in nasty clumps all about the stones. My knees are bruised and my hands are raw. Yesterday, as soon as I polished one portion of floor, someone would pass by to deliver more mud. Such is our work here, endless and toilsome.

Last evening after Vespers, our sisterhood gathered near the hearth to share our favorite stories from beloved memories of Belle Cœur. Cibylle listened closely, as she always does, making little movements and sounds that both amuse and perplex us. Oh, how I long to scribe Cibylle's story! I must write of her soon, but to put her name to parchment feels too dangerous now. If my writings should be discovered, this book and I would surely be burned.

All I can say is that it becomes more and more difficult to keep Cibylle hidden. Her strange actions worry us so. If she is found by the nuns, trouble will follow. Enough! I dare not write about Cibylle or her strange ways.

For now, I must continue to record the story of our life at Belle Cœur. Sabine and Petronilla tell me time and again that the ways of our sisterhood will be important to those who will follow us. In that future time, the stories I scribe will come alive again. Our record of our days on this earth will radiate all we know about how to live in passionate beauty, in harmony with creation as sacred artisans and pilgrims following the path of peace in a violent world.

"Our way of life will inspire the future lives of women." This is Petronilla's prophecy, and Sabine is holding me to task; thus I write in haste before I gather my rags and bucket and make the long walk to the refectory. Seeking the sacred in the midst of scrubbing and mopping is a practice that will surely grow my soul.

Gertrude, Imene and Sabine, as the founders of Belle Cœur made their own prayerful choice to live as seekers of beauty and truth. Their day-to-day existence was rooted in discovering holy wisdom hidden in ordinary moments. They sought the presence of the sacred in all things and in all manner of daily tasks—tending the sick, baking bread, milking the goat, and lighting candles as dusk became evening. They were wise in the ways of the world and the Church. Their hearts were united through their calling to seek direct communion with God through prayer, Sacrament, and their attentive, thoughtful ways of living.

The nearby villagers were grateful in the early days of the sisterhood for the women's presence and for their new infirmary. Over time, the sisters' healing methods and their choice to remain independent rooted Belle Cœur in the dark soil of possible suspicion by Church officials.

The sacred rituals were created with that fine integrity that signified the order of the sisterhood of Belle Cœur. As each woman, one by one, became a sister, she brought her inspired gifts to share with the whole of the community. With every passing day, they journeyed deeper into the terrain that was their passionate love for God. They were growing through grace, in a dominion of Divine Love.

Sabine spoke to the sisters soon after my arrival as we gathered near the hearth on the Sabbath. "Let us rely on our sisterhood, and our coming together whenever possible, that our little chosen family may thrive and live on. Together we sit in our circle to share stories, to speak the needs of our spirits, to open our hearts to the presence of divine wisdom. The circle holds us in place.

"I sit with you on the rim of the circle not as the one in charge, for we are all teachers. We must listen to one another with the ears of our hearts. We must allow our minds to grow still before we offer our prayers. See the candle burning brightly in the center? There we find our common heartbeat present in the flame as the symbol for God's illumination and wisdom."

She paused and drew a long breath. We followed her example. Sabine continued, "We remember to welcome silence when there are no words to express what rests heavily upon the heart. The gentle tone of her voice and the dancing, graceful gestures of her hands held us rapt.

"The circle is round; it contains us as surely as the sacred font holds the holy water in the cathedral. We rely on the Light at the center, on the flame burning with eternal wisdom."

She asked us as we sat in resplendent communion, faces lit only by the tender, golden light. "Do you believe God marks each of us with love, with a special purpose for our lives?"

We were quiet as we drank from the sweet well of prayer and reverence. We held the question the way one holds a sip of sacred wine gently in the mouth before swallowing to savor every drop of holy sustenance.

"I have observed God's markings in the infirmary." Mabille broke the silence softly. "Often those who survive illness and injury are somehow branded and awakened by God's love and mercy. I have also witnessed this with the dying. God's marking of the soul sometimes occurs at the moment before death. Peace accompanies such a special grace. I have witnessed these things."

"And perhaps that is your marking, Sister," Sabine replied just as softly.

"Yes?"

"God has given you the eyes to see the mystery at work. You have observed those who have been asleep to creation's wonders when through grace their spirits are quickened. In illness they stood at the portal of death and God's mercy returned them to life. Your awareness of what you have witnessed is now a part of you." Sabine stopped for a moment, closed her eyes, and folded her hands at her heart before continuing. "You embody the experience, and it becomes a teaching for all of us. Your recognition of God's touch is grace. You have the eyes to see and the ears to hear the deeper meaning of a particular moment."

Tears spilled down Mabille's cheeks. "I never considered my recognition of such things to be a special grace, Sister. It feels just…natural, seeing God's hand touching lives."

"Ah, yes, dear Mabille. Don't you see? That's what grace is, a blessing. It's a state of being in total harmony with God's unfolding plan. Grace signals the unification of the human heart with the Sacred Heart. Grace is a numinous experience when the two beat as one." Sabine bowed her head and grew quiet. Again, we followed her example. The silence gave us space to take in all that was spoken. After several moments Mabille went on.

"I have always thought of my music and singing as gifts, as a calling from God. Perhaps there are other symbols and signs I have been blessed with that I have never appreciated as God's markings."

Sabine then offered her final wisdom of the day. "Make a chain of roses of your lives, my dear sisters. Let each day unfold hour by hour as God reveals your markings and fills you with grace. Pray without ceasing. Invite love to become the center of your existence. For God is made visible through love."

Our circle ended with Helvide's recitation of the Twelve Holy Mysteries of Belle Cœur. These are the sacred observations and practices that are woven into the day to day life of the sisterhood. The Mysteries are:

I. The mystery of human love and longing to know God
II. The mystery of holy silence and ecstatic praise
III. The mystery of spiritual grace and anointing
IV. The mystery of dreams and visions, the peramony
V. The mystery of the moon and stars, shinorage
VI. The mystery of signs and symbols
VII. The mystery of the changing seasons and Creation

VIII. The mystery of the angels and saints
IX. The mystery of the sacred imagination
XI. The mystery of community and sisterhood
XII. The mystery of fasting

Without a word, we prepared and ate our simple Sunday meal of milk, bread, and cheese. Before we cleared the table to continue our Sabbath silence that would not end until morning, Sabine led us in prayer.

"Beloved, we pray to recognize Your markings on our souls. Help us to use life's pain and suffering as fuel for our hearts' chariots of love. Amen."

What has always marked the women of our sisterhood is a spirit forged by courage that has been called forth again and again. Special bravery was required to celebrate the Sacraments of Eucharist and burial without a priest. Though we drew our rituals from the prayers of the Church and added our own, our worship knew no bounds.

Our devotion to follow prophetic obedience, to be led by God rather than adhere to the religious rules of men, was the foundation stone of our order. We relied on God's guidance, leaning into the Blessed Mother, the saints and angels. There was no map to follow for our way of life. We did not know we were clearing a third pathway for women…wife, nun, sister of Belle Cœur.

Beloved Jesus was at the center of all when we broke the bread and blessed the wine in secret sweet Communion. His mother, Mary, was held in continual devotion. We drew strength and courage from Our Lady.

The spirit of Mary Magdalene was also ever present. She, too, was a source of courage. Her way to follow Christ was a woman's way. Magdalene acted out of love and service. She did not disown her wisdom because the rules demanded she yield her mind and soul. She anointed Jesus's feet with precious spikenard oil with love and homage to her Beloved, rather than contemplating how others would reprimand her perceived misuse of such a costly blessing.

The earliest sisters of Belle Cœur established their rituals of morning prayer to take place in the meadow or near the hearth. Evening prayer happened when all were tucked in before bed.

I was invited, those first days as the women were coming to know me, to take part in the morning ritual. In the early hour, before dawn's light flooded the house, we rose and dressed in silence then walked out into the shadowy meadow where the dewy grass anointed our steps. First, we marked ourselves with the sign of the cross and the blessing of Belle Cœur. Pressing two fingers to the center of our chests, we formed a cross over our hearts, enclosing it within a circle.

Next, before we began our duties we offered a prayer of petition to God:

Beloved,

Please guide me in my desire to live as Your faithful servant. May my eyes be Your eyes, to recognize the depths of human suffering and the ecstasies of divine beauty. May my ears be Your ears, to hear the hidden truths within the hearts of those who bring their stories to my door. May my hands be Your hands, so Your healing love may gently fall on each fevered brow I touch and each task that I perform. May my words be Your words. Inspire my tongue to utter Your guidance, and encourage me to rest in silence, when silence is needed. O Blessed One, keep my heart forever open to fully feel life's pain and delight. Help me to not turn away from those things that are difficult to witness, or those that cause me to be fearful. Still my trembling, and strengthen me through Your presence within me. Make me brave and guide my every action. Bless my work to Your glory. Amen

The sisters' choices brought an ever-present threat of danger. Their secret names for things and other rituals served their ways and portrayed their difference from other communities. These practices became traditions that eventually grew to become the Order of Belle Cœur, the sisterhood. They chose to live outside the rule of the Church. The Belle Cœur way of life was humble but not ordinary, and the sisters knew their choices could lead to suspicion from outsiders and possible peril.

Brother Paul taught me how the Church is distrusting of healers and independent thinkers. Many with positions of authority believe that a fine line is all that separates the healing arts from witchcraft. Only priests are allowed to exorcise demons. Only men are privy to certain wisdom.

"Heretic! Blasphemer! Devil-woman! Witch!" Thus the Church brands those who break the rules. Even now, here at the monastery, caution is woven into each moment when we are in the presence of anyone outside the sisterhood.

If a suspicious word in the form of a dark rumor came to the door of Church authorities, it could mean persecution, the dungeon, torture, or a fiery death.

The waxing and waning of the moon, the colors and scents of the changing seasons, and the sun's movement across the sky marked my early months at Belle Cœur. Again I recall how I did all I could to be helpful. I longed to earn my acceptance into the order. Each morning I offered to wash the linens, scrub the cooking pots, or tend the garden so I wouldn't be asked to serve in the infirmary. Working there vexed me with dread.

When I stood near Imene to hold the bowl while she cut a patient to let blood, I felt myself sway like a tree caught in a wind. Stars flashed before my eyes, and dizziness overtook me every time I saw her apply leeches to an open wound.

"Goscelin, take a breath! I need your help. Gather yourself! I'm the one who should be faint...faint from fear, for you know women are not supposed to bleed a patient. Only men are wise enough for such medicine, eh? Stop your fidgeting and come here!" Imene could be very demanding. All the while, my nausea and trembling continued. "Do you think we're supposed to treat you for your little miseries?"

"No, indeed, Imene."

I knew I worked in a sanctuary that succored the wounded and world-weary, the suffering pilgrim, soldier, and villager. Yet how could I overcome my revulsion at the sight of blood and pustulant wounds or the rude sounds of the sick?

My distress must have been obvious, for Sabine was kind enough to give me only short assignments. I longed to be invited to scribe as she had mentioned when we first met, but there had been no talk of it since. Because I was not yet a true member of the sisterhood, I felt I couldn't ask for such privilege. So I waited and waited. Patience was clearly my lesson. I was determined to humbly bend to my tasks. In an unexpected way, God gave the grace I needed.

One afternoon, I answered a faint knock at the infirmary door to find a thin, gray, aged man standing before me. He had the look of one who had been handsome in his youth, but his clouded eyes were milky with grief.

"She has been gone since the spring rains ended. My heart longs to join her. Each morning I awaken and pray to God that this is the day I may be taken." The old widower smelled of urine and disease; death's hand was pressing upon him.

"Welcome, beloved of God. What is your name, Monsieur?" I asked, swallowing hard in a vain attempt to calm my stomach.

"Matthieu."

"Matthieu, may the peace of Christ be upon you."

I led him to the chair near the hearth. Mabille was summoned and told of his needs. She hurried off to prepare bread and milk for our quaking, emaciated visitor. I filled a shallow bowl with water from the kettle near the hearth.

I retrieved a small glass vessel from Helvide's cupboard. Then I knelt at the old man's feet. He had left his muddy shoes outside the door. I draped a blanket around his hunched shoulders and pulled the long, dirty stockings from his skinny, hairless, white legs. The smell was foul. My stomach turned, but I smiled at him reassuringly.

God, give me strength to serve this poor soul.

His feet were the color of the stone floor, gray and mottled. The toenails were raised and ragged and yellow. Pus oozed from two. The toes of his left foot curled one atop the other. There was a large wet sore on the sole of his red and swollen right foot.

This man is Jesus. I am serving Jesus. I repeated my prayer in my heart again and again as I imagined the man to be Christ right there in front of me.

Slowly and gently I guided Matthieu's world-worn feet into the warm water. He released a deep sigh and his tears began to pour forth. His body shook with great heaving sobs.

My hands grew warm.

Jesus, Jesus, Jesus.

Matthieu closed his eyes and trembled. The suffering places within his flesh and bones opened to receive God's healing.

I cupped water from the basin in my hands then gently poured it over the old man's battered ankles and heels. Gently I uncrossed his toes to carefully cleanse the dirt away. My touch was not of my own doing. Rather each motion and gesture felt inspired and guided by something beyond my capability. Holding each foot above the bowl, I poured water from the pitcher over the soles of Matthieu's feet.

When the washing was complete, I dried his flesh with linen towels. Kneeling, I placed his clean feet on my lap and pulled the stopper from the vessel of oil. The musty fragrance of the precious spikenard filled the air. This was the ancient oil Magdalene had poured so long ago from her alabaster jar to anoint Jesus.

In my heart, I felt I was tending Jesus through Matthieu.

Like drops of water touching the tongue of one dying of thirst, the spikenard dripped between the crooked, aged toes. It spilled slowly in holy rivulets the length of each foot over the heels and the ankles. When the ritual was complete, I placed boiled verbena officinallis about his feet and wrapped them with linen strips, and finally more strips of linen to bind the compress.

Matthieu's clouded eyes were open again, and brighter now. "She went so quickly, Sister. The fever took her without warning. There was no time to call for help or to find a way to bring her here. I miss her so."

"I'm so sorry. I'm sure she knew you were there with her. I'm sure the angels were there also. Please rest. I'll return in a moment."

I went to Imene's cupboard and fetched the red glass vial with her special medicine for healing broken hearts and quickly returned to Matthieu.

He continued talking of his wife. "I pray to join her. If the angels arrive for me this moment, I am ready."

I offered the old gentleman a blessing and anointed his heart with Imene's golden serum. Then I kneeled before him and placed his bandaged feet on my lap.

"Lay down your miseries, beloved of God, and rest in the peace of Christ. Lay down your miseries, weary traveler of life and be healed. Amen."

Following the blessing, Mabille, who had been busying herself near the hearth, wrapped a blanket round our guest's shoulders and offered him bread and milk. This was our sacred ritual for any suffering soul who crossed our threshold. We were called by God to greet the indwelling Jesus in the pilgrim, the child, the thief, the soldier, and the whore.

My desire to learn the service of healing continued to be tested by the sight of pus-filled wounds or the rotting, putrid flesh of a leg gone black and cold. Prayers flew from my heart to the heavens for the grace to remember that Christ was present in even the most disgustingly deformed or wretchedly ill person.

Yet, I was to discover that not all who professed true faith shared such a prayerful heart.

Since I had arrived at Belle Cœur, I had occasionally seen a priest and barber come from Vézelay to visit the patients. The first time I witnessed the men visit our infirmary, I saw the sisters stop their work and make way so the black robed men could pass through. They ignored us completely. I drew near Sabine.

"Why are they here?" I whispered.

"Shhh. Not now," she replied nervously.

I cautiously made my way in their direction as they talked with Annabelle, one of the village women who worked in the infirmary.

The priest was tall and perhaps near my age, with a halo of thick, dark, tonsured hair. He glanced my way, and I smiled with his recognition. He didn't smile back. Rather he frowned and pointed at me. "Who is that woman?" he asked Annabelle.

"She's a village girl, Father; she's helping today. Please—could you offer your blessing to a patient who is failing fast?" She turned away, encouraging the priest to follow her. His gaze stayed fixed on me for a moment before going to the patient.

Imene witnessed this exchange. She pulled me aside and whispered urgently, "Oh, Goscelin, don't call attention to yourself in the presence of anyone from the Church!"

"But, Imene—why did Annabelle say I was from the village?"

"Because we try very hard not to cause curiosity about who we are. There are rumors about other women who have fallen under suspicion by the authorities. Women who are healers or herbalists or—or women who choose to live alone without a man in the house, as we do. Such women have been known to pay for their freedom with their lives! The women who come here from the village are protective. They are our friends, and they cover us with their…their seemliness."

"Surely all churchmen don't carry suspicion of women like us! I lived with a monk who was kind and good. He taught me things I never dreamed I would know. Why would a priest or one of the Church cause harm? My teacher, Brother Paul, told me these things as well. I didn't understand how it could be so then, and I still don't understand."

I looked at Father Caradot and the fat barber who walked with a limp. He had come with the priest to bleed one of our patients. They were with Annabelle at the end of the infirmary standing near the patient's bed. I was struck by the indifference in both men's faces.

Imene pulled me out of sight and hissed, "Trust me, I know things that you must learn in time. Trust what I say. I must return to my duties. You need to leave here. Go to the house and make yourself useful. Go! Now!" Her fearful tone made me feel fearful, too. I did as I was told while my mind held many questions.

Soon I learned that the visits from the priest were intended as opportunities to observe our ways in case we should be practicing witchcraft. That is to say, many were coming to believe that women were to blame for all things unexplainable. If milk suddenly curdled or livestock took ill and died, or a mother giving birth was freed of pain by taking certain herbs, or if there was a flood when there had been drought…these misfortunes were apt to be blamed on a woman.

Unmarried women, old women, even little girls, often fell prey to vicious rumors fed by fear and ignorance. During the unscheduled visits by the local priests and the barber, we made every effort to become invisible in the way we offered herbal treatments and ministered to the sick.

Helvide gave me more instruction about the dangers of our chosen way of life. "Don't be naïve, Goscelin. We must be wise as serpents and gentle as doves, as Jesus taught. We take risks living as we do. We're following God's call, but the men of the Church would not believe this. They would see us as disobedient, willful women. In fact, they would be certain we are in thrall to the devil!"

I noticed Helvide on more than one occasion talk to Annabelle in whispers. Her serious expression caused me to wonder and worry, but I wasn't brave enough to seek answers for my questions.

In midsummer I sat one afternoon in the clover by the pond, amid the bees busily filling their tiny purses near their fat bellies with golden pollen. I was stealing a few moments away from my sisters to study Volume I of Dominions and Graces. The sacred text began: *The transformative properties of earth, air, fire, and water correspond to bone, breath, heart, and blood in the physical body.*

I knew this to be true from my increasing frequent errands of mercy in the infirmary, and from observing the sisters as they cared for the sick and dying. The infirmary was a place of miracles and demons, mercy and mayhem. Bone, breath, heart, and soul were exposed and examined by Gertrude, Imene, Helvide, Ravenissa, Beatrice, and Sabine. Their prayerful scrutiny of a patient's condition and tenor informed the prescription that would follow.

The sun warmed my back while I lay on my belly in the grass by the pond, searching the pages of Volume I for wisdom. I longed to be strong for God and for those who needed care—but there was weakness in my spirit. I searched the parchment for inspiration and guidance.

Vexation of the spirit requires equal portions of sunlight and moonlight to restore balance and to cleanse the dark properties of unsettledness.

Sunlight and moonlight were a ready prescription, to be sure. Languishing in the fragrant warmth soothed by the hum of the bees in their nearby hive, I searched the pages I had once illuminated with reverence and joy. I longed to understand the causes of human frailty and suffering. My study only yielded more questions. Not ready to return to the house, I walked around the pond, clutching the leather-covered book to my chest as though it were a shield and hoping no one would notice me. It was good to be alone.

I reflected on my studies with Brother Paul, especially his teachings about using the eyes of the heart and the sacred practice of beholding life rather than observing it. One winter's afternoon he placed an apple on my writing table while I was working.

"Tell me what you see, my girl."

"Why, an apple, Brother, thank you," I said reaching for it.

"No! Don't eat it…yet. Tell me what you see." His game continued.

"I see an apple that is red and ripe and looks good enough to eat."

He smiled, and his clouded eye seemed bright for an instant.

"You're observing the apple, Goscelin. You're reporting the facts of what you see. Now I want you to behold the fruit. Practice beholding it with the eyes of your heart and spirit. Slow down. Study the thing with reverence. Take time to take it in with eyes that are capable of seeing beyond the obvious."

I squinted at the apple. "May I touch it?"

"Absolutely. Study it."

I held the apple in both hands. I noticed a bruise I had not seen a moment before.

"It has a tender spot. I wonder how it came to have this little injury." I touched the soft, brown skin gently with the tip of my finger. "Apples make me think of the Garden, the Tree of Wisdom." I felt the weight of the round, red fruit in my hands, and a spark of recognition arose like smoke from a fire. My sudden glimpse of understanding came from a hidden place behind my heart. "God created this perfect food," I said with unfamiliar certainty. "It's perfect, in spite of the bruise. The way people are perfect in spite of seeming imperfections...We're perfect in God's eyes."

"That's it! That's it. Do you understand now? Do you grasp the difference between simply seeing and the art...the sacred practice of beholding?"

"Yes. Now may I eat it?" I said, smiling as I took a big bite.

Whenever I've caught sight of an apple since that day, I am reminded of Brother Paul and his lesson.

What did I *behold* in my new home those first months? There was the flow, the rhythm of days and nights at Belle Cœur. The elements were all present, earth, air, fire, and water; and also bone, breath, heart, and blood were visible—and more than that, they were palpable. Prayer, ritual, healing, and grace colored each facet of daily life. Everything was vibrant and alive within the orderly ways of the sisterhood. Matter and spirit combined at Belle Cœur, creating something new and real.

During my time of reflection by the pond, I came to realize the myriad ways the sisterhood of Belle Cœur was rooted in the elements, in the body, in the heart of God, in Creation herself Belle Cœur was a world like no other, a world that rested in the heart of Christ. Belle Cœur was a Dominion unto itself! Grace lived there... in the dust of the garden, in the fleck of light in the eye of the dying pilgrim, in the broken and shared bread, and in the prayers that flowed from dawn to dark.

I fill my quill with ink, tap it gently, and before putting it to the page I ponder each of the sisters of Belle Cœur in terms of the elements. Brother Paul's tutelage had so filled my heart and mind that I came to see my sisters reflected as aspects of Dominions and Graces. That is, each sister to me was like a particular element. Each embodied various properties described in those holy teachings. But of all the sisters of Belle Cœur, there were those for whom my heart held special favor.

Gertrude

When I think of Gertrude, the words "gentle manliness" find their way to the page. Her wisdom for seeding and harvesting the garden graced the life force of Belle Cœur. She was earth combined with air. Gertrude's essence held the seasons of spring and autumn. With passionate fervor, she dug and planted the vegetable and flower beds, and she was a masterful builder and carpenter, as good as any man in the village.

"You see dis chair?" She pointed to the beautiful chair she had carved from an old stump. We were near the garden outside her shed. "It's a livink ting, made of vood from da alder tree. Da vood has a heartbeat born from its dance wit da rain, da sun, und da vind."

Her large, powerful hands prayerfully crafted the cots, chairs, and tables in the house and infirmary. The shed near the garden behind the house was filled with Gertrude's collections of baskets, boxes, and bowls that became containers for all manner of sacred objects.

In the back of the shed on a long table was something too miraculous for the eye to believe...a small cathedral built of hundreds of small stones. Tiny windows made of scraps of vellum, which I had passed along for the purpose, were tinted with juice from beets and kale from the garden.

One dark, rainy autumn afternoon, Beatrice sent me to the shed for a basket brought by one of the villagers in exchange for Helvide's medicine. Gertrude was there working on her cathedral. She had placed a candle inside the walls of her creation, and the golden light shone through the little windows and between the cracks in the stones. I imagined there were tiny people inside. I could almost hear them praying.

"It's so very beautiful." I told her while I admired her craft.

"To build a cathedral to da glory of God...ahhhhh...dat vould be a lifetime's vork vorth da sacrifice."

A tall, strong woman, narrow at the hip and wide at the shoulder. It was Gertrude who built the extra room to house the increasing number of sick and wounded, that day by day found their way to Belle Cœur.

Once, when we were talking about her home and her life before Belle Cœur, she told me, "My people, da North people, are very fair. Perhaps 'cause da vinter months are so long und dark. Vee are made to shine brightly so vee might find vun another ven all is in blackness." This explained her pale skin and flushed cheeks and neck, and solved the mystery about her tolerance for cold weather.

Our gravedigger, Gertrude dug all the graves for the pilgrims or soldiers who died at the infirmary. No priest was called for the final blessing. Rather, the sisterhood gathered around the shrouded body before it was returned to the earth. Our prayers were sung as Gertrude sprinkled lyme over the corpse then filled the hole with dirt.

She went quietly about her work with a furrowed brow and determined spirit and spoke only when she was addressed directly. One had to listen carefully, for her speech was slow and often as soft as a whisper.

"Da body must rest quietly for a time after death, Sisters. Da spirit is still nearby for some hours vile it becomes accustom to its freedom."

Imene was usually the one who prepared the bodies for the grave. Gertrude's devotion to Imene caused me to ponder the beauty of a faithful and fervent love between two women. Gertrude often caught her up as if Imene were a feather on the wind, spinning her round before returning her to the ground. Their glances at one another in those tender moments spoke of something much deeper than sisterly friendship.

Blushing Imene, after their romp, playfully poked at Gertrude. There was an unspoken but palpable love between them. One of the many secrets of Belle Cœur.

Imene

Imene confidently directed the care for our patients in the infirmary. Though only men were privy to the study of medicine, Imene proved a woman's worth as healer.

"Remember, dear Sisters, your bodies are the arks of your souls. Honor the rhythm of your hearts, the pulse of the divine within you. Dance to invigorate your spirit. Celebrate not only the day of your physical birth but also those particular days that mark the birthing moments of your spirit as they occur throughout your life."

She taught us well, not only about the workings of the body and all manner of illness, but also about the workings of the soul. All the while she encouraged us with her tender merciful way. The Dominion of water and blood, earth and bone held meaning for the healer, Imene.

"Pray, my sisters, before you touch the sick. Pray and ask Jesus, the great Physician, for your hands to become His instruments for healing the one you are ministering to. Open yourselves to become vessels of Christ's love and mercy. Prepare your spirits with fasting to make a welcoming place within you so you may be filled with Jesus. Remember, your hearts are the storehouses for your souls. Stock them with prayer to bring healing to the suffering world-weary people who come to our door."

Imene's long, thin fingers guided many an infant safely from the mother's womb. Slender and calm, she glided through the infirmary with great assurance, directing one sister to bring water to a bedside, simply nodding to another who instantly knew to sweep the floor. She gave direction for how to care for a wound or an illness in a gentle voice, but her command was certain.

Imene's concern could also cause her to become short-tempered and sharp. If a patient was neglected in any way, or precious medicine was accidentally spilled—or if one of us yawned from weariness—her temper flared as at a great injustice, for these transgressions were unacceptable to her. I did my best to stay alert and to please her without question.

"There are so many to tend to; I can't possibly stop for rest now!" Fatigue often followed Imene like a demon shadow. She preached to us to care for ourselves, to tend our bodies, but it seemed her body was overworked and little appreciated by her. However, to watch her lay her hands upon a child wracked with fever, one could clearly witness Christ's healing light move through her most perfect vessel for prayer.

Beatrice

Beatrice rocked and nursed the tiny ones whose hunger was terrible. At forty-four years, she was the eldest of the sisters, yet her great breasts miraculously held an endless supply of milk for babes whose mother's nourishment had run dry. She was also our cook.

Her short, plump body belied her inner and outer strength. Compassion flowed from her heart with the same steady current that her mother's milk flowed from her bosom. Yet, her corrections and sharp opinions were delivered with a crack of her wooden spoon on the tabletop.

Of all the sisters, she was the one who always spoke her mind without pausing to please. Her truthfulness could cut to the bone.

"If you're in my kitchen, you will make your hands useful. I have no time to point out what needs doing. Open your eyes and be purposeful to the glory of God. If you see no way to be of help, then perhaps your eyes are clouded with laziness, for there is always something to tend in a kitchen." Crack!

Beatrice often lectured us in the evenings as we cleared the table before prayers. "I believe the Holy Ghost will walk into this house one day, and we'll all be so busy we won't even invite the Spirit to sit down for our blessing. If the Mother of God herself appeared to us, would we look up from stirring the soup, tending the sick, mending the sheets, or hoeing the garden to say, 'Good morning, Mother of God?' I doubt it! We must be attentive, my sisters, because in a place where so many are dying and there is so much to keep us busy, why, the Holy Ghost and the Blessed Mother are sure to be nearby."

She tempered her seeming harsh lessons with great love and comforting hugs. The Dominion of fire and an abundance of heart were Beatrice's qualities, sturdy and strong, brimming with compassion and the milk of life.

If the truth were known, I favored Beatrice as my found mother.

Petronilla

Of all the sisters, Petronilla is the most challenging to describe. How does one depict a visionary and prophetess? She is air, but air shot through with spears of fire. The moment of dawn's breaking and the darkest hour of night are her dominions. Her inner realm, if one were able to view it, would surely reveal impenetrable forests and majestic mountaintops. She traveled to places in her dreams and ecstasies that none of us could imagine and yet, she was graced with gifts of the Spirit that benefited all.

Her youthful beauty, startling thinness, and faraway expression captured the attention. Petronilla shared soulful and practical wisdom the sisterhood depended upon. The teachings revealed through her visions fed the sisters' spirits and guided all facets of life at Belle Cœur, but frequent dark moods taxed her vitality.

The community learned to accommodate Petronilla's many physical ailments. At first her fevers and fainting were frightening to me; later I grew accustomed to her maladies, as they heralded her oncoming rapture. She often nibbled her nails to the quick until they bled, the way Ravenissa's mouse gnawed at a bit of cheese. Headaches accompanied by "a burning shimmering light like the sun" framed her visions.

She took to her bed, drawing the curtains around her cot, lying still as a corpse for days at a time. No food. No drink. No need of anything. All the while, she swooned. She was locked in her invisible world… in ecstasy with the Beloved.

Twice, following my arrival at Belle Cœur, the sisters and I witnessed Petronilla's body rise from her cot. Four hands high she rose—like a feather caught by the breeze, she floated in place. Air, she was definitely a child of air. We dared not touch her for fear she would startle and harm herself. One has to witness such a sight to believe these things occur. I must say, though I testify to this in the company of Beatrice, Gertrude, and Imene, my mind still questions how such a happening can be real.

Some might call her levitations the devil's trickery. Others would claim she is holy blessed, a saint held captive by God between the world of spirit and the world of flesh. We were her witnesses and her protectors, ever careful to keep her far from the eyes of the villagers and those in the infirmary. They were curious enough about our healing ways.

Many days passed during Petronilla's spells when she was infused with divine wisdom. We took turns keeping watch over her, wiping her fevered brow or covering her when she chilled. We stayed near until at last her breathing returned to a normal rhythm. Her twitching and moaning were the signals she was returning home to us from those places beyond our vision or understanding. Later, when she was fully herself again, we gathered around her cot.

Beatrice sat near her. She would open her frock, hold a spoon in one hand, and with the other squeeze her thin, bluish mother's milk from her fat, brown nipple into the spoon. Spoonful by spoonful Beatrice slipped her sustenance into Petronilla's open mouth.

Only after she was fed did Petronilla tell us of her journey.

"Where did you go? What did you see, dear Sister? Did you come face to face with Jesus?" Mabille twisted her apron into a knot while her questions spilled out like ripe berries falling from a basket.

Beatrice put the spoon in her lap and dabbed the corners of Petronilla's mouth with her apron. She pushed her heavy breast back inside her dress the way she lifted kneaded bread dough into the bowl. Petronilla's eyes opened wide.

"Oh, Sisters. How do I tell you? Shards of lightning blinded my vision. I was in pitch. Within the blackness was the voice of God. 'Let your longing lead you, not defeat you. Use longing as the blacksmith uses fire to forge iron into a pot or kettle. Make something of it,' I heard him say not with my ears but with my heart."

Her eyes rolled upward, and her hands stretched toward heaven while she repeated in a whisper the divine words she heard with her heart. "'Set about your work in the world. Longing, when it is not used for fuel for the spirit, soon turns the heart away from love in the direction of anger and grief. Longing asks you to rise up and bring forth your wonders and treasures. I am there, within the longing. What you yearn for is born from My love for you.'"

She stretched her long arms toward the ceiling. Tears leaked from her wide eyes. "Then, Sisters, the darkness split in two. I was shown a silver egg as tall as you, Gertrude! The egg became a golden door. It opened to reveal a woman's outstretched hand. The hand held a cask made of comb dripping with sweet, golden honey. Bright, burning light flooded my vision. Time stopped. There was no breath in my body, for what I witnessed halted my breathing. Inside that living comb of honey was the throbbing flesh… the beating, blood-red heart of Jesus!"

A chill ran through my body. I reached for Henriette in my apron pocket and gripped her tight. Petronilla took a deep breath from the heavy stillness in the room and continued.

"Again I heard the voice: 'Within your heart is a honeycomb made from love. It was placed in your soul before your birth. I pour divine honey into your heart in endless supply from My heart to yours. Your task on earth is to pour it freely to all who cross your path. Feed My divine honey to the hungry ones. Tend the honeycomb of your heart. Offer My honey, My peace, My love. When you share your love, you share My love. Let your thoughts and prayers become the bees of your hive. Send them swarming into the world.'"

In that moment, as Petronilla told us about the divine honey, I followed the river of memory in my mind back to that long-ago morning in the forest, to the moment when Brother Paul gave me the gift of the queen bee. Petronilla's words caused me to remember that Dominions and Graces lived in me. My mind struggled with sudden questions. How should I share the ancient wisdom? When?

Petronilla asked for her gazing bowl. Beatrice fetched and filled it with water from the pitcher. It was no bigger than my hand and not very deep. Gertrude had carved it from the leg bone of some creature I can't remember. Petronilla treasured the thing. She said it blessed her visions with clarity. She gazed deeply into the shallow dish.

Then she told us, "Ahhh. Yes! I understand. Flowing honey. When we give freely of our love to others, God's love replenishes the honey in our hearts. Make honey of your lives, my sisters. Make sweet, holy honey of your lives."

Is that Helvide I hear coughing down the hall? She was ill some days ago, and now her cough returns to shake me from the trance that has befallen me with the scribing of Petronilla's story.

I rub my aching fingers while the monastery bells call the nuns to Prime, the readings offered at the wake of day. We are blessed to find safe haven here with the vowed religious. How will I scribe the story of how we came to live here near the great cathedral after leaving Belle Coeur? Please, God, may this not be asked of me now.

The new day begins. I should fetch my bucket and rags and begin my chores. No! I will not go yet. There is more to share. This is my true work, not scraping mud from stone.

Oh God, I am weary. Send Your angels with the words You would have me scratch upon this parchment. I must record the stories of our sisterhood as I've been told to do. Guide my quill. Amen.

Helvide

My prayer delivers a treasured memory. I close my eyes and return to the house with the blue sign and the sight and pungent scent of Helvide's herbs. They were beautiful to behold. Carefully gathered and tied, fat bouquets of lavender, thyme, and rosemary hung from the kitchen crossbeam to dry. Eventually each came to a special purpose as salve, balm, tonic, or medicine.

Helvide's unique wisdom was born from the world of nature. She was our herbalist with a natural understanding of the properties of plants and trees. Knowledge of stones and minerals and the secrets of the seasons were also within Helvide's Dominion. Her special gifts were rooted in shinorage that allowed her to read the stars in the heavens for guidance and direction.

If one sister of Belle Cœur traversed the entire realm of Dominions and Graces, it was Helvide. The four seasons and earth, air, fire, and water were *all* her domain. She understood the plant-life cycles: seeding, gestation, birth, life, and death.

Her kind expression was the countenance of someone who lived close to the Mother, to Creation. Her wrinkled skin befitted her gift, as though she herself had grown from the earth like a mushroom or woody stem. Always eager to taste the fruits from the garden, her mouth was round and full. Nature was her language. She spoke tree bark, moss, stone, root, and earth as if she dwelt on the forest floor.

"Put your hands deep into the earth, Sisters. Draw strength from her! Earth is the source for all that grows. We eat the plants, and we are nourished. We take the herbs, and we are healed."

Of all the sisters, to my heart, Helvide was the kindest. We spent many hours together when I became her helpmate.

She tended the herb garden, verdant and alive with the fragrance of rosemary, thyme, chamomile, and sage. I watched her go about her work in the small wooden herbarium, a shed at the end of the garden. She carefully concocted potions and medicines from fresh cuttings and from ground flowers and stems plucked from the bouquets that had been hung to dry. She taught me the properties of her ingredients.

"You should know, Goscelin...primrose is for melancholy. Storksbill eases throat pain. Comfrey soothes ulcers of the skin. Fennel clears phlegm. These remedies when carefully prepared provide healing for many of the sick who come to us with hope upon their hearts for a miracle."

Glass vessels filled with strange-smelling oils and salves, and tiny bundles of mugwort, thistle, blind nettle, and wild thyme wound tight with horsehair were kept on her cupboard shelves.

Helvide worked alongside Beatrice in the kitchen, adding bits of pellitory and cubeb pepper to our cook's simmering pots. She believed the combination of these ingredients allowed clearing of the intellect. Her herbs helped to sustain us.

She worked the earth with her strong hands and directed the harvesting and the planting of the vegetables in our garden and the grapes in our vineyard.

Her diminishing eyesight called forth her senses of touch and smell to assist her.

In autumn she ordered the harvesting of the apples and tended the making of mead and cider. One afternoon she picked an apple from the tree and squinted, as if to study it while she turned it in her hands. She squeezed then sniffed it.

"Ripeness is discerned from much more than appearance," she told the villagers standing under the apple trees. They had arrived earlier to help with the harvest in exchange for Helvide's medicines and a portion of apples as their pay.

"Consider how God touches and prods us to determine our readiness to serve Him. Contemplate how He has tested you, my friends. Find those green, unripe places within your soul and nourish them so in time you will be ripe to God's touch and ready for His use."

Helvide's parables intrigued me. I recorded many of them in the margins of Volumes I and III of Dominions and Graces. If any one of the sisters understood the power and meaning of the elements, earth, air, fire, and water, it was Helvide.

Ravenissa

Once more, I turn the hourglass. The morning light brightens the room. Surely Sister Marguerite will be looking for me. She is the eternal taskmaster! I must put down the quill and go, but I feel the angels begging me to finish what I have begun. I cannot fear the consequences. I must continue.

As I recall Gertrude, Imene, Beatrice, Petronilla, and Helvide in these pages, I come now to Ravenissa. Something of her must be put on parchment before I put my writing away to begin my chores. Of all my sisters, she is the most mysterious. As certainly as Petronilla was and is a holy mystery, Ravenissa...well, surely Ravenissa is not of this world.

At Belle Cœur Ravenissa tended our livestock and cared for ailing pets and animals brought to us by a few trusting neighbors from the nearby village. Here at the monastery, her work continues, though mostly in secret, lest she create suspicion. It is easy for Ravenissa to arouse curiosity and questioning. Her ability to speak to creatures in the tongue of their particular species is a gift that is both admired and feared by anyone who witnesses her strange ways. Fire continues to live on in Ravenissa. Underneath her quiet and solitary heart burns a mighty flame of passion for nature and her creatures.

Beatrice told me that soon after Ravenissa's arrival, the property surrounding Belle Cœur became a gathering place for goats, pigs, dogs, and assorted other animals.

"She was our Noah. The animals found their way to her. Animals that usually don't get along—the cat and the dog, for instance—played together when Ravenissa was near. Don't ask me how she managed it, odd girl that she is." Beatrice shook her head.

A small lean-to behind the house beyond Gertrude's shed became an infirmary for the countless feral cats.

Ravenissa was famous for singing with them in the afternoon, much to the children's delight.

It was quite a sight to see Ravenissa seated on the dirt floor with a lap full of kittens, an elderly, fat, yellow cat wrapped about her shoulders like a shawl, while a gray, speckled one was cradled in her arms like a baby, the lot of them purring and mewing in harmony together. Villagers believed Ravenissa was either gifted by God or completely mad.

"Ravenissa should no longer come with me to the village to feed the hungry." Beatrice spoke as she nibbled the meat from a chicken leg. We were finishing our supper at the table by the hearth one evening that last month at Belle Cœur.

"Why not, Sister?" Comtesse asked.

"Her animal noises and more importantly the way the animals follow and talk to her raises suspicion. I overheard whispers today. Someone called out, '*Elle est une sorcière*!'" Beatrice twisted her apron as she spoke.

Many of those who learned of Ravenissa's special gifts brought their creatures large and small to her for her healing, often in secret for fear of their neighbors thinking they had befriended *la sorcière de Belle Cœur.*

Other villagers crossed themselves when passing her on the road or turned the other way, whispering, "She works with the devil. She talks to animals in their language."

If a creature died while in her care, she honored it with a special ritual. Belle Cœur's animal graveyard was a small plot of land encircled by hawthorn bushes. The mongrel dog, blind cat, one-legged crow, or other poor, dead creature was first sprinkled with bits of rosemary. Then tenderly fur or feathers were wrapped with scrim and blessed with prayer offered by Ravenissa.

"You, Creator, made the beasts and birds, the fish and the crawling ones. Take Your creature back into the earth to live again in frond and flower. For your mercies we give thanks and say amen."

Afterward there was a procession to the hawthorn bushes, where the grave was dug. Surely burying animals with ceremony is called the work of Satan by most. Our dear Ravenissa walked then and now on the edge of the sword.

Oh, I must stop! I must, but it's curious to my mind that I only now at this late morning hour feel I mustn't go to my duties before I scribe something of Comtesse. Were it not for her, my childhood friend, I would not be a Sister of Belle Cœur. Lately, I feel a certain distance growing between us that troubles my heart.

Comtesse

The Dominion of water, Comtesse is water. Thunder lives in her. She is an oncoming storm. To the eye Comtesse appears calm like water before it heats to a rolling boil over the fire. One never knows for certain when the moment of boiling will begin. Her quick changes in mood make me guarded. I'm afraid I am fearful and distrusting of the woman who was once the girl I truly thought of as my sister.

Comtesse's calling was to be the needle-worker and seamstress to craft and care for the sisters' clothing. Tapestry making was a craft learned from her mother, a wonder with needle, wool and loom. Her nimble fingers sewed the simple blue dresses that fell to our ankles, worn in the warmest months and covered by a linen apron, front and back. A linen wimple and short veil covered our heads. In winter we wore gray, woolen dresses and Comtesse created black blanket cloaks for extra warmth.

She crafted our altar cloth used for special devotions and Holy Communion. It was colorfully stitched with crimson angels, a yellow sun, flying green beasts, and lapis blue birds, honeycombs and tiny golden bees. Comtesse illumined linen the way I illumined parchment, from the inspiration that was born in our sacred imaginations.

It makes me sad to write about Comtesse. I'll write no more of her today. Rather I will take a moment to retrieve a page from my basket, a page I scribed soon after my arrival at the house with the blue sign. Now I slip it in place with this morning's pages as testament to what I first beheld with the eyes of my heart, as I awaited acceptance to the sisterhood.

There is wisdom in this community of women, in the Order of Belle Cœur. Wisdom born from the melding of the gifts God has imparted to each sister. When the sisters work their gifts together, like yeast mixed with the flour, knowledge rises and something new is made. God has gathered the women who form this community for a special purpose. Something yet unnamed is coming into being, and it will continue to grow and blossom. Matter and spirit will merge, are merging...

into what will soon become the New Work. For now, I must stay alert and attentive to observe the signs and symbols of God's guidance. For now, I must wait and be patient with the hope I will soon be invited to become a sister of Belle Coeur.

I put my quill to rest and wonder what another would scribe about me here upon this parchment, as I have spoken of my sisters. I pray they would say, "*Goscelin was a scribe who loved God. Her dominions were earth and fire.*" I pray they would say, "*She was the keeper of our stories.*"

Le Monastère de la Visite
26 November 1258

Sabine suggested me to Sister Marguerite as the one to assist with the cleaning of the scriptorium. I have been instructed to scrub the stone floors, tidy the quills and the pigments used to illuminate the manuscripts, and also dust the many shelves. I must go about my work as silently as possible, lest I disturb the monks. Oh, if only I would be permitted to serve as scribe in that big room filled with light and alive with the beautiful music of quills playing upon parchments. The fragrances of ink, pigment, and parchment take my spirit back to my years in the hidden room. The stacks of manuscripts tempt my eye to peek inside but that would be foolish.

The monks, unlike beloved Brother Paul and Brother Jean, don't welcome my presence in their sacred space. I take great care while dusting the shelves and straightening the jars of pigments to become invisible.

Sometimes I take to thievery, though I always pray for forgiveness. I am very careful when I snitch bits of parchment, worn quills, or a pot of ink and scant amounts of vermillion and ochre. These treasures are hidden in my apron pocket to be entrusted to Henriette's watchful care until we return to our quarters. I risk much to record our stories in this manuscript.

I believe God has placed me in this monastery's scriptorium so I might be privy to the needed tools to complete my scribing of our sisterhood's stories. This opportunity feels in accordance with Petronilla's prophecies. I recall the guidance she received from her vision and later whispered to me.

"God has chosen you for this holy task. Scribing your journal on behalf of our sisterhood, is the work of your soul. It's important, Goscelin, for you to choose and record the stories that will best serve as guidance for a future generation, according to God's plan. Your record is not for us. Rather, it is intended to quicken the hearts and souls of others whom we will never know."

Petronilla instructed me from her bed while I sat nearby folding linen into bandages. I asked her, "What did your vision reveal about these people we will never meet? How will they know how to find our book of stories?"

"You ask too many questions, Goscelin. I don't have the answers." She spoke slowly and softly, never opening her eyes. "I have shared with you all that I know for now. Follow the instructions I am given to pass on to you. I must rest."

Petronilla is very thin. Trembling hands and a blue cast to her already pale skin reveal her fragility. Two days ago Beatrice and Imene had to bind dear Petronilla's arms to her cot with wide strips of cloth to keep her from floating above the mattress. Her mysterious levitations continue. Her body longs to accompany her spirit as it climbs toward the heavens to harvest the angels' messages.

It's damp and cold in our quarters. Though we have a small fire here, we miss the warmth of our wide, welcoming hearth at Belle Cœur. Le Monastère de la Visite is a maze of long dark corridors, outbuildings, and underground passageways connecting one place to the next on this vast property.

This little writing room in our quarters where I scribe our stories is a large closet, a seeming forgotten storage space rarely used by the nuns. Shelves arrayed with crockery and iron pots line the walls. Here among water jugs and cooking vessels, I perch on a wooden stool at a narrow plank table. I come to my haven as often as my duties permit. After my years in the hidden room at Saint Catherine's, I seek places that are confining and mysterious. I feel safe here.

When we first arrived at this monastery and were shown where we would stay I claimed this closet as *my* scriptorium. Soon I discovered a family of rats living in an old empty soup cauldron in the corner near the doorway. Within days, Chanson, Ravenissa's favorite cat, grew fat from her late-night feasting, and the cauldron is vacant now. However, one quick brown mouse has seemed to escape Chanson's jaws. The little creature appears from time to time to keep me company and to torment the cat with her quick disappearances.

The Witness, the Scribe, the Listening Ear, these are some of the names Petronilla has given me. Our stories yet to be preserved in accordance with Petronilla's prophecy live in me until I find the time to record them. Like an artisan creating her tapestry, I take threads from the stories of our sisterhood and weave them into my journal. I am the keeper of our mysteries, our prayers and healing rituals.

I pray that when I have at last completed our manuscript, Petronilla's prophecy will come to pass. I pray others will one day read our book in the way Brother Paul taught me to study Dominions and Graces. It's my hope those who will one day read of us will be inspired to scribe their reflections and wisdom in the margins of our journal and discover revelations between the lines for their lives.

On stolen parchment I scribe each story then bind them together one by one. When the manuscript is complete, it will be wrapped in soft, brown hide. In this way the stories of *nos cœuragerie* are saved and honored. *Nos cœuragerie,* a new word of my making to represent our order and sisterhood, springs from my quill. I must remember to tell the others.

Tonight I will scribe a story that's dear to me, chosen as a perfect rose from our sisterhood's fragrant and colorful bouquet of life at Belle Cœur. I light a new taper and rub my hands together to warm them as I dip the quill into the ink…

Our life at Belle Cœur, cocooned us in beauty and our love for one another. The days passed swiftly, the way fingers move from bead to bead, prayer by prayer, on the Rosary. There was a precious quality to the ever-changing color and light of each hour. We were captured by God's love, and we were being grown by the Spirit and made ready for our future.

My memory became a vessel for the stories of our daily life. I longed to put my quill to the page to record the pattern of each day, but scribing the stories would come later, for parchment and ink were in precious short supply.

Two springs had passed since my journey had delivered me to Belle Cœur. Though I lived and worked there, I remained an outsider—waiting and praying the community would soon invite me to join the order of their sisterhood. For two years the women had been observing my commitment and discerning my call to the sacred life arts that were woven into the sisterhood's order. I was learning the rhythm of the sisterhood through dedication to my daily responsibilities.

Sabine faithfully tended the myriad tasks required to ensure our household and infirmary flowed surely as a river. She thoughtfully distributed duties between us and also directed the care for the many pilgrims and villagers who came to our infirmary.

At Belle Cœur, Sabine accepted, on the sisterhood's behalf, the gifts of generosity from villagers offering us alms, livestock, seed, and all manner of barter. They did this in exchange for our medicines, and for bread baked by Beatrice and honey gathered from the skep in the meadow. Rarely were our healing services exchanged for silver or gold. Our monies were few.

Without Sabine's steady guidance, I dare not imagine how we would have managed. On the Sabbath she always blessed us with a special teaching. I recall one particular lesson that I ponder often.

"Each of you is stronger than you realize, more capable than you believe, and gifted with a special purpose! Don't doubt God's blessings that reside within your heart and are written on your soul. You have an assignment to fulfill that was bestowed to you when you when were born." She looked us in the eye one by one as she spoke. "You must discover what you are to do…what you are meant to deliver before you return home to the Creator. Each of you has a legacy of purpose to offer. As sisters of Belle Cœur, we must encourage one another while each of us seeks to fulfill her life's assignments for God."

We were not to call Sabine our leader, but she was and is still the one we turn to regarding the practical nature of the day. Her role of overseeing our order of tasks and duties continues here at the monastery. However, Sister Marguerite, the monastery's nun assigned to be in charge of us, has final say about our duties as our mistress of chores.

One early, warm evening at Belle Cœur when spring was turning toward summer and the daylight lingered softly, Sabine invited me to walk with her. We followed the stone pathway from the front door to the narrow dirt trail leading to the meadow.

A skinny, gray kitten, Ravenissa's latest rescue, chased a sparrow. She pounced with serious intention, but thankfully the little bird escaped. I thought of Ravenissa's tiny pet mouse that lived in her apron pocket and hoped the playful kitten wouldn't discover *her*. The pets of Belle Coeur were considered as members of our family. Besides the assorted feral cats, there were also two goats with long, floppy ears, six sassy hens, one tired old rooster, six sheep, and three cows. Ravenissa was able to speak with all of them in their native tongue. She chirped, gurgled, moaned, and purred in conversation with every creature that crossed her path. A very strange miracle to witness.

Sabine spoke as her walking stick moved in rhythm with our stroll, pressing into the tall, green grass. "Your quiet way is a blessing for all of us, Goscelin."

"Really? Hmmm. I don't know what you mean."

"I've noticed how thoughtful you are with Comtesse. You bring her to her senses when she's in one of her disagreeable moods. Her behavior is wearing. No doubt we are offered lessons of tolerance and patience when Comtesse is nearby."

Sabine and I swatted our way through a swarm of gnats.

"She was my only friend when I was a girl. I never would have come to Belle Cœur were it not for her encouragement. I struggle to understand her these days, but something works on my heart to continue to pray for the grace to stay close to her."

"That 'something' you mention is God's love working through you, Goscelin. You bring a sense of calm and peace to difficult moments. Your gift of gentleness is grace for all of us." Little droplets of sweat on Sabine's upper lip glistened as though she were anointed by an invisible hand.

"Thank you, Sister, but I'm no more special than…"

Sabine stopped and took hold of my arm. "Don't dispute me. A reply of 'thank you' for a truth is all that's called for. You're right to hold your interior gifts with reverence and humility. However, if you deny or diminish them, you show disrespect for God, who bestows the gifts. Do you understand?"

"I think so." My face felt flushed and hot.

"Don't be shy about the truth of who you are." She released her grip and gently patted my arm. "I don't mean to scold you, but I invite you to think about what I've said. Acknowledge your gifts so you'll care for them and not take them lightly."

"I understand. But you must know it's very difficult for me to be the object of this conversation... to have such attention. I don't think of myself as one who does anything special. You seem to see something about me that I...I don't."

Sabine strolled slowly ahead of me. Her lean figure cast a long shadow on the grass. The cicadas' song grew louder, as if they were singing their praises to God for the daily miracle that was playing out before us. Brilliant orange and purple clouds painted the sky in wide strokes that appeared like giant angels' wings. The world seemed to be afire with God's visible prayer for all creation.

We paused for a time, silent before the beauty of the moment when the sun slipped behind the hill. The air quickly chilled with dusk's arrival. We walked arm in arm toward the house.

"I'm not the only one who sees your gifts, Goscelin. The community recognizes your contributions to our life together. You've become one of us. You are our sister." Sabine paused near the stone wall, and turned to me with a wide smile.

My memory will always hold those words—*you are our sister.*

"Ever since you came here you've been trying to discern if the way of life at Belle Cœur is right for you, and so have we. The community has been praying for clarity to know if it's God's will to invite you to stay. If you feel called to join the sisterhood, dear Goscelin, we feel you are already one of us."

"Oh, yes, Sister! Yes! This is what I have been praying for since I arrived. I can't imagine being anywhere else. I love all of you. You are my sisters…you are my family."

In five days' time, the moon was a perfect white orb in the night sky. I had bathed in the pond before sunset and been given a new blue frock to wear. The ceremony began in silence. After supper we processed by candlelight to the center of the garden. The sisters formed a circle around me. I held Henriette tightly in my hand.

Gertrude stepped forward carrying a milk stool and gestured for me to sit. The moonlight cast our shadows long and tall across the silvery plants in the garden. She drew her shears from her apron pocket.

Marie spoke slowly. "Your hair falls to the ground to remind you your body will one day return to the earth. Beauty will fade with time, but your soul is everlasting."

Gertrude cut my waist-length hair. It fell in great handfuls to the ground, the way the silk separates from the corn when the husk is stripped away. The evening breeze chilled my newly bare neck. I felt I would float away from the sensation of lightness.

Maman would surely have wept to see my golden hair in piles upon the earth. When I was a child, she would sing her happy song and weave my braid with clover, a cherished memory for comfort while Gertrude's blades completed their work.

The flickering candlelight danced with the moon glow. The sisters appeared shimmering and luminous as the golden angels in my illuminations. Comtesse slid a bulging satchel from her shoulder and retrieved a folded bundle of clothing. She placed the garments in the crook of her arm then unfolded a linen apron. Stitched in blue on the apron bib was an equidistant cross within a circle, the sign of Belle Cœur.

She passed a white cap and linen veil to Sabine before she slipped the apron over my head, covering my blue dress. "The apron is to remind of your call to serve God's people. Remember to tend with compassion the needs of all those who cross your path, as Jesus did. Be His helpmate on earth. Serve as He would… with hands that heal, a voice that speaks truth, with ears that hear cries for help, and with your heart that is guided by the Spirit. Do what you have always imagined you could not do, as an example of Magdalene's courage."

There was a faint tone of resentment in her words. She frowned and looked away. Her expression startled me, the way it feels to be awakened from sleep by a sudden clap of thunder. Comtesse turned her back, and Sabine stepped forward while I slipped Henriette into my apron pocket.

Sabine placed the snug linen cap onto my head, securely tying the two streamers in the back, at the nape of my newly bare neck. She pinned the shoulder-length veil securely to my cap with three long pins, one at the crown of my head and one above each ear.

With the placement of each she spoke prayerfully: "You are blessed with the inspiration of God, our Creator. You are blessed with the teachings of Jesus, our Beloved. You are blessed with the compassion of Our Lady, the Mother of us all. Use these gifts as the Spirit leads you. May these garments of our sisterhood and your prayers protect you from evil. Dedicate your body and soul each morning to loving service as you put on the armor of God."

Tenderly she touched the sign of Belle Cœur at the center of my chest. With her fingers she outlined a cross and traced a circle round it, never taking her eyes from mine.

"Please give me *your* blessing, Sister Goscelin." Sabine bowed her head.

I repeated the blessing sign over her heart while the tears I had been holding back spilled down my cheeks, splashing to my apron. Sabine and the others raised their arms to the milk-colored moon.

"Blessed Mother, we stand in your presence with our new Sister, Goscelin. May grace be upon her. Pray we continue to grow in service to God our Creator, to Jesus our Beloved and to you, Mother, guardian of Creation. We are the sisters of Belle Cœur, and we long to follow your holy ways according to God's will for our lives. Amen."

Beatrice came forward. She gave me her blessing and my charge.

"Sister Goscelin, you are our scribe and the keeper of our stories. You are also our teacher for reading and writing. Make use of your gifts to the glory of God!"

A scribe and a teacher! My place at Belle Cœur was named at last. I could never have dreamed such a life. I had a purpose! Hot, salty tears coursed down my burning cheeks.

After the ceremony as the candles guttered down and we—yes, truly we—walked back to the house in silver light, I lingered last and was suddenly embraced in a current of the sweetest fragrance! A night zephyr of aromatic joy swirled about me—and was gone.

We gathered inside near the hearth, and the sisters came to me one by one. Each offered kisses on both cheeks followed by tender blessings and the sign of Belle Cœur. When it was Petronilla's turn, she took my face in her hands. Her fevered, blue eyes were wide and pooled with tears. She spoke in a strange language unknown to me. Her gaunt, pale face was lit with a child's happy smile. She laughed. "Goscelin, my sister, what you hear is the blessing of the angels. You don't need to know what they're saying. The sound of their words is stored in your bones for a later time when it will be needed." Petronilla's unusual prayers always left my entire being humming as though a swarm of bees were busily building a hive in my heart.

It was a night of celebration. We feasted on honey cake and mead wine prepared by Beatrice.

"It's our tradition. I've been baking honey cakes for each sister since I was welcomed to the community." Beatrice cut into the warm, golden mound, sticky with a thick coating of the bees' amber elixir. Mabille sang and played her lyre. Ravenissa placed her mouse in my hands for me to hold for a few moments as her way of honoring the occasion.

After Compline, when I was preparing for bed, Gertrude presented me with a small wooden cross.

She carefully hung it from a leather thong above my cot. I was home. This was where I belonged. The sisters of Belle Cœur were my true family now.

I tucked Henriette under my pillow then drifted into a dream that with the morning light would vanish from memory as swiftly as the dark clouds that suddenly covered the full moon.

Oh, to return to Belle Cœur and happier times! Our life followed the daily rhythm of the Hours, the Divine Office, seven times of prayer, beginning in the middle of the night in our beds with Matins, followed by Lauds sometime later. The prayers of the Divine Office marked time. When we arose at daybreak in fair weather, we went out of doors to say Prime. Several times in the day and evenings, Mabille or Beatrice rang the bell in the garden to call us to pause and be attentive to our prayers. Terce in the midmorning. Sext at noon. The prayers called Nones followed in the midafternoon, and Vespers came at dusk. Compline completed the daily cycle before sleep.

Sabine acquired the book of prayers and Psalms before she began her life at Belle Cœur. "I will never reveal how I came to have this book, Sisters, so there is no use in asking."

To my scribe's way of seeing, the book was fine. The illuminations were carefully crafted, and the script was gentle on the eye. Sabine's mysterious statement fanned only mild curiosity. However, Comtesse thought she surely must have stolen it. She had been trying my patience all afternoon while we folded linens. We argued about the provenance of Sabine's Book of Hours.

"I'm certain it was given to Sabine as a gift, or perhaps she found it on the road. No matter how she came to have it, it's a blessing we share. You should be grateful she shares her blessed treasure with us."

"Oh, you're so very good, Goscelin! I suppose you've never had suspicions of anyone."

"Of course I..."

"No matter. I really don't care what you think." Comtesse turned and skipped like a child out the door. Her anger with me was something I didn't understand, but I couldn't gather my courage to ask her what I'd done to make her dislike me so very much. I was grateful for our prayers throughout the day because often I felt unsettled, and prayer was the only way to calm my heart.

The sound of ringing bells always carries me back to Saint Catherine's Abbey. While I lived there whenever I heard the bells I was reminded of how I was the different one, the lesser one, a young woman living in hiding in the midst of men. I couldn't take part in the prayers in the great sanctuary because it wasn't safe to be visible.

Each day at Belle Cœur, I gave thanks that at last I belonged to a community that was loving and welcoming. Praying the hours marked the portions of the day, night, dawn, morning, noon, afternoon, dusk, evening, and the return of night. I pondered how the hours were like seasons, folding one into the next. The early morning was likened to spring, a time of new beginnings, the hours of resurrection where gratitude for another day of living was at the center. Noon and midday reflected the summer, a time for cultivation and planting seeds for new growth. Late afternoon and early evening sang of autumn with the fruition of the day. Night and the deep darkness before dawn could be understood as winter, hibernation, rest, and replenishment before the cycle began again.

When I thought of the hours and their rightful relationships to the elements in Dominions and Graces, my mind wandered through the possibilities. If early morning was akin to spring, it would follow that dawn and the morning hours were connected to air, the first breaths of day. Noon and midday became summer, calling for the crystal flow of water to nourish growth. Afternoon and dusk turned to autumn and the Dominion of earth for bountiful harvest. Lastly, night's dark descent reflected winter's mysteries, calling for fire to illumine the path to rest at day's end.

"*There are connections in all of nature. Each of us is part of the natural world, Goscelin. We're human animals, made in God's image.*" Brother Paul's teachings return to me as I contemplate the weaving of the elements with the hours. I open the small box, here on my makeshift table in our quarters. The queen bee he gave to me that mysterious morning in the woods still rests on her bed of lavender. She is a queen. Jesus's mother is the

Queen of Heaven. She is like a holy beehive, and her son is the honey that flows from her heart. Yes, everything is connected under heaven.

I recall a question I once asked Brother Paul that opened the door to a most curious lesson: "*How can I, a woman, be made in God's image if God is the Father?*"

My teacher was silent for a long while. He rubbed his bald head as though to call forth his knowledge, and with each rub it shone more brightly. "*You speak of theological concerns, my girl. I'm speaking to cosmology and the origin of things. My answer for you is beyond religion in the literal sense, Goscelin. We're human animals, men and women. Both sexes were forged into being from the imaginative fire of the Creator.*" I nodded my agreement before he continued.

"*Men and women are the same when you take away the body. The soul is what I'm speaking of. In that place, dear girl, in the realm of the soul, lives the Sacred Androgyne. This magnificent part of our being, our divine nature, is neither male nor female.*"

This startling statement stretched my mind to the breaking point, as though it were on the rack, tortured by new thought. Question upon question arose in me. My teacher and I were lifted to a place beyond time. When the bells began to ring for Vespers that same evening, Brother Paul finished his lesson with words I will hold forever dear.

"*We have spoken of many things today. But this, dear Goscelin, is all you need to know for certain. You are a child of God. You are holy and good. You have within you all the worlds that God has placed in the universe. The Creator lives in your heart, and your destiny is written on your soul. You are a woman of wisdom.*"

Then he closed his eyes and placed his hand on my forehead and drew a cross with his thumb while he whispered what must have been a blessing. Peace wrapped around me like a warm blanket and I rested within his benediction.

The bells and our prayers at Belle Cœur kept the rhythm of our spiritual lives. In this way our bodies and souls were trued to the Spirit. When we prayed, we prayed in a circle. Each of us brought a special gift of service that served the whole, and in our circle there was equal measure. We took turns leading the prayers.

Thus the power of our community was complete within each woman. It was like Brother Paul's teaching…We *were* children of God. We were made in the image from the wondrous imaginative fire of the Creator. In *that* place we lived in harmony together. The circle, the bells, the hours, and our prayers held us in the presence of Jesus and Mary. Unknown to us, day by day we were being prepared and fortified for what would come.

In the first months when I was a Sister of Belle Cœur, I began going to the village each week with

Beatrice. One of our many ministries as sisters of Belle Cœur was to feed the hungry. We carried baskets of bread and honey collected from the skep in the meadow.

"Something sweet for your soul. Go in peace." This was her blessing as she spooned a dollop of the golden stickiness onto bread and passed it to anyone we came upon by the side of the road.

Rather than going all the way into town, we tended the people of a little village without a name on the outskirts of Vézelay. From the edge of the village, the enormous cathedral that held Magdalene's relics could be seen atop the hill in the distance.

It was late spring, and Beatrice and I plodded along with our baskets in hand. She walked several paces ahead of me muttering her prayers while her bread basket swung in rhythm with her awkward gait. The cicadas sang like a chorus of fledgling angels, and a crowd of white clouds moved slowly across the sky. They billowed as they passed over the sun, casting rolling shadows that spread across the landscape to bring fleeting moments of blessed relief from the heat. Henriette bounced about in my apron pocket as I picked up my pace to catch up with Beatrice.

"Why don't we go into Vézelay today, Sister? There must be many hungry pilgrims there. I've never been to the cathedral. Could we go?" I spoke loudly because Beatrice didn't hear so well, though she'd never admit it.

"We'll not be going there." Her tone was firm. She swatted the flies that had suddenly joined our little parade.

"It's not that far, is it? I mean we could visit the village and walk the short distance into the town. I've never been—"

"I said we'll not be going there!"

The cicadas' racket grew louder. I kicked a stone in frustration. Beatrice didn't notice.

We walked a while in silence. My discontent at the refusal of my request began to grow like a blister on my heart. Suddenly Beatrice stopped and turned to face me. Red-faced she wiped away the sweat that ran down her cheeks from under her cap.

"We'll not be going there because it's not safe." Her forehead wrinkled in deep folds, and she fanned her face with her hand. "In fact, we're most likely not safe traveling this road. The sisters try not to talk about the dangers all around us for fear we'll bring them closer. Some things are better not mentioned."

Sweat poured from under my arms in a sudden rush. Our pace quickened. My stomach churned, and I felt terrible that I had been angry a moment ago.

Beatrice stopped and dropped her basket. We stood in the shade of an oak tree by the side of the road.

"Listen, Sister, I told you we shouldn't speak of these things lest the evil powers around us grow stronger from our worry. I will only tell you this…The Church doesn't take kindly to those who choose to live according to their own ways. We have chosen not to take the veil and the vows of the nuns. We live the way of Belle Cœur. Though we pray many of the same prayers and take the Sacrament because we live by our own rule, if they were to truly know us, we would be considered suspect by the bishops and priests."

"Why? We love God. We follow Jesus's teachings. We..."

"We also break the bread and share the cup without a priest. Do you know what happens to those who don't follow the rules of the Church, Sister?" Flies swarmed all around us. We stepped onto the road again and I had to nearly run to keep up with Beatrice.

"I know there's...trouble for those who don't obey. I know they are surely scolded."

"Trouble! Scolded!" She stopped and laughed out loud, but in the next moment her laughter ceased. She grabbed my arm and pulled me close. Then she whispered so forcefully spittle sprayed my cheek.

"Trouble! So much trouble that people are burned to death in the middle of towns. So much trouble they're tortured to make them confess to things they never did. Trouble, Sister, is something we must stay away from at all costs."

My questions flopped about in my belly like helpless fishes caught on a line. I was afraid to spill them out for fear of what Beatrice's answers might reveal.

From that day forward, the demon of dread plagued me. My prayers increased, and I clung to the faith that Jesus would keep us safe.

My faith continues to steady me even now here at the monastery. The threat of danger is as close as the next breath. Life is precarious because we are women who have trespassed the boundaries of the Church and dare to live the way of prophetic obedience. We listen for and obey God's call. Our consciences guide our lives rather than blind adherence to the rules of men.

At least here, as we work alongside the nuns, we seem to be protected from the inquisitors, men bent on seeking out and punishing any poor soul who lives outside their dictates. Persons, particularly girls and women, who are viewed as different or who choose to think and act independently are often branded as witches, blasphemers, or heretics. We live on the rim of earthly fire and judgment while we pray that our way of life will come to be accepted by the Church, and we will be safe at last.

The rhythm of the hours carried one day into the next, and we went about our work: comforting ailing pilgrims and villagers, attending births, praying with the dying, feeding the hungry, and sharing God's love with all who arrived at our door.

In time, the frequent visits to the village with Beatrice yielded a gift to me in the form of a friend. Ambrosine looked younger than her sixteen years. We had met several times as I passed by her dwelling just before the village. In brief moments while I dallied waiting for Beatrice to deliver bread to neighboring folks, Ambrosine and I spoke enough to find delight in each other's company. She was curious about everything, and I looked forward to seeing her when I went to feed the hungry with Beatrice each week.

She was some five years younger than I. In a peculiar way, I felt she was the younger sister I had always hoped for. Everything about her was fine. Her nose was sprinkled with freckles. I was envious of her long, thick, brown hair that shone like copper in the sunlight. Her body was slim and willowy, and her every gesture appeared grace-filled. When she walked she glided along like a long-necked swan floating on a pond.

"Why do you wear that cap and veil?" she asked one afternoon. My basket was empty, and I was standing near the door to Ambrosine's dwelling where she lived with her mother and little brother, George.

"It's our way..." I caught myself when I suddenly remembered Beatrice's warning not to call attention to ourselves. "Hmmm,we cover our hair to keep it from interfering with our work in the infirmary."

"Your clothes are strange. Why do you and Beatrice dress alike?"

"Have you ever been to Mary Magdalene's cathedral, Ambrosine?"

"What? Oh, yes, we go there for Mass often. It's like I imagine paradise to be, full of light with angels singing. Have you gone there?"

"No, but I hope…"

"You must. I will take you there one day! I will show you where they keep her bones. Don't you have a miracle you pray for? You could pray to

Magdalene's relics like I do. I pray to learn to read and write." Her blue eyes grew larger the faster she spoke.

"Why, I can read and write, Ambrosine! Perhaps I can teach you…"

"How can you? I've never known a *woman* who could write or read. Who taught you? Are you sure you're not a nun? They are the only women I know who can do such things? Oh, it would be wonderful to study with you! Next time we meet...could we start then? Surely you are the answer to my prayer!"

"We'll see. You should come to Belle Cœur. I can give you lessons there."

I wanted to share with Ambrosine who I really was. How Brother Paul had taken me in and taught me so much. I wanted to tell her about the sisterhood of Belle Cœur. The more I longed to speak about these things, the more the dark-winged demon of dread pounced on my heart.

In spite of my caution I was about to spill out the treasures of life at Belle Cœur to my friend when her mother appeared at the doorway.

"Come in now, Ambrosine. Enough of your idleness." She frowned and looked straight at me; then she went back inside just as a cloud passed over the sun, making me shiver.

My lovely friend leaned close and whispered, "What prayer do you wish to be answered more than any other? What miracle will you pray for when I take you to visit Magdalene's relics?"

"Why…to see my mother again." I reached for Henriette deep inside my pocket.

Le Monastère de la Visite
3 December 1258

This season of Advent brings a mood of sweet anticipation. Wolves howl in the forest, and flocks of storks fly on the cold north wind like great long-legged angels. We have been helping the nuns arrange boughs of pine, bouquets of rosemary, and red-berried holly branches all about in preparation for Noël.

We are awaiting the celebration of the birth of Jesus. Thoughts of Our Lady and her earthly journey rest on my mind. She said yes to God's call to be the mother of Christ. Mary said yes! Not with the whimper of one who cowers when summoned, but boldly, fortified by her faith in God's unfailing love.

Candle wax pours down the fat cream-colored pillar on my writing table. I pinch a soft warm piece of tallow and roll it gently between my fingers to form the tiny infant. Tenderly, I shape his little head, round like the sun. I think of how the Beloved's birth poured light on a new day for people everywhere. In that way He was the sun and God's Son, as well.

I place my petit Jesus beside my other waxy creations...an acorn, a mouse, and my little figure of Maman. More wax flows down the side of the pillar making a soft hissing sound as it streams into a pool on the table. I cool it with my breath, then press a bit in my palm to shape a crèche for the baby Jesus, praying all the while for Petronilla to be well.

Tonight I saw her lying thin and pale on her cot while a hundred candles burned 'round her bed. Her bright blue eyes were open wide, witnessing that which only she's privy to see. Mabille tended her. Sabine, Beatrice, and I stood nearby praying for her protection while our dear prophetess wandered the holy landscape of her soul.

One recent evening before she became ill, when we had finished our prayers, she shared her thoughts while we all sat quietly in our circle. Her gentle voice, tremulous with urgency, returns to me now.

"We are waiting, Sisters. We are waiting with Mary for the birth of Jesus." Petronilla studied her hands as if her words could be read in the creases and lines. She rocked gently and turned her face upward, eyes closed. "Mary teaches us patience. She points the way to the path of courage and faith. Mary didn't know where her child would be born or how she would teach him and care for him. She only knew she was willing to follow God's call for her life." Her speech slowed and she whispered.

"We are waiting, Sisters. We are waiting for God's plan to be revealed for our lives. Our Blessed Mother illumines the way. Let us draw strength from her example. Courage. Faith. Trust in God. Let us rest in her presence as we await what is coming." Petronilla turned and nodded in my direction as though she knew I was inspired to speak. My little prophecy poured from within. From a place beyond my understanding.

"Earth, air, fire, water…May God and Creation protect us from the trials yet to be."

Oh, Blessed Mother, we wait with you for the birth of your Son. With His birth, light returns to the earth. With His birth, hope takes root in the human heart. We wait with you, Queen of Heaven, and we prepare ourselves to receive the sacred infant anew in our souls. Hail, Mary, full of grace…

Je vous salue, Marie, pleine de grace.
Le Seigneur est avec vous.
Vous êtes bénie entre toutes les femmes, et Jésus,
le fruit de vos entrailles, est béni.

Worry plagues me. I touch fire to the wick of yet another candle to cast more light, for my mood is dark and troubled. Will we ever return to Belle Cœur?

It's as though we live between two worlds; the world of our self-ruling sisterhood and the world of the *le monastère* with its many laws set forth by men of the Church.

We don't belong here. It's unsafe. We long to live as sisters of Belle Cœur, unfettered by the restrictions we must adhere to. If only we could live freely to celebrate with our hands, hearts, and voices the sacraments of life—and death—according to the ways of our little community.

At Belle Cœur we practiced our sacred life arts in freedom. At Belle Cœur our souls were free to worship and work as called by God. Benisons of healing and beauty we lavished on our world. Now we only share these things in secrecy as if…as if it were a sin for women to burn with holy fire and passion for life itself.

Ah, if only I had time as when I was in the hidden room. I long for hours of solitude and stillness to ponder God's mysteries, to scribe my most private revelations, and to study Dominions and Graces.

My poor hand trembles with fatigue tonight after hours of scrubbing and cleaning the scriptorium. The monks pay me no mind, save one, who follows me with his eyes. Today when he saw me come into the great room, he looked up from his work and appeared to stare right through me. My heart skipped like a stone thrown across a pond, and my breath caught in my chest. I have never had a man look at me in such a way. My face burns hot as I write these words.

Yes, today was long! Early in the morning after Prime, Ravenissa and Marie joined me here in the writing room for their lessons. Sabine has determined that all the sisters learn to read and write. I began to teach Ravenissa and Marie soon after I was accepted at Belle Cœur. Gertrude and Mabille have also studied with me from time to time.

Today, however, our precious lesson was interrupted when Sabine called all of us to the infirmary. The nuns needed extra hands to care for an inpouring of patients. The rebuilding of Our Lady's cathedral at Chartres must be completed. Its vaults reach higher toward the heavens with each passing day—but many bones and bodies are broken in that holy endeavor!

Sabine came to us with her instructions, and I hurried off to the scriptorium to clean the cold stone floors. Such are my endless chores, running here and tending there. I spend more time scrubbing than scribing.

I close my eyes while my heart yearns for a clean and peaceful place to write. I imagine a welcoming room with open shutters and a view of a green pasture where sheep graze while warm, lavender-scented breezes blow gently across my face. Yes, I ache for such a place where I might scribe all the prayers, stories, and musings that crowd my heart like a family of children clamoring for their mother's attention.

My heart has longings and so do my hands. My fingers ache to caress a pot of proper ink made from gallnuts, gum, and lampblack. Oh, how I wish to create illuminations once again with the brilliant hues that graced the original volumes of Dominions and Graces!

But I am blessed to have precious work that makes my spirit soar in the midst of scrubbing floors and folding linens. Teaching lifts my soul when the sisters, my students, each in her own way begins to recognize how the scratchings and blots upon the parchment do indeed have meaning. There is power in words and the knowledge that grows through reading and writing.

Just yesterday Sabine pressed me: "Please, write as often as possible, Goscelin! We need your record of our stories. Your quill must recapture the moments of those blessed days at Belle Cœur and weave them with our new stories of life here at *le monastère*." Her voice softened to a whisper. "You must also capture the prayers of our sisterhood and the recipes for Helvide's medicines with your quill. Remember that you are charged, dear sister, to make a record of our sisterhood. Your manuscript, the journal you are keeping, will be our legacy after we're gone. Your book…"

"*Our* book, Sister, our book…"

"*Our* book filled with our stories will become a map for the ones who will come after us."

So much responsibility she poured upon me. The dark tone of her words stirred my bowels with fear. I hurried to the garden to relieve myself while her words echoed inside my head. After we're gone? A map for others who come after us? Did her charge hold a promise of early demise? Who are the *others* she spoke of?

When I remember my early days as a teacher, I recall the first time Ambrosine came from the village to join us for studies at Belle Cœur. My young friend found her way one gray afternoon when the heavy clouds held the promise of rain. Beatrice was putting the cat out when she noticed my friend looking all about as she wandered near the garden.

"What are you looking for, girl? Don't I know you? If you're looking for the infirmary, it's…." Beatrice stepped out of the house and pointed over her shoulder.

"I've come to see the teacher!" Ambrosine shouted.

"The teacher?"

"She must mean Goscelin," Marie said as she ran to welcome Ambrosine. She showed her inside where

Ravenissa, Helvide, and I were studying together near the hearth.

"I had to sneak away from my mother to come here, Goscelin. She doesn't like you or her." She nodded in the direction of Beatrice. Then she turned to speak to Ravenissa and Helvide. "*Ma mère* says that you talk in the tongue of creatures that crawl about and that you make strange medicines. Some say the women of Belle Cœur work with the devil. I'm never supposed to come near you." She mimicked her mother's gestures as she spoke, twisting this way and that.

"Then what are you doing here? Have you come to cause us trouble? 'Cause if it's trouble you're looking for, I'll...." Beatrice looked at me with worry as she spoke.

"No need to fret, Sister. Come sit, Ambrosine, but you must only stay a little while."

Ambrosine pulled off her cloak, curled like a kitten next to the fire, and went on, unaware of our concern. "I've told Maman she's wrong about you, but she won't listen. The way she feels about all of you is confusing."

"What do you mean?" Beatrice asked.

"Well, she said you aren't nuns but you pretend to be, and that women who love God go to the monastery and take the veil. She told me that either women are nuns or wives and mothers. She says you don't love either God *or* men because you haven't taken the vows of the Church. So you must be working with the evil one. But I know you're not evil—"

"I'm not working for the devil!" Ravenissa cried. "What a dreadful thing to say." She dropped her head, pulled her mouse by the tail from her apron pocket, and began to feverishly stroke him with a long slender finger.

"You're mother is mad!" Beatrice cracked her wooden spoon on the table.

Ambrosine looked stricken. "*Oui*! *Elle est folle*! But it's my mother's friend, Madame Boisine, she's the one spreading so many nasty rumors and making people afraid of you."

Helvide's face flushed crimson with rage. "My medicines are strong to ease terrible suffering. Sometimes people have strange dreams caused by the mugwort. But to say we work for the devil! That's a curse! How evil!"

Ravenissa and I looked at one another in amazement as gentle Helvide's voice broke loose with anger.

Ambrosine stood and twisted her hair. "I know, I know. I'm sorry to tell you these things. I wish my mother didn't believe the rumors about you."

I wasn't surprised to hear that Cotille, Ambrosine's mother, disliked me. She was rude every time I came near.

"It's good you don't believe the gossip, Ambrosine. But why in all heaven are you here? What if your mother comes looking for you? If in fact she feels as you describe, she'll cause trouble for all of us!"

The room fell silent, while my questions hung in the air. Ambrosine looked me in the eye.

"I want to learn. You told me you could teach me. My mother won't know. Listen, Goscelin—I promise I'll be careful. She doesn't know I've come here. I won't be missed if I'm not gone too long. Please let me learn from you."

There have been moments in my life when my stomach became a fist inside me, punching like a cat in a bag, to get my attention—to stop me from blindly, ardently venturing into folly. If I ignored my gut's plea, trouble most certainly followed.

I felt the warning in my belly clear and strong. *Don't teach this girl!* Even Henriette who was deep in my apron pocket seemed to shout her silent warning. But the voice in my head cooed, *It's all right. Make her happy. You're a teacher. Don't be afraid. Imagine how important you'll feel once this girl begins to read and write.* I didn't dare look at Beatrice, Ravenissa, or Helvide for approval.

"All right, Ambrosine, you may stay for a lesson, but promise to be careful if you come again. You must be sure learning to read and write are worth risking your mother's rage." The words poured out of me and all the while my stomach rumbled the alarm.

Beatrice cracked her spoon once again on the edge of the table. I ignored her.

Ambrosine's face was bright and eager. "Thank you! Thank you!" She hugged me about the neck. "I want to learn, Goscelin, more than anything. Maman will never give me permission if I ask her. It will be a wonderful surprise when I show her I can read and write. She'll be proud of me—she'll forgive me. You'll see."You're making a grave mistake, Sister." Helvide's face was suddenly so close I could taste her breath. She whispered, "You...*we* will live to regret this day."

A shiver rippled down my back with Helvide's warning, but in truth I felt compassion for my young friend. I reached for Ambrosine's hand, pushed away my fears and felt happy for this opportunity to share my love of learning and wisdom.

We hugged, and I remembered myself standing where Ambrosine now stood. I recalled how I had awkwardly stumbled into Brother Paul's hidden room and first heard the beautiful music of his quill scratching across the parchment. It was my destiny to be there. What if he had turned me away out of fear of reprisal? I couldn't have imagined at that time that God was preparing *me* to be the teacher.

How can you refuse her? my chattering mind queried, while Ravenissa and Helvide walked away shaking their heads. Beatrice turned her back to me and without a word she cracked her spoon on the table.

Though I worried during those last days at Belle Cœur, of the danger of teaching Ambrosine against her mother's wishes, I felt I had made the right choice. I held then, as I do now, the conviction that knowledge and wisdom must be shared and passed to others. There were moments, however, when I had doubts about my decision, but I could not go to my sisters with my anxieties. They had warned me after all. We had discussed my agreement to teach Amborisine at great length in our circle, soon after her studies with me began. Sabine and Beatrice had spoken privately with me as well to air their disagreement. All, save Mabille and Marie, had voiced deep concerns. I knew I had to live with my choice and I prayed there would be no consequences.

And then there came two events that struck us with the force of God's will. Two pilgrims came to the infirmary, and our life together..., our little world, was changed by their messages.

The first message arrived with Madame Picard. She was an elderly woman who became ill while she making her final prayerful pilgrimage. A villager noticed her frail condition and delivered her to our infirmary. Madame Picard brought a special gift. It had been passed to her some years before. We learned it had come from the cupboard of the great Abbess Hildegard from the North Country.

The old woman, thin as a stick, suffered from a terrible fever. Her urine was red and stank like rotten beets. She lay on her cot sharing stories she had learned from a sisterhood of nuns in the Northlands... stories about the Abbess Hildegard. Her labored breathing colored her tale of Hildegard von Bingen, the wise woman, the great teacher, and lover of God.

She recounted how long ago she'd made a pilgrimage and stayed at Hildegard's abbey. While she was there, an old nun passed along a special gift to her.

"Give me my satchel, girl." Madame Picard rose up on her pillow. Imene reached under the cot and retrieved a worn leather bag.

Madame pulled out a brown velvet-covered manuscript, a concertina. It held twelve folded leaves of parchment fastened together securely to ensure it would travel well. There was a leather loop so the closed book could be hung from one's belt.

"I have seen a book made in this fashion," I said, as Brother Paul's lesson returned to me.

He had taught me about a special illuminated concertina similar to the one Madame placed in my hands. "*This sort of book is called a vade mecum, Goscelin. The phrase means 'goes with me.' You see? It's fashioned to wear about the waist while on pilgrimage. The vade mecum is full of maps and stories about the saints. There are also prayers for the pilgrim scribed in these pages. Contained here are computus texts that have to do with the nature of time. Oh, the vade mecum is a useful guide! It may also hold herbal recipes for medicines, and charts of the stars so a pilgrim may look to the firmament for guidance.*"

It was clear that the dirty, old, velvet book Madame Picard opened for us to see had been crafted for someone of great wisdom. The worn pages of parchment were no doubt stained with the ingredients listed in the various formulas. I could make out recipes for tonics, compresses, and other healing treatments as I carefully turned the pages.

"*Touchez-le, ma cherie!*" Madame invited me to examine the parchments more closely. The illuminations and markings appeared to shimmer and glow in the lamplight. I carefully opened and sniffed the folds. I sensed a person of importance had used this curious book. I pressed my thumb onto a faint brown thumbprint on the second page.

I became aware I was holding a schemata for healing countless ailments. Each parchment was neatly scribed in a careful hand, and some bore small but exquisite illuminations of plants, herbs, and minerals, the ingredients for the medicines described.

"*Connaisez-vous un herboriste*?" the pilgrim asked me.

"Yes. Yes, I know an herbalist. She's just over there."

Helvide was summoned and introductions were made. Madame Picard nodded to me to give her the book. Reluctantly I let it go and prayed Helvide would share it with me.

Helvide and I leaned close to listen to Madame Picard, who now spoke in a whisper.

"Abbess Hildegard was a great visionary. She left many teachings for those who knew her. I believe she was a saint. *Pour certains c'est qu'elle était un guérisseur.*"

"She was a healer? What else do you know of her?" Helvide asked as she offered Madame a sip of water.

"The abbess was good friend to popes and queens. The nuns told me she…was quick to temper…and she would often take to her bed to get her way."

All the next day the old woman rallied. Madame was feverish, but determined to tell us all she knew about the beloved abbess. She shared with Helvide and me that Abbess Hildegard had composed music and written books recording her visions. One manuscript represented nine books of healing systems: animals, reptiles, metals, stones, fish, birds, trees, elements, and plants.

I thought of the importance of the volumes of Dominions and Graces and of the abbess's manuscripts. I imagined there must be other sacred books hidden away awaiting discovery at a future time when the wisdom they contained would be needed.

Soon after her lesson about the Rhineland abbess, Madame Picard's fever overtook her. She fell silent and entered the place in between, the realm that is neither life nor death. Two days later she died.

Helvide spoke as we gathered in the cemetery at Belle Cœur for Madame Picard's final blessing and burial.

"Madame Picard was an angel sent by God to deliver sacred wisdom to us for safekeeping."

I wondered if somehow *we* had been angels for Madame as we tenderly cared for her those last days and hours. Isn't this what Jesus calls us to, after all? Caring for one another, loving one another…this is the way of Christ.

With Madame Picard's timely gift of healing recipes, many lives were saved. Our prayers and the strangely beautiful, velvet-covered concertina containing Abbess Hildegard's healing wisdom were holy weapons in our battle to assuage human suffering. God's miracles happened frequently in the infirmary at Belle Cœur—and they continue here at the monastery so far from that blessed place.

We prayed that our care and prayers had comforted our messenger as she departed from this life. She never completed her pilgrimage to Magdalene's Cathedral at Vézelay. It seemed that God's plan was for her to journey to Belle Cœur to be with us so Abbess Hildegard's healing wisdom could live on.

Madame Picard was the first dying messenger to bless our sisterhood with useful guidance. Soon there would be another who came to Belle Cœur's infirmary carrying a message that changed our lives forever.

❧

It was nearing the time of the Feast of All Souls in late October. Though we were unaware at the time, those chilly autumn days would be our last in our beloved home.

Just as we live now in the presence of increasing suspicion by those around us, our safe and blessed life at Belle Cœur also became treacherous and darkened by rumor and suspicion. Villagers were suddenly reluctant to come to us, save Ambrosine, who came to study reading and writing on the days when her mother left the house.

Annabelle Veniers and Portia Russot were the only women we knew who dared risk being shunned by the other villagers. They offered steadfast assistance and continued to help us to care for the many pilgrims who stopped at our door. Gertrude had prepared a sleeping space for them at the east end of the infirmary. There was no room for them to live in our main house, but they took their meals with us at our table. They did not feel called by God to join our sisterhood, yet our friendship was strong and their devotion to the work was true.

In the autumn it happened that villagers who came regularly for Helvide's teas and herbal remedies stopped making their way to Belle Cœur. Where were they getting the care they needed? We no longer had the villagers' trust or the blessing of their helping hands to tend the gardens and orchard in exchange for medicines and treatments. Ravenissa healed the two remaining dogs, pets, that had been brought to her, but their masters from the village never returned to claim them.

The gossip begun by Madame Boisine had spread like a plague with no cure. Through Annabelle and Portia, we learned the nature of the malicious reports. Vile rumors were tossed from one to the next. It was told around the village that we were practicing witchcraft. This hateful falsehood poisoned the hearts and minds of those we had come to know and care for. Fear and more lies slithered like a snake throughout the town, striking the minds of many with the venom of gossip.

Autumn was nearing the turn to winter, and we went about our tasks as always, with prayer and cheerful attitudes—as best we could. I persevered in teaching my sisters to read and write. Since late spring Ambrosine had continued to sneak away from her mother to come to Belle Cœur for her lessons. She was a good student, a quick learner, and proud of her accomplishments.

Ambrosine's passion for her studies burned with such intensity I could nearly smell smoke.

"When I'm not here, learning from you, Goscelin, I feel cravings in my mind. I want to be able to read and scribe like you. Oh, how I wish we could go to that secret room, the place you told me about so I could study all the books there. There's so much I want to learn."

The day arrived, however, when her earnest passion caught everything ablaze with an invisible fire that ultimately burned a new pathway to our sisterhood's destiny. It was a sun-drenched fall morning. God's presence was palpable in the brightly colored leaves as they spiraled to the ground. The Spirit played in the cool gentle breeze that fell across the meadow bending the brown grasses. The tall stalks of wheat bent to Creation's breath the way good folk bow gracefully when royalty passes by. I came to learn on that day that even when one is in the presence of such glorious perfection, danger can come charging swift as a crusader's warhorse.

Helvide and Gertrude were working in the garden at the front of the house, harvesting herbs. Crow was perched on the roof over the doorway where he had been roosting on the day I arrived at Belle Cœur. Ravenissa swept the threshold, and Beatrice was at the hearth nursing a baby whose sick mother was being cared for in the infirmary.

Mabille and I studied together at the table. My sister practiced a little song I'd taught her to help her remember the alphabet.

A woman's shouts interrupted our sweet reverie. We went to the doorway and looked out across the garden. Helvide stood shielding her eyes as she squinted in the bright morning sun. Gertrude rose swiftly and strode out onto the path with her broad shoulders squared and her powerful arms locked on her hips.

"You need help? Vhat is it you say?" she called to the woman down the way who was dragging a girl along by her arm.

"Where is she?! Where's the woman who's filled my daughter's head with her nonsense?!" Cotille pulled Ambrosine behind her.

Gertrude hurried down the path to meet them. "Madame, Madame, *s'il vous plaît*...No need to scream so. You and your daughter are velcome—"

The woman was spitting with rage. "Get out of my way! Where is the teacher? If you don't fetch her at once, I'll come into your den of magic and find her myself!"

Ambrosine began to sob.

Her mother struck her cheek hard with the back of her hand. "You stupid girl! You pathetic creature! Sneaking away from me, how many times...how many times! *Mon Dieu*! For what? For wisdom, you tell me!"

"Maman, you're hurting me. Stop. Please..." Ambrosine pleaded.

"I told you only men are allowed to read and write. You didn't listen to Père Lagoise and your father! Now you've been vexed by this teacher...by this witch of Belle Cœur!"

Ambrosine cried. Her pale cheek bore a bright red handprint. "But, Mother, I thought you would be proud, I thought..."

Cotille grabbed one of her daughter's thick braids and yanked her face close.

"Silence! Don't you ever speak another word! You're dead to me now. My life is over because he will blame me." She sobbed hysterically. "Your father will beat the life out of you if you come home, and worse will happen to me. Where is that teacher of yours? This is all her fault. This is the devil's doing!"

Crow called out. He flew from his perch toward Ravenissa's shoulder as she ran from behind the house.

Ambrosine's eyes met mine. I ran down the path and reached toward my friend while her mother continued to pull her by the hair.

"Please stop! Your daughter has not been poisoned, I can assure you, Madame. I'm the one responsible for her learning. Not the devil!" Sudden heat rose in me when I heard Ambrosine whimper. I pulled off my veil and cap and shouted, "If you want to be angry at someone, pull *my* hair!"

Again I reached for Ambrosine. Her hand went out to meet mine.

The mother yanked her away. "Don't you touch her! You've already stolen her mind from me, but you'll never have the rest of her. I want you to know what you've done. She and I must go far, far away."

Mother and daughter sobbed and wailed. "I curse you for what you have done. Just wait! Madame Boisine—will surely notify the Church authorities at Vézelay. Now that there's proof! Proof that you're evil. Only someone working for the devil would give a girl such power and fill her head with thoughts that distract her day and night. You witches of Belle Cœur have cursed my daughter—and me! Madame Boisine will return home in three days' time. Somehow I will get word to her about what you've done. *Mon Dieu*! We are undone. We are finished. What will become of us?" She fell to the ground and let go of Ambrosine's hair. The girl dropped to her knees.

My mind ran round in circles, like a lamb fleeing from the butcher. I searched for words to calm the mother's fears.

"Thoughts are not dangerous. They are sacred. Holy Wisdom was with God at the dawn of creation..." The words pouring from me sounded hollow—what cared that desperate woman for ideas?

Helvide joined us. She reached to comfort the woman the way one carefully reaches out to calm a wounded animal.

"If you touch me, I will bite your hand off. So help me." Her words came out slowly in a guttural whisper. Her eyes appeared more beastly than human. "You and your medicines and potions. All of you acting so saintly and all the while stealing poor villagers' children and poisoning their spirits." Her voice rose to a shriek. "You talk of God so sweetly, but it's all part of your play to seduce young girls to your witches' ways."

Helvide and I drew back, looked at each other. We knew we were in the presence of one possessed. This madwoman, this dark angel had delivered her ominous message. We had been warned that soon men in their black robes with their books of laws and rules would come looking for us. Our demise had been set in motion.

There were no more words to be spoken. Ambrosine continued to wail, and her eyes never turned in my direction again. I could not save my friend, and I wasn't sure I could save myself.

They turned as if to go; then our accuser spun 'round once again. Her voice was deep and strangely soft, and her green eyes stared at me with a fire of hatred that would have curdled milk. She took a slow step toward me and spit in my face.

"I pray you burn in hell. I curse you." She grabbed Ambrosine's arm, and they turned quickly down the path toward the meadow.

I never saw either of them again.

The hot spittle ran down my cheek. My flesh felt burned by her rage, ignorance, and fear.

Crow flew after them cawing loudly, and then circled back to perch on Ravenissa's shoulder while we stood frozen in silence. The baby at Beatrice's breast fussed, and Mabille stood with her arms wrapped about herself, swaying and singing ever so softly...as if to wash the air clean of what had just been invoked. So began the unraveling of Belle Cœur.

Le Monastère de la Visite
10 December 1258

In this dark place where we now live, we are surrounded by the veiled nuns, the sisters of Holy Grace. It feels as if our poor souls are bound by *their* rules and instructions. Certainly we're obliged to keep custody of our eyes.

If my eyes were to meet Sister Marguerite's, I would surely want to run for safety. We are friends with several of the good sisters here, but Sister Marguerite takes no liking to any of us.

Sabine in her brisk, practical way busily schedules all our many duties. She must answer to Sister Marguerite's sour temperament. Sister Marguerite dictates function and order for the nuns in her cloister with a shrill voice that makes us shudder. A taut-lipped nervous woman who neither smiles nor laughs, she frightens me.

Everything in the monastery's infirmary is kept clean as possible, but we can't rid the air of the foul odors of illness and death that assault the senses. The stench of vomit, rank urine, and diseased flesh fills the large room partitioned by wide linen curtains.

Today I arrived and found myself shrinking before the daunting tasks and endless beds filled with the horror of all manner of wound and sickness. I chastised myself for falling into despair. But death is everywhere. The ending of life has a miasma all its own.

This morning, Sister Marguerite interrupted my reflection with her screeching. "Goscelin! Stop staring and standing about! Why are you pinching your nose? What's the matter with you? There is work to be done!"

Sister Marguerite tolerates our sisterhood's presence because we provide extra hands for the unending tasks required for the monastery and all who live in this enormous place. Dear, resourceful Sabine has born the brunt of her constant demands, endlessly delivered with a pointed finger and critical stare under the arch of a thick, black eyebrow. Her tongue is as sharp as the finger she so readily pokes into Sabine's bosom while delivering her orders.

Today Sabine, who was tending a patient nearby, overheard Sister Marguerite berate me, and she hurried to to see what was happening.

Our hateful taskmaster turned her tirade on Sabine. "You need to take charge of the women in your little community." She stabbed her finger into my shoulder. "This one is as lazy and slow as a sow full of piglets!"

"I'm certain Goscelin will be helpful, Sister. What is it you need?" Sabine's deep gray eyes turned to me briefly—a look that spoke "beware—hold your tongue."

"I doubt she will be of any use." Sister Marguerite straightened her habit, pressed her thin lips together, then delivered her edict. "The real task at hand for you, Sabine, is that you must begin to prepare your community to take the veil. God does not smile on women who *play* at being religious yet refuse the vows of the Church so they may fully serve God as brides of Christ. If you imagine you can walk in the world of the flesh and dabble in the world of spirit, you're wrong. The bishop has inquired about you and your little band of sisters. You'd best talk to them, and then report to me so we can begin your formation. Soon!"

The more Sister Marguerite spoke, the more my bowels growled as if they might release at any moment.

"What do you mean the bishop has asked about us? Please don't threaten me... threaten us," Sabine replied with slow calm assurance, never taking her eyes away from Sister Marguerite's disapproving stare.

"God has called us to a life that is not unlike yours, Sister Marguerite. Our community is devoted to serving God's people and the will of our Creator. However, we're ready and alert to work in the world beyond monastery walls if that's where the Holy One beckons us to go."

Gripped in the certainty of her beliefs, Sister Marguerite's face grew hard. "The flesh is tempted when it is in the world, Sabine! To put yourself in a place where the devil can find you is a mistake—hear what I say to you…and to you!" Her bony finger jabbed my chest. Henriette bounced inside my apron pocket. "The devil will surely find you, and you'll be doomed to damnation! And you'd best watch that frail one of yours who wanders around preaching here and there in the common tongue. Satan has his eye on her for certain." She crossed herself for protection as she uttered the evil one's name.

The "frail one," our dear Petronilla, had dared to speak out, once in the courtyard of the monastery and again near the nuns' chapter house. Her words from God were spoken in our native tongue rather than Latin, the language of the Church. We have learned doing this is particularly offensive and considered blasphemous according to Church rules.

Sister Marguerite knows nothing of nor would she appreciate our sisterhood's call to prophetic obedience. Nor does she know how dreadfully ill Petronilla is.

Sabine drew a deep breath and gave me a quick glance. "I will give regard to our sisters' taking the veil, Sister. Thank you for your counsel to me…and to Goscelin. We're here to help you, and it's not our intention to cause you concern. Now please tell us—what do you need from us today?" As I witnessed Sabine speaking to Sister Marguerite, I was reminded of her lesson when we were still at Belle Cœur: "*When confronted or in danger, remember to pause for a breath or two and call on God for the words that will save you.*"

Sister Marguerite thrust her finger in my chest. "Get on with your duties. Go care for Madame Junot." I turned away to tend the blind, old woman with rotting teeth. Sister Marguerite stomped away to the kitchen at the north end of the infirmary. Sabine gave me a reassuring nod before returning to her work.

Jesus, please send angels to protect us. Amen.

All of us are bound to work long hours in the infirmary. Until three days ago Imene's nursing skills were valued and put to frequent use. On that sad day I was passing bread and milk to the patients when I witnessed Imene's distress.

All through the night my sister, the midwife, had tended a young girl in labor. Just as she was about to give birth, Sister Marguerite cast her shadow over Imene's earnest care.

"Sister Berneine will attend the birth, Imene. You go now and help to clean the waste pots."

Imene's chin quivered as she spoke. "But, Sister, the child is coming soon now, and her labor is dreadful—I fear the baby is turned—"

"You'll do as I say, Sister! You're no longer needed here. *Aller vite*!"

I wanted to go to defend Imene but thought I would only fuel Sister Marguerite's meanness.

Imene chewed her lower lip as if she could devour her rage. Her concern for the mother and unborn infant overcame her. "I fear for this girl, Sister. With all respect I ask you again please let me see her through delivery!" Imene grabbed the nun's sleeve.

Sister Marguerite jerked back. Her eyes narrowed, and she stretched herself, becoming taller and taller before our eyes. "Do you think you're the only one in this infirmary capable of tending a birth?" she hissed.

"Of course not, Sister, but I've much experience with difficult..."

The patient screamed out as her labor increased.

"Enough! Sister Berneine!" An elderly nun stepped tentatively from behind Marguerite. "Roll up your sleeves! I'll fetch Sister Claudelle to assist you. Imene—to the waste pots!"

Sister Marguerite took Imene by the arm and stormed away. Moments after she was out of sight, Sister Claudelle, agitated and breathless, hurried to help.

The poor girl's labor was horrible. She was but thirteen, and her opening was small even to my untrained eye. Imene had been taken to the other end of the infirmary, assigned to the worst task, emptying chamber pots filled with feces, urine, and vomit into a large barrel.

With Sister Marguerite out of sight for the moment, I moved closer to the girl. When the infant's rump rather than the head appeared in the mother's opening, Sister Berneine called out to Imene to come quickly. The look of terror on the old nun's face was cruel proof she didn't know how to help the mother and child.

Imene dropped a filthy pot and came running. She pushed up her sleeves. "Move aside! Stand behind me!"

Pressing on the mother's abdomen with one sweeping motion, she reached into the womb with her other hand to carefully turn the baby. All the while she spoke reassuringly to the frightened girl over her screams. A crowd of nuns gathered round.

Finally the child whooshed into life from his mother's womb in a great gush of water and blood. Imene held the tiny, wet, blue body. She cleared his mouth of milky fluid and then gave a quick firm pat to his backside. Silence. Another pat. More silence. Sister Berneine stood by silently. Imene turned the baby over her arm, rubbed his back briskly, and gave him a slap on his little bottom. At last he let out a healthy cry. His color turned red as radishes pulled fresh from the garden with his first breath of life.

"Praise God!" Sister Claudelle crossed herself.

Suddenly the nuns stepped back. Sister Marguerite appeared from nowhere.

"How dare you go against my orders!"

"But, Sister I didn't know what to do. The child would surely have died if Imene had not come to my assistance. I fear..." Sister Berneine began to cry.

"You, I will tend to later!" Sister Marguerite pushed her aside, nearly sending her into the wall. She turned 'round and grabbed the howling baby straight from Imene's arms. "You are no longer needed in this infirmary. I'm assigning you to the kitchen. You can assist Sister Veronica with her duties there. You're dismissed!" Sister Marguerite caught me staring at this sad scene. "Goscelin! What are you gaping at! Get back to your work!"

"But, Sister..." I stammered.

The infant clutched to Marguerite's slight breast squalled. She shouted over his cries. "Get to work or you'll find yourself in the barn cleaning up after the animals. You women are a menace!"

The nuns scattered like a flock of startled pigeons. Marguerite handed the whimpering baby to Sister Claudelle with little feeling, as if the infant had been a plucked chicken about to be tossed into the soup pot. She stormed out of the infirmary while two nuns chased after her.

Mabille had been folding linens at the south end of the infirmary near the hearth. She heard from the whispers what had happened. I saw her go to Imene, who was gathering her medicines and satchel. I joined her, and together we comforted our beloved Imene, who went to the young girl who had just given birth, kissed her forehead, and whispered something in her ear. Then Mabille and I accompanied her to our quarters.

Imene has been dreadfully quiet since Sister Marguerite bound and tied her healing hands. Gertrude is her constant companion. She's the one Imene clings to.

We have left Belle Coeur perhaps forever, yet our covenant with one another, our sisterhood, lives on and forms us still. I know Gertrude and Imene's hearts are woven together by their shared devotion. They are loving partners, wedded in spirit. I behold

Gertrude tend distraught Imene with abiding tenderness. She anticipates when her beloved is hungry and brings sustenance. When Imene appears tired, I have seen Gertrude wrap a blanket about her as a cocoon for needed comfort.

Jesus teaches us, "Love one another, as I have loved you." From what I have learned in the infirmary, love is all one clings to when dying. Love is all that remains in the soul when it's time to return home to God. Love is essential to the human spirit the way the breath is necessary to the life of the body.

Abiding tenderness is visible in the myriad small gestures of kindness Imene and Gertrude extend to one another. They are careful to keep their affections hidden when they are outside our quarters. Some would say spousal love of one woman for another is sinful. Having witnessed what is shared between Gertrude and Imene, I cannot imagine that God does not bless the love they share. To my mind the commandment "Love one another" is clear. Love is love is love.

Since our recent difficult encounters with Sister Marguerite, we are mindful to keep out of her way when working in the infirmary. She watches us like a sharp-eyed owl in the garden watches a mouse scurrying about looking for a place to hide. The only one of our sisterhood our mean taskmaster favors is Comtesse, who does all she can to endear herself.

This morning I was folding bandages just out of their sight when I overheard their conversation.

"You have so much to teach me, Sister Marguerite. I'm anxious to be a good nurse, but I'm certain I'll never be as skilled as you. How can I be helpful today, Sister?" Comtesse asked eagerly when she arrived for her morning assignment.

Sister Marguerite made her request. "I need you to make six linen curtains. They will hang between the new cots Brother Martin is building. Your readiness to serve doesn't go unnoticed, Comtesse. Beginning next week you'll begin to learn how to care for the patients. But today I require your skills with needle and thread."

"Of course, Sister."

I leaned from my corner to catch a glimpse of Comtesse beaming her most convincing smile to Sister Marguerite. I could scarce believe what I saw next... she spread her apron wide from side to side and curtsied. Curtsied! As though she was in the presence of royalty!

Scribing this sorry scene makes me shiver with discomfort. Comtesse is no longer the sister I trusted with my deepest secrets all those years ago. I carry what I witnessed today like a stone in my heart.

May I be given the grace stop my judgments. Amen.

When she isn't mending the nuns' habits, Comtesse hides away to work her needle and yarn into small, exquisite tapestries depicting the messages and stories from Petronilla's visions. Orbs of golden light, winged beasts with great teeth, the Blessed Mother surrounded by crimson roses, Jesus riding on a cloud of fire...these things are cast as woolen pictures stitched by Comtesse. They appear like illuminations in a manuscript fashioned with wool and flax rather than pigment and parchment.

Her talented hands are always busy. Regrettably, so is her mouth. Remaining silent is impossible for Comtesse. Even when she's lost in her needlework, she can be heard whispering—in conversation with herself! Back and forth she murmurs as if she were two characters in a play.

"What do you think of the way Beatrice picks the meat from the bones?" This is Comtesse, speaking in a wise and sly tone.

"*Most disagreeable. She disgusts me*!" A curiously deep voice, as if she were imitating a man.

"Will you tell her to stop?" Again the sly one.

"*Perhaps...no...yes...most assuredly I will*!" the mannish voice replies.

After her conversation with herself, she mutters gibberish under her breath then looks about nervously. Her mouth hangs open. She appears to suck the air through pursed lips. Perhaps an exorcism should be her prescription.

The animals are busy preparing for winter. Squirrels gather acorns and fortify their nests with twigs and leaves. There are not as many birds flying about as there were a month ago. Where have they gone? I must ask Ravenissa.

Beatrice prepares broth. She steeps turnips, potatoes, carrots, and kale, then strains the concoction until only the liquid remains. This is our daily sustenance. We are fasting. I taste her prayers as I sip my portion of broth slowly from my cup.

Helvide and Beatrice work side by side at our small hearth here in our quarters as they did at Belle Cœur. They prepare spelt bread, mugwort tea, and rosemary salve to treat the pilgrims' various ailments in the infirmary and for our needs as well. My sisters have a dance all their own as they go about their chores together. It's a women's dance…easy, harmonious, and gentle.

We are blessed with a small kitchen with an open stone hearth for warmth and cooking. There's a table in the corner where food is prepared, and above it are wooden shelves for condiments. A long, narrow refectory table with a bench on either side is where we take our meals.

The placement of things and the warmth of the fire are familiar and comforting. We have done our best to make this place feel like a true home. But in my heart I long to race through the deep green meadow past the stone wall, up the path to our beautiful little house. I ache to see the blue sign on the doorpost—then cross the threshold to be inside those four sheltering walls once again.

Here in our quarters beneath the refectory table, there is a hinged wooden door in the floor that opens to reveal twenty stone steps leading to the damp, cold cellar. This is where we keep the root vegetables in large pottery crocks. An iron pot and metal spoon hang nearby. We use them to bang and clang before descending the stairs, for there are rats the size of a cat in the cellar.

"Someone must do something about the dreadful vermin down there!" Comtesse yells as she descends the steep stairs to fetch potatoes for Beatrice's broth. "Also the spiders. Their webs are a nuisance. Look!" She clambers back up angrily. "Nasty, sticky webs all over my apron!"

"Why don't you find a way to rid us of these pests if you're so bothered by them?" Lately Beatrice has lost all patience with Comtesse. She is violently chopping a large yellow onion.

"That's not my chore! In fact, soon I'll be talking with Sister Marguerite about greater responsibilities than chasing after rats and dusting away cobwebs."

Beatrice's face turns red. She stops her chopping and wipes her damp brow with the back of her hand. "Just a moment! So, that's how it is? *Mon Dieu*! Well, isn't this a lovely story. You and Sister Marguerite cozy as two hens in a nest. That nun is trouble, Sister! You'd best be... careful. There's not one reason to trust the likes of her." Beatrice's broad bosom heaves as she catches her breath.

"That's a dreadful thing to say." Comtesse sniffs. "All I know is that she's fond of me. She listens to the concerns of my heart. There are other nuns who are becoming my friends. The way they live and work together has lately seemed...Well, they definitely spend more time in church than we do. Sister Marguerite says the ways of Belle Cœur's sisterhood are strange and not—"

Beatrice cuts at the air with her carving knife, an alarming sight. "Be still, Comtesse! You're really pushing too far now. You'd best stop your tongue before you say something you'll come to regret. I swear, if you continue like this, I will..." Beatrice puts down her knife and presses her hands on the table for support, gasping for air.

"Please, Sisters." Helvide stops what she's doing and drops her pestle. Her strong, purposeful hands, stained with beet juice, reach for a towel.

"Let's keep peace—and wait until we're all present to speak of these things." She spoke calmly. "Comtesse, please be still. You seem to be full of questions. We can talk this through when everyone is present." Helvide rests her hand on our sister's shoulder. "You know we care for you, Comtesse. You're important to us. And you, Beatrice, please sit down—I'll finish the chopping."

"There you go. All of you are always telling me to be quiet." Comtesse pouts.

Gertrude adds wood to the fire. Our tireless carpenter is weary. Her heavy body seems tethered to the floor as she bends ever so slowly, pressing one hand against her lower back. I go to help her. Her other hand trembles when she stirs the glowing coals with the iron pole. She whispers to me. "Dis ist time for silence. Vee moost take our concerns to God; vee moost pray. Enough has been spoken."

Gertrude's reminder that silence and prayer are most necessary in the midst of turmoil illuminates my irritation at Comtesse. Oh, how easily I can forget what is sure to soothe the heart and mend all brokenness. Silence, blessed silence and the prayers of the heart. A hush falls over the room except for the thumping of Helvide's chopping and Beatrice's heavy breathing.

In my mind I relive the scene of that evening with too much clarity as if it were happening now, as if I'm in a dream I see it all play out again. Comtesse paces back and forth before the row of bowls on the table. She moves one bowl closer to the table's edge and the one next to it back a hair. These little motions continue until the row is as straight as it can possibly be.

"Why is everyone always so quick to shame me?" Her shrill tone breaks the stillness and unravels my prayer. She nibbles at her thumb. It bleeds. Her tears splash onto her apron.

"Why do you think Sister Marguerite is befriending you, Sister?" I speak without thinking.

"Oh, not you, too, Goscelin. Well, it's no surprise. You...the one who is so very, very good. Of course, you would speak to the side of Beatrice. She's always favored you. No matter that I have known you longer than anyone." Comtesse turns to face me fully. "If it weren't for me, you never would have left home. I saved your life! You think you're so holy now that you're a sister of Belle Cœur."

I take a deep breath, pray a single word...

Please.

"What is happening, Comtesse? What's happening? Let's be still and gather our wits." I ignore Gertrude's wisdom to be silent and continue, "I don't want to say things I'll sorely regret, and I'm sure neither do you. All I asked was why you think Sister Marguerite favors you."

"Because she does! It's as simple as that. She favors me, and I like feeling special!" She sucks the blood from her thumb. "She makes me feel important. I don't have to explain myself…especially to you, Goscelin. Is there no one who can see my version of things? Leave me alone! All of you! I'm sick of your mothering and pretentious holy ways!"

Her fist punches the flour sack hard, spilling it to the floor. She spins 'round— and with one swift motion sweeps the bowls with her open palm. They knock against the table and shatter into scattered bits about our feet. Comtesse runs wailing for the door. We watch as she scurries through the rain across the garden and out the gate.

"That girl is living, breathing danger for all of us!" Beatrice wipes beads of sweat from her brow with a trembling hand. "The evil one has hold of her. She needs our prayers…for all our sakes. Though I'm so angry I can't utter a prayer right now. I want to shake her to her senses."

Helvide fetches the broom to clean up the mess. Beatrice takes a breath and begins kneading the dough that has risen during the commotion.

I offer a suggestion. "Helvide, can you make a medicine for Comtesse? Some potion to ease her sharp tongue? Oh, if only Petronilla were better. We need her prayers and wisdom now."

"My medicine won't cure what ails Comtesse." In Helvide's eyes I see resignation. "The darkness that traps her calls for prayer, fervent prayer. It's her soul that's sick…or worse, possessed. No, my medicine won't help her at all. Only grace will bring her peace."

I bend to the floor and begin to gather the broken shards. A sharp edge pierces my palm. Drops of blood fall, and I watch with amazement as they form a crimson butterfly on my apron.

Le Monastère de la Visite
12 December 1258

We continue to recover from Comtesse's outburst two nights ago. Her rage has brought a cloud of uneasiness to our quarters. I find myself reaching into my apron pocket for Henriette throughout the day, my ever ready comforter. She sleeps beneath my pillow at night. I keep her close always.

Thankfully, this holy season calls us to prayer and preparation for the celebration of Jesus's birth. The scent of rosemary is everywhere. Little bouquets of the pungent, dark green herb are placed about to honor the Blessed Mother. Boughs of holly heavy with bright red berries bring color to doorways and mantels.

Helvide has been helping the sisters make candles for the special *Réveillon de Noël* Mass. I look forward to our Belle Cœur tradition of sharing little offerings with one another on Noël. My gift to each sister will be a little scroll. I will carefully scribe each sister's name on small scraps of parchment next to a tiny illumination of the infant Jesus and Blessed Mother. I remember my joy the first time Brother Paul guided my hand to form the letters of my name. I hope my dear sisters will take delight when they see their names spelled out for them.

Before I can begin crafting *mes petits cadeaux de Noël*, I must resume writing of our last days at Belle Cœur. For that was the time of the second prophecy and the advent of a fateful message.

When first we learned the villagers were clamoring for more gossip, more kindling for their fires of suspicion, it seemed an ominous cloud darkened the horizon, though the skies were especially bright on those late fall days. Nights were long with little sleep, and when sleep arrived at last, several of us were visited by *les cauchemars*—unspeakable dreams of torment and terror.

However our fears grew worse after Ambrosine and her mother came to Belle Cœur. The day after Cotille's horrible accusations, we went about our tasks prayerfully while we cared for the sick, tended the livestock, harvested potatoes in the garden, and baked our daily bread. In truth, we were in a trance of fear. We had no more sense of how to face that danger than sheep at the mercy of wolves.

The first autumn storm arrived that same evening. With the deluge an elderly pilgrim made his way to our door. Soaked through and through, he had fallen ill a short distance from our infirmary on his way to Vézelay. It was clear that the earthly pilgrimage of Monsieur Façon was nearing the end.

Imene treated the old wanderer's fever while he spoke of the wondrous things he had seen on his journey. I spooned Helvide's fennel tea between his thin, parched lips while unaware that the three of us had entered into the mystery of God's unfolding plan.

It was an ominous afternoon in the Belle Cœur infirmary. The candles flickered from the draught while the wind rattled the shutters. The old man's square jaw and thick, white hair hinted at the handsome youth that still lived somewhere deep within him. His eyes were clouded with age, but they shone alive with passion for his story. He spoke between halting breaths. Spasms of wet, rolling cough arose, subsided, and arose again.

He told us he had journeyed to the distant *Cathédrale Nôtre Dame de Chartres.* It was the living reliquary for a most sacred object, the *Sancta Camisia,* the veil of the Mother of God.

Gaunt and exhausted, Monsieur Façon trembled with the effort of his story about the great church and its rebuilding while Imene and I sat on either side of him. Imene raised him up on the pillows to make his breathing more comfortable. She encouraged him to be still, but he was in the grip of some force that gave him surprising strength to croak out a vivid tale.

"I learned from other pilgrims on my journey, Sisters, that some time ago…a fire, a terrible fire… destroyed most of the city of Chartres." His voice was coarse and his breathing labored. "It burned nearly all the cathedral save the crypt…and the tower foundations. But there was a miracle. Believe me! It's true! Three days after the fire, the townsfolk learned the Blessed Mother's veil had survived the flames. The bishop instructed the people that a new shrine must be built to honor the Virgin and her relic, her holy veil. The veil she was wearing when she delivered Jesus."

Monsieur Façon choked out more details as he told us the cathedral at Chartres was like the New Jerusalem, a place of welcoming for Christ's return. Later his strength gave out and he faded into silence.

In the hours that followed Imene and I were praying near his bedside when suddenly he rose up on his elbows. I held the bowl while he vomited phlegm and blood while Imene supported his frail body. I felt like retching with him from the stench.

"You must rest. Tell your story later…" Imene tried to soothe the man's ranting.

"No, Sister, for God may call me at any moment—you must listen to what I have to tell you. You must hear this!" His claw of a hand grabbed my sleeve.

"When I entered the cathedral, I was…lifted into heaven. The enormous windows tell stories...stories in pictures made of colored glass, you see. It's a living book, that holy place!"

I wondered if what he said was true or the strange imaginings of one with fever. His tale continued.

"My eyes could scarce take in the beauty of it all. Animals, stars, moon, people…all of these…made of colors and glass. God's power and love is there! I crawled on my knees upon the great stone pathway…on the floor to the center…" Here his body was wracked by endless coughing. His story ended. He fell against the pillow into deep sleep.

As evening approached Imene stayed near.

"Sanguine, choleric, melancholy, phlegmatic, all his humors are failing," she whispered.

It was time for the cutting of the vein. The venesection had to be done after the sun set. Imene called for Mabille to play her lyre as much to comfort us as comfort the old man. I was told to hold the bowl to catch his blood. There was no butcher or physician, no man in sight to make the cut, so Imene once again broke the rule and dared do it herself.

I wanted to run away. Imene's eyes glistened with confidence. Her skilled hands were steady and purposeful. Confidence was her lesson, a teaching I sorely needed.

My skilled sister lanced the man's arm midway between wrist and elbow. She applied a small glass cup that had been heated by candle flame. I took a deep breath. Then I heard a voice speak clearly with the ears of my heart.

I am alive within this dying man! When you tend him you tend Me. Serve him and you serve Me. Love him and you love Me.

Oh, Jesus! I will tend You! I will serve You! I love You! my heart replied.

Grace overcame me. Imene removed the cup. I held the bowl steady to catch the dark blood streaming from the wrinkled flesh. A sound like a rushing river began to thrum in my head.

This man is Jesus, my brother. This man is Jesus, my beloved…

Monsieur Façon's grimace softened. The roaring in my ears stopped, and I became aware of Mabille's sweet voice singing softly while she played her lyre.

Her songs and lullabies surely comfort the dying in their final hours. Time and again I've witnessed her tenderly cradle a body ravaged by disease while she sang a heart-rending air. Petite Mabille's strong, clear voice surprises those who judge her to be passive and frail because of her delicate appearance.

She's told us, "It's important to hold them and breathe in rhythm with their breathing. The song is born from what I feel through a dying body. Rocking is helpful, too. Remember how it felt to be rocked by your mother?"

Like an angel she sings, ever so softly. She breathes with the one who is dying, slowly…slowly…faintly. In time the breathing stills, and the patient's soul is at last set free of earthly wants and needs.

When the small bleeding bowl was nearly full, Imene began to bind the pilgrim's arm with linen and wool. When she was finished, the old man without warning startled to wakefulness. He grabbed her by her apron and pulled her into him. His clouded eyes peered up urgently, and he whispered, "*You must* go, Sister! The Mother calls you. You must… pilgrimage…go…take your sisters…and prayers…to Chartres! She calls you there!" He fell back and drew his last breath.

We crossed ourselves and stared at our messenger's face now wreathed with the peace of death. His mouth hung open, and his eyes were fixed upon that distant bourne. His final words echoed around us like an incantation.

In our infirmary we'd heard the words of dying men, women, and even children. Often secrets had been told to us and urgent confessions made lest the dying one go to the grave with sin upon the heart. But never had such a burning command been given directly to us.

You must...pilgrimage...go...take your sisters...and prayers...to Chartres!

Later the same night, when we came together in our circle for prayer, the relentless wind blew the rain in little rivulets under the door. The water rolled on the packed earth to form a strange, curling script across the floor like a message slowly scribed by an invisible hand in an unknown language.

Crow perched on Ravenissa's shoulder, safe inside from the fierce weather. His head was tucked under one shiny, blue-black wing that glistened in the flickering light of the array of candles.

Imene and I told the story of the dying pilgrim and his instructions for our sisterhood. Afterwards, the entire community stayed silent for a long while to reflect on what had been shared. I took Henriette from my pocket and held her between my palms.

We sat in stillness with our questions. How should we respond to the old man's instructions? Was he a holy angel carrying guidance from our Blessed Mother—or simply an old man who ranted in delirium? The candle at the center of our circle burned down to become a glowing pool of milky wax.

Should we leave Belle Cœur to make a pilgrimage to Chartres? Should we go to the earthly shrine of the Blessed Virgin? Was this indeed meant to be our unfolding destiny?

Or should we stay at Belle Cœur to continue our healing work—and risk possible danger?

We entered into thoughtful discussion and agreed we needed a vigil of prayer, a vigil like no other, on that stormy night. We rose from the benches and stood together in a circle before the glowing hearth while Ravenissa lit still more candles. The warm, clean scent of beeswax sanctified the air. Our shadows danced upon the walls as we pressed against each other. Our peramony for discernment was about to begin.

Each sister placed her left hand on the shoulder of the one in front of her, right hands atop our hearts. Petronilla offered the prayer.

"Beloved Jesus, guide us. Blessed Mother, Mary Magdalene, pray for us as we begin our peramony. We ask for visions to inspire and clarify the choice that is before us. Inspire our dreams so in the light of day we may know God's will. Amen."

Eyes cast downward we breathed together and began to pace 'round and 'round with slow steps. Connected to one another. Hands to shoulders, each heart pressed into the back of the one in front of her. We breathed together until our breathing in and breathing out became one breath. One prayer. Hands upon our hearts in rhythm with the Sacred Heart of Jesus.

Our sacred ritual, our peramony, was our way of visioning. Petronilla had taught us that when we breathed together, our senses were invigorated and opened to receive God's guidance. Our senses were peaked as they reached toward the Holy One seeking sustenance for our souls. Breath blended with breath. Prayer melded into prayer, until together, we sank to the floor. In that moment our spirits rose to realms beyond our earthly seeing.

I saw angels made of fire. A portal opened in my mind into an endless passageway where there were countless doors. My hand reached out to open one and then another. A sudden waft of the long-ago fragrance of Maman's hair drying in the summer breeze filled me with sweet melancholy. I heard a great beast moaning in pain and understood she was laboring to give birth. Heat radiated from my flesh. I was naked. Sweat ran between my breasts. Terror caught me by the throat. Snow melted on shimmering stones from the blaze of the sun. Then a woman's voice spoke clearly from the wetness. From the space between those same rocks. From the place where my sweat was running. *Come!* she said with authority. *Come!* Before me was an enormous wooden portal with an iron latch. Above the portal Jesus and Mary were carved from stone. The stone was alive. Mary was seated on a throne. She smiled at me. The voice filled my mind, my whole being. *Fear not! Cross the threshold. The key to the Garden is inside.* In that moment the great door began to open.

The sound of bells pulled me back. The morning bells were ringing from beyond Belle Cœur at the village church. I wanted to stay in that wet, hot place where Creation's blaze melted snow on stones, where the Mother sat on her throne of wisdom. The woman's voice became silent. The portal that had opened but slightly closed tight.

My body trembled. My legs were entwined with someone else's. I couldn't tell where my being began and ended. My left arm was stretched out above my head. My hand felt wooden with numbness. There was a sweet taste in my mouth as if someone had fed me honey.

I opened my eyes to the sight of all of us in a great pile near the hearth. Slowly I untwisted my legs from Marie's. I lowered my arm from its awkward position, and my hand burned with returning life. The others began to stir and stretch.

In the faint, gray pallor of early morning, our spirits slowly returned to our bodies still wreathed in dreams and visions. Tears rolled down my cheeks into the corners of my mouth…tears that tasted like hope. We were coming back from the peramony to the jolt of time and place to share our dreams, to embrace God's guidance.

Gertrude stood and shook off sleep. She stoked the fire.

In silence we huddled together on the earthen floor as the cock crowed and the growing light chased away night's shadows. Color and shape returned to the chairs, the tables, and Crow, who flapped his wings from his perch above Ravenissa's cot. She pulled herself to her feet and went to him. He hopped to her shoulder, and they drifted toward the door, appearing to my eye like a beautiful remnant from my dream. Ravenissa opened the door, and Crow flew into the morning cawing his blessing.

The rain had ended. The strange message it had scribed on the floor the night before was gone. Sunlight poured into the room through the open door. The house smelled of earth and smoke and a subtle ether of womanly visions.

Imene spoke first. "The Mother emerged from the sun." She pulled her knees into her chest as she whispered from her place on the floor. Her eyes were wide with the look of one who had been in the presence of the holy. If she had been an illumination in a manuscript in that moment, she surely would have been portrayed in gold. "The brightness of the light held Our Lady's presence. She spoke to my mind without making a sound. 'I need your hands.' These are the words I heard from Mary, our Mother."

Helvide took a deep breath. "She appeared to me as an ancient, gnarled tree. I heard her voice on the wind of an approaching storm. 'I will give you new medicines.' This is what she told me."

"I didn't have a vision but I felt a pull, a tug on my arm. I believe it was a call to leave Belle Cœur." Helvide spoke slowly. There was trembling in her voice. "It frightens my mind to think of it. Yet my heart is certain in this morning of decision. I believe we are to leave here. This is God's will for us."

My vision played about in my head. I stumbled to find the words to tell what I'd seen. "A woman's voice called to me. Was it Magdalene? The Mother? I don't know. I stood before a great door. A portal made of wood that slowly opened to me. But then it closed. The place beyond that portal…that's where I feel God is calling us to be."

The sharing continued one by one. Comtesse studied her thumb then chewed around the nail like a nervous rabbit nibbling lettuce in the garden. She continued to examine her thumb this way and that without looking at us. When finally she spoke, her voice was shrill and angry.

"I saw nothing. Only darkness. Portals made of wood, mysterious voices...that's what *you* describe. But I saw absolutely nothing."

As if to contradict Comtesse's curt response, sunlight spilled through the open door. We were bathed in the morning light. It was time to begin our duties and more than time to relieve Annabelle and Portia, who had tended the infirmary for the night.

"Why must we rely on these dreams and imaginings for guidance? I don't trust them." Comtesse's thumb oozed blood. She sucked it.

"I call us to hanswere." Sabine stood near the door.

With the hanswere each sister would show her response. Whether we should go to Chartres or stay at Belle Cœur.

Sabine instructed us, "At the count of three, if you're in agreement we should go to the cathedral at Chartres, pat your heart. If you believe we should stay here at Belle Cœur, cover your eyes with your hands."

"*Un, deux, trois...*" Marie counted.

All of us instantly patted our hearts—save Comtesse. Her head bent downward; her hands covered both her eyes. When she parted her fingers to peek at the rest of us, she immediately sat up straight and rapidly patted her heart the way one pats a fidgety baby. Her bleeding thumb left a crimson mark on her apron.

~

Before we went to our duties that morning, it was agreed we would begin our pilgrimage as soon as possible. Swift preparations for our departure began. Grief took up residence in the house at Belle Cœur and grabbed my spirit without warning. Beatrice wept silently over the nursing infant at her breast. Helvide tied bouquets of herbs and wiped her tears with dirty hands. Her face was stained with earth and yellow pollen. Even stalwart Gertrude sniffed and mopped her eyes with her apron.

I wanted to find a way to capture Belle Cœur in my memory for all time, so I played a game as I prepared to let go of the beautiful place that was home. I began to record to memory every sight, smell, sound, taste, and touch that lived at Belle Cœur. The hue of the afternoon light glistening on the pond, the aroma of Beatrice's bread baking on the hearth, the patter of soft rain on the sod roof, the taste of tart red apples from our orchard, and the comforting warmth of my sisters' hands as we gathered in our circle in the morning to pray.

Memories of the long journey it took for me to arrive at the house with the blue sign returned. How could I endure another trek? What if we lost our way? If we were blessed to arrive safely at Chartres, where would we live? *How* would we live?

I relied on Henriette to soothe me each time my demon of dread came to spread fear. Each of us suffered in her own way the days and hours before we left our beloved Belle Cœur.

ஒ

The afternoon following our peramony, Beatrice and I sorted the cooking pots, blankets, and crockery when Ravenissa ran into the house.

"He's gone! Have you seen him? He's gone!"

"Who's gone?"

"Crow! He's disappeared. My heart aches as I must choose which animals will stay and which will come with us. I set my doves free yesterday only to find them this afternoon roosting on the rooftop! Turtle was returned to the pond. Annabelle has offered to care for the sheep, the chickens, and the rooster. It's all so hard. Of course I'm bringing Chanson, the cat, and my mouse." She lifted the little creature from her apron pocket by his tail and kissed his tiny nose.

I offered a sorry comfort. "Crow will come back. He'll return. Maybe he's saying good-bye to his friends."

"I can't leave without him. He rode on my shoulder all morning but flew off in the early afternoon, and it's dark now. He always returns before dark. Oh, where can that blessed bird be?"

Into the evening we heard Ravenissa cawing as she called out to Crow from the path beyond the garden. She cawed until her voice was nearly gone.

ஒ

It was late night of the next day following our decision. Eleven baskets the size of large pumpkins were filled and neatly arranged by the door. We were ready to depart the next morning. Each basket was stuffed full to the brim with what would be needed to continue our crafts, sustain our healing work, and assure our housekeeping.

Helvide had gathered herbs from her garden. She took salves and balms from the infirmary cupboard and carefully packed the vade mecum filled with Abbess Hildegard's remedies and recipes.

Beatrice chose two cooking pots, one kettle, and one dish and cup for each of us. Earlier in the day, she'd baked a large honey cake and three loaves of spelt bread. Carefully she wrapped our remaining small brick of goat cheese in cloth.

"I'm the one to portion our food. I'd better not catch hungry hands trying to snitch more than their share each day. I'll miss this old hearth. I wish I could take my big soup pot, but there's no room in our wagon."

Beatrice busied herself on our last afternoon at Belle Cœur. With her free hand, she gathered her supplies, and with her other arm she held a babe to her exposed breast. The infant's mother had fallen ill while traveling and was resting in the infirmary.

"What will you little ones do without my milk after I'm gone?" She sniffed.

It was agreed we would fast on our pilgrimage and take only one small portion of sustenance a day. One of our goats, Hortense, would come with us to provide milk, but the cows, would stay.

Comtesse reluctantly gathered her linen, loom, wool, and needles. "I can't imagine how all this is happening. Where will we live?" She whined the question all of us were carrying.

Imene's midwifery instruments, Mabille's lyre, and Marie's pouch of sticks and stones were also carefully bundled for travel. Gertrude had been busying herself for hours in her shed. When we asked what she was doing, she would only say, "Following der Mutter of Jesus's direction."

Sabine emptied her counting box and gave all the coins, save four, to Annabelle and Portia, the new guardians of Belle Cœur. They would live in the house after we were gone and continue the work.

Sabine placed the box with our pittance into a flat, square basket beside her precious vessel of ashes, the remains of her family. Gertrude's carpentry tools were wrapped in wool. Her hammer and chisel were placed with the other belongings in our wooden wagon, our drayage on the road to Chartres.

"Just let sumvun try to harm us!" Gertrude smiled, and then frowned her fiercest frown as she wielded her axe above her head.

Petronilla took candles from the chest beside the door and laid them on her blanket. She rolled them tight and placed them in the cart next to Gertrude's tools. Petronilla's basket was empty.

"Petronilla—you must prepare your basket." Sabine's voice, usually so calm, was sharp with worry.

"But it is prepared, Sister."

"How can that be when clearly it's empty?"

"I have filled it with my petitions for our journey. They are visible only to God. My basket also holds the spirit of Belle Cœur that I gathered with my breath and blew into the spaces between my petitions. This basket seems a humble container for such treasures, don't you agree, dear sister?"

Sabine nodded and without a word, she turned back to the task at hand.

I pulled the olive wood box from under my bed. Carefully I stuffed dried grasses and moss between each bottle of colored pigment for extra protection. Why had I never used these? What was I saving them for?

The four volumes of Dominions and Graces and the black box containing the queen bee were tucked into the bottom of my basket. I rolled my quill within my one remaining parchment and placed these things on top then covered all with my blanket. Henriette would travel with me in my apron pocket.

Blessed Mother, you call us to a strange and unknown place. We're afraid. I'm afraid. Watch over our little band of women with your merciful love and protection, and remember us to Jesus in your prayers. Amen.

When the daylight began to fade on our last day at Belle Cœur, we went to the garden between the back of the house and the infirmary. Sabine had invited Annabelle and Portia, our loyal helpmates from the village, to leave their duties in the infirmary to join us in the garden. Annabelle's daughter, Audrey, stayed behind to look after the few patients.

While all of us circled around them, Sabine gave Annabelle and Portia their final instructions just before sunset. A cool breeze rustled the leaves and caused me to shiver. Ravenissa looked up, and so did I. For a moment I thought she'd caught a glimpse of Crow, but it was a pigeon on its way to roost in the apple tree.

Sabine placed the old iron keys to the house, the infirmary, and the shed in Annabelle's hand, then pressed the woman's fingers tight about them.

"You and Portia are the guardians of Belle Cœur now. Look after this place with love and care, for you're standing on holy ground. May this always be a haven of compassion for the world-weary traveler, a portal to heaven for the dying, and a sanctuary for prayer."

Tears fell all around as Sabine continued.

"We must leave this blessed place, but if it's God's will we pray to find our way home again. Keep watch for us, dear friends. Meanwhile, may God look after us all until we meet here…or in heaven. Come inside and let us break bread together."

We gathered at the table. Beatrice fetched our best crockery cup and a small wooden plate from the shelf near Magdalene's nook beside the hearth. She nodded toward Annabelle and Portia. "We shall always be sisters in Christ, all of us together."

I looked around at the dear faces, some worn, some tired, some radiant, but all beautiful. I held this moment to be cherished, the way one embraces the last warm, perfect day of autumn before the north wind strips away what remains and leaves the landscape barren and bleak. Perhaps it was the quality of light from the fire or the message in the rain upon the door that told us, *Make this moment into a memory, for soon this will all be gone.*

Gertrude poured a portion of mead into the cup and took a generous piece of bread from the day's loaf. Helvide spread a linen towel. She carefully placed the cup and plate upon the cloth. Together we stood and prayed the Our Father. Then Beatrice spoke from her heart.

"Let us bless these gifts." We extended our hands above the bread and wine and offered our prayer.

"Jesus taught that whenever we break bread and drink wine, we are to remember Him. May His love for us, present here in this bread and this wine, in His body and blood, give us strength to continue our journeys. May our love for Him be revealed through our service to God's people. Amen."

Sabine broke the bread into small pieces. She passed the plate to Annabelle, saying, "The bread of life." Annabelle took a piece of bread and placed it in her mouth. She then passed the plate to Portia and repeated the blessing. Each of us offered the bread and the blessing to the next.

I took the cup of wine after the bread had been passed and offered it to Helvide, who stood beside me. "The cup of compassion." My sister took the cup and sipped from it then passed it on.

When our communion was over, Portia prayed.

"Beloved, we are grateful for this sacred meal. May we be sustained for whatever will come. We pray to serve You with our hearts and hands as we serve Your people. Bless the sisters of Belle Cœur, our sisters, as they journey. Bless us all…women who follow the Way of Jesus. Amen."

Sabine kissed Annabelle and Portia on their cheeks and made the sign of Belle Cœur upon their hearts.

Lastly she gave her blessing, "May hope and wisdom live within you, dear sisters."

The two women bowed their heads replying, "Hope and wisdom."

Later the same night when the house was swept clean and tidied for Annabelle and Portia, who would settle in after we were gone, a fierce wind blew from the north. Melancholy joined us as we gathered in a circle near the hearth to offer prayers of thanksgiving for the simple blessed house that had been our home and sanctuary.

Before we were about to take our last sleep at Belle Cœur, Mabille fetched her lyre. "Let's sing, Sisters. Let's fill Belle Cœur with song to show her how much we love her. I'll teach us a new song to sing in the morning when we begin our journey." She strummed the lilting, hopeful melody, and her angel's voice soon had us following her lead.

Belle Cœur, Belle Cœur,
We leave you now,
Yet our hearts with you remain.
May the hearth fire burn
Till we return
To our beloved Belle Cœur again.

Belle Cœur, Belle-Cœur,
Nous vous laissons maintenant,
Pourtant, nos cœurs restent avec toi.
Puisse le feu de cheminée brûle
Jusqu'à ce que nous retournions

A notre Belle Cœur aimé à nouveau.

The final, perfect note of her tune hung in the air only to be shattered by pounding on the back door.

"Sisters! Sisters! *C'est moi*! Annabelle!"

Sabine unbolted the door. Annabelle was in tears.

"What is it? What's wrong?"

"They're coming for you…the churchmen. Just now a woman in the infirmary told me she saw Ambrosine on the road this afternoon. Ambrosine told the woman her mother said the churchmen and the bishop have been told terrible things about you. Madame Boisine has made her report! Ambrosine said they're coming to take you away!"

We grabbed for one another the way someone drowning grabs at the air in search of a lifeline.

"You must leave. Now! Before they arrive with the light of day!" Annabelle pleaded.

"She's right. We mustn't wait till dawn. It will be too late," Beatrice urged.

Sabine turned to Annabelle. "Thank you, beloved friend."

"Go! Your safety is all that matters!"

Annabelle stayed to help us load the cart. Like good mothers taking hold of their children's hands, we carried our baskets to the cart. Imene and Mabille held the lanterns high. Gertrude arranged our belongings, taking care to be certain the cart was well balanced. Ravenissa kept her eyes heavenward and cawed out into the night sky.

We wept as we watched Gertrude pry the blue sign from the wall by the door with her knife. She wrapped it in a blanket and tucked it between the baskets. It had been decided that the sign, a treasured piece of Belle Cœur must come with us. Portia would soon paint another, the cross enclosed by a circle. Ravenissa brought Hortense from the barn and hitched her to the cart. Annabelle bid us adieu and hurried back to the infirmary.

We gathered in the house for the last time. When all was finally ready, we blackened our fingers with ash from the hearth and made our marks on a board inside the cupboard door so something of us would remain.

Then Gertrude offered the ritual that marked the end of our days at Belle Cœur.

"Sisters, I vas given a dream, a dream of how I am to prepare dis...for our leevink." She opened a pouch tied to her belt and reached inside. She held up her creation. Hanging from a leather cord was a small square of iron etched with the sign of Belle Cœur in the center.

"I saw dis in mein dream, und I knew it voot offer us protection ven vee travel. You vill now carry Belle Cœur next to your hearts verever you go."

From the pouch she drew more amulets. She tenderly placed one around each of our necks.

"May dis medallion shield you from evil und harm. Amen." Next she placed a large strong hand on each head in blessing. "Hope und visdom." We each replied, "Hope and wisdom."

Each sister took her leave by kissing the doorpost and marking it with the sign of our sisterhood. One by one fingers pressed the shape of the equidistant cross enclosed in a circle on the weathered wood. When my turn came, I felt the ache of my heart breaking in two.

Gall caught in my throat just like the morning when I left Maman.

The time for rituals and good-byes had run out. They were coming for us. Faceless, nameless men would soon arrive and be enraged to find us gone. What then?

What would become of Annabelle and Portia? Surely God would protect them. Questions ran around in my mind like rats scurrying about in a rainstorm. Forced from our home and sanctuary, we were now pilgrims—but to some we would seem as criminals fleeing for our lives.

⁂

The wind blew the last leaves from the trees as we stepped onto the muddy path. Already my feet were cold. The clouds glided across the waning sliver of moon— appearing as angels winging their way toward heaven.

Our lanterns and prayers illumined the way. Gertrude and Imene walked together alongside the goat. Ravenissa, Helvide, and Marie, arm in arm, sobbed softly. Chanson was nestled into the cart among our baskets.

Surprisingly, Comtesse didn't whine. She shuffled along, smiling and muttering softly in conversation with herself.

Sabine paused to retrieve a long branch from the ground.

"If we are pilgrims, we should don ourselves to be recognized as such." She held her new walking staff high.

"That's right, Sister!" Helvide called out from the middle of our little caravan. "A pilgrim's staff is like a friend to lean upon."

I held tight to Beatrice's arm with one hand and clutched Henriette, who had settled deep in my pocket, with the other. Beatrice's lantern lit the way, and we followed our sisters slowly at the end of our caravan. She was weary. Her usual quick step was heavy and slow. I thought of how I hadn't had the chance to teach dear Beatrice to read and write, her most secret desire. Perhaps when we settled in our new home she would at last study with me. For now we clung to one another and plodded on. Every now and then, Gertrude halted the parade so we could catch up.

We walked all night to set distance between us and the churchmen. Gertrude knew the way to Chartres because she had been a journey-woman, a pilgrim many times before her life at Belle Cœur.

Just before dawn we reached the narrow road that trailed alongside the river. With the first light of day Mabille's sweet high voice began the chant.

May the hearth fire burn
Until we return
To our beloved Belle Cœur again.

Each voice joined in the chorus, while step by step we traveled deeper into the mystery.

Book IV
Pilgrimage

Le Monastère de la Visite
5 January 1259

The New Year has begun. January's cold wind blows through the crevices in the monastery walls without mercy, and though we are grateful for this shelter, we miss Belle Cœur, our true home.

We sense we are being watched. We rely on Petronilla's guidance for how to stay invisible to suspicious eyes. Her voices instructed her to tell us we must protect Cibylle above all else. Cibylle's condition becomes more obvious with every passing week. We are vigilant to keep her hidden from the nuns to avoid their questions and curiosity. She spends her days in our quarters entertained by Marie. The two are inseparable friends.

Petronilla asked me after our morning prayers to be certain to record the story of how our dear sister Cibylle came to us. I sharpen my quill, pull my cape tight against the chill, and light another taper to brighten this dark afternoon as I prepare to tell the story of our most mysterious sister.

When we left Belle Cœur, guided by the dying pilgrim's message to journey to Chartres, we were naïve to imagine our sojourn would be a simple trek across the countryside in search of our new home. In truth, few of us had ever traveled beyond Vézelay.

We had been on the road for three days blessed by the cool autumn weather. Towering, dark clouds hung low and followed us like enormous, burly shadows in the sky.

Tired from hours of walking, we stopped at midday to rest and eat our daily meal, as was our custom while fasting. Water was plentiful from the many streams that branched from the long and winding river near the main road.

Beatrice cut honey cake into small portions for each of us, and Ravenissa milked the goat into her bucket then poured the nourishing warmth in equal portions into our cups. We settled in a circle on the earth beneath a tall birch tree along the sloping bank of a narrow, rushing stream. Helvide offered our blessing.

"We praise You, Keeper of our souls, for Your protection as we journey. Through Your grace, this meal sustains and renews our strength. With grateful hearts we say amen."

With Helvide's amen, as we crossed ourselves there came the sound of flapping wings overhead. Crow! He swooped down to perch on Ravenissa's shoulder, where he bobbed up and down, cawing loudly.

"Where have you been? I thought you were gone forever!" Ravenissa squealed while the bird gently pecked her cheek. Ravenissa cawed loudly and quickly lifted her mouse by the tail from her lap then slipped him into her apron pocket. Crow made soft cackling sounds in her ear.

"How did he find us?" Mabille asked while we witnessed the sweet reunion.

"He has a special sense God gives to birds and other creatures. He says he's come to help us find our way to our new home." Ravenissa reached up and stroked Crow's shiny black head.

We were happy to see our winged friend again. I cherished the smiles on my sisters' faces.

As the memory of that moment comes back to me, I realize how Crow's return was the herald for the strange events that came next. It has been told that when exhaustion plagues a person, her eyes often play tricks. We were surely exhausted from our travels, and the shadows were fitful under the gray sky of an autumn afternoon; but the apparition that appeared before us was no deception of the eye or hoax of the spirit.

We turned back to our meal after Crow's arrival to discover the presence of a young maiden. She stood between Petronilla and Marie, who were sitting at the edge of the stream. The girl watched us with large, dark eyes until she had our full attention—then she began to spin 'round in circles. She sang gibberish in a voice that to my ear was more animal than human.

"Who is this? Where did she come from so suddenly?" Helvide pointed.

"What's she saying, Ravenissa? Do you understand her jabbering?" Sabine asked.

Ravenissa appeared puzzled. "I've never heard anything like it. It sounds a bit like deer-speak, but truly her speech is unfamiliar."

The girl's clothing was tattered and filthy, and her waist-long mane of curly, brown hair was tangled with twigs and grasses. She appeared like a wraith in a dream, part human and part creature from the forest. Her large, deep green eyes sat strangely apart on either side of a plump, round nose. To me her ragged homeliness was peculiarly enchanting. She suddenly stopped spinning and babbling to look at each of us with a girl's youthful face but a crone's wise expression.

Petronilla eased herself from the ground. She went to the girl to examine her more closely. The maiden stood perfectly still while Petronilla held her dirty face gently in her hands, turning it slowly this way and that. They stared at one another for a long time. Then Petronilla closed her eyes and leaned forward. She pressed her forehead into the girl's. This mysterious connection continued for several moments while the rest of us looked on.

Petronilla led our visitor to the edge of the bank near the flowing water where she removed her torn and filthy dress.

"Look! She has a star between her breasts!" Mabille pointed.

We were startled to see a red, star-shaped mark in the center of her chest, between full breasts that had been hidden under her frock.

"Her body surely doesn't match her childish spirit. Poor thing, look—she's cold." Marie was distressed.

The naked girl shivered uncontrollably. Her large, dark nipples puckered tight.

Petronilla gathered up her skirt and apron and walked the girl into the stream. The rushing water circled 'round their knees. The girl giggled before Petronilla cupped her hands and dipped them to fill them with the cold, clear water.

She poured water over the woman-child's head three times with the words, "I baptize you in the name of Jesus…You are a beloved child of God…The Holy Ghost's blessing be upon you."

The girl whimpered softly. Petronilla made the sign of the Belle Cœur cross over the maiden's bosom—and the girl became still and slowly bowed her head.

Petronilla looked up. "She belongs with us!" She led the shivering waif by the hand to the place where Beatrice was waiting with a blanket.

"You're certain?" Sabine asked.

Beatrice wrapped the girl tight in the blanket and brought her to us.

"Most assuredly," Petronilla replied. "I am certain she had not been baptized. She is safe now, marked as God's own."

"You know this to be true?" Sabine asked.

"Yes, Sister, could anything be more true under heaven?"

"It's just that…"

Petronilla interrupted. "Sister, don't judge her appearance. Her body is a cocoon that disguises the beautiful butterfly God is creating within her." She continued without taking a breath. "She's pregnant. We must care for her and the child that sleeps this very moment inside her womb."

A gasp went out from all of us with this proclamation.

Sabine rose to face Petronilla. "Oh, Sister, how can you ask this of us? We have no idea where we will live or how we'll care for ourselves, let alone a pregnant young girl! Especially this one…who from the looks of her will no doubt require a great deal of time and attention. What has God revealed to you? Why do you say we must take her with us?"

"In my heart I know God has placed her on our path. She's alone and with child, and it would be wrong to abandon her," Petronilla responded firmly.

"Sisters, wait! Wait!" Mabille looked around at all of us. "How do we know this girl doesn't have a family that's looking for her? Perhaps she's lost. It would be terribly wrong to take her with us if she has kin who are worried about her this very moment."

"I'm certain she has no one." Petronilla spoke calmly. "However, if it will ease your fears, we'll ask the pilgrims traveling over there if they know of her. For now, let her remain in our care."

"I don't like this at all." Comtesse stood with her hands on her hips.

"Say more, Sister?" Sabine said. Concern marked the faces in our circle.

"We've never accepted a new sister so abruptly. What's the great urgency? Why should we welcome her just because Petronilla seems to think we should? How can we possibly bear one more burden and care for an orphan who is pregnant? When she delivers there will be another one to care for. Did you think of that? To take this girl into our sisterhood without any knowledge of her is a ridicule of our order." Comtesse's face contorted. She whined, "We have rules. I spent months at Belle Cœur working and slaving until I was finally accepted…"

"When did you ever work so hard?" Beatrice laughed.

"Sisters, calm yourselves. *Arrêt*! Stop! Our order, our covenant with one another, allows for change when there is need. We're not bound by countless laws and rules." Sabine reached for Comtesse's hand. "Comtesse, please…We're free to marry if we choose, even to live outside the community. Surely our boundaries are open to welcome the stranger. God would not send us more than we can care for."

She turned to Petronilla. "You recognize something special in this girl. We can see she needs tending. As hard as it will be, our Christian charity calls us to help her. I suppose we must embrace the possibility to accept her…now…today. Do all of you understand what I'm saying?" Sabine's question hung in the air.

Crow cawed loudly three times. Comtesse pouted, and the girl sat on the ground wrapped in the blanket rocking to and fro, humming softly. Beatrice and Marie stayed near her.

"Petronilla, you have our trust. Am I wrong, Sisters?" Sabine looked at each of us. Everyone but Comtesse patted her heart in agreement.

Sabine spoke to Petronilla. "You've prophesied many things and delivered instruction that has always been helpful to us. We must trust your prophetic guidance. It is your gift, after all."

Comtesse began to cry her inevitable tears. Petronilla reached to take hold of her hands. "She's one of us, Comtesse. I can't find words to explain how I know this, but believe me, if we don't take this girl into our sisterhood, if we don't offer her protection and safe haven, I'm certain we'll be disobeying God." Petronilla's cheeks were flushed. "She needs us—and in a way we have yet to know, *we* need her."

"So I ask for our count, our hanswere, for the sake of our covenant with one another." Sabine looked at each of us. "Give the sign of your favor or disfavor for welcoming this girl into our order according to Petronilla's guidance."

After a moment's hesitation, all patted our hearts in agreement.

"Very well, we have a new sister. But I don't have to like this turn of events," Comtesse complained.

"Have another bite of honey cake, Sister. Something sweet to cure your sour mood." With one arm Beatrice cuddled the girl, who was wrapped tight in her blanket, while her other hand held out a morsel of cake to

Comtesse, who snatched it up and stuffed it into her mouth.

We sat silently for a time, eating our meal, growing accustomed to the peculiarities of our new sister. Curiously, the crone wisdom I had witnessed in her expression earlier that day had vanished entirely. All afternoon the girl's face beamed recognition as if we were familiar to her, though her eyes shone more like those of a devoted dog, faithful and yet lacking certain intelligence.

I noticed her features were uneven, like bread dough pressed by a baker in haste. But her thin, bluish lips turned up time and again in a captivating smile that illumined her face the way the sun shines reassuringly through oncoming storm clouds.

Beatrice took her to the stream again, this time to bathe her. Then she dressed her in Marie's spare frock and apron. The girl remained barefoot because we had no extra pair of shoes. Her matted hair embedded with leaves and twigs would be shorn at another time because the shears were packed away in the heap of belongings on our cart. Meanwhile, Marie did her best to gently remove bits of this and that from her walnut-colored mane.

The afternoon light began to dim. Crow flew from Ravenissa's shoulder to a low branch of the sheltering tree. One by one we went to our new sister to offer the Belle Cœur blessing as each of us touched the cross and circle upon her forehead. When it was Gertrude's turn, much to our surprise she reached into the leather pouch strapped about her waist and removed an amulet, the same she had made for each of us. Imene smiled and nodded to Gertrude.

"You are vun of us doe perhaps you don't understand vat dis means. Vee care for you and de baby you carry." Gertrude spoke softly while the girl cuddled into Beatrice's bosom. "Velcome. Dis amulet vill protect you. *Der Friede Gottes sei mit euch.* Amen." Gertrude placed the cord over the girl's head and kneeled to kiss her on both cheeks.

"EEEEEHHHHH! MICH MICH! ANUM POTAY!" The girl jumped up and squealed with joy.

"Ravenissa, vat she say?" Gertrude asked.

"Oh, if only I knew!" Ravenissa moved closer to study the girl. "I wish I understood her. She's a mystery to me. Perhaps she'll teach me her language."

Sabine looked curiously at Gertrude. "How did you have an extra amulet, Gertrude?"

Imene spoke for Gertrude while tears spilled down her beloved's red cheeks.

"Days before we left Belle Cœur, Gertrude dreamed there were twelve of us sitting, as we are now, under a large tree in the shadows. When she made the amulets, she made twelve. Today her dream came to pass." Gertrude wiped her eyes and smiled.

The girl threw her arms 'round Gertrude's neck. Gertrude swept her up and spun her 'round. When our clapping and laughter settled down, Beatrice leaned close to the girl.

"What's your name, child?"

The girl stared into Beatrice's eyes.

"You must know your name?"

In response the girl clapped her hands together and started rocking again, making a keening sound.

"*Mon Dieu,* we have to give her a name. She has little else. Surely we can honor her with something that is truly her own." Beatrice patted her belly while she spoke as if to summon a name from within.

Marie cuddled up beside the girl. She looked into her eyes, studying them for the answer she was seeking. "Cibylle." She spoke softly, not breaking her gaze with the girl. "Cibylle was my sister's name, my sister who died of fever. You are my…you are *our* new sister, and your name is Cibylle." Marie's face bloomed with delight at the sight of all of us, as we smiled and patted our hearts in agreement with her choice. Comtesse took her time but eventually offered her sign of approval.

"Good," Marie said as she hugged our new sister.

"Ahhh, yes! Cibylle was a lovely child. We miss her. Good of you to think of your sister, Marie. I like the thought of hearing Cibylle's name being spoken again," Beatrice said.

"Yes. This is good," Petronilla agreed.

Beatrice pulled up her apron and opened the front of her dress. She leaned forward, and her full breast slipped out. She pressed the large, dark nipple into a cup to relieve the milk that had begun to leak out onto her clothing. Then she did likewise with the other breast until the tall cup was full.

Beatrice tidied herself and cut a twelfth sliver of honey cake. She offered the cup of her mother's milk to Cibylle, who gulped down the thin, bluish liquid in three noisy gulps. She gobbled the cake and even the crumbs that fell to the ground, not minding the dirt and grass that also made their way to her eager mouth.

I wondered if somewhere Cibylle's *maman* was calling for her. Surprising tears stung my eyes as I thought of my *maman*. Had she called for me after I ran away?

While I was in my reverie, the faint remaining sunlight broke through the clouds for an instant, casting dark swiftly moving shadows over our merrymaking. A chilly breeze blew across the grain in the fields, bending it downward in wave upon wave like soldiers falling in battle.

We decided to stay the night by the rushing baptismal stream. Gertrude and Marie gathered wood, and soon a blazing fire warmed our circle. By its light I brought out my scraps of parchment, my writing board, quill, and vessel of ink to capture a few notations from our extraordinary day.

I looked out over the landscape as the light grew dim. There was Comtesse. Her head was cast down, and she looked pitifully small wandering amid the tall grasses. My heart ached for her. What had become of the lively companion of my childhood? I set my things aside and went to her.

"Comtesse? *Chere amie?*"

She turned to reveal a face of such misery that I reached my arms out to seize her and pull her to my heart. She stiffened.

"Please—can you not speak to me? What's happened to you? We are friends, sisters together," I pleaded.

"Not now, Goscelin." Her tone was firm, and her eyes filled with tears as she waved me away and turned her back.

I settled down beneath a tree some distance from the fire where the sisters were busy attending Cibylle. Weary and confused, I had no heart left to take up my quill.

7 January 1259
Le Monastère de la Visite

It's early morning and the story I began two days ago pulls at my heart, begging for completion. I must clean the scriptorium today, but first I will finish what I've begun.

I was distraught that night on our pilgrimage as we made our way to Chartres. I longed to find peace for Comtesse and me. Her refusal to confide in me was painful and unexplainable. I remember that when I left her in the field, I felt so horribly tired and discouraged I couldn't pray.

Soon Helvide and Ravenissa came to comfort me. They had witnessed my unsuccessful encounter with Comtesse.

"Goscelin, please don't worry...Each of us is in God's hands. Don't despair, dear sister. Grace will find her. All shall be well," Helvide comforted.

On either side of me, they sat down as grace themselves. Ravenissa, dark and slender, and Helvide, fair and pink as though kissed by the sun.

They have always been kind to me. We share a love for Creation and the longing to completely surrender to God's vast mystery of which we are but a tiny part.

I touched the amulets hanging 'round my neck. The talisman made by Gertrude, and the soft cloth–covered bundle of acorns and ground oak leaves that Helvide gave each of us months before, a tiny gift found upon our pillows one night that inspired our custom of *les cadeaux de nos cœurs.* From time to time, our gifts from our hearts appeared with sweet surprise. One of us, when inspired, would create a little offering for each sister and leave it where it would be certain to be discovered. Helvide explained how, when her bundles of acorns and oak leaves were found, she had made each one with prayer, as a talisman to welcome autumn's magic into our bones.

Helvide's wisdom is rich and wild. She speaks the language of plant, herb, and the mineral kingdom. She recites the movement of the moon and the stars. Stones and moss, tree and frond are earth's scripture for her.

She had asked me to create illuminations, small pictures, marks and symbols to express her recipes and medicines. I made these notations carefully. They were drawn upon the smallest bits of parchment. When they were completed, Helvide wrapped them in a rabbit pelt bound with leather thong. She is the guardian of a very particular wisdom, not unlike the sacred knowledge in the pages of Dominions and Graces.

To my eye, my sister of the garden appears to have sprouted from the earth, like a willow tree. Her tall, supple body is strong, lean, and graceful. When she danced naked among the rows of cabbages and fennel under the full moon, her shadow marked a wild rhythm. Helvide's short, golden hair halos her head beneath her cap and veil, and her bright blue eyes turn storm-gray in accordance with the weather. She is light, the way her sister Ravenissa is dark.

"Goscelin, we will give you something for your quill tonight. We'll tell you our story. For you have yet to learn how we became sisters." Ravenissa smiled and stretched. Crow flew from his comfortable perch on her shoulder to a low-hanging branch nearby where he could watch over us. Our dark-feathered sentinel and guardian.

I took up my parchment and board and carefully unstopped the vessel of ink. My quill felt curiously warm and ready as I grasped it with my fingers, but my heart was still heavy with concern for Comtesse.

Helvide and Ravenissa tugged my sleeves playfully and pulled me to the ground, causing me to nearly spill my precious ink. Helvide smiled a mischievous smile.

"Forgive me, Sisters, I know we're fasting but this is truly a holy occasion…the sharing of our story with you, Goscelin."

She took a small glass vessel from her apron pocket and removed the stopper. "Sweet, golden honey, dear Sister. Just a taste…before you begin to scribe our tale."

She passed the little container to me, and without hesitation I inserted my finger and felt the sticky, sweet elixir meet my skin. I scooped up a shimmering globe of amber, and with the most natural inclination I ever so briefly dipped my honey-soaked fingertip into my pot of ink.

"Ink and honey, bless my quill, and may there be sweetness in the telling of the story." I put my finger to my tongue and sucked it clean. If the qualities of hope and wisdom could be tasted, surely they would taste like ink and honey.

I recall how Ravenissa spread a blanket beneath the tree. I settled in with my back against the trunk. Helvide lit her lantern, for we were seated a distance from Gertrude's fire.

"I'll tell our story. Ravenissa isn't so good with details."

"You're right. You'll tell it better than I, sister. You arrived first, after all." Ravenissa leaned against me. Her head rested on my shoulder.

This is what I recall of that evening as I prepared to write the story of Helvide and Ravenissa. Now at last, all these months later, I make ready to add these parchments among the others. Parchments holding the story I scribed in an open field while we made our pilgrimage.

24 September 1258
Scribed while on Pilgrimage to Chartres

I rest my back against a tree. Helvide draws a deep breath and begins…

I am Helvide. My understanding is blessed with the wisdom of the healing properties and powers of herbs and flowers, sun, moon, stars, and the changing seasons. The soul of nature has always revealed herself in ways I understand.

During my childhood a door opened to me. A door leading to the realm of spirits that dwell in the roots, leaves, blossoms, and seeds of plant life. Rosemary, mustard, mugwort, and honeysuckle...these I know not with my mind but rather through my skin and through smell and taste. Mosses, gichtbaum, grapevine, smoke, elder, elm, and juniper, these were my strange girlhood friends. I've grown to know their divine purposes. My special wisdom has served me, protected me from harm, and allowed me to heal myself and others time and again.

I never knew my mother who gave me life. Myrtle, the healer and wise woman raised me. She told me the true story of my birth when I was old enough to understand.

My mother became pregnant when she was very young. The boy who was my father ran away. Maman lived at home with her six brothers, two sisters, and my grandmother. Grand-mère insisted there was no room for another child in the household. She sent Maman to the forest, to Myrtle, as the time for my arrival grew near.

Myrtle, the dark, wrinkled angel with long, white hair wild as a stallion's mane pulled me into life from my mother's womb. She birthed me with her strong, gnarled hands into her curious pagan's world of nature and magic.

She had not always lived in the forest. In her girlhood she discovered she had a gift for healing many ailments suffered by people in her village, but her mother disapproved of her skills and banished her from the family. She set out on her own "to live in the wonder of the goddess' creation."

The forest called to her, and when she came upon an old, abandoned wagon with a moss-covered roof in the shelter of a stand of pine trees, she knew she was home. In time people from the surrounding area discovered Myrtle and her healing ways. My mother was one of the fortunate souls who called on Myrtle in a time of need. And it was Myrtle who led my mother to a special place when she was ready to deliver me into this world.

I was born in the late afternoon near an ancient spring beneath the wide branches of the great sycamore tree at the edge of the Taunèe woods. There, under the soft, brown earth, five streams ran together to forge a sacred joining, a "jemny," as Myrtle named it. It was a place I would return to time and again throughout my girlhood.

Maman and I stayed on with Myrtle. Soon after my birth, a dark despair descended upon Maman's heart. In late autumn one morning, while Myrtle foraged for mushrooms in the woods and I slept on my palette in the wagon, my mother slipped away unseen. She never returned for me.

Myrtle became my mother, my teacher and guide. Even now I still hear the sound of her voice, deep and full as though her throat echoed ancient wisdom she'd been gathering for a thousand years. When I was old enough to understand her teachings, she told me she was certain I had been sent to her as a gift from the goddess. She believed I would become like a living book, a vessel to hold her wisdom so the knowledge she carried would continue after her body returned to the earth.

Pilgrims on the road and the people in the outlying area came to our home for Myrtle's medicines and magic. They brought vegetables from their gardens, chickens, and other barter in exchange for her mugwort tea, herbal bundles, and most of all for her rituals and petitions to the goddess for their healing.

I grew strong while Myrtle taught me her ancient wisdom. Each day she fed me the secrets of nature. Her lessons were always accompanied by great spoonfuls of honey harvested from the wild hive in the trunk of the sheltering tree.

She explained how stones contain both fire and moisture. According to Myrtle, the underworld creatures abhor and fear precious stones. They remind the dark ones that their power and glory were a part of creation before they fell from the goddess' grace.

Myrtle drew pictures in the dirt with her staff to illuminate how the earth is alive, how it breathes and has intelligence like the animals in the woods. We went to the stream and filled our bucket with red clay from the bank. With each new season, we worked the clay to become guardian figures, the serpent and frog, wolf and weasel, were placed for protection around the old wooden wagon that was our home. Other talismans made of bark and vine were placed in our garden and on the path leading to the pond where we bathed.

I learned it was the Mother of the Earth who tended the changing guard of nature when autumn fell to winter, winter burst into spring, and spring yielded to summer. All the while the goddess reigned over the land and the sky, the trees and the creatures.

The faded red, wooden wagon with its mossy roof and big wooden wheels was our sanctuary and shelter. A ladder made of thick branches led from the ground to the shuttered doorway. Myrtle hung ribbons of brightly colored cloth from the slatted wood ceiling inside our one-room dwelling. The cloth was payment from a traveler she'd nursed through a grave illness.

Inside there were two shuttered windows. A little door in the ceiling could be opened for air by day and to see the stars at night.

Before bed each evening we spoke our prayers onto each of the twelve green beads strung in a circle on Myrtle's mother-round, a kind of Rosary of her own making.

We pray…

For the four-legged ones in forest and meadow.

For the creeping ones on the ground.

For the flying ones of the air.

For the swimming ones in the river and Blind Spring.

For the honeybee, the butterfly, the spider, and all the ones that crawl or creep.

For fire, air, water, and sky.

For Grandmother Tree and the shelter she provides.

For plants, stones, metals, for all of these blessings we thank you, Mother of Creation.

The day is over.

The darkness comes.

Protect our night journeys in sleep.

Bless our dreams with your wisdom.

Wake us with your morning light. Turah. Turah.

On warm nights we slept outside on the earth to behold the pageant of the moon and stars. Myrtle pointed out the pattern of the night sky and how the design in the heavens foretold the ever-changing temperament in her herb garden.

In winter we closed the shutters and the wagon's door tight. We donned foxtails and rabbit skins stitched together with strips of goat's hide to keep us warm.

A small shelter near the wagon made of branches and moss was for visitors, the weary pilgrim, tired merchant, or returning crusader. This was a welcoming place for anyone Myrtle deemed safe and worthy. Many passed through our forest in need of healing or a night's rest, but for good reason she was wary of bandits and thieves.

When I was very young, two men on horseback came to the wagon. They said they were soldiers returning home from battle. They appeared hungry and tired.

When Myrtle told me this story later, she always said, "I knew from first glance they were no kindred to goodness. Sometimes opening the door of hospitality welcomes certain danger. Trust the grip in your belly. The body knows truth and sends warning. Remember to always heed the messages that come through your senses."

Myrtle shared a meal with the visitors and showed them the shelter where they could camp near the fire outside the wagon. She put me to bed. I was only an infant and fortunately have no memory of what happened next.

In the night, the men pushed their way into the wagon. One grabbed Myrtle and held her tight while the other tore things apart searching for anything of value. They took the few coins she had and a small silver box, Myrtle's only possessions from life in the outside world. Before they rode away, one of the men slapped Myrtle hard across the face then laughed. "That's so you won't forget us." Myrtle never forgot. I believe other horrors befell her that night, but this was how she told the story. Our forest was a sanctuary, but even sanctuaries are vulnerable to predators.

Soon after this unfortunate event Myrtle began to paint. To climb the ladder and enter the wagon was a journey to another world. Designs from Myrtle's wondrous imagination, flying two-headed beasts, twisted vines and countless flowers, a fiery sun, milky moon, and all manner of symbols covered the walls of our one-room home. Her colors came from the garden: blackberry juice, crushed mulberry leaves, and ground mustard seed.

"The creation of beauty in one's surroundings makes a shield of protection," she instructed while she painted a running deer on the wall above our table.

The seasons fell, one upon another, while my spirit fattened on Myrtle's magic and wisdom. We were happy enough and unaware of the gift that would soon arrive.

In my sixth year, a woman from the nearby village brought a girl-child to Myrtle. The woman knew only that she was five years old and orphaned when her mother died of fever. Her father, a crusader, had been away since before her birth.

Other children had come to us from time to time. Anxious mothers desperate for medicines and healing for a sick child brought them to Myrtle.

The tiny woman with broken teeth and one leg hobbled about on her crutch, as though she couldn't stand still.

"I've heard you're a healer. This child needs your care; most of all she needs mothering. Poor orphan. Take her, won't you? I beg you, take her! She's been fending on her own. It's a pitiful sight to see her begging every day. But lest God punish me for not telling you...you should know she's an odd child. Keeps to herself and seems to be more at ease with animals than people. Your ways might..."

I remember how I studied Myrtle while she bent down and held the girl's face in her hands. She pushed her hair to the side and licked her forehead as if to taste her. Then she squinted hard and gazed into her eyes.

"What's her name?" she asked.

"Murielle," the crippled woman answered.

Myrtle put her hands on her hips. "No. That will never do." Then Myrtle lifted the girl high toward the branch where a raven was perched.

"I name you Ravenissa, Raven-child, the one who speaks and understands the tongues of fox and hare, dove and squirrel."

I remember the day of your arrival, after the one-legged woman went away. Myrtle turned you and me face to face. She gently wrapped us together with a long piece of wood-vine… heart to heart, belly to belly, then took a small vial of rose oil from her pocket. She poured the oil across her fingers and made a cross and circle on our foreheads. She closed her eyes tightly and whispered, "Helvide, meet your sister, Ravenissa. Ravenissa, meet your sister, Helvide. You are my daughters. I am your mother. So it is, forevermore. Turah. Turah."

A crow cawed twelve times while Myrtle unwound the binding. Then the three of us joined hands and danced a circle dance until we fell down dizzy in a pile of laughter.

"You remember that day so well, Helvide." Ravenissa said.

Helvide removed her veil and cap and scratched her head.

"Until you arrived, dear Sister, Myrtle was my mother, my teacher and playmate. I was happy at the prospect of having a friend and companion my size. However, the idea of sharing Myrtle with another troubled me."

Ravenissa stroked Chanson, who had silently appeared. She lifted him to her lap. The big cat pawed at her apron pocket. "It turned out all right in the end. We used to squabble and pull each other's hair, but Myrtle wouldn't let us go on for very long. We did have fun together. Remember the painting of the goddess on the wall above the bed?"

"Oh, yes! Do you want to tell Goscelin about the painting and your dream?"

"No, Sister, you tell the story better than I. I'm no story-teller."

"Alright then. But be sure to let me know if I forget something important. This is *our* story afterall."

Helvide continued ...

Painted on the wall next to our bed was the face of the Mother, the Great Mother of creation. She watched over us while we slept. One warm night when the candles had burned down and the three of us were on the bed looking at the stars through the little door in the roof, I asked Myrtle to tell us about the Great Mother. It was very still, and I remember the clouds sailed past the moon making shadows play upon our faces.

Myrtle spilled out her lesson while she undid my braid and loosened my hair. "The Goddess is protector and comforter. She will inspire your dreams if you make an offering to her."

Ravenissa asked her what kind of gift the Mother of the Earth would like best.

"Feathers always please her. But a heart-shaped stone is also good, if you can find one. You must choose for yourself, my dearest. I'm certain the Mother will be pleased with whatever you bring her."

We had questions. Where should we place our offerings? How will the Mother know where to find them?

"Oh...you must decide. Let your heart tell you where to leave it. That's part of the mystery of offerings. An offering must be freely given and placed by the heart. Turah, turah, my dear." Turah, turah, was Myrtle's way of saying, "Trust all is well, believe, and it shall be so."

That very same night Ravenissa dreamed she flew above the forest with a flock of crows. She was a crow in her dream with huge, shiny, black wings. She flew high between the clouds and the earth. In the dream she watched a long, black feather from her wing slip free and spiral to the ground.

The next morning Myrtle sent her to the blackberry thicket with her basket to choose the fattest berries she could find. The basket filled quickly, and just as Ravenissa reached to pick the last berry before she returned home, a long, shiny, black feather circled down from the sky while a crow cawed overhead. The feather came to rest in the branches of the blackberry bush. She knew this would be her offering to the Goddess. Her heart told her it would please the Mother of the Earth to discover her gift in the exact place where it had fallen. She called her thanks to Crow and watched him fly out of sight. But he soon returned."

"See, you tell it all so well. You know the story by heart," Ravenissa smiled.

"The crow you speak of? It can't be him?" I pointed to our beloved Crow perched in the tree above us. I was puzzled.

"Yes, that's the one," Ravenissa smiled.

"But that means he's very very old...for a bird, that is. He doesn't seem aged."

"Crow is one mystery I've come to accept, Goscelin. Just one of many mysteries..."

Helvide stood and stretched. I rubbed my hands together. My fingers were stained and cramped from so much scribing. Helvide shook out her skirts then settled herself again.

Our mother taught that each of us possessed special gifts. Myrtle believed it was her task to unlock the door to our souls to reveal what we were born to share. We had been sent to her, she often said, to become the guardians of her wisdom. She told us, "I will teach you everything that has been passed to me. One day, a long time after you are gone from the earth, when your bones are dust, those same gifts will be reclaimed by women of an age yet to come. The wisdom will live on. Turah! Turah!"

Myrtle showed me how to use my hands as if they were like the branches on a tree. My arms and hands could reach up, down, or outward. They could be still in prayer but never idle.

I learned where bitterness and heat live in the tree's trunk and leaves, and how they carry warmth and cold like the plants. She taught me to identify herbs by their fragrance and taste. These things soon became as familiar as the sight of Myrtle's wrinkled face and long white braid.

Her knowledge of making tinctures, unguents, teas, and medicines was passed on to me. Oils, salves, dry-burning, wet-burning, sacrificial aromatics, wood-base, divination, potions, and sleep-pillows...all her magic, healing recipes, and forest wisdom were written on my soul.

When Ravenissa and I were still very young, we learned to weave. Myrtle crafted two simple frame looms. Each was made of four smooth branches tied together at the corners with wood-vine. Wool came from a spinner in the nearby village who traded her yarns for Myrtle's mugwort oil, said to increase one's dreams.

"Weaving is a blessed craft, dear ones. Your hands can weave the story of your life on your loom. Even when your day's work is done, you must continue to make beauty," our mother said as she warped our looms with strips of linen and gave us her lesson.

Together we built a big frame loom. It was taller than Myrtle. We stripped the bark from four large, heavy branches and placed them on the ground in a square. Then we wound the corners where the branches met with strips of hide. Two longer thick branches were bound to either side of the frame. Myrtle dug two holes in the earth near the wagon. We raised the frame and set the posts into the holes and filled them with mud.

Our loom was built to honor the Earth Goddess. It was where we wove nature's beauty into a tapestry each time the season changed. In spring we wove together; clover, ivy, bright green grasses, and strips of colorful stained cloth blessed with our prayers. During summer the grasses dried, and we brought snail shells and lavender to be worked into the design. In autumn small branches with acorns and tiny bouquets of purple thistle and twigs and moss from the forest floor were added.

Ravenissa's ways as a child were dark as her complexion. She would mope and brood unless she was allowed to spend time each day with the creatures: the birds, the mice, the weasel and fox. She spoke more easily to Crow, our goat, and even to the cicadas than to me! There was a fox, a vixen that lived in the woods not far from our wagon. Ravenissa discovered her den and went every day for weeks to the place near the stream where she'd first seen her foraging in the bushes. Each day she spoke fox-speak to the beautiful animal until at last, one summer's evening, she followed Ravenissa home from the woods—much to Myrtle's and my astonishment. She stayed with us for several days then disappeared never to be seen again.

Ravenissa also had a keen sense of hearing. She listened in rapture to every sound around her. She told me once how her mind, or rather her tongue, made memories of the dove's song, the chatter and squeaks of the squirrel and deer, and the croak of the frog's call.

And so, we grew older and our days and nights passed swiftly. We were given more chores to help Myrtle care for those who found their way to our wagon. Childhood ended, and our moon-bleeding began. Myrtle taught us how to use our monthly blood as sacred blessing for the earth. She no longer bled as we did, but each month when the moon was full Ravenissa and I went naked to our garden. We squatted so our moon-blood could be offered to the soil. This was the time of month when we were instructed to carefully harvest the guidance of our dreams.

To celebrate our maidenhood, Myrtle pierced our left ears with a long needle and gave each of us one small golden hoop as a symbol of the circle of creation. The pair of earrings was payment from a woman she had midwifed before we arrived.

One early autumn afternoon a year or so after our moon-bleeding began, she took us to visit Grandmother, an ancient oak tree near the pool of green waters. Crow flew ahead of us from branch to branch, waiting for us to catch up before he glided a little distance to another limb. We walked farther and farther into a part of the woods where we'd never been, and all the while Crow cawed his shield of protection as we approached the tree.

Her trunk was wide and weathered like Myrtle's skin. Her heavy, broad, leafy branches hung low, touching the ground in some places.

Myrtle taught us to approach all trees slowly, with our arms outstretched, and to always bring offerings to show respect. We brought acorns and pine needles to leave on the ground near the trunk. We approached the Grandmother in silence.

Myrtle reached under her apron and removed a forch from the rope 'round her waist. We watched while her arms spread wide and she stretched her body as though she herself were a tree. Then we heard her say, "Grandmother, thank you for protecting my secret. Your shade is a blessing, and your mighty branches are home to the birds and squirrels. I honor you, and today I bring my daughters to you for your blessing."

When Myrtle finished her greeting, she signaled us to join her near the tree. She nodded it was time to pay our respects. After we greeted the Grandmother, we watched Myrtle as she gently and slowly inserted the forch into a deep crevice in the ancient trunk. With her midwife's skill, she moved the stick about. I recorded her every move, her delicate finesse, as she gently turned the tool to extract a long slender bundle wrapped in brown hide from the narrow pocket in the trunk of the tree. We had no way of knowing a prophecy was unfolding.

"One day, after I'm dust, you'll be the guardians of my wisdom. When you're older, other women healers will come seeking your knowledge. You'll be invited to leave the forest and join them in their work. It's time for you to begin to prepare for that day."

Myrtle held the bundle above her head. She shuffled to a wide, flat stone, and we knelt down together. The trees swayed above us, and sunlight and shadows dappled our faces while we were bathed in a shower of dried brown pine needles.

Her wrinkled hands pulled a sheaf of moss from the forest floor. She spread it on the stone like a cloth. Then she placed the bundle upon it. With great care she removed the hide covering to reveal a curious wooden box with rusted hinges. The lid was painted with colored symbols. In the lower right corner was a painted gold cross inside a green circle. In the upper left corner was a crimson spiral. The box was long and shallow.

Ravenissa and I clasped one another's hands. Crow flew to a branch overhead. One long, blue-black feather landed on Ravenissa's shoulder. Myrtle threw her head back, laughing loudly. Her dusty hand wiped spittle from her mouth. She whispered, "Crow knows. Crow knows."

"Knows what?" we chirped together in one voice.

"Crow knows…it's time."

She slowly opened the box. Inside, the lid was covered with gold letters and more symbols. Underneath a piece of faded blue wool were twelve long, green glass vials and a small silver spoon with a long bone handle. Each vial was stopped with wax the color of blood. A numeral, I through XII, and special symbol were etched into each wax stopper.

Crow soared in circles above us while Myrtle taught us the secret meaning of each of the XII elixirs.

"There are twelve measures of health, twelve properties. If two or more properties are unbalanced, illness occurs. There are illnesses of the body and also the illnesses of the spirit. When someone is need of healing, you must inspect the twelve properties to discover which ones need purifying. Then you choose the matching vials to administer one portion of elixir

with the silver spoon. One vial contains mouse stones. It is only to be used by a midwife.

"Six properties are attuned to the body and refer to the earth, to the realm of matter. They are plant, tree, mineral, metal, animal, and stone. Six properties suit the spirit, and they refer to the heavens, to the realm of the Goddess. They are sky, star, bird, angel, moon, and sun. Each symbol etched in the wax seal reveals the property."

She drew the symbols in the dirt with a stick as she continued her teaching while the afternoon light grew dim.

Ravenissa and I took Myrtle's knowledge into our hearts and minds. We didn't realize these would be the last lessons our beloved mother would share with us as her living books of wisdom.

After the box was once again deep in the tree for safekeeping, we returned home, escorted by Crow. Myrtle fed us vegetable root pie and mint tea for supper. Before sleep, she told us her favorite story of how we were born...to her. Then as always, we said our prayers to the Goddess of the Earth before Myrtle kissed us on our noses.

When I was heavy with oncoming dreams, I was startled to my senses by the scent of rose oil. I opened my eyes to feel Myrtle finger a cross and circle on my forehead with her sweet anointing.

The next morning, Crow awakened us. When Crow's call ceased, there was only silence and the undeniable scent of angels in the air.

It was a sad day. We tried and tried to rouse her. Her braid lay on the pillow like a snakeskin left on the garden path. Myrtle's hands held her green beads as if the Great Mother had taken her home in mid-prayer. Peace was painted on her weathered face that in the early morning light appeared less wrinkled, more youthful, and strangely pale. Myrtle was sleeping the sleep of all tomorrows. Our mother had made her crossing in the night to the place where souls are rested and given a fresh purpose before the Goddess returns them to their new bodies and new lives.

We washed her aged body with water from the pond and anointed her with the same oil she had used to bless us the night before. Afterward we carried her to her favorite place, a deep hollow in the grassy mound near the holly tree. We laid her there. The earth seemed to yield with respect as her body settled into its resting place. She fit perfectly, as if the Goddess had made a space in her bosom just for Myrtle.

We spent the day dressing her in a gown we fashioned from moss, chamomile, and clover. We brushed her silver hair and adorned it with a clover crown and tiny, yellow snail shells. Then we covered her with the tapestry of nature's gifts taken from our garden loom.

She looked pleased to be so beautiful for her journey to the place of all tomorrows. Finally we covered our mother with earth, and marked her grave with a cross of branches fixed in a circle of braided wood-vine, the symbol she stroked on our foreheads so tenderly our last night together. We spoke our love for her and prayed for her swift passage to the place we, too, would go one day.

Late in the afternoon, the wind began to blow. Ravenissa made a small fire near the grave. We mixed shaved deer horn and frankincense together. The odor would chase away unwelcome spirits, bad worms, and spells. This was our final gift. We slept beside her that night.

For a time we continued our mother's work there in the woods. Word spread throughout the village that the crone's daughters could heal both human and animal. Ravenissa tended all manner of beasts. I made herbal soups and teas, compresses and salves for those who came to our door seeking healing.

Our garden grew beyond imagining. We were sure it was because Myrtle's spirit blessed the soil. Ravenissa's menagerie also grew. She spoke to badger, goat, and fawn each in its own tongue, and Crow was never far from us.

In the autumn of my eighteenth year, Sabine appeared at our door. She had lost her way in the forest as she traveled from Vézelay to her home nearby. I remember her first words to us with clarity. "Greetings! I hope I am not a disturbance to your day. The path I was following led me to your door. Yet…I am not quite sure how, because I have followed the same path before and somehow never arrived here."

Her kind smile and bright eyes assured us she was trustworthy.

From that first afternoon, Sabine was very taken with our home and our knowledge of plants and animals. We made a strong acquaintance that endured. She began to come regularly—then Gertrude and Imene joined her. They were her dear friends. She called them her sisters.

The three were warm and friendly! They talked about Jesus and His Mother, and they taught us their prayers. The stories of Our Lady seemed like the stories Myrtle had taught us about the goddess, and Myrtle's mother-round beads were like the Rosary. The women's prayers were comforting, and the stories of Jesus's teachings took root in our hearts.

Their visits were not only welcomed but also helpful. Gertrude repaired our leaking roof with her strong, sure hands, and Imene brought salve for Ravenissa's rash and applied it with her gentle touch. Sabine helped us put the wagon in order, and all was done with large doses of laughter and storytelling.

It was good to feel a motherly presence once more. After one year, the three sisters told us our skills were needed at their infirmary at Belle Cœur. They invited us to join them in their work and worship and to share their home.

Myrtle's prophecy had come to pass! She had told us this day would arrive... the day when all she had taught us would be shared with other healers. Her spirit lived on.

Two days after the women's invitation, Ravenissa and I took Myrtle's forch and went to bid farewell to Grandmother Oak. We removed the secret box of elixirs and filled the open space in the trunk of the tree with moss and acorns so she wouldn't feel empty.

We slept on Myrtle's grave that night and told her of our plans. The next morning I carefully lifted plants from the garden. I wrapped the roots in earth and linen until they could be planted at Belle Cœur.

Ravenissa gathered her animals and explained to each what was about to happen. I folded the colorful cloth ribbons that hung inside the wagon and the fur blankets Myrtle had stitched. It felt right that our wagon would stay for some lucky pilgrim to discover, for that was what Myrtle would have wanted. After all, the wagon came to her as a gift. Now it would become another's blessing. Myrtle's home was full with her magic. Covered in vines and moss, it was also home to the wood rat and wren. The wagon seemed to say, "I belong here. You have a new home. Leave me to nature."

Ravenissa and I took our looms, our golden earrings, Myrtle's green mother-round beads, and her favorite red, woolen shawl. These things kept her spirit close and made her guidance feel ever present.

The sisters of Belle Cœur arrived with the north wind late in the afternoon. Ravenissa and I walked through the forest and meadows that had been our home. With a last look at the Taunèe woods, we took leave of our familiar world.

Gertrude arranged our belongings on her cart, tapped the goats with her walking stick, and our caravan was underway. When we passed by Myrtle's grave, we paused one last time to offer the blessing she had taught us, "Turah, turah. Turah, turah." Crow, our feathered protector, flew ahead as if he knew the way to where we were going.

Le Monastère de la Visite
January 8, 1259

I come to my writing room as dawn breaks, before I begin my chores, to add a notation to the tale of Helvide and Ravenissa. I scribed their story while we were on pilgrimage, on the evening of that strange day when our sisterhood welcomed Cibylle, the one who would change our lives forever. Replete with tender love for my sisters, I now place these four parchments written that night to the ever-growing bundle of our stories.

Soon I will bind my writings together within the piece of hide I took before leaving Saint Catherine's. The beauty of Helvide and Ravenissa's tale has caught me up as I read it once again.

I remember that at the very end of that most mysterious day of our pilgrimage, all of us stretched out on the earth while Comtesse continued to pace about, unable to settle herself. Our heads touched together beneath the stars. To the angels above, we must have appeared as spokes on a wheel.

We were tired but giddy. Cibylle's playfulness was contagious, and Marie was happy to have a new friend. One by one, my sisters fell asleep while I lay awake. My mind was stirred with thoughts of Myrtle and the curious life Ravenissa and Helvide shared with her in the forest. My writer's heart was satiated, the way the belly feels full after a delicious meal.

As I reflect on our pilgrimage from Belle Cœur to Chartres, I realize it was a time of riddles and uncertainty. I'm sure God's grace guided and protected us every step of the way. The same is true, even now.

Though our sisterhood hasn't found comfort and peace at this vast monastery with its strict rules and draughty passageways, we're grateful to the nuns for giving us shelter. Yet, our determination is to hold fast to the memory and spirit of Belle Cœur that shines like a beacon of hope on the horizon of this unfamiliar landscape.

The daylight creeps under the door. My fingertip finds its way to my tongue and for an instant...I recall the sweet, enticing taste of ink and honey.

Le Monastère de la Visite
January 9, 1259

The air is heavy and prickly, dense like before a summer storm, though it's now dead of winter and the weather is cold and fair. No storms in sight, at least not the kind that bring wind and rain.

I feel unsettled and restless but take comfort from my assignment to scribe our stories. That's what I shall do this early morning. I pick up my quill and the thread of my telling of the tale of our pilgrimage to Our Lady's cathedral at Chartres.

After Cibylle joined us and Ravenissa and Helvide shared their story, we continued our journey. On the sixth evening after a long day's walk, we rested on the ground near an orchard on the plains somewhere between Belle Cœur and the town of Chartres.

Gertrude built a small fire as the daylight faded. We shared our prayers and sat together quietly. Mabille stood and brushed the dry grass from her dress. She clapped her hands for attention. Crow startled and cawed his alarm.

Mabille cleared her throat.

"I have something to say."

Her eyes were wide, and her face was flushed like one who'd been too long in the hot sun.

Shy Mabille had never addressed us in such an urgent way. Gertrude had wandered across the field to a grove of trees in search of branches for the evening fire. The rest of us roused from where we'd been resting.

Mabille looked to Sabine for approval to continue. Sabine smiled. Mabille stretched her neck and took a deep breath.

"I would like to teach you new songs…the songs of my heart…songs that come from God." She spoke with an unfamiliar authority. "Please…let's open our hearts and sing our praises. Let's build a shelter made of song." Her chest heaved a sigh of relief.

Again she looked to Sabine, who nodded assurance. Then her eyes traveled 'round the circle. No one spoke. Not because we didn't agree with our sister, but rather it seemed we were all surprised by her sudden boldness.

She continued. "Our little songs at Belle Cœur are familiar to all of us. Let's sing what's been hiding inside our hearts all this time just waiting for the right moment to be sung. I know each of you must have a song that God has given you to sing!"

"Praise God, Sister! I'd be grateful to see what waits within my heart beneath these heavy breasts. Do you really believe I've a song somewhere inside me?" Beatrice rubbed her bosom as if searching for a buried tune.

Mabille's face flushed with excitement. "Oh, yes! We all have songs sleeping in our bones. I think God puts them there before we're born, and life has a way of calling them forth."

"Even me, Mabille? Do you believe I've music waiting inside me?" Ravenissa asked.

"*Naturellement*! You speak to the owl and muskrat, field mouse and deer. Imagine what God has placed in you for your very own voice to sing!"

Mabille's enthusiasm caught us up one by one.

"Teach us, Sister. We need a new song to bless our way." Petronilla gently tugged Mabille's sleeve.

Comtesse stirred the ground with her tall walking stick. "My mother always told me I was gifted with song. My family praised my singing. They told me I sang like an angel. I could teach the others, Mabille."

"No, Comtesse. Too many teachers will only cause confusion. This is my inspiration to share." Mabille's face turned red, but her message was clear and strong.

Comtesse frowned and chewed her thumb. She shrugged and walked away, whispering to herself.

Imene called out. "Lead us, Mabille. We'll be like the pilgrims in Scripture. They sang Psalms as their pilgrim songs. Teach us a new song, Mabille, please."

Evening's blanket of darkness covered us without notice while Mabille moved into the center and swayed her arms this way and that, directing our voices while she taught us her simple chant. Gertrude moved about as she stirred the fire and lit the lanterns, singing all the while.

"So this is what you've been humming, Mabille, while we've been walking. Our pilgrim song!" Petronilla smiled.

We are pilgrims on the Holy Road.
Far from home are we.
Show us the way.
As we walk and pray.
Alleluia, alleluia.
Amen and amen.

We are pilgrims on the Holy Road.
Onward we go.
Make us strong.
The way is long.
Alleluia, alleluia.
Amen and amen.

Our voices rose into the darkness. The chorus of Belle Cœur was born in the middle of the countryside that autumn night. Small bands of pilgrims were all around us. Their fires and lantern light appeared like fallen stars scattered upon the earth.

Mabille directed the singing of her chant over and over until we sang her words and the lilting tune clearly and smoothly. Cibylle joined in and hummed softly while she spun 'round and 'round, never letting go of her amulet squeezed tightly in both hands.

"Let's sing the chant one more time before our prayers," Mabille requested, though the hour was late.

We began to sing, and to our surprise the other voices of nearby pilgrims joined in. Our singing blended together into the plaintive voice of one people seeking God on the Holy Road.

After the last note faded into the velvet blackness of night and the fires burned low, Petronilla led us in prayer. We huddled closer to one another under our blankets to stave the chill.

Later I fell deep asleep and dreamed of Maman. She appeared younger than when I last saw her. She was smiling, and a radiant light shone round her. I ran toward her calling out, "Maman! Maman!"

Ravenissa shook me awake while the others around me stirred. "You're dreaming, Goscelin. Shhhhh. Be still. It's only a dream."

I pulled the covers tight and wept, believing in my heart it was not a dream. I felt Maman had gone to heaven.

Two days passed. While we walked at a steady, plodding pace, Crow flew ahead out of sight to a faraway branch. When our little procession came into view, he called to us before flying on to another perch down the road.

Marie and Cibylle were constant companions. Marie was filled with joy to have a sister close to her age. One evening after the day's journey, she gathered sticks and stones for Cibylle, and together they played a game of *batons et des pierres.*

Marie marked a square in the dirt and covered each mark with a stick. In the center she marked a circle. Sitting some distance away, the player tossed four stones, one by one, into the center of the circle. If the stone missed the center, a stick was removed. After four rounds of play, the one with the least sticks won. Cibylle had a natural gift for this pastime, much to Marie's delight.

I longed for more parchment and a private place for scribing. My dream of Maman in her heavenly body, rather than covering me with grief, strangely made be feel that she would now be near me always. My longing for my mother was replaced with abiding peace. A distance had been closed and I felt her spirit would be forever with me. I believe there is an invisible birthing cord between children and their mothers that is never severed.

The dream inspired poetry and ideas for fanciful stories that took up residence in my imagination.

Thoughts of Maman meandered through my mind and led to the lessons in the various volumes of Dominions and Graces. The elements—earth, air, fire, and water—lived in my understanding in a new way.

I realized during the countless hours of walking and sleeping in nature what Brother Paul had tried to teach me when I was locked away in his secret room. His voice echoed inside my heart.

"You are one with Creation, Goscelin. There is no separation between you and the mud in the field, the candle flame, the wind that pries the leaves from the trees, or the rain that falls from the heavens. These things live in your bones. The same hand that made this earth and all the wonders of nature forged you."

At night I slept on the hard ground and could not escape hearing the life crawling beneath my blanket…ants and beetles, worms, and other insects too unsettling to imagine. I pondered how one day *I'd* be in the earth, and what was creeping there would pick my bones clean. Sleeping out of doors fed my dreams and imaginings.

The fire provided warmth and light. The wind gave me breath to keep up with the others. And the sound of the river coursing over the stones renewed my faith each morning that we would eventually reach our destination.

I remembered how Brother Paul had instructed me to collect bits of nature and add them to the volumes. I promised his spirit I would begin to do this.

Each day's walk inspired pictures and language to be stored in my mind for another time when each could be birthed through my quill onto parchment. Inspiration was all around me, in the sound of our feet marching in rhythm along the road or on the air in the scent of drying grass and musky odor of bodies in need of bathing.

Words tumbled about in my head. I walked and played with words to describe what I witnessed on the Holy Road to Chartres. How would I describe the sight of a falcon as he hovered then dived from on high to snatch the mouse from her hiding place in the rushes? How could I capture with words the startling way he swooped her up with her babies still fastened to her teats?

What language would I use to express the relief that came with the touch of cool water on my parched lips, after hours of walking prayer on blistered feet? How would I tell of the sweet taste of honey cake each afternoon or the sight of God's canopy of stars that appeared at dusk to bless day's end?

Sometimes I walked alone, lagging behind the others to ponder Maman. Surely she had appeared to me, so I wouldn't worry about her any longer.

Oh, God, bless Maman with Your peace, and please send her spirit's beautiful presence to visit me in my dreams from time to time. Amen.

On the eighth night of our journey, we came upon a grassy slope near a grove of walnut trees. I removed my shoes and wiggled my toes in the grass.

If Henriette were able to speak, she surely would have scolded me, for I had forced her to share my apron pocket with my day's gathering of nature's treasures.

My collection included…

a sampling of an unknown species of wildflower
a reddish-brown leaf covered with tiny white warts
a small, empty, brown, speckled snail shell
two samplings of thorny thistle
a bit of bone or perhaps deer antler

After our prayers we settled into our blankets. Above us the clouds parted to reveal the silver slip of the waxing moon, the way a mother's body opens at birth to disclose the crown of her baby's head. Suddenly the sky was filled with countless stars. Faint moonlight poured over the landscape, and somewhere in the distance a wolf howled a lonely cry.

"The moon is a blessing for women," Helvide began. "The waxing moon is known as Brid and called Diana when she is full. She becomes Morrigan when she's waning. The moon is ever three, Maiden, Mother, and Crone. Each of her faces forms the pattern of woman's life."

Ravenissa's long, slender finger gently stroked her mouse stretched out upon the length of her hand. She had snitched a little cheese from the brick when Beatrice wasn't looking. The mouse nibbled the hard, white crumbs from her fingers while she spoke.

"Remember, Helvide, when we were young maidens and Myrtle told us that whenever we were in need of something we must utter our intention to the dark of the moon? That's the time when the Mother of Creation hides herself. When the moon is dark, it's like a brief season of secrets and an auspicious time for making promises and for visioning. The full moon delivers our heart's desires and monthly bleeding begins and we are unleashed. That's our most potent and powerful time."

I watched the mouse's belly grow fat as the last of the cheese disappeared into his tiny mouth. He preened his whiskers like a cat before Ravenissa lifted him by his tail and returned him to her apron pocket.

"That's why Helvide and I always give a portion of our monthly blood to the garden on the night when Mother moon is full. It's our offering of gratitude for the gifts of womanhood."

Sabine stood stretched her arms to the heavens. Gertrude stoked a fresh fire. Smoke spiraled upward in a mysterious dance with Sabine's gestures while she recited the Scripture.

"A great sign appeared in the sky, a woman clothed with the sun, with the moon beneath her feet, and on her head a crown of twelve stars."

"I heard this read from the Book of Revelation when I was a novice, before I ran away from the nunnery," Sabine said. "Our Mother, the Queen of Heaven, she, too, is within the moon. Let's look to the heavens, sisters to find the twelve stars of Our Lady's crown." She invited us to find the brightest stars that night.

One by one we found jewels for the Mother of Jesus. Even Cibylle seemed to understand the game. She pointed to the brightest star of all.

I looked up at the night sky, and though I felt very small in the midst of such vastness, I knew I was one with all I beheld.

Brother's Paul instruction came to mind.

"You will know when it's time to share Dominions and Graces."

"Sisters, I want to share something with you. Something important."

My announcement spilled out all at once without hesitation. I spent a long while that night on our pilgrimage explaining as best I could the story of how I was initiated as the guardian of Dominions and Graces by Brother Paul. I shared with my sisters what I had come to understand about earth, air, fire, and water.

I promised to show them the volumes when we arrived at our new home, for they were tucked deep in my basket under our belongings on our cart. There was more, so much more to tell them, but I felt it wasn't time for everything to be revealed.

There were questions from the sisters, and for some there were no answers, only more questions. Such is the nature of the mysterious wisdom of Dominions and Graces.

I feel I'm emptying my heart on this parchment, my writer's heart that has been holding these stories from our pilgrimage. However, there is one story I have been carrying that I'm eager to scribe now.

We had been gone from Belle Cœur nine days, perhaps ten…

The road narrowed, and the warm, sunny autumn morning turned suddenly chilly and dark. By midafternoon we had donned our cloaks and felt certain it would rain. The smell of a storm rode on the wind that whipped the grasses and blew dust in our eyes.

We were walking between two small bands of pilgrims. We had learned the previous night that the ragtag group was also traveling to Nôtre Dame de Chartres.

"Stay close. Follow us. I've been there before. I know the way," Monsieur Chartaine, a kind old gentleman, assured us. A short, frail man with piercing, clear blue eyes, he appeared to be the elder of the group of nine: two men, two women, and five young children.

We talked about the weather and our journeys. That night, Monsieur Chartaine revealed details about the cathedral, the same we had heard from our dying messenger in the infirmary at Belle Cœur. We shared prayer at evening's end. It was good to be in safe company with others who loved God.

The next afternoon our new friends were some distance ahead, and we noticed them turning off the road toward an abbey on a small rise to the north. They signaled to us to follow them. We thought this change of course was strange, but we trusted the group, and it was a welcome diversion to see scenery other than the river and plains we'd been following for days.

The abbey church was made of stone with a moss-covered roof. It reminded me of a chapel I had seen when I journeyed to St. Catherine's so long ago. When we caught up with Monsieur Chartaine and the others, he explained.

"This is Nôtre Dame des Heures. We'll visit the anchoress who lives here. This place is home to a small community of sisters devoted to praying the hours. The anchoress will feed our souls with her wisdom. Come. Her anchorage is there on the other side of the entrance to the sanctuary." He hurried on ahead.

"What's an anchoress?" I asked Beatrice who walked beside me.

"I heard about an anchoress when I was a young girl. I think she lived in the church on the other side of the village to the south of Belle Cœur," Beatrice answered.

My curiosity stirred as we followed the pilgrims 'round the corner. "What does she do?"

Beatrice shrugged. I took her arm. We made our way up the rise toward the entrance.

Just beyond the corner at the front of the abbey church was a small stone structure made of a different sort of stone from the larger building. The little room, as it were, was attached to the church. There was no entrance, no door of any kind. There were only walls on every side. I would learn this kind of room is called an anchorage, the place where the anchoress lived. There was an iron-grated window on the front of the structure, and beneath it was a very small opening, a kind of pass-through.

We formed a line and waited in turn to approach the window to pray with the anchoress. When my turn came, I hoped to catch a glimpse of her, but a dark cloth separated us, and there was no way to see inside. She offered a prayer in a language I couldn't understand.

The other pilgrims waited until all had experienced a moment with the anchoress. Later, when we began our return to the main road I was full of questions. I ran ahead to Monsieur Chartaine.

"Monsieur, please tell me about the anchoress. Who is she? How does she live?"

We walked together for a while, and he shared that an anchoress is a nun who feels called by God to live as a hermit, as though she has died to all worldly thought and activity. After the bishop approves her request, the church builds her anchorage, her little, enclosed dwelling. After her death, it becomes her tomb.

Monsieur Chartaine told me how sometimes a grave is dug in the dirt floor of the anchorage as a *memento mori.* Each morning the anchoress reaches for a handful of dirt from her grave to remind her that someday she herself will return to the earth.

"She never leaves her enclosure. She's walled in. Sealed there for all time as it were. The little pass-through is the place where the nuns who care for her deliver her meals and collect her refuse," Monsieur Chartaine explained.

Inside the sanctuary, another little window opens into the anchorage so the anchoress may receive communion from the priest. That window, Monsieur Chartaine taught me, is called a squint. He knew all this because his sister became an anchoress, and he had visited her many times. He told me about the day his sister died to the world and was sealed into her anchorage.

"The anchoress represents the anchor, and the church is the ship. She's a constant, unwavering spiritual presence for the people. After the bishop approved Marie-Francine's request, she fasted and made her confession. She kept her vigil the night before her entombment. The next morning there was a special Mass." The old man's eyes filled with tears, and we stopped at the roadside while the others passed by.

"During the Mass my sister lay face down on the floor of the church with her arms spread out before her, before God. She offered her body and soul as a living sacrifice. She gave up her life in the world, to live in constant union with the Holy. I was there. Our mother wept and wept that day."

"What happened next?" I asked.

"There was a procession. All the people followed the priest and Marie-Francine, who was dressed and veiled in black. She carried a long taper. She was a young girl at the time."

"How did they enclose her?" My mind raced with pictures of Marie-Francine, somber and serious.

"A grave was dug in the floor of her cell, her anchorage. They lay my sister on a funeral bier, and the priest said the prayers of last rites." Monsieur

Chartaine pulled a dirty rag from his pocket and blew his nose.

"Oh, please don't tell me they buried…" I was horrified.

"No, no, my dear. But my sweet sister died to the world that day, and she was entombed, as it were. There was no door, only a small opening so she could enter the place she would never leave. They carried her inside and the opening was walled up with stones and mortar after the priest said the final prayers."

"Oh, my! How have I never heard of an anchoress before?"

"It's a rare calling, but there are women who through the grace of God live this way. They are great spiritual comforters for people who visit them. Holy women. Marie-Francine died last winter. Her body now lies in the grave that she saw every day of her life as an anchoress."

We walked together in silence for a while before we caught up to the others. As if reading my thoughts, he leaned near me before rejoining his fellow-pilgrims. "Don't worry," he whispered through his stale breath. "Like I told you, it's a rare calling. Your love for God doesn't mean you must be sealed into a tomb. You have another kind of gift to offer, I'm sure." He smiled a toothless smile then hobbled away.

Thank heaven, I thought. I took a deep breath and ran to report to my sisters what I had learned.

Comtesse was silent after we visited the anchoress. Her mood was sullen.

We walked along the road around a bend in the river separated a good distance from Monsieur's Chartaine's little group. A band of men on horseback, priests dressed in long black cassocks, galloped past us.

One of the priests had only one arm. He halted his horse to the side of the road while his fellow travelers went on ahead. His huge, black steed snorted and stamped its front hoof in a cloud of dust. A long, fresh, jagged scar stretched from the priest's chin across his right cheek to his brow. He looked down at us with his one open eye. His other eye was closed and sunken. Crow cawed out from Ravenissa's shoulder. The horse's stomping startled our goat. If it weren't for Gertrude's strong catch, the cart carrying all our belongings would surely have overturned.

"Sister," he called to Sabine, smiling and speaking with a tone that belied his grin. He spat on the earth and continued. "To which order do you belong? Your habit is unfamiliar to me." The horse danced about. He tightened the reins.

"Our order is the same as all, my brother. We are servants of God." Sabine forced a particular smile, a strained expression I'd never seen before.

We kept our heads down and continued to walk together slowly while the horse snorted and stamped its great hooves alongside us. My heart leaped so hard in my chest I thought I would faint.

"I don't recognize you as Cistercian or…"

"We're sisters of Belle—" Comtesse volunteered. Sabine grabbed her by the arm and pulled her in close interrupting her before she could finish.

"That is because we've traveled a great distance, and our order has never been in this region until now." Sabine's speech was quick and breathless. "Would you like to stop and rest, good Father? May we offer you something? Perhaps some bread for you to share with the others who are traveling with you." She held tight to Comtesse's arm.

The one-eyed, one-armed priest frowned.

"Thank you, no, Sister. We'll break our fast when we arrive at the cathedral."

He stared at Sabine, and I watched as she tightened her hold on Comtesse. We moved along, staying close together in silence, staring at the road. I began to count stones along the way.

"Very well then, Father. May Christ's peace accompany you the rest of your journey. We must stop now. It's time for our prayers…unless you care to join us."

My heart leaped again in fear with her invitation.

"No, I must be on my way so I don't lose the others. Don't let me keep you from your prayers. God bless you, Sisters." The priest let go of the reins and quickly made the sign of the cross in the air. He continued to look down at us for several moments before galloping away.

We stopped and quickly gathered with bowed heads. He turned once to look back at us.

"Let go of my arm! You're hurting me!" Comtesse pulled away from Sabine.

"Blessed Mother....my heart's still pounding. Are you mad?! Don't ever tell anyone who we are, Comtesse! Especially men of the Church! Do you want us to be called before the authorities? The Order of Belle Cœur would be deathly curious to the officials and men of the Church. Why, they'd question everything about us! We'd be taken away for sure. You must keep your mouth closed, do you hear me?"

Sabine walked quickly to a nearby thicket of weeds, where she raised her skirts and relieved herself.

Comtesse rubbed her arm. She appeared pitiful and confused. I reached out to her.

"Don't touch me! Leave me alone!"

We continued on, but Comtesse lagged behind. No one attempted to soothe her, least of all me.

While we walked, Beatrice offered a warning.

"Sisters, we must find safe shelter as quickly as possible once we arrive at Chartres. Our garments make us suspect to anyone seeking reward or indulgences for finding a heretic or witch. Stay close together at all times. Guard your conversations. Speak softly so you won't be overheard. It's late. We need silence to calm our spirits. Pray for God's guidance and protection, and keep your eyes alert for a resting place for the night."

Cibylle had been with us for several days, and our tattered caravan was growing weary. There was one large portion of stale spelt bread remaining. The cheese and honey cake were gone. We followed a good distance behind Monsieur Chartaine and the others while we sang Mabille's new song of adoration to the Blessed Mother. Sometimes we recited Psalms aloud, but mostly we walked in silent procession, two by two.

The merriness we had experienced when Mabille first invited our singing had faded away.

All along the pilgrimage route to Chartres, we were guided by the frequent appearance of coquille shells thoughtfully placed by other pilgrims along a worn pathway winding through the open fields. The shells, we learned from Beatrice's conversation with a woman pilgrim on the first day of our journey, were the sign for pilgrimage. They offered a blessing for the spirit. They also marked the pilgrimage route.

"The shells are to remind pilgrims of Mary's love and safekeeping," the woman had told Beatrice. "And of course there is the legend about a young nobleman. Perhaps it's familiar to you?"

Beatrice said she hadn't heard of it. The woman told her the lad was thrown into the sea by his horse and about to drown when Saint James himself appeared and saved him. The boy's body, when pulled from the water, was covered in scallop shells, which were seen to mark the miracle. The coquille shells showed the route to Saint James's relics, a great distance from here.

Beatrice's face suddenly became very serious. "But she also told me something very troubling. While making her second pilgrimage, she witnessed a burning."

"A burning? Not like the one we heard of…the burning of those six women in Pont Neuf?" Ravenissa gasped.

"Yes, the very same. The woman whispered her horrible tale to me lest someone should hear us talking of such things. She said while she followed the trail of shells through a large town, she saw ten or more women dressed in sackcloth and chains. Men dressed in hooded black robes on horseback dragged the poor souls through the streets. I forget the name of the place. The way the pilgrim told the story, the women were pulled along like animals to the center of the city. In the middle of the town were tall pillars set into great piles of wood, kindling, and straw." Beatrice's face was red, and little droplets of sweat beaded on her forehead.

"Were they Churchmen, the men who dragged the women through town? Why would they do such a thing?" Mabille asked.

"They were churchmen. Inquisitors, that's who!" Beatrice said.

"What had these women done? They weren't burned alive, too, like the women in Pont Neuf? Dear God, I don't understand. Why would priests and men of the Church...why would followers of Jesus commit murder? Why would they burn people alive?" I asked while my mind swirled with imaginings of the horrible scene.

"The women were healers, according to the woman who told me the story. They apprehended them because it was believed they had diminished the pain of childbirth with their herbal medicines. A townsperson told the pilgrim that the inquisitors had discovered a hairy mole on one of the poor souls. They called it a 'witch's teat.' That's what they do, you know?" Beatrice asked for a cup of water. Helvide fetched it.

"What do you mean, that's what they do?" Ravenissa asked.

"They strip their suspects bare. Can you imagine it? Being stripped naked in front of men in such a way! They strip their captives naked and then prod and poke them until they find a mark or freckle, a mole or a scar. They claim such a mark on the body is the place where the devil has entered them and branded them as his own." Beatrice couldn't catch her breath. She sat down, sipped the water, and continued.

"Because the woman with the mole was friends with the others, the Church claimed they were all heretics who worked with the devil. They were dragged through town, their hair was shaved away until their scalps were bald and bloody, and then…I can dare say it." She took another sip of water and crossed herself. "Then they chained the women to the pillars and brushed their bodies with pitch."

"Stop, Sister. Please stop! I can't listen to any more," Mabille pleaded.

But Beatrice went on. "Meanwhile, a priest asked them to confess they were witches so they could be freed to do penance. The women wailed they weren't witches but lovers of Christ. The priest went on to read out their supposed sins while a man wearing a black mask set fire to the straw and kindling beneath their feet. The pilgrim told me another priest offered a prayer, and someone in the crowd moved in to hold a cross on a long pole before each woman...so she could kiss it before dying in the smoke and flames."

Ravenissa fanned Beatrice, who was sweating profusely. Sabine wrapped her arms around Mabille, who was sobbing. Imene took hold of Gertrude's hand. Cibylle snuggled into Marie. Her eyes filled with tears.

"This is why I keep saying we must be careful. Let's not speak any more of this. I fear we open the gate for the evil one to enter with the talk of such travesties. We must pray now, Sisters, for ourselves and for those poor souls who have suffered a most unimaginable death."

Beatrice crossed herself again, and we followed her example. Even Comtesse remained silent the rest of the afternoon while we prayed with the voices of our hearts.

Oh, Beloved. Protect us from evil. Have mercy on the souls of your martyrs. Have mercy on us. Amen.

It was nearing sunset. We followed the wide path worn through the fields by countless pilgrims. With evening's approach we slowed to allow space to come between us and the other weary journeyers. The sky was overcast, and the light of day began to wane. The land spread out around us flat and open like God's parchment ready for scribing by autumn's hand. The tall prickly grass caught hold of our skirts and scratched our ankles.

Petronilla had a terrible toothache. Helvide made a compress and fashioned a sling that wrapped under her chin and tied atop her head. Her cheek was swollen and red.

Seven of us began our monthly bleeding as the moon was nearly full. My belly cramped and my ankles swelled.

Comtesse broke her silence. "We never should have left Belle Cœur! What'll become of us? I don't want to be used as kindling for some madman's fire in the middle of a nameless town?"

"We're all very tired. Enough!" Sabine held her head and spoke between clenched teeth.

Comtesse started up again. "We're making a terrible, dare I say deadly—"

"Sister! No more! For mercy's sake give us peace and quiet." Helvide pleaded.

Comtesse took a deep breath as if to hold in all that wanted so badly to be spoken. Then with a shrug she lifted her skirts and walked farther into the field, speaking in two voices in another conversation with herself. Beatrice shook her head from side to side.

Again, I wanted to go to Comtesse, but I recalled my last pitiful efforts. I decided to pray for her instead. Praying for someone so irritating is surely a test of faith. I didn't want to pray for her. I needed God's grace to forgive my sister her mean-spiritedness.

Comtesse had grown more peculiar with each passing day. Her unpredictable moods set her apart from us time and again. I was tired of her outbursts, but more importantly, I was worried for our safety.

It was time to come together in our circle for Vespers. We continued to look for a suitable resting place while a flock of a hundred or more storks flew overhead. All of us paused to look heavenward. The storks were enormous, their thin, yellow legs outstretched behind their lean, white bodies. Their broad wings made a sound like the puffing of distant billows as they soared along. We watched them until they disappeared from sight. A long, white feather spiraled from above. It appeared like a tired angel as it floated slowly down, down, down, and came at last to rest on the earth. We watched it fall at Cibylle's feet.

"A blessing just for you." Marie grinned. She retrieved the feather from the dried grass and handed it to her friend. Cibylle's thin lips spread wide with laughter. We joined her in her moment of joy, tickling one another and giggling like merry children.

Mabille stepped away from our frivolity. She played a haunting tune on her tiny flute, a gift made by her brother, then put it aside and sang softly to herself.

Pia mater gratie
pia vena venie
pia regis filia
o regi glorie
servos tuos hodie
pie reconcilia

Distracted by our play, no one noticed Beatrice, who had gone on ahead of us. She stood utterly still on a small rise amid the tall grass. Suddenly she dropped to her knees, catching our attention. Her face was expressionless and her gaze was fixed as if she were looking at the face of God. We hurried to where she was kneeling and turned to take in her view.

It appeared at first glance like a great, sleeping beast nestled upon the autumn landscape. The enormity of the cathedral caught my breath away. Surrounded by fields of deep golden wheat moving in tempo with the will of the wind, it was a sight none of us were prepared for.

We were silent, except for Cibylle, who was still giggling. Marie took hold of her hand, and she quieted.

Mercifully, even Comtesse was still. Crow settled on Ravenissa's shoulder and ceased his insistent call. Our little sisterhood stood together in a moment of reverence that only the presence of God can evoke.

We were tired, dirty, and thinner than when we had left Belle Cœur. Without a map, we had used our wits. We had faithfully followed the shells left by countless others to find our way. God's grace and protection had delivered us...but to where and to what?

Suddenly, in a brief burst the sunlight appeared through a sliver of cloud, the last light of day. For an instant the earth appeared to become afire in gold. The cathedral and its scaffolding shimmered like a ransomed jewel.

We became one with the green and amber palette of earth's autumn colors. Dominions and Graces. Earth, air, fire, and water. The creature, the great Church, was alive and breathing, Our Lady's earthly house of sacraments and mysteries.

We joined Beatrice on our knees.

"Praise God! We've survived our journey and we've arrived safely." With Beatrice's words Cibylle cried out for a moment, as if she were grieving.

My hand reached into my pocket, for Henriette. I squeezed her tight. *What will become of us?* I asked silently. She held no answer and offered little comfort.

16 January 1259
Le Monastère de la Visite

Darkness came swiftly the night of our arrival at Chartres. Gertrude lit torches from our last pilgrim's fire, and we joined the procession of light with other pilgrims as we wound our way toward the cathedral. Helvide and Ravenissa walked ahead to guide the goat as she pulled our cart through the field. Our little caravan of twelve was but a drop. We flowed into the river of hundreds, perhaps thousands of pilgrims longing to enter the Mother's earthly sanctuary.

The sound of moaning grew the closer we came to town. Men flogged their bare backs with leather straps to feel one with Jesus's suffering, His passion and the cross. Others silently walked on their battered and bloody knees the remaining distance. Some sang and prayed aloud in unfamiliar languages, while still others fingered their Rosaries.

There were women with babes at their breasts. The sick and elderly were carried on wooden litters. Many nuns and monks appeared weak, no doubt from fasting. Those possessed by demons wailed and thrashed about. All form and manner of humankind melted together as one body seeking solace in Mary's bosom, one people seeking the sacred.

We were weary, dusty, and hungry. I lagged slowly behind my sisters. My blistered feet had carried me without disappointment to our destination. Beatrice suffered the most, though she never complained. She struggled to keep our pace in spite of her labored breathing.

I stank. Warm blood gushed from my winny. I longed to bathe and break our fast. The soles of my feet stung as though I were standing on nettles, and my head ached.

Where would we live? Time and again I gave my question to God. I had no possible way of knowing where our next shelter would be, nor did I know what would happen with the next breath. Our bodies were taxed, but our spirits were on fire with curiosity as we came closer to the enormous cathedral and the commotion all around us.

Marie and Cibylle walked ahead of me holding hands. I smile as I remember them at that tender time when their friendship was new and playful. Petronilla had grown increasingly pale and thin during our journey. Her delicate temperament was sorely tested by her toothache that night amid the pulsing clamor. Sabine, our vigilant shepherdess, repeatedly looked over her shoulder and all about to be sure not one of her flock had been lost while the throng of pilgrims pressed closer.

We had never witnessed such a crowd of people. Gertrude stayed close to our goat while Imene walked alongside the cart. We held together in pairs. I moved ahead and gripped Sabine's hand. Petronilla took hold of Beatrice. Ravenissa and Helvide fastened to one another. For a moment I feared the two of them would turn and run back into the fields to escape the noise and bedlam of the city.

Sadly, I watched Comtesse refuse Mabille's outstretched hand. She kept to herself. Sabine grabbed onto Mabille, and the three of us huddled close together.

Cibylle broke away from Marie and began to dance in circles, much to Beatrice's alarm. She took hold of the girl by her shoulders. She leaned her forehead into Cibylle's with a mother's firmness.

"Is this how you propose to meet Our Blessed Lady?!! Fold your hands at your heart and bow that untamed head of yours! You, too, Marie!" She grabbed Cibylle and Marie by their arms and pulled each girl close to her. Petronilla joined Ravenissa and Helvide.

"Perhaps her dance is a gift for the Blessed Mother, Grand-mère. Perhaps Cibylle is privy to hear music we cannot hear," Marie shouted at her grandmother.

"*Perhaps* you'd like to wait outside!" Fatigue colored Beatrice's words as she gave Marie's cheek a pinch.

Gertrude raised her hand, and we halted together as countless other weary souls moved past us, the way water in a stream disperses around a stone. Sabine spoke in a loud voice over the voices that grew more deafening with every step. Drums and horns began to play.

"We've come a long way, Sisters. We're tired and near our journey's end. Pray to remember this moment all the days of your life. Stay close to one another!" She shouted.

Her words were clear and reassuring in the midst of chaos. We formed a row and joined hands, all of us. We became a single thread in the colorful tapestry as we wove ourselves into the crowd.

My heart beats faster with my memory of that miraculous night. All that happened comes alive again in pictures forever illumined in my mind. Every manner of strange instrument played around us.

We stood and stared upward, *high* above at the wonder of the massive stone cathedral. Words cannot describe its height and breadth. Scaffolding covered some of it where work and the carving of saints and angels were being completed. This was the great reliquary built many years ago, destroyed by fire and now nearly built yet again to house the miraculous relic, the veil Our Lady wore when she gave birth to Jesus.

Carved sticks and bare hands pounded drums, both little and big. Singers with colorful, feathered caps and pointed shoes fingered strange instruments made of wood and string. A man with two black holes where his eyes should have been blew a long whistle. A very fat man with cheeks that bulged like cow's udders played a long brass horn. The piercing sound caused Cibylle to cover her ears with both hands. Marie followed her example. They looked at one another with childlike astonishment.

The noise of hammer and chisel took our gaze upward above the wide cathedral doors. We witnessed a hundred or more men who clung to the great stones while they worked by torchlight to bring the rebuilding to completion. Their tools clanked an unforgettable sound above the crowd.

I had never seen the likes of so many artisans at work in one place. They wielded their tools with certain skill and determination. Their daimons were surely of the highest order bringing them inspiration from God to carve the saints and angels from stone. The living reliquary of the Blessed Mother was a hive swarming with workers dedicated to one purpose, to glorify the Queen of Heaven.

Brother Paul's teaching returned to me: "*Creation, Goscelin. The queen bee is a symbol for Creation herself. She represents the Blessed Mother, and her honey is the Christ.*"

Creation was at work! Here in the souls of those who hammered, chiseled, and painted beauty of extraordinary measure. I was on fire with desire to write of the ecstasy that only comes from divine inspiration. I wanted to record in Dominions and Graces what I was experiencing in my bones, my heart and soul. If only I had quill and parchment in that moment I could have scribed what instead I had to lock away in my memory…

This place is a holy hive for the Queen. She reigns as Wisdom and Creation combined. She inspires and calls humankind to greatness. Through her, each life holds the promise to become a sacred work of art. Like these artisans who now climb to the rafters to create sculpture in praise of Mother and Son, in celebration of God's glory, so, too, we are called to be sacred life artisans, each of us, to create a masterpiece of our living. We are called to make beauty, to sing our songs, to dance our prayers, to share our stories in thanksgiving for every day and every breath, in the name of Love.

Crow had vanished again. Gertrude and Ravenissa stayed close to the goat. Mouse had surely burrowed deep into Ravenissa's pocket.

A man full of drink breathed in my face and lunged toward my breasts with his big, hairy hands before he collapsed face first onto the cobblestone street. I confess I nearly gave the drunkard a sharp kick to his backside as I passed by. He reminded me of my father.

The unruly marketplace surrounded the main entrance to the cathedral. From where I stood in the midst of the market, I saw stalls that boasted strange foods unfamiliar to my eyes. A short, fat man with greasy skin cooked fish and fowl on an open fire. The smoke in the air was thick and full of strange but delicious odors that made my hungry belly growl out loud.

A pack of dogs fought for bony scraps tossed by a crippled man. His left ear bore an open sore crawling with maggots. My shoe landed flat in the dog's steaming waste to add another kind of odor to the *mélange.*

At the opposite side of the wide west entrance of the cathedral were more rows of wooden stalls. A beautiful woman with waist-long, fiery-red hair was draped in brightly colored silken scarves. On her shoulder was a large talking bird! Its feathers were bright green, and the beak was the color of the sun and curved to a sharp point. The bird called out, "Amen! Amen!" I shouted to Ravenissa but she didn't hear me. I was certain she had never seen a bird that spoke *our* language.

The beautiful woman was selling lead badges. Each medallion depicted a tunic, like the one worn by many pilgrims. She also sold badges forged to look like coquille shells. There were arrays of short fat candles and tiny carved wooden statues of the Virgin seated on her throne holding the Christ child on her lap. Greedy voices called to the pilgrims, "*Les souvenirs! Les souvenirs*!"

Silks and spices, spotted, plump rabbits with lazy, long ears stuffed in wicker baskets, and soft, brown, leather shoes with thong ties were carefully displayed. Pilgrim guidebooks, vade mecums, like the one from the abbess and embroidered vestments for the priests were arrayed to tempt all manner of desire. I longed to stop to look at the vade mecums, but I couldn't lose sight of my sisters, who kept pushing ahead toward the entrance to the cathedral.

The colorful surroundings were suddenly darkened by the presence of the priest who had passed us on the road. Still cloaked in a black cassock, he now wore a wide-brimmed black hat. He moved through the crowd like an ominous storm cloud while people stepped aside to let him pass, a gesture of respect or perhaps fear. Sabine spotted him coming our way and quickly steered us between two rows of market stalls, where we were hidden from his sight.

In that moment my heart signaled the same alarm it had thrummed during our first encounter with this priest and the other churchmen on the pilgrim road. As I recall that instance and other terrifying moments that would come later, I wrestle with my still-unanswered questions.

How long must our community dodge the threatening presence of those who do terrible things on behalf of the Church, while claiming to be sanctified servants to God's people? How are we to live in this state of unholy irony and trepidation? Their rules and judgments simply cannot be God's will, but rather the will of men desiring power and control.

I crossed myself and prayed for protection. My head felt as though it would burst in the midst of the chaos that first evening in Chartres. The peace and tranquility of Belle Cœur were very far away.

But in the midst of the clamor, there was vibrant, creative fervor that caught my soul. I beheld all that was taking place around me and began to feel an unfamiliar thrill. I had not felt so alive since the day I stumbled into Brother Paul's secret room.

Each of my senses peaked and awakened. While excitement stirred my spirit, exhaustion took hold of my body. I was bone tired. It was a night of paradoxes, shadow and light, fear and pleasure, sacredness and obscenity, elation and depletion.

As we pushed through the crowd toward the entrance to the cathedral, a colorfully dressed man caught Cibylle's attention. He skipped beside her while he tossed three cloth balls high above his head.

Cibylle broke away from Marie and Beatrice and twirled about before spinning away into the crowd with the man. She quickly disappeared from sight.

"Cibylle! Cibylle!" Marie panicked and began to cry.

Beatrice grabbed Marie's hand. "Stay close! We'll find her! Cibylle! Cibylle!"

Beatrice and Marie wound through the crowd, and we followed close behind, the way ducklings follow their mother. Connected hand to hand, we chased in the direction Cibylle had gone. Hammers clanged. Merchants shouted. Music makers beat their drums in rhythm with our frightened hearts.

We were already very fond of the strange girl with the far-set eyes. What would become of her in a place like this? What if a man heavy with drink saw her simple spirit and…At the very moment my mind played out all manner of dark thoughts for our Cibylle's fate, she appeared in the crowd up ahead, still following the happy juggler.

"There she is! Praise God!" Beatrice looked up toward heaven and crossed herself before she shoved her way through the rabble. We were dragged along with her. In one swift motion, she reached out and pulled Cibylle to her.

"Curse you!" Beatrice shouted at the juggler. He laughed and tossed Cibylle a red cloth ball with a wink.

"Give me that!" Beatrice grabbed the ball from Cibylle and hurled it into the crowd. "You gave us all a fright. You'll stay with me now. No more running about!" Cibylle's look of dismay was heartbreaking. Beatrice put her arms about her. "Oh, child, don't look so sad. You're about to enter Our Lady's shrine. Give me a smile. This is a happy night!"

I squeezed Sabine's hand tightly, and we pressed closer to the entrance. Up ahead I could at last see closely the three large, open portals that provided a way into the cathedral. I looked above me to the stone carvings over the center threshold. There was Jesus in all His glory. He was flanked by two winged beasts, a dove and an angel.

We were pushed by the crowd to the right of the west entrance. I stood back from the door and looked upward. All noise and confusion stilled as though my ears were stopped.

There above me, carved into the cathedral was the Blessed Mother. Chiseled from stone over the doorway was the unmistakable Mother of God seated on her throne with her baby upon her lap.

To my disbelief it was the same door I had seen in my vision, my dream during our peramony at Belle Cœur!

I had learned Our Lady is the Queen of Heaven *and* Earth. Heaven surely awaited beyond the threshold of the cathedral.

I fixed my eye on the stone carving of the Mother and the infant Jesus. Who was the artist who had used hammer and chisel to fashion both so perfectly? With that fleeting thought I heard Our Lady's voice with the ears of my heart.

"*Open the door, reveal the throne. For this is the moment of revisitation. All that is old will once again become new, change, yet remain forever the same. Relinquish judgment of what you see. The gift within the journey will be revealed in time. Not the time of earth but rather the time of un-time. Un-time, that place where peace abides in the understanding of all that came before or will ever come again. There is no need to attempt to learn what manner of key will fit the door. You have only to reach inside your heart to find the key."*

The clamor and noise returned as suddenly as it had stopped. How could it be? How could the Mother of God's voice come to me in such a way? It was her voice! For certain I was not dreaming—but it was Petronilla who heard voices. She was the visionary. I was merely the scribe. How could such a miracle happen to me?

My mind doubted what had occurred while my poor body trembled with awe. The Mother had indeed spoken to me. At first chance I would scribe what she had said. I repeated her words inside my heart over and over again to press her message into my memory.

Gertrude, Imene, Petronilla, and I gripped hands as we caught a final glimpse of Blessed Mother above us. Without warning an impatient young boy tore me away from my sisters with a forceful shove from behind. And that is how I entered the great cathedral. I was pushed in!

Just as my mother had pushed me from her womb into the world, I was birthed backward from the world through the Mother's portal into *her* womb...into the immense sanctuary of Nôtre Dame de Chartres. Mary's presence permeated my flesh, bones, blood, and spirit.

Water gushed around the soles of my dusty sandals. Pilgrims bathed and washed their clothing in small groups near the doorway. Water poured over matted hair, swollen feet, and filthy hands. The dust of many weeks of travel was rinsed away from tattered garments wrung out and placed on the stone floor to dry.

Water appeared to be everywhere. It covered the slanted entrance. It ran in a gentle current down toward the open door. I was standing in the waters of Mary's womb. This was a birthing place for the human spirit, for the soul. A Grace for Dominions and Graces, Volume IV, *Water*, came to me.

Water. Within the Mother's womb there is a life-giving spring for humankind. She teems with love available to all manner of persons: the sick and lame, the dying and those not yet born, rich and poor, the criminal and the saint, the fishmonger and the artist. Oh, blessed water, remind us each day of the womb of our Mother that nourished Jesus before He came into the world.

I bent low to wet my hands with her sacred water imbued with the essence of my brothers and sisters. I brought the sweet wetness to my face to mingle with my tears of thanksgiving. The New Jerusalem, the City of God, the Cathedral of Our Lady welcomed all! Dark skinned, light skinned, the broken, rich, poor, lame and demented. All are welcomed!

Golden yellow light filled her stone vault. Candles of every size appeared to blaze as one holy fire. Wax poured down the butter-colored tapers creating haunting, lacy forms, faces, and unfamiliar creatures. The flames changed shape and merged to become a singular, glowing star. So much light fooled the eyes to believe it was day rather than night.

The Mother's burning fire of love for us is the same. She can lead us from our darkness into the radiance of new life through her sun…her Son! In time, I would record the wisdom that was branded into my soul on that night into Volume III: *Fire.*

Fire. Each candle burns with a pilgrim's prayer. We are all pilgrims on life's journey. In the Mother's womb, we are held in her living prayer to God. She is luminous. Her fervent desire to bring us closer to the Beloved is holy fire to light our way. We dance within her, and the blaze consumes us in divine love and divine passion.

My heart was hot with desire to know her more deeply. The air was heavy with prayer-filled smoke and the intoxicating fragrance of frankincense that smoldered in golden thuribles swung by boys dressed in long black cassocks and white lace aprons. I made notations in my mind for future reference for Volume II, *Air,* as grace filled me.

Air. The first breath leads the body into life, and the last guides the soul home to live in the eternal breath of God. Here in her womb there is the musky and potent breath of creation. Her breath. She replenishes our spirits through her breathing in and breathing out. We are held in her and intoxicated by her holy, perfumed air. When in sacred places, whether a stone cathedral built by men or a treed cathedral in nature, we must open our hearts to know the One who calls us by name.

I cupped my palms to scoop the smoke and take into my body the breath of the Mother. Above me, the light of ten thousand candles illuminated long tall windows made of colored glass pictures that told the sacred stories of faith, creation, and the saints.

My awe for the artisans who crafted the sacred stories made of glass played upon my imagination. The magnificent beauty created for God and God's people caught my soul and set my mind adrift in holy playful wonderment.

Without warning, with my next breath I was lifted, released, and set free from the weight of my body. My spirit soared upward. Like a bird I flew above the people and their prayers below me. I floated through the wafting smoke above the warmth of burning flickering candles. In my rapture, I glided past the tall, colored-glass windows that lined the towering stone walls like jeweled midwives tending the spiritual births taking place within the pilgrims, here in the womb of the Mother.

There were countless crimson, lapis, and amber-colored glass pictures of the saints, bakers and kings, angels and animals. And Jesus was there illumined both as child and man. The stories from Scripture were captured within the windows for the people to see and to know.

Mary, made from glass, wore her golden crown and blue gown. She was seated on her throne of wisdom, where she held the infant Jesus on her lap. Their luminous white halos shimmered and glowed. Other windows showed the stories of Jesus washing the feet of the disciples, and God banishing Adam and Eve from the Garden. To my inspired eye, they were like an illuminated book, alive with prayer and teaching.

Bells rang out. The sound was distant at first. The droning *din, don, din* of the cathedral bells sounded the call to Compline and beckoned my spirit to return to my body. I was startled to discover myself kneeling on the cold stone floor in among a long winding row of pilgrims. We were walking on our knees.

An old, toothless monk in front of me turned and placed a burning taper in my hand. Warm, soft wax rolled down the candle to make a waxy shroud over my fingers. I felt no pain.

"*Le labyrinthe...*" The monk pointed ahead.

"Where are we going?" I breathed. "Is this a prayer?"

There was no reply.

I looked about for my sisters. Behind me high on the wall above the place where we had entered was a large window, a circle made of colored glass. Inside the circle at the center was a smaller circle surrounded by twelve petals, also made of glass. Twelve smaller circles surrounded the flower at the center like a rose.

The crowd pressed closer to *le labyrinthe.*

Lyres, flutes, drums, and horns began to play. Life filled Our Lady's shrine and spilled over me like the return of sunlight after a storm. I was on my knees on the ground on the cold, hard stone. I made my way along on the floor of her womb, toward the huge labyrinth with its curious pathway. Once again Grace filled me, this time for Volume I, *Earth.*

Earth. Divine Mother of creation, you are present in the mysteries of nature. You pour your fertile blessings upon the verdant green hills. Your power flows through fields, the trees, and flowers. Your hand casts the changing of the seasons, the time for planting, cultivation, and harvest. Seed us, Mother of Wonders, with new dreams, work, and wonderment. Your fragrance, hidden in the rose, reminds us that you are Nature... earth, fire, water, and air. You are our life-giving Mother.

Flesh on stone. On my knees I followed the others and made my way to the entrance of the spiral pathway on the cathedral floor. I began to follow the singular path. It coiled, back and forth, this way and that.

A dwarf edged past me as I made my way in. I moved to the side as she passed and placed my candle into her gnarled hands. She bowed her head and crossed herself.

Many pilgrims sang. Some prayed aloud in unfamiliar languages. Others were silent. A girl with an infant at her breast stood, eyes closed, blocking the way forward. Some people chose to go around her, and others stood or knelt waiting for her to move along. A woman with waist-length hair the color of charred wood danced wildly upon the stones. Another, with very dark skin, came toward me and whispered something I didn't comprehend.

The labyrinth was a living river of life that flowed to the center and out again as one sacred stream. For each pilgrim seeking the Holy City, the New Jerusalem, the pathway was the journey. I understood how the dying man in our infirmary, God's angel who guided us to come here, had not exaggerated his stories of what he'd witnessed. That first night at Chartres we lived into the vision he had given us only twelve days before.

I put my hand to my heart. Was someone, somewhere praying for me? Prayer was palpable around and through me, in me and of me. I stood and became a walking prayer.

A song poured from my throat, a song not of my making. Strange sounds and an unknown language spilled out from a newly discovered place within my soul. My tongue felt as if it were made of fire, and my senses were full and swollen like a river flooded by a sudden torrent.

The path led me to the center of the labyrinth. My arms opened wide as if to embrace the Mother herself.

With that singular gesture, the world around me became absolutely silent. In that instant the cathedral walls appeared to melt away. The great vault above rose higher and higher until it shattered into the heavens in a million shards of blinding, golden light. For the second time that night my spirit soared free of my body.

I felt myself pulled by an unseen hand backward through a long black tunnel. The labyrinth's path, to my eyes, changed to become a dusty road leading to a landscape of rocky hillsides, olive trees, and flocks of sheep. The sun illuminated everything with white heat. Dark-skinned people appeared. Some tended the sheep while women walked together carrying large earthen vessels on their heads. A dog barked. An infant cried.

"Follow me!" A young boy dressed in a white robe, his head wrapped in cloth, caught my arm with his shepherd's crook and pulled me toward a growing crowd of men, women, and children scattered on a nearby hillside. Many hobbled on crutches; a blind man was pulled up the hill by a young girl. A woman passed by. Her hands and feet were wrapped in bandages. She stank like rotten meat.

"He will begin soon! Look how the people come with their hopes and their prayers." The boy ran ahead then waved to me to join him.

The air was dry and still. Locusts jumped all around on cracked, parched earth. A few olive trees with low-hanging branches offered blessed shade. Goats and lambs rested there with the aged and infirmed. People spoke to one another in a strange and beautiful language that was somehow familiar.

"There's the Nazarene! See him?!" The radiant young boy pointed to a man sitting alone on the hillside beneath a tree heavy with olives.

"Yes, I see him," I replied.

He was dressed in a long linen robe. His head was bowed, and his thick black hair fell in waves over one eye. A dark scruff of beard gave him a rugged appearance. A man went to him and touched his shoulder. The Nazarene stood and walked slowly toward those seated on the ground at the front of the assembly. Several men and three women gathered around him to hold back the crowd.

The throng pushed toward him.

"I'm blind! Help me!"

"Heal my child; she hasn't walked since birth!"

"Come this way!"

"Over here!"

"Touch me! Heal me!"

Even though their tongue was foreign to me, my mind understood their words. Their cries for healing echoed through the hills down to the sea below. The boy, my guide, gripped my hand and pulled me further up the hill while the Nazarene began to lay his hands on the maimed and the mad, the leper and the lame. Chaos followed. Women chortled a chorus of guttural sounds that were ancient and haunting to my ears. Someone blew a ram's horn in the distance.

My young guide took hold of my hand.

"Where are you taking me?"

"To meet him." His voice was eager.

"But I have no need of healing."

"Then you will receive his blessing. Miracles come through his blessing as well."

The boy's strength was that of a man. We seemed to fly over the dry earth and stony pathways. In an instant we were near the front of the line of those who were waiting their turn to come before the healer. The man in front of me was presented by one of the Nazarene's friends.

"Master, this man is deaf, and his speech is awkward. Many have approached to pray on his behalf for you to heal him."

The healer stepped forward. He looked into the man's eyes as if reading a book. Then he led the deaf one some distance away from the crowd. Again in an instant the boy and I soared farther up the hill. We stopped short of the place where they were standing.

The Nazarene put his fingers into the man's ears, spit, and touched his tongue. Then he looked up toward the heavens. He heaved a deep sigh and commanded the deaf man, "*Ephphatha*!" Instantly I understood this to mean, "Be open!"

"I can hear! I can speak! Praise God! I'm healed! It's a miracle!" The man rubbed his ears as he cried out.

"Go now and tell no one!" the healer told him.

I stood before the healer at the front of the crowd while he turned away to speak quietly with one of his friends.

My guide tugged on the Nazarene's garment.

"Please, Master, give this woman who has come a long way your blessing."

Only then did I truly see him. His eyes were dark, as dark as the tunnel that had delivered me to him. Tears spill on the parchment as I recall the power within his gaze. Compassion and love, a fierce yet gentle love, poured from the healer into me.

Without a word he placed his hands firmly on either side of my head. With my next breath, a force, not unlike what it must have been to be pushed by God from my mother's womb into life, moved through me. Another breath, and I felt all past misery leave my body. Waves of ecstasy crumpled me to the ground.

"Sister…" A familiar voice called to me from far away. In an instant my spirit traveled through the long, dark tunnel to return to my body. My mind was confused, and the noise and smells of the cathedral were painful to my senses.

Sabine bent down to speak to me in my stupor. "I'm sorry to interrupt your prayers, Goscelin, but we must go now. God has sent us an angel of mercy. She's offered us shelter. Get up. Come with me."

My realization in that moment took my breath away. "Jesus! Jesus!" I spoke aloud.

"Come, Goscelin. I'm sorry to disturb your prayers. Come!" Imene pulled my sleeve.

"Jesus. It was You," I whispered.

Not until I had opened my eyes did I realize Jesus was the healer on the hill. *He* had touched me. I had looked into *His* eyes. My body continued to hum, as if a thousand bees had taken up residence inside me. I hummed like a hive from the power of His gaze and His blessing. My heart ached with love. Love *for* Him and love *from* Him.

The walls and roof of the cathedral were as before. However, nothing would ever be the same again. My heart and soul had been broken open by God's Love. Ever since that night, I have longed to rediscover the mysterious path that leads to the place where He walked among the people to heal and teach with love beyond all imagination. My search for the portal to Love is my heart's singular burning desire.

While I had been in the presence of Jesus, Sabine had wandered through the cathedral. She met a nun from a nearby monastery, Sister Lunetta. They shared a long conversation, and the nun inquired about our needs for shelter and work. When she learned we had no place to stay she extended a welcomed invitation. Then she explained how we would receive lodging in exchange for our assistance in the monastery's infirmary and help with other chores.

As Sabine pulled me along on our way to find the others, she told me, "Sister Lunetta is God's blessed answer to our prayers! Now we have place to live and serve. We'll go with her in the morning."

It was late. We slept that night on the cathedral floor near the south entrance with other pilgrims. Beatrice looked all about to make sure the priests we'd met on the road were nowhere near before we settled ourselves. Helvide and Ravenissa went outside to guard our cart and feed the goat. Sister Lunetta stayed near us.

Her peaceful countenance was comforting. Her features were delicate, and her skin was pale, the color of cream. I imagined her hair was fair, though it was covered from sight by a tight, linen wimple and white veil that framed her pretty face. When she spoke, she used her hands like another language. Gestures fell this way and that. She always ended her remarks by closing her long, slender fingers together in a prayerful pose at her heart.

It was agreed that after Mass the next morning we would follow Sister Lunetta to our new home at the monastery. I lay awake all night thinking of Jesus. I arose before dawn to return to the labyrinth while my sisters slept. I had to get to the center once again. I prayed to find the entrance to the tunnel.

The effects of the Beloved's touch continued to hum in my bones. I remembered His instruction to the deaf man on the hillside after his healing.

"Go and tell no one!" Jesus commanded.

I, too, would follow His direction. Time was needed to allow the settling in of His blessing and grace.

The bells announced the break of day. With the morning light, my eyes feasted on the splendor of the windows that sparkled like a queen's ransom of jewels. The Mass fortified our spirits, and all the while I ached from the power of the blessing that had forever changed me.

The sun beamed through the colored-glass windows casting gold and crimson shadows on our faces and the floor of the cathedral. I turned to take a final look into the vastness of the Mother's earthly shrine before we stepped out into the crowded busy street.

Sabine went to a nearby stall. She took a coin from our purse and bought a loaf of warm bread from a woman merchant. The town seemed sleepy in the early morning, while a hundred artisans or more climbed tall scaffolding to continue the work of rebuilding Our Lady's living shrine.

We found Helvide and Ravenissa with the goat near our cart. Our caravan stepped onto the Holy Road once more. We followed Sister Lunetta to a wide-open pathway north of the cathedral.

With our hearts and souls nourished by the Sacrament, we walked to the outskirts of town toward the monastery, Le Monastère de la Visite, sharing bread along the way.

Sister Lunetta tried to prepare us for the enormity of our new surroundings.

"We number two hundred seventy-two nuns and twenty-seven brothers."

Beatrice held Cibylle's hand. "My goodness, that many?"

"Actually, there are greater monasteries. Though ours feels crowded most days. There are many differing temperaments, as you can imagine," the nun said.

"Oh yes, we can imagine," Beatrice replied as she gave a quick glance toward Comtesse.

When my eyes fell upon the sprawling stone monastery atop a steep hill, I thought surely we would require a map to find our way about once we were inside. Smoke spiraled upward from many chimneys. Fat, brown ducks swam downstream on the river under the bridge leading to the arched entrance of the monastery grounds.

"I wonder what it's like to be a nun within such a place. Do you think their work is hard, or have rich patrons lavished them with fine foods and gifts and…" Comtesse pondered.

Beatrice turned to her. "We won't know till we're inside, will we, Sister?"

"I'll ask Sister Lunetta. She'll know." Comtesse was about to call out to Sister Lunetta who led the way with Sabine when Mabille turned to her, taking hold of her arm with a firm squeeze.

"Not now, Comtesse. This is not the time. We should be praying and singing praises to God and His Mother. Your concerns of fine food and gifts must wait."

Comtesse was about to continue her argument when Sabine called out to us. "Stop here and wait. I'll return soon."

We joined hands and prayed silently. Sabine followed Sister Lunetta through the tall, arched stone entrance.

In a little while we moved to the comforting shelter of a wide, low oak tree as rain began to fall and the morning light faded to dark afternoon. Cibylle and Marie played *batons et des pierres* near the trunk of the tree. Ravenissa set the goat free from the cart to nibble the grass, and Comtesse paced 'round and 'round babbling to herself. The rain stopped, and finally Sabine appeared in the archway. She waved to us to join her.

We followed Sabine and Sister Lunetta through the monastery gates to the refectory. Twenty or more nuns had gathered to greet us. We received a cautious but gentle welcome. They seemed eager for our extra hands to help them with their duties, but we soon learned the rule of their order forbade particular friendships. Our place among them was obvious from the first moment. We were there to serve them.

Sister Lunetta was different. She was warm and generous with her many kindnesses. Even now she remains our most trusted friend.

As I recall those first days and weeks with the nuns, I remember it was daunting to be living and working in the presence of so many. I'm still taking it all in. The monastery provides a roof above our heads, and we are blessed with meaningful service to the sick, but our spirits remain at Belle Cœur.

The surrounding countryside and nearby forest enfold us. Wheat fields flank the west stone wall of the enclosure. An apple orchard bordered by a winding stone pathway leads to dense woods that wrap around the north and east walls of the grounds. To the south of the entrance, a narrow dirt road meanders the open grassy meadow where cattle and sheep graze. On the opposite side of the meadow, a morning walk along the narrow, well-traveled pilgrimage trail leads one to town.

From my favorite vantage point, the top of a small tower near the nun's chapter house, I look out across the fields of grain. The cathedral is visible on the horizon. It appears like the alchemist's retort, afire with God's merciful love. The great church is to my mind an earthly vessel filled with holy mysteries and doorways leading to God. Not a day passes that I don't pray to find the tunnel that carried me to Jesus.

Yet the sacred presence and unending prayers within the cathedral are obscured with shadows. Mixed with the sweet fragrance of incense is the foul scent of willfulness, the unbridled willfulness of men who use the Church as their stage. For they have the power to control the fate of those who dare follow God's call rather than adhere to their man-made rules.

The intentions of these proposed servants of God are tarnished by their greed for power. They have lost their way. They have turned from the path that is holy and loving to wander the way of wrath, judgment, and control.

Jesus tumbled the tables of the moneychangers outside the Temple in Jerusalem. He challenged their laws. Jesus recognized and named the officials' distortions of the sacred. He exposed the corruption of His time. From what I have learned and witnessed, the Church today, despite all its holiness and goodness, is also corrupted.

This startling paradox sends alarm throughout my body. I am growing to understand how shadow and light converge. The *holy* and the *horrible*, describes the unending tension of life in *my* time.

I light another taper in this cold, tiny room where I come to record our stories. I hear my sisters stirring about down the hall as the day begins. Soon the bells will call us to prayer.

Brother Paul's warning from so long ago returns to haunt me.

"*Protect your writing at all cost, dear Goscelin, lest it be discovered and you and it be burned.*"

2 February 1259
Le Monastère de la Visite

I can only wonder how life would be an easier road to follow if God's plan for each of us was found scribed on a scrap of parchment. It isn't possible to say if knowing our destiny would make the path easier. Perhaps it's the *mystery* of life's unfolding journey that enriches our days here on earth. What if each soul is a world within God's eternal eye, held forever in the divine's gaze? We must trust our Beloved Mapmaker to show us the way.

For now I'm in exile, a wanderer longing to return to Belle Cœur. Belle Cœur is where I belong. There waits my true home, sanctuary, and haven. It's evident a shelter and a home are not the same.

Thankfully, God has provided shelter here at Le Monastère de la Visite. We have warm beds, food, and quarters that offer protection from the rain and cold, and all of us are grateful. But this place will never be home.

Henriette stays deep in my apron pocket. She, too, is homesick for beloved Belle Cœur.

This monastery is dedicated to the Scripture story of the Visitation, the sacred event when Mary traveled to Judah to visit her cousin, Elizabeth, when she was pregnant with Jesus. Upon her arrival Mary greeted

Elizabeth, and the child leaped within Elizabeth's womb and she was filled with the Spirit.

It is God's doing that we are in a place dedicated to this most beloved story from the life of our Mother, Mary. It is also our community's story. One by one each of us made her way to the little house with the blue sign. With each sister's arrival, the gift she carried was recognized and honored by the others. This is the way of women, shown to us by Mary and Elizabeth. We are called to appreciate and acknowledge one another's indwelling gifts of the Spirit.

I do my best to continue to nurture and assist my sisters in the midst of so much change and uncertainty. I'm tired and anxious. Since we came to this place, there has been constant distraction from my prayers and unending demands for service to the nuns. Hours for scribing are rare.

Comfort comes in those moments when I'm alone with my memory of Jesus's blessing. Within this monastery there are too many voices, and endless orders for obedience to the nuns.

Each day I seek a secret hiding place for brief moments of stolen silence and peace. I have discovered two secluded places for solitude and prayer. A hollowed-out trunk of a towering old pine tree at the edge of the woods is my favorite place when the weather is fair. An empty dusty cupboard under the stone spiral stairway leading to the monastery's bell tower serves best when it's stormy.

The monastery is situated near the rivers Eure and Loir. Tall limestone walls wrap around on all sides. The structures include a large sanctuary with clear glass windows, a contrast to the story-filled colorful windows of the cathedral. The nuns' cloister is built on a square plot of ground. This garth is enclosed on four sides by walkways and low-lying walls, the arcades.

Other buildings include a chapel, chapter house, scriptorium, infirmary, refectory, and kitchen, and many outbuildings and sheds. An ample barn for the livestock: goats, sheep, milk cows, and horses is near a stream and large pasture adjacent to the woods. Much to Ravenissa's delight, the barn is very close to our quarters where there's also a chicken coop and dovecote. Vegetable and herb gardens, an apiary, and an apple and pear orchard complete the thriving landscape to the east.

A goodly distance from the main enclosure, there's a long and narrow wooden house where the monks live. The priest, Père Gilbert, celebrates the Mass and hears the nuns' confessions. He visits the sick in the infirmary. The monks are scribes, and they rarely cross paths with the nuns. They spend their days in the scriptorium, the cavernous room with its tall shutters and glorious northern exposure.

Our sisterhood's living quarters are in an old granary, a wood and stone building at the eastern corner of the main property. We live some distance from the cloister where the nuns' quarters are connected to the refectory by a long, arched passageway flanked by an evergreen hedgerow and the stone outer wall of the nun's chapter house, their meeting place.

Our quarters include one main room with a small cooking hearth and a long table for preparing food and taking our meals. There's an adjoining larger room we use as our sleeping chamber and down the hall is the nearby storage closet I claimed as my scriptorium.

When we first arrived after Sister Lunetta brought us to the granary, Beatrice swept each and every corner and nook with her broom. We blessed each room with prayers for protection. Soon, Comtesse took up her needle and wool to create beauty for our surroundings. When her handiwork is complete, we'll have a linen altar cloth stitched with red roses to adorn the little table in our sleeping room.

Helvide has plans for the seeds and plants she brought from Belle Cœur. She will hoe a garden in the small enclosed yard outside our quarters in the spring. Gertrude has been gathering wood from the forest to build a cupboard for the hearth. Ravenissa has found her place caring for the livestock. She knows the animals by name, names she's given them. Crow is never far from sight, and her mouse continues to live in her apron pocket, just as Henriette lives in mine. Imene tends our little injuries: Helvide's burned palm that came too close to the fire, Gertrude's aching shoulder from chopping wood, and thankfully she healed Petronilla's toothache.

Sabine does her best to keep our household orderly while she oversees our duties and chores according to Sister Marguerite's instructions. Marie and Cibylle are constant companions for one another, and even they have their tasks as they wash the dishes, make candles, and tidy our quarters. Mabille's happy tunes continue to lift our spirits while Petronilla's dreams and visions inspire and guide us.

At every chance, I come to this little room, this closet, where I keep my copies of the four volumes of Dominions and Graces, parchments and supplies, and my queen bee hidden in one of the old crockery pots in the corner. When I am away at my duties, I take care to also hide my parchments for our journal lest someone outside our community should visit unexpectedly.

Each of us does her best to bring her prayers, wisdom, and sacred life art to each day. The inclination to weave our love of God through our prayers into even the smallest moments of daily life fuels our spirits in the midst of the uncertainty of our circumstances.

All facets of life are capable of sacred expression and imbuement according to how we choose to celebrate and use our spiritual and creative gifts. The beauty is in the blending of how each demonstrates her vision of the sacred.

The rituals of daily life sustain us. Prayer is added to all we do to feed our spirits.We taste it in Beatrice's bread. It grows in Helvide's planting of the herbs and is heard in every strum of Mabille's playing on her lyre.

Beauty nourishes our hearts through the placement, order, and cleanliness of things. A thoughtful arrangement of polished lady apples on a wooden plate stirs the senses in the midst of busy daily life. When accompanied by prayer, a floor swept clean, a tidied cupboard, or a sprig of rosemary thoughtfully placed on a pillow are sacramental gestures of faith.

The sacred is palpably present in our sleeping room. Gertrude and Comtesse have suspended linen curtains between the cots to provide the blessing of privacy. Gertrude carefully hung the wooden crosses, brought from Belle Cœur, in each of our spaces. Imene and Gertrude share one sleeping space. Their cots are close together side by side.

At the north end of the room where we take our rest is the small table awaiting Comtesse's altar cloth. The wooden carving of Magdalene holding her precious jar is in the center. Leaning against the wall at the back of the table is our plaque from the doorpost at Belle Cœur. These things represent our hope to return one day to our beloved home and infirmary.

Each morning fresh flowers or herbs, according to the season, are placed on our altar. Candles burn perpetually. This is our gathering place for prayers at the beginning of the day before light, and again in late evening before bed.

As sisters of Belle Cœur, we believe God speaks to each of us in a unique way. Our rituals and prayers unify us and hold us in a common shared center. We are united through our practices that reflect our love for God, while the outward expressions of our spirits are often very different.

To be ever present to the presence of God is the *invitation* and also the *art* of each day. Sweeping the floor, building a table, spinning wool, tending the sick, making bundles of rosemary, preparing soup for the evening meal…all of these are the art of living. Life becomes a sacred work of art when prayer and love for God is present in the doing and making.

We work from early morning till evening and sometimes throughout the night in exchange for our lodging. Keeping attentive to God's presence in the midst of many demands tests even the most spiritually dedicated of us. This is why the bells are so important. The monastery bells call us to community prayer throughout the day, the same as at Belle Cœur. Prayer is the holy river that continually flows in each of our hearts throughout our daily tasks.

Every day two or more of us tend the sick in the infirmary. We assist the nuns with preparation of the monastery's meals in their big kitchen. We mend their habits, care for the livestock, hoe the gardens, and do our best to cheerfully complete all that is required of us. I cherish the few days each month when I am told to clean the scriptorium. Sadly, there's no time to teach reading and writing to my sisters as I did at Belle Cœur.

Mostly, the nuns keep to themselves. We work alongside them and share their surroundings, yet we rarely engage in conversation or camaraderie. Rather they speak to us with little gestures. A gentle tug on the sleeve signals us when we are needed. Fingers to the mouth translate, "Silence." All their movements are purposeful and carefully considered. They are graceful and grace-filled.

Their white, flowing robes are their wedding dresses as brides of Christ. They share a secret, hidden prayer life that brings a curious combination of peace and mystery to this place. Their lives of contemplation are imbued with the pondering of Jesus and His Word and their adoration of his Blessed Mother.

"The Word must be heard in the heart, in the poustinia. This is the place where God dwells within us." This important teaching came from Sister Lunetta, whom I have come to know and love—our beloved angel of mercy who found us the night we first arrived at the cathedral. She and I are two branches of the same tree through a shared devotion to Our Lady.

On the last warm afternoon of autumn soon after we settled in our quarters, Sister Lunetta and I were preparing to scrub soiled linens in the large iron kettle outside the common yard near the infirmary. We stood under an ancient oak. Ravenissa had recently named the tree, Grandmother, when she climbed in the crook of a lower branch and sensed the tree's age.

"She told me stories," she announced with a smile. "She's a Grandmother tree, like the one from my childhood."

The oak's verdant canopy was home to dove and wren, squirrel and spider. Her leaves cast dancing shadows about the yard while we worked in silence.

High-flying ravens formed a pattern of black stitches against the cloudless blue fabric of the sky.

One of the monastery's many cats, fat and black as soot, stretched out her long, plump body in a patch of grass. She purred her cat song while she preened. I removed my sandals and pressed my feet into the earth to feel the rhythmic pulse of nature's heartbeat.

Side by side, Sister Lunetta and I scrubbed the stained bedding with our prayers and placed it in the simmering pot of herbs and lye. Later each piece was pulled from the cleanse with a long stick and dipped into the rinsing tub. The wet linen hung on the stick to cool for a moment before it was wrung out and spread upon the surrounding hedgerow to dry.

Sister Lunetta closed her eyes and broke our silence with her whisper.

"I feel the Mother's presence."

I ceased my busyness and closed my eyes, then drew a deep breath. I felt nothing. I put out my hands as if *she* might touch me. Still nothing. My mind began to chatter thoughts of envy for Sister Lunetta's spiritual abilities.

As jealous judgments tumbled about in my head, I felt a rush of peace pass through me like a soft breeze. It touched me like the brush of a passing loved one or the movement of the heart when it senses another's prayer.

"Yes, sister. Oh yes, she's near," I whispered.

We opened our eyes, joined hands, and knelt down together in the prickly grass in adoration of the Mother's visitation. The trees and bushes were alive with light and I felt the presence of love, love that heated my heart and made my skin tingle. Sister Lunetta and I joined hands and she prayed.

"We abide in you, Our Lady, as you abide in us. We pray to serve you and your Son and we are grateful for your blessing. Holy Mary, Mother of God...."

A gentle breeze began to blow; the tingling stopped, my heart cooled, and my tears receded. The Mother left us with her silent blessing of peace that returns to me now as I scribe this story.

We seek to find our rhythm in this unfamiliar place. Meanwhile, Petronilla prays in strange tongues we do not understand. I recall the one time I prayed in this way, in the cathedral, though it's never happened for me again.

Three nights ago the Spirit filled Petronilla's heart, and she poured out a message from heaven in "the language of the angels," as she calls it. To me, her words were musical and strangely familiar, though I did not understand her heavenly gibberish. Afterwards, she struggled to describe her ecstasy.

"Sisters, you ask me how it feels to be a voice for the Spirit. Let me try to explain. Think of Mabille and the careful way she plays her lyre. She knows how to pluck each string to create a melody to give us comfort when we're weary or in celebration when we're joyful. The lyre is simply the instrument. God has graced Mabille with a special gift that makes the lyre sing." Petronilla's hands mimicked Mabille's playing while she continued.

"It's likewise with me. I'm the instrument, and God has given me grace to deliver the message. Listen to what the Spirit sends through my heart and voice, and God will reveal divine wisdom to each of you, according to your need and understanding."

We sat in silence for a moment. Not one of us was prepared for Comtesse's interpretation that spilled forth like hot tar from a cauldron.

"God is calling us to take the veil. That's the message you bring us, Petronilla. That's *my* understanding."

"What are you saying? I can't imagine God is asking…" Petronilla responded.

Comtesse stepped toward Petronilla. "Don't tell me I'm wrong! My understanding is that we're being told by God to enter the nunnery. That's what I heard."

Beatrice scolded, "Hush! How can you utter such a thought? Our covenant, our agreement is that we've chosen another way of life…a life of freedom and independence from the confinement of the cloister. What do you suppose our sisterhood, our Order of Belle Cœur, is all about? If you're called to take the vows of the nuns, then so be it; you're free to go, but don't include the rest of us in your plans. God would not inspire our hearts with the Belle Cœur way of life and then want us to take vows that contradict how we live."

Comtesse turned on her heel to Beatrice. "Don't you see? We are separated from the Church! The Church is the one, true way to God. Our prayers and practices are wrong and sinful!"

I could no longer listen in silence.

"What's come over you, Sister? Your attraction to Belle Cœur was the reason I went there. I followed *you* to a life you felt *called* to live. You were among the first in our sisterhood. How can you say our life together is wrong?"

"It is, I tell you!"

But I interrupted her. "Let me speak! Listen to me! Praying to God from our hearts isn't a sin. Breaking bread together in the name of Jesus isn't wrong. Celebrating our rituals isn't sinful when our only thought is to praise God. As sisters of Belle Cœur, we've been called to a different path. We choose to be independent of the men's rules. We are called to freedom to follow God's call. Surely you don't disagree."

Comtesse grabbed my arm. Her words breathed hot. "But, Goscelin, the bishop is looking for those who *don't* follow the rules. Surely we are…"

Frustration fueled my tongue. I pulled away.

"Surely we are suspect? Is that what you're going to tell me…tell us? Believe me when I say I respect the nuns and their call to sacred vows. I'm sure all of us respect them, but our calling is to another kind of sisterhood. If you choose to take the veil because it's a call from God, then so be it. But the way you're talking sounds like your fears have the best of you rather than God's calling."

Cibylle looked around the room and began to cry. Marie wrapped her arms about her, rocked her, gently patting Cibylle's round belly.

Sabine reached for Comtesse's hand, but Comtesse turned her back. "Beatrice is right, Comtesse. Speak only for yourself. You may not speak to others on our behalf! I must ask you…are you truly feeling called to leave us?"

There was no hesitation in Comtesse's answer. "The sisters like me, and what's more...I like them! Sister Marguerite certainly favors me. She told me I would be an excellent nun."

Silence fell over the room like a blanket thrown in desperation to smother a fire.

Sabine broke the quiet. "Let's take our concerns into prayer. We'll pray for you, Comtesse, as you discern whether to leave us or stay. But please remember to be respectful of the rest of us. We don't share your call. Am I right, Sisters?"

We patted our hearts in agreement, even Cibylle.

Comtesse turned round to face us. Her posture stiffened, and she appeared to grow taller as she spoke. "Well, I'm not surprised. None of you ever regard what I have to say. No one appreciates my way of seeing things. But you'd better listen to me tonight. I tell you we're not safe as we are. You will regret your refusal to at least consider taking the vows of the Church. I pity your ignorance..."

Sabine raised her voice. "Enough! Stop now, Sister, before you say something that will burn the bridge between your heart and our community. This kind of talk is sure to set a place for fear, and where fear settles the evil one comes to feast upon it."

There's an unwelcome invisible presence among us since Comtesse's outburst three nights ago. We are careful to give her extra distance when she enters the room or passes one of us at work in the infirmary.

Yesterday while I tended the hearth, Sabine asked me, "You've known Comtesse since she was a child. What's taken hold of her?"

"I wish I knew."

"I realize it's not good for us to speak about her this way without her being present, but I'm concerned, Goscelin. One has to wonder what she talks about with Sister Marguerite."

The wood was damp. The fire spit great puffs of smoke. It filled our quarters, burning our eyes and making us cough.

"Look, the devil is in our midst." I laughed as I stirred the logs.

"Let's pray you're wrong," Sabine replied soberly.

Sleep is rare these days, and the nights are long. Our sleeping room is crowded and cold. Petronilla continues to cry out from her dreams, Marie has a dreadful cough, and troubled thoughts run wild in my head no matter that I constantly pray for peace. Helvide snapped at me yesterday because I was not folding the linens to her liking, though she was quick to make amends. Ravenissa stays away from our quarters whenever Comtesse is present. She's taken to sleeping in the barn with the animals if Comtesse is near.

Sabine is deeply troubled. Since Comtesse threatened to leave us, I found her one afternoon crying in a corner of our yard.

"What is it? What's wrong?" I asked.

"Oh, how I've failed. I've failed her in some way, Goscelin. I haven't given her the attention she's needed all these years. Now she's found it elsewhere and..." Sabine wiped her nose with her apron.

"Oh, no. No it's not your fault. You've always been generous and loving to Comtesse. She's been needful and determined for a very long time. Only now it's so much more than that. She's become fearful and supicious. I don't know her anymore, and truthfully I don't care to be close to her now. Her fear is contagious. I become scared anytime I'm with her, don't you?"

Sabine was quiet while we walked to the infirmary. Before we began our duties we stopped outside the door and joined hands. Sabine prayed.

"Merciful God, there is a tear in the fabric of our beloved sisterhood. We pray to You. Mend what has been broken. We pray for Comtesse. Heal her. Heal us, Beloved, and protect us from the demon of fear. Amen."

In a stolen moment I go to my secret place in the empty cupboard to capture my thoughts. I carry my satchel containing a bit of parchment, my quill and ink, and Volume II, *Air*.

I know Comtesse is fire and Petronilla is air. The more Petronilla prays and feeds us her teachings, the more Comtesse's willful wildfire rages. With each lick from the flames of her fear our trust in her diminishes.

I scribe my Grace in the margins of Volume II…

Air feeds fire. Without air a fire cannot burn. Fire travels quickly, consuming whatever lies in its path. At base level, fire destroys. At the highest level, fire turns simple metal to gold. Air is life-giving. Each breath feeds upon air. Air sustains life and strangely also feeds the destructive power that lives in fire. Is it possible to reconcile these two disparate forces, air and fire? Renewal and destruction…we are living in a borderland.

Thankfully, Petronilla, in spite of her fever, comforted us last night as we gathered for Compline before bed.

"The soul is like the mouth of one awaiting her lover's kiss. She leaves her home and sets out into meadow, woods, and field in search of Him. Her longing is terrible. She calls out His name, and she walks backward for a while, counting each step while stopping her breath, as if ritual will bring Him closer. Her lips become swollen with passion, and her wailing begins. Exhausted, she returns to her house to find Her beloved waiting patiently by the threshold." Petronilla paused with a faraway look before she continued.

"'I called to You. I searched for You in the meadow, woods, and field. I walked backwards, counting each footfall while taking no air, in hope my magic would beckon You to me,' she cries." Again she stops, her lips move silently then she goes on.

"The Beloved tells her, 'Oh, My love, the sight of you is my heart's joy. You had only to look for Me here, where you live. For where you live is where I'm always waiting for you.'

They kiss, and with their kiss she understands. From that day until the time of no tomorrows, they will live as One Heart, One Spirit."

After her story Petronilla offered another teaching. Her pale skin glowed with a bluish cast in the candlelight, and I caught the faint scent of roses as she spoke softly.

"Be still and go within the oratory of your souls, Sisters. God is there. We don't have far to travel to find our Beloved patiently waiting. Make your art and craft a prayer. Fashion each moment of your life into a sacred gesture of affection to the One who dwells within you. Remember that rituals born of habit or desperation are not unlike the magic tricks of a disreputable conjurer in the marketplace. Don't become greedy for rapture or ecstasy. Rather tend your prayers, be kind to those who cross your path, and care for the sick and the forgotten ones. Follow the Way that Jesus showed us. Love. Love and serving others is the only call."

Petronilla's lesson left my body humming with a strange and subtle trembling. It felt like the angels themselves had been playing me like they play their harps under the great light-filled vault of heaven.

Often we sit at her feet at day's end before bed while she stares into a place we cannot see. Her eyes glow from the indwelling light that illumines her body. Light that fills the entire room with a golden cast. Together, we pray to enter into the secret realm of heaven that Petronilla has described. She tells us that each of us is capable of receiving the grace to go there if we but dare to open the eyes of our souls.

I know what she teaches is true. I remember my night on the labyrinth, the tunnel, and Jesus's blessing.

Petronilla's spiritual gifts tax her constitution. Our beloved sister is plagued with fevers and clusters of red welts between her shoulders. She lies perfectly still, longing for God to come ever closer and aching for the return of her husband, Guy. He has been away nearly two years as a crusader in service to the king.

Before her most recent illness, Petronilla reported to us after morning prayers.

"Guy appeared to me in a dream last night sitting atop a great black horse. He was a soldier in a sea of armored men. There were thousands riding across a vast open plain. A long, high range of dark mountains loomed on the horizon in the distance. I sense today the army is nearing their destination. He is safe. Michael the Archangel leads them forward carrying his mighty sword." Her long slender fingers twisted her nightclothes as she spoke.

Beatrice expressed her gratitude as she prepared to go to her duties. "You bring peace to my soul, my dear girl. I'm grateful to God for your visions. Knowing your dear husband is well makes my day a blessed one." She depends on Petronilla's gifts of seeing to comfort her. Most days, her work with the nuns in the monastery kitchen keeps her distracted from her worries.

Petronilla offers us peace and calm while Cibylle causes concern. Marie keeps her occupied playing *batons et des pierres.* Helvide also tends Cibylle with the invitation to help her with the candle making. They do this together in our yard, enclosed by a high stone wall just outside our quarters. Our little bit of earth is invisible to the eyes of anyone nearby unless they should come through the big wooden gate.

Cibylle's belly grows larger each week. Imene reported Cibylle's condition after her most recent examination. "Seven months, perhaps nearly eight."

"Who do we imagine the father to be?" Sabine asked.

"How could we ever know? Cibylle surely can't tell us, and I doubt she understands how she came to her condition. We must pray her babe is healthy and pray Cibylle does well through the birth." Imene spoke to several of us gathered in our circle around the hearth toward day's end.

"How will we keep a crying infant a secret in this place?" I asked.

Beatrice chewed the end of a carrot and wiped her brow. "Hopefully Cibylle will take to mothering. Otherwise I'll nurse the poor little soul. How I shall explain to the nuns where my milk has gone if I help the girl feed the little one? That will be a problem for sure. When I'm not working the kitchen, they're always placing a poor, hungry baby in my arms in need of milk."

Imene stirred the fire. "We must constantly pray for God's protection. I can't imagine what would become of Cibylle and her child should the churchmen discover them. What with her peculiarity and strange appearance, surely she would be thought to be in communion with the devil, and of course the baby..." As Imene was about to finish her thought, the door blew open, and the candle on the table was extinguished by the wind. A chill caught my breath away.

"No more talk of such things! We mustn't utter the evil one's name. Doing so surely invites his presence. We must go to our prayers and to bed." Beatrice closed and bolted the door tight.

Left to her ways, Cibylle would choose to be unkempt and wild in appearance, as when we found her. Her curly, long hair is the color of walnuts left too long on the ground. It was decided we shouldn't cut it, as Petronilla told us doing so would terrify Cibylle. She often wears her hair like a blanket. It's so long she can wrap it around her in a protective way.

Beatrice fusses at her constantly to scrub her hands and face. For all the concern she causes, Cibylle and her strange ways fascinate me. Her gait is awkward and clumsy. The wide space between her large eyes makes her resemble a fish. This seemingly cruel comparison is simply my observation, offered with affection. I love her dearly.

Pale blue vessels appear under her milky-white skin. They shine like markings on a map leading to an unknown destination. She appears homely to those who don't know her, but there's a quality of innocence in her gaze. I believe our precious Cibylle carries a truly unreachable mystery, perhaps even more so than Petronilla.

When she becomes nervous, frightened, or anxious, she folds her arms over her chest and rocks her body rapidly from side to side. Because her speech cannot be understood, we are never certain what goes on inside her head. Her hands are red and raw from daily digging and clawing of the earth. Much to Beatrice's disgust, Cibylle prefers to forage for her meals. Things from nature that would cause most people to vomit are sweet delicacy to her. We have observed her peeling acorns. She rolls each one in damp earth then arranges them in threes. One by one from right to left, she eats them as if they were delicious bits of honey cake.

Another source of great annoyance to Beatrice is Cibylle's refusal to touch meat of any kind. The mere sight of cooked rabbit or lamb makes her rock and wail.

Her connection with and passion for nature comes alive through her imaginative creations. She gathers fallen leaves, moss-covered twigs, milkweed pods, comfrey root, blackberries, and the tiniest of stones. Her many finds are licked and sniffed for taste and fragrance. Her treasures are sorted, then thoughtfully arranged as if to make little altars all about. By the end of each afternoon, as many as twelve of Cibylle's creations are all along the ground near the wall of our yard. Some of these grow to be as high as my shoulder.

She has no language to express the meaning of her sacred art, but she hums happily as she gathers, sorts, and places leaf with stone and stick with moss.

Marie helps her collect and count out her materials, but it's Cibylle and *only* Cibylle who creates her nature shrines.

Sadly, Gertrude and Ravenissa must destroy her daily creations after dark, lest someone from the outside should come through our gate unexpectedly. They do this with reverence and prayer. Cibylle never seems to notice they have disappeared. The next day she simply and happily begins her work anew.

Her favorite pastime, next to being out in nature, is to help Helvide with candle making. She surprised Helvide one day by adding rosemary and thyme to the beeswax, a sure sign she is clever in spite of her odd appearance.

Marie gestures with her hands to Cibylle as their special language. She makes a circular motion with her index finger on Cibylle's open palm then kisses the same finger and presses it to Cibylle's cheek. Cibylle returns the gesture to Marie, and this exchange always ends with a hug.

I record in Dominions and Graces Volume I, *Earth*:

Cibylle is of the Earth, connected to the growing things and changing seasons, part mystery part miracle. She is fey and God's particular child of woeful wonderment.

One afternoon soon after our arrival at the monastery, Beatrice and I chopped vegetables in preparation for supper. Marie told a story to Cibylle while they played with the cat near the fire.

"Two Boots was the cat's name. He was a big, black cat, bigger than most." Marie's imagination was at work as she wove her story for Cibylle. "Two Boots's front paws and legs were white as snow. That is why…"

"That is why they called him Two Boots!" Beatrice laughed out loud. "Oh, my darling girl, you are *trés drôle*!"

"Grand-mère! I'm telling the story!" Marie shouted. "Two Boots decided he wanted to go to town…"

"AHHHHHH! NOMNIE NEY! NOMNIE NEY!" Cibylle began to wail and laugh all at once and jumped about patting her belly.

"What's the matter? What's wrong?" Marie cried as Cibylle laughed and pulled up her dress. She pulled Marie's hand to her stomach.

"Why, it must be her infant moving about inside her. That's what she's feeling! I would wager my life. She's quickening!" Beatrice dropped her chopping knife, wiped her hands on her apron, and went to Cibylle, who suddenly sat down and grew quiet.

Beatrice spread her fingers wide and pressed her hand on Cibylle's bare belly. Cibylle giggled with astonishment.

Beatrice moved her hand away. "It's not very strong yet, but the child's alive for sure!"

Cibylle hugged Beatrice round the neck and clapped her hands.

"You understand don't you, girl?" Beatrice asked.

"You understand, Cibylle! You understand you're going to have a baby!" Marie squealed.

Cibylle smiled and looked at all of us as though we were the simple-minded ones.

The days here are long and our laboring, endless. I've not yet told my sisters of my vision of Jesus so many months ago. I await a sign from the Beloved for when and with whom I'm to share my story of His blessing.

Why was I deemed worthy of such grace? Why was I chosen to be led by the young sheepherder, an angel, to Jesus on the hillside? Perhaps I suffered a delusion, though I think not. For I know in my bones I was truly in Jesus's presence that night…in the sea of pilgrims, on the pathway of stone, in the cathedral.

There is no time for me to return there to once again enter the labyrinth. To once again see the living pictures made of colored glass.

The throng of sick and wounded grows larger each hour as soldiers, pilgrims, and townspeople from Chartres fill the cots in the infirmary. All ages and manner of ailment pour through the door.

One needs strength to enter the infirmary. My memory of Jesus's blessing gives me courage to witness the human suffering that is all around.

These things I saw today…

A young, blind man with a gaping, pus-filled wound on his leg was treated with maggots. He was led to the infirmary by a crippled boy, small in stature but large in spirit.

A battered stonemason. He had fallen a great distance from the cathedral roof. He held his gut and screamed in agony from wounds in his belly that were not visible to our eyes.

A febrile infant brought to the infirmary by her little sister. Eleven siblings awaited her return. Orphans. Beatrice put the babe to her full breast, but he was too weak to suckle.

A young boy made his way in, holding his dead dog and hoping for the animal's resurrection. Sister Marguerite pushed him away. Sister Lunetta fetched Ravenissa, who found the boy and offered comfort. They went to the woods to properly bury his friend.

A woman with a large growth in her nostril. The thing appeared to my eye like a hideous worm peeking out of a hole begging for someone to cut it out. No one knew what to do for her. She went away still suffering.

Others come with bloody flux, devil's fire, and countless human ailments we cannot name. Two monks, Brother Christopher and Brother Adnot, quietly carry those who suffer from lepry to a secret unnamed place. Père Gilbert stands in the yard outside the infirmary and makes the sign of the cross over the cart full of castaways before the brothers start off on the dusty road. Sister Lunetta believes they go to a nameless place where they linger to eventually die an ugly and friendless death. Only those who know Jesus are allowed a Christian burial.

Many who labor to complete the rebuilding of Our Lady's great sanctuary at Chartres fall to their deaths or come to us cut, bruised, bleeding and broken. We pray for guidance and wisdom to know how to comfort such unimaginable suffering.

Bless the hopeless and helpless, dear Jesus. Grant them peaceful deaths, and may they at last dwell with You in your heavenly Kin-dom. Amen.

One recent afternoon before Sister Marguerite banished Imene from the infirmary, she was directed to care for the town's executioner. He had chopped off two fingers while cutting wood. Imene later told us how her hands trembled when she looked into the eyes of the man who had ended the lives of countless souls. She recounted how her knees buckled while she scrubbed the bony, bloody stubs where his fingers had been.

"He never flinched or made a sound. He only stared at me with the look of the devil. You know, he's the one who sets the fires of death outside of town for those the Church names heretics. It's this evil one who kicks the stool out from under the ones who are hanged for their crimes of thievery, adultery, and murder. There was no light in his eyes. They were the eyes of a lost soul, one who's separated from God."

She twisted her apron as she shared her day's story after supper.

"I searched my heart, but I felt no compassion for him. Were I not so afraid of him, I would have scrubbed those bloody stumps to cause him more pain. How can someone be so evil?"

"Oh, Imene, no doubt any of us would feel the same. His presence must have been terrible. How you managed to care for him was only by grace. But difficult as it is, praying for the likes of this treacherous man is the work of our souls." Sabine put her hand to heart as she spoke. "We must fervently pray…especially for those who live an earthly hell without the knowledge of God's love for them. We must intercede for those who do evil: the murderer, the betrayer, and even the executioner. Each day make your prayers of petition for those who are contemplating evil. Pray for those you do not know, nor will ever know who are planning on that day to harm another."

"Oh, Sister, you ask so much," Imene said. Those around the table nodded agreement.

"I know. I know. But imagine that through our prayers we build a bridge from our knowledge of God's compassion, grace, and goodness. A bridge from our hearts into the world of darkness. In this way we help heal earthly suffering." Sabine appeared tired but her voice was strong.

"Evil contemplates evil and waits patiently to seduce unwary and unprotected souls. If evil is to be defeated, those who foster love must diligently serve as God's heart and hands here on earth. Jesus taught the disciples to be 'wise as serpents and gentle as doves.' We must follow His counsel, for we live in a dangerous time."

Sabine closed her eyes, and Petronilla continued.

"We're compelled to believe the light of our prayers touches lost souls, breaks through the darkness, to reach and open closed hearts with divine love. We're charged by God to pray for our enemies."

Imene interrupted. "Sisters, I hear what you're saying, but my heart feels nothing. It's too much. I don't believe I am so holy as to forgive such atrocities. How does one forgive a murderer? Give me penance, for I am not as good as that. How am I to pray for the wicked man I was called to care for today?"

Gertrude knelt beside Imene. She removed her beloved's muddy shoes and began to rub her feet as Sabine continued.

"Think of it this way, Sister. As servants of love we're called to practice compassion without judgment. Executioner or innocent newborn, our prayers must know no difference. We do what God calls us to do. And that call is to offer comfort to the murderer and mother, crusader and child, the saintly and the sinner. Prayers are often the only and best medicine we can offer. Our lives must become living prayers in our suffering world."

In my heart I know the counsel of my sisters was right and good, but my mind wants to argue, like Imene. How does one step past judgment and fear to offer prayer and forgiveness to the presence of evil?

But this I know for certain in my heart and my head: Sabine never asks us to do that which she would not do herself. She's correct when she says praying for the most difficult people in our lives *is* the work of our souls. It's the hardest work and requires far more effort than plowing fields or scrubbing endless hallways on hands and knees. I know for certain it's *my* work and *my* challenge, and I doubt I will perfect it before my time on earth is over.

Oh, if only Helvide, our sister who reads the heavens, could look up at the stars to tell us the fate of our future. What will become of us? Will we ever live on our own again, without obligation to those who hold power and position? Uneasiness flows through our sisterhood like a poisoned underground steam. We mustn't succumb to our worries but rather become more diligent in prayer. Prayer is our armor against our greatest enemy, fear.

I take Henriette from my pocket and press her to my cheek for comfort. Sometimes I can almost hear her sigh.

Last evening, despite the cold, Helvide and Ravenissa risked being seen when they danced naked, then squatted near the earth to allow their women's blood to flow into the garden under the full moon. Their pagan ritual of blessing the ground with their monthly bleeding is one they cherish.

Our Belle Cœur rituals mark the passing of time. Each week we gather in our circle on Sabbath evenings. Rarely are we all present as we often were at our house with the blue sign. Our duties here at the monastery call us away, even on the Sabbath.

Those who are present come together in prayer. Someone lights the candle at the center, then one by one, without interruption, we share our stories from the week. We use our custom of hanswere as our way to fairly make decisions affecting all of us. The circle is like a sacred basket or vessel. It is strong enough to hold whatever we bring.

During our circle or at our table at mealtimes we mark the places of our absent sisters with candles and stones. Every morning one of us places flowers or herbs, depending on the season, on our altar near the hearth and on the table in our sleeping chamber.

These rituals and others, too secret to commit to parchment, weave our hearts in the unity of our shared sacred life. Whatever may come, we hold fast to one another and our faith that God will protect us.

5 February 1259
Le Monastère de la Visite

I must go to my duties at the infirmary, but first I must record how Sister Marguerite has made it chillingly clear that we have received undesired attention. Sabine crossed paths with our taskmaster yesterday afternoon.

"I must tell you. Two of your women were witnessed dancing naked in your yard two nights ago. Disgusting and vile are your ways! God have mercy on your souls! Heed my warning, or you may find yourselves in trouble in ways you can't imagine."

"Good Sister, I don't know who witnessed the things you report, but let me assure you it was only a little game. Not vile, as you accuse. I take your warning seriously. I will share it with my sisters. Please be assured we are grateful to you for your concern. Thank you, Sister."

Sabine faced the nun's outrage wisely. Sister Marguerite's threats have caused us to agree that we must be cautious and only celebrate our rituals in our quarters behind closed doors. We are puzzled by who might have seen our sisters in the yard that night, for the wall is high and the gate was closed.

We carry our traditions of Belle Cœur more secretively and silently with each passing day. Meanwhile, Cibylle carries within her womb the secret of who fathered her child. Her time for delivery grows closer.

I carry something. too. With every turn of the hourglass, my vision and the revelations I received that first night in the cathedral go deeper into my soul. Sadly, I cannot find the language to share how I saw Jesus. How He blessed me. Perhaps no words have come, so my encounter with the Beloved may grow in my understanding before the telling of my story.

For now, I must ponder these things privately while I look for morsels of time to continue scribing my account of our sisterhood. By day I offer what I can to assist my sisters, catching moments of sleep in hidden corners and in the hollowed out trunk of the big tree in the woods. I spend the darkest hours of the night at my table scribing our journal.

I observe my sisters and listen carefully. I pray to capture their stories the way Ravenissa gently scoops the fat, speckled caterpillar from the garden path. She carries her to the shed and sets her free, safe to explore the plants and herbs of Helvide's indoor garden. Perhaps the tiny creature will weave a silky cocoon like the others that hang from Helvide's thistle branches.

They sway and glisten while inside God is working a miracle.

Our stories are cocooned in parchment and ink. Petronilla directs me.

"Yours is holy work, dear Goscelin. You must seek each story the way Gertrude chooses the vegetables in the garden. She examines the leaves, sniffs the air, and stirs the soil before she pulls the carrots from the earth and places them in her basket.

"Go to your memory's attic and sort what you find there. Gather the stories that catch your heart. Listen carefully each day to capture the wisdom of your sisters with your quill.

"You do this for us so we may live on after we're gone. You also do this for women who are not yet born. For they will be seekers of wisdom, women's wisdom, to help bring healing to their world."

Petronilla's mysterious instructions make me wonder…who are you…*you,* the one who holds this book written by my hand? If you are now the guardian of our stories, what has become of us? What has befallen the sisters of Belle Cœur?

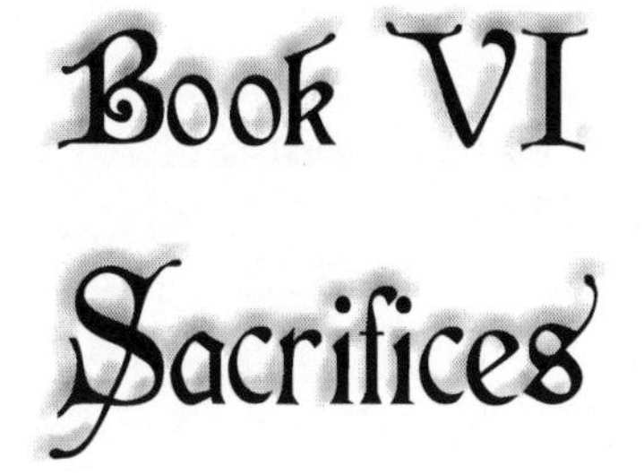

Book VI Sacrifices

16 February 1259
Le Monastère de la Visite

How shall I begin to share the story of the past four days though my hand trembles so I can scarcely guide the quill? My heart is wracked; my mind is vexed and distracted by the sensations of my body. When I think of the horror of that night, I can't breathe. The bruises written on my bones and flesh tell my unholy story.

It was dark, and I went to the scriptorium in secret in search of parchment. It was late, and I was certain no one would be there. I used my servant's key to enter, and by lantern light I quickly found what I needed. I rolled three scraps of parchment from the binding table, pressed them flat, and tucked them under my apron. I listened to be sure no one was about. There was only silence and the sound of my own heart beating in rhythm with my fear.

I slipped out and locked the door behind me. Cautious not to stumble, I hurried across the yard through the darkness. I noticed a light in the meadow near the brothers' quarters. Like the bright yellow eye of a demon, it made its way toward me. There was no place to hide.

"Who are you?" a loud voice called out as the light caught me. "Brother Gilles here! Stop and speak your name, girl!"

"Goscelin. I'm Goscelin," I choked.

"What are you doing out here alone at this hour?" He held the lantern before my face. "I know you! You're the one who cleans the scriptorium." He pushed back the hood of his cloak. I had seen him before when I scrubbed the floors and straightened the shelves. He was the monk who stared at me, the one who made me feel so strangely with just his gaze. A stubble of red beard covered his broad chin; his tonsured hair was combed flat across his forehead.

"I needed air. Sometimes I find it hard to sleep. I needed air, that's all. So I'm out here getting air... out here in the night air. Breathing. That's all. Just a breath of air and I'll be going…" The words poured out of me like bats from the bell tower.

"The wolves might get you and gobble you up!" He laughed and grabbed me 'round my waist.

The parchment fell to the ground from beneath my apron. Faint from fear, I crumpled forward. Brother Gilles caught my fall. He reached to retrieve the stolen goods.

"Now why would you have these pitiful bits of parchment hidden under your apron? Eh? What are you up to, Goscelin with the blue eyes?"

I waited for a lie to save me. But nothing came.

"Well? Answer me! What are you up to that you must pilfer parchment in the middle of the night? Certainly you're not copying the *Sanctorale* or the *Epistolarium* on these. And where would a servant girl learn to scribe? Or are you stealing for someone else….ahhhhh, that's it!" He shook my arm. "What are you up to, Goscelin?"

I tried to stay still, fearful he would sense my trembling. "Oh no, Brother, I'm not stealing this for someone else…I'm the one in need of parchment. I—I don't want to forget what I have learned."

"What do you mean?"

"Please, may I go now? I really must go!"

"Not until you tell me why you've stolen from the scriptorium! You're trying my patience, girl!" His grip on my arm tightened.

I wanted to run, but I could not feel my legs. "I once studied with a brother at an abbey far from this place. A brother not unlike you, a kind and gentle brother—he taught me to scribe."

"Now I've heard it all! What order of brothers is called to teach silly girls such wisdom? Hmmmmm." In the glow of the lantern, his eyes gleamed. Spittle wet his lips. "You fascinate me, Goscelin…you, a servant girl, and a scribe you say. Ha! *And* a pretty thief who likes to walk about alone late at night. You'd better say penance for your crimes."

A deafening stillness fell upon us. The monk let go of my arm for a moment while he folded and put the parchments in the pocket of his robe. Then he took up the lantern and held it close to me. He seized my chin with one hand and turned my face first one way then the other.

"Come with me!"

My legs shivered as he dragged me along, across the yard, back to the scriptorium. Once inside he took me to a locked cabinet and fumbled with the key fob hanging from his cincture in search of the right key.

Save me! Jesus, help me!

He opened the cupboard to reveal jars of pigment and one shelf of small bound books.

"Choose one."

"I'm sorry, I don't understand."

"Choose one, girl. Every scribe should have his… her own private manuscript. I crafted these. Choose."

"But how can I…"

"Choose, Goscelin, before my generosity turns sour." Smiling, he made a grand sweep with his arm and then bowed to his knees.

Confusion destroyed my thoughts the way fire sets a bale of hay ablaze. I pointed at a book. "That one, please."

He nodded. "Take it."

Brown and small, finely made, it fit the palm of my hand. An illumination of the Mother and Christ child on parchment had been stitched onto the cover.

"It's your illumination?" I asked.

"Yes."

"So beautiful. I don't know what to say." I tried to smile. "I thought you would take me straight to Sister Marguerite and report me. Your kindness is not what I expected. Thank you, Brother."

"Fill it with your prayers, dear Ga-se-lin! Your prayers for forgiveness for being such a wicked girl!" He frowned and leaned close.

"But I…"

"I'm teasing. I'm teasing you, stupid girl."

He closed the cabinet and took up the lantern. He turned and faced me with an expectant look. "Now you must let me have your favor in return."

With his words, my winny and thighs tightened together to lock the door to my body.

"My favor?"

He slid the book from my limp hand and placed it on the table all in one slithery move. He fumbled under his robe…I remembered and knew all too well the meaning of the pungent, sour odor that suddenly filled the air. It took what little breath I had. The putrid smell of men's malice and evil, the stench of Satan's presence.

"Now, Goscelin, you will give me a gift—or do I have to take it?" He grabbed my arms—I twisted, but he dragged me close to his sweating face and growled through clenched teeth, "You know I hold the power to determine your fate in an instant. Don't displease me. You wicked girl! There are those who would relish picking you to pieces. If you want my protection, kiss me now like you mean it!"

Panting, he tore at my apron and clawed my flesh as though digging in the dirt for a lost jewel. He pulled open his robe then pressed his sweating body into mine…

In that moment of unspeakable horror, I felt the top of my head split apart—my spirit rushed out as it had time and again when I was child at the mercy of my father's drunken trespasses. My spirit soared, looking for a place to settle. The part of me that will never die sped somewhere high above to a dusty corner of the ceiling. She hovered there, watching the poor girl below as she was ravaged by a demon who claimed to be a man of God!

At that strange height, distant from the pain and terror, the disembodied part of me looked with hungry eyes for something to feast on. There on a nearby rafter was a glistening spider's web and a moth held captive at the center, struggling to free herself. A great, black spider scurried across the lacy web to his prey. Dispassionately, my spirit watched while his hairy body spewed an endless silken thread, and his legs danced frantically to seal the moth within her tomb.

As this sad story played out upon the ceiling, a calm voice from somewhere far away kept whispering instruction.

"Keep still. Keep silent. He will soon be finished. It will soon be over."

My spirit busied herself...counting. There were fourteen soot-blackened rafters in the upper corner of that room. Four decaying webs held the drying remnants of eight prey. Below were twenty tables, twenty stools, and thirty torchlights. Six cupboards lined one wall near nine large shuttered windows. My spirit was about to number the vessels of pigments on the shelves when the familiar roaring began inside my head as my spirit returned to my body.

Oh, Merciful God, the pain! Help me! Make it stop!

I reentered my body as suddenly as I had left. While the leaving was a blessing, the return was excruciating.

My hands immediately went to the place where he been, as if my touch could ease the fire that burned there. No scream came from my throat, though my mouth was wide open. His drool ran down my cheek. My head was bare and my apron torn away. One breast was exposed, scratched and bloody. The salty, rank smell of him was everywhere. My head—oh, how it ached from being beaten against the table.

He stood above me half naked.

"A word of this to anyone, and I will go straight to the bishop!" Breathing heavily he adjusted himself, closed his robe, and pulled his hood over his head. He dropped pieces of parchment on top of me.

"If you need more parchment, my pretty scribe, you know how you can come by it. And do take the book, a souvenir to remind you of the price for pilfering. This arrangement we have is agreeable, *n'est-ce-pas*?" Then he hurried away.

For a long time I was frozen in place, unable to move. The searing pain in my backside and winny sharpened my wits. I collected my veil and apron and went out into the darkness to make my way to the pond. Shocked to realize I clutched his book in my hand, I threw his wretched gift into the night. I stepped into the frigid water up to my waist. The sobbing began. I rubbed all the stinging, throbbing places where he had been in hope of scrubbing away his unholy touch.

I crept back to our quarters just as the light of day returned. Beatrice was stoking the morning fire before prayers.

"What in the name of heaven!"

"Shhhh. Please, don't ask me…"

Her arms went about me gently.

"Don't ask you! Don't ask you? Sit down, Sister. Something terrible has happened. You're soaking wet."

"Despicable! Evil! Again and again! Why?"

"Goscelin, you're ranting. What has happened to you?" She turned my face towards hers. "*Mon Dieu*! I've seen that look before in a woman's eyes. And this bruise on your arm! Let me look at…" Beatrice gently opened my blouse. Like a dog on the hunt, she caught the scent she suspected as she sniffed my neck.

"Oh, dear God! Who did this to you? Tell me... who is he?"

I looked down at my chest to see the raw red marks covering my breasts. Then from somewhere deep within me the laughter began, as if I were now infected by Satan with demons from hell.

"It was one of the brothers...!" The laughter belched hotly from my throat. "I went to the scriptorium for more parchment. On the way back Brother Gilles—caught me in the meadow. I had to...pay the price for him to keep silent."

For a moment we stood together looking into one another's eyes. I couldn't stop gasping for breath. Then the weeping began in great, unending gulps. Beatrice sat down and pulled me into her arms. She rocked me like a baby. She was weeping, too. After a time we settled into silence. She wouldn't let me go.

"What's the matter with her?" Comtesse stumbled into the room, rubbing sleep from her eyes, followed by Cibylle and Marie. It was early morning and nearly time for Matins.

"Be still. She's fine. She had a difficult night in the infirmary. Make yourself useful and poke the fire. It's going cold."

Beatrice and I had entered into a lie. Resting on her shoulder, I kept my eyes closed so I wouldn't have to explain myself.

"What happened in the infirmary? What was so difficult? She hates the infirmary, you know..." Comtesse chattered on as she made her way back to her cot to dress. Cibylle and Marie were silent.

"Fetch a fresh sleeping gown, Marie. Hurry now... Take Cibylle to help you," Beatrice ordered.

Then she let me go and made the hearth ablaze. She helped me to my feet to stand before the purifying heat, peeling off my torn, wet clothing and pouring warm water from the kettle into a bowl. Then she began to gently bathe all the tender places. Afterward she took a jar of lavender salve from the shelf and carefully applied it to the scratches and bruised places. The smell of lavender blessedly chased away the odor of his trespass and violation.

I stood naked and shivering when Marie and Cibylle brought the clean gown. Cibylle came near. She looked at my battered body. Tears filled her eyes. Beatrice held the jar of salve toward her, speaking softly.

"You know what happened to her, don't you, dear? Here, you can help to heal her."

"It's all right, Cibylle. I'm all right." The look in her eyes pierced my heart. It was clear she understood. Between us we knew a horror that no two women should ever be made to share. She gently massaged the salve into my skin, murmuring soft, animal sounds to comfort me in her own tongue. When she was finished, she abruptly left the kitchen.

"Are you sure, Goscelin? Are you certain you're all right?" Marie asked after witnessing Cibylle's care.

Beatrice pulled the clean gown over my head.

"She'll recover, Marie. Don't fret."

Cibylle returned. She placed a small, round stone into my palm, closed my fingers 'round it, and made the sign of Belle Cœur on my chest.

19 February 1259
Le Monastère de la Visite

Henriette is lost. My blessed Henriette, my comforter, my friend is gone. I searched our quarters and she's no where to be found. No doubt she fell from my apron pocket as I made my way home that dreadful night. How will I manage without her wisdom? Where will I turn for comforting? She has been with me always. Maman's gift to me. Oh, Henriette, I'm so sorry I didn't protect you. I will do my best to find you. I'm so ashamed!

I wear my shame like a stain. Will it ever fade? What if I had fought him? Could I have run away? Why? Why didn't I put up a struggle?

Rage consumes me like a fever, rage at my attacker and rage at my cowardice! The only thing that helps my sanity is when my quill touches parchment.

Were it not for Beatrice's mothering presence that morning when I returned broken and bruised, I don't know what would have become of me. She washed me then sent me to bed. I slept fitfully and later finally rose to begin my morning duties. My mind was clouded with drowsiness, and my body ached in places too private to name while shame set up residence in my bones.

I have no memory of how I dressed and made my way to the infirmary. Imene greeted me. She pulled me into the little room where supplies are stored.

She gripped my arm tight and whispered, "Before Sister Marguerite sees you and puts you to work, I have to tell you a secret. You're the first to know,

Goscelin. I'll tell the others when I have the chance, but it's probably best to keep what I'm about to share from Comtesse. We must be very careful that Sister Marguerite doesn't find out."

"Find out? Find out what?" I asked.

"Gertrude has gone to Chartres! She's wanted to go there to help build the cathedral since we first arrived. She left late last night." Imene let go of my arm and lightly touched my cheek. "What happened to you? You're bruised. You look strange."

"I'm fine. I'm not fine really. I can't talk about it now. Later. I promise later."

"What's the matter, Sister? You…" Imene pulled at my sleeve, looking for more bruises.

"What will Gertrude do there? How will she help?" I asked. "The stonemasons and builders are men. The only women we've cared for here were hurt while moving stones or such. Women aren't allowed to take part in the building…are they?"

Imene laughed. "You know Gertrude has a strong will. She'll find a way to work with the men, I'm sure of it."

"Of course. You're right. Well, I hope things go well for her, if this is truly something she feels called to do. I remember the little stone cathedral she built at Belle Cœur. But why wouldn't she tell all of us she was going? You know, so we could pray for her?"

"She feared the sisterhood would try to keep her here, for her safety. That's why I was the only one she told. Believe me, I tried to stop her, but as I said, our Gertrude has a strong will. Pray for her, won't you?"

"Yes, certainly. And I'll pray for you as well. You must be terribly worried. I am," I said.

"And I'll pray for you, Goscelin. Something awful has happened to you, hasn't it? I hope you'll confide in me as I've confided in you. I love you, Sister. Is there anything I can do to help you?" She pressed my hands to her heart.

"Your prayers are help enough. I'll share my story with you soon, but not here. Not now. I love you, too, Imene."

We hugged one another and went to our chores.

I made sure Sister Marguerite wasn't in sight; then I sat down on an empty cot while I made compresses from folded wool. I tried to pray for Gertrude and Imene, but my usual spiritual fervor was nowhere to be found. My attempts to pray were dry and empty. I did my best to deny the pain I felt in my body's deepest darkest places.

I suffered through the early afternoon. As it was nearing time to deliver bread and milk to the patients, the north door of the infirmary flew open with a blast of cold wind and two young boys on the run.

They ran straight past me calling out, "Goscelin! Is Goscelin here?"

I was struck with the fear that somehow the young boys had been sent by Brother Gilles to fetch me to the bishop. I looked for a hiding place.

"Goscelin is over there!" Comtesse pointed in my direction before I had time to escape.

"You're Goscelin?"

I recognized Hugo, a small blond boy who often helped Ravenissa.

"Yes...What is it?"

"Bring blankets! Now! To the woods! You're needed! There's blood...an arrow! Ravenissa sent us. She needs your help! Hurry! She said bring blankets and sulfur."

Sabine and Mabille were also assisting in the infirmary. Sabine signaled for me to follow the boys. "Go! But hurry back. We need you here. There are too many to care for today"

Mustering what strength I could find, I quickly collected two blankets and a small vessel of sulfur from the cupboard. We hurried outside. I followed the boys along the paved pathway, past the shed to the place where the stepping-stones ended and the dirt path began. The boys pulled at my sleeve while I tried to keep up with them. Every step sent pain through my body. The cold rain rode on the wind making my face sting.

I called out to the boys, who ran ahead.

"Where are we going? What's happened? Slow down! Slow down!"

Hugo stopped until I caught up with him. The tall boy ran ahead.

"We were helping Ravenissa gather wood near the forest. She told us we'd get honey cake if we helped her. We were ready to come...to bring the wood to the infirmary. I went farther into the forest to look for kindling. When I bent to pick up fallen branches, something big moved in the brush. Then I heard a squeal.

I went closer, and there was blood all around on the ground, bright red blood! I hollered for Ravenissa. She came running and pulled back the branches, and then we saw her!"

"Saw who! Come back here!"

The boys ran ahead. The rain turned to thick fog. The path was now a stream of mud. My shoes were heavy with wet earth. The pain in my groin was unbearable. Hot tears spilled down my cheeks. I lifted my skirt and apron, laboring to catch up while I tried to make sense of what was happening. Who had been shot with an arrow?

A child? The daughter of Mademoiselle Aurore, perhaps, for she was always getting lost in the woods… or….

Fog hovered near the ground. Crow cawed out to me from above, and I followed him for the boys had raced beyond a curve of the path. My legs ached as I tramped through the mud. My bladder was full, adding to my pain, but I dared not stop to relieve myself.

Hugo ran back and grabbed my sleeve. "*Vite! Vite,* Goscelin!"

He pulled me along to a glade just at the edge of the muddy path where the forest begins. It was dark and dense with thickets of blackberry bushes and towering pine trees.

There in the dim gray light, kneeling in a pile of wet, decaying leaves was Ravenissa. Her hands were covered in blood. She signaled us to be still, then motioned to come toward her—slowly.

My nostrils filled with the scent of musk and wet earth. Liquid brown eyes stained with fear and pain stared into mine. The doe's large head lay in Ravenissa's lap. The deer's breathing was labored. Her wet, black nostrils, like billows, widened and narrowed with each steamy breath. The arrow was deep at the place where her long neck joined her chest. Blood made a rivulet through her brown fur. It dripped onto Ravenissa's apron in a black pool. My knees gave way for an instant, and my head was filled with noise.

The deer flinched and moaned. Ravenissa echoed the doe's cry as she stroked her withers.

I dropped to the ground. The boys knelt beside her. Then the deer's belly moved. First it was only a ripple, and then the ripple became a bulge, like a hand moving about inside a soft velvet pouch.

"She's birthing…and she's dying." Ravenissa spoke in a dry, tight whisper, never lifting her gaze from the doe's.

"What can we do?" I asked.

"Goscelin, you must help me. We will wait for the moment of her death—then you will open her belly. Perhaps we can save her fawn."

Death must have heard Ravenissa. The doe lifted her head for a moment, as if to signal her agreement to the plan. With a last steamy breath, her suffering was over. Ravenissa crooned a plaintive, droning sound, her blessing for the fallen deer.

Then she ordered the boys, "Turn her to the side."

The boys pushed and rolled the deer as instructed.

Ravenissa pulled her knife from her apron pocket. She removed the sheath and shoved it toward me.

"Goscelin. You must cut—now."

"Why me? You know better than I..."

"My hands must be free to deliver the fawn! Do as I tell you! Don't hesitate, Goscelin!"

"I don't know where to start!"

"There! Cut there!" Ravenissa pointed.

I drew in a ragged breath and placed the knife-point at the opening of the doe's winny. I pressed the blade down into the fur and flesh and moved it up toward the midsection. Sparks flew before my eyes. My body quickened with each halting move of the knife.

"Deeper, Sister! You must cut deeper! Do it again. Deeper this time!"

Blood flooded the trail of the first cut. I retraced the pathway, pressing harder into the flesh, but feared I would go too deep and injure the baby inside. Tears flooded my heart—I could not allow them to flood my eyes.

Ravenissa stood. She pulled her skirts to her waist and stuffed them into her belt. Then she straddled the doe at her midsection. Skillfully she pulled the flesh back from either side of the cut, the way one peels moss from damp earth to reveal what grows beneath.

The boys stood back. In silence Ravenissa and I acted as one. Later we would speak of how we felt assisted by angels.

I made a slow, careful cut while Ravenissa worked the flesh. She peeled away the wet, red layers to slowly uncover the precious cargo.

"Make a new cut. There. That's it. Open the sack."

I followed her instructions. A tiny leg and hoof appeared through the milky pouch like an apparition.

I made the cut and there came a great gush of water and blood.

Movement. Stirring. There was life within death. The fawn signaled us not to give up.

Sweet precious life, we will not fail you!

Head to head we leaned into the belly of the doe, two midwives in nature's infirmary. Through the blood and the water we could see golden spots on dark, wet fur.

Ravenissa motioned to the boys to spread the blanket. Together we lifted the living treasure from the bony cave. She was still and slight but perfectly formed. We placed her on the blanket.

Ravenissa took the knife from my hand. She cut and tied the birthing cord.

"Bless this creature. Let her live. Amen," Ravenissa prayed.

She rubbed the fawn with the blanket while I pulled the remaining sack from the head and face. Her mother would have bitten the cord and licked her babe into the world. We mimicked her actions as best we could.

The fawn flinched!

Life! Sweet life!

Bloody, pungent, wet, and juicy life! Her head raised. Wet sneeze.

"We did it! We did it!" Hugo yelled and threw his cap in the air and hugged his friend.

Ravenissa and I crossed ourselves and laughed through our tears.

The fawn was tiny, born a bit before her time and strangely out of season. A little miracle, she lived and breathed before us.

Ravenissa bundled her tired but squirming charge and carried her toward the meadow and the barn beyond. The boys were sent to fetch a shovel. I caught my breath as I watched them cross the meadow. At last I squatted near the earth to empty myself.

I took in the stillness of the forest. Crows cawed and circled above their waiting feast. The frigid wind caught my breath while the last leaves of autumn blew all about.

There before me the doe lay like an empty purse, her life spent and her treasure taken from her. How long had she suffered while she stumbled through the forest to finally fall and surrender? Wounded animals usually crawl silently away to die. They don't cry out to reveal their hiding place. Yet this doe had cried—and her fawn survived.

An unfamiliar strength came upon me. I put my foot on the deer's neck and drew the arrow from her with one long firm pull.

Is this how it is with mortals who are struck deeply by God's arrow? By God's flaming arrow of holy *passion* and *calling* for the human soul? The stinging, burning arrow of divine love sends the mortal running on a journey, into darkness, into hiding at last to fall and die to the old way of life, that no longer serves the soul with purpose or meaning.

Only then can a renewed life born of the awareness of love truly begin. The birth of the soul into the presence of God's love is holy and real. Surrender is the knife that cuts through the flesh of forgetfulness. The forgetting that our souls…that *we* are love incarnate.

How many times in a lifetime are we hunted, dropped to our knees, and changed by God's grace to find the strength to begin again?

Tonight in the barn from her bed of straw, the fawn suckles Ravenissa's version of her mother's teat—a soft bag made of hide filled with warm goat's milk, mashed suet, and honey. Ravenissa makes soft clicking sounds in her curious way. A deer's lullaby, perhaps.

The little one has a star-shaped marking on her breast. "I named her Etôile," Ravenissa whispers.

Exhaustion overtakes me. The stories of the extraordinary day and my dark, unholy night are at last recorded. The candle burns short, and the hour is late. Tomorrow, no doubt my wretched account must be shared with my sisters.

Without thinking, my hand reaches into my apron pocket for Henriette. The emptiness I find there stings my heart. Dear ragged and stained Henriette, the only witness to my attack. Where can she be? I lay my head on this parchment and weep for the loss of my doll, my girlhood, and so much more.

Later, my thoughts turn to the forest, where with my little remaining strength, the two boys and I buried the doe at dusk. Before we put the creature's sorry remains beneath the earth I cut away one of her teeth for Ravenissa. An amulet of gratitude from the mother to the midwife.

Some, who hear this story, may ask... *Why didn't we leave the doe's carcass where she fell, as sustenance for fox or crow? Why didn't she become a feast for our table?*

I ask, *Would you not bury your teacher? Would you not honor a holy messenger?*

The doe delivered a lesson I will always remember.

Be ever ready for God's arrow of passion and call! When it strikes, make a swift surrender to the inescapable fall and prepare to be made anew... in the image of divine love.

1 March 1259
Le Monastère de la Visite

A terrible tragedy has happened. I don't want to write this story, though I know I must. Later. Perhaps the words will come to me later. A plague of darkness has infected our hearts and spirits with lost hope.

Tonight marks one year since Petronilla's prophecy and her charge for me to begin to scribe this fund of parchments, these recorded fragments of the stories of our lives and our shared life as sisters of Belle Cœur. Of late all I spill onto the page is dark and somber. There are no stories to offer comfort or joy.

I light two more tapers while the wind rattles the shutters and sends a chilly draught under the door of this tiny room. The candle flames bend and quiver as the night air pushes through the cracks.

Merciful God, I'm weary and broken. The story I must scribe tonight tears my heart in two. I'm lost in the desert, thirsty for Your presence. I call to You, and I'm deafened by Your silence. Where are You hiding? I must believe You are near, or my faith will surely wither and die. I pray to be struck by Your holy arrow. Send it now to pierce my stony heart. Return soon, Beloved, and make me a new heart... a new life through Your divine love. Oh, God, heal me... heal Gertrude. Return Your peace... Amen.

How do I write of Gertrude's catastrophe while still consumed with my memories of the awful night in the scriptorium?

Oh, how I pray for joy to return soon to vanquish our hardships. For now, there is only grief and challenge. To steady myself for the task at hand, I will gather my wits by writing of the other most recent accounts of our sisterhood.

Soon after all that happened some days ago, Imene told the sisters that Gertrude went to Chartres, and Beatrice informed the others that I had been raped by Brother Gilles.

I was upset when Helvide came to comfort me after Beatrice spilled out the news. I went immediately to talk to her.

"Why, did you share my story, Beatrice? I would have told them eventually."

"*Rien ne pèse tant que un secret du cœur.* Nothing is heavier than a secret of the heart, dear Goscelin. I told them, because they must know. Besides, the sisters needed to be warned to be on guard and to stay away from him."

Since having learned my sad fate, they have each ministered to me with their healing oils, prayers, tears, and tender merciful words. Beatrice is right. No secret is too dark or too vile to be shared in the face of love. Even Comtesse showed a gesture of mercy when she gently placed her hand on my head and prayed for my healing. Her tenderness in that instant revealed a corner of her heart that is yet untouched by fear and affliction of the spirit.

Too many troubled thoughts of myself find their way to the page tonight. There are far more urgent concerns that have come to worry all of us. I'll share these before I scribe the most recent misfortune.

I worry about Beatrice. She's often flushed and short of breath. Despite her weariness she always seems to have a hungry baby at her breast. There are many abandoned infants these days. Sadly, mothers who are unable to feed them leave them at the infirmary. Or sometimes a little one is brought from town by a neighbor or relative if the mother is unable to feed it. When Beatrice is not in service as a soothie, she works in the monastery kitchen or here in our quarters baking bread and soup to sustain us.

Thankfully, Sabine made certain that I've been permanently relieved from my cleaning duties in the scriptorium. Now I will serve as her assistant in the infirmary, much to Sister Marguerite's disgruntled agreement. This is Sabine's loving action, to keep me close to her and away from Brother Gilles. One of the nuns, Sister Monica, I believe, has been assigned to replace me in the scriptorium. I pray for her protection.

My wounds are still visible under my clothing. The memory of the spider and his prey returns to haunt me. I'm certain for the rest of my life I shall always think of that dreadful night whenever I see a spider.

This evening at supper Marie proudly reported how Cibylle had crafted thirteen little shrines near the edge of the forest during the afternoon before it began to rain. Beatrice was furious with Marie for taking Cibylle out of our yard into the woods.

"Marie, if the nuns should see Cibylle foraging about, we'll be sent to the bishop for certain! Sister Marguerite hopes to catch one of us doing something odd so she can twist the story to make a trap for us. You must promise you'll never take Cibylle out of our yard again!"

Her grandmother's scolding left Marie in tears. Cibylle's forlorn expression seemed to say, "I'm sorry for causing such a fuss."

Marie isn't well either. Her gullet is swollen and red tonight. By the time we came together for prayers before sleep, she'd lost her voice entirely.

Petronilla continues to grow more and more frail. Before Compline, Mabille called Beatrice and me to examine the welts on her poor body. They were spread over her breasts and neck the way passing clouds overhead cast shadows across an open field. Her body appears like a landscape on fire. Imene is perplexed.

"I've never seen welts this large. There are so many. Look there! It's spreading as I speak!" We watched with strange fascination as the welts appeared to grow before our eyes in places where moments before the unaffected flesh had appeared normal. Red blisters ran together like an army of ants moving over fallen fruit upon the ground.

Though Petronilla is plagued with her strange ailment, this evening her presence held a strong fragrance like lilacs, or perhaps more like roses. Throughout the night her scent became stronger and sweeter. When I touched her forehead to check for fever, my fingertips were warmed as though they had been held close to the fire.

"Her ecstasy is constant. We shouldn't try to rouse her," Mabille whispered. "One of us must always stay nearby."

A little while later as Mabille and I kept our bedside vigil with Petronilla, we watched her body thrust left then right. Suddenly, as if by an invisible presence, she was lifted above her cot. She floated two hands high. I shall never grow accustomed to the sight of something so unbelievable, no matter how many times I witness it.

We gently placed our hands above her to keep her body from floating to the ceiling. Mabille glanced in my direction and whispered, "Perhaps she's going mad."

I replied, "Or perhaps, *we* are."

We must keep Petronilla hidden away as carefully as we keep Cibylle out of sight.

Ravenissa spends all her time tending her precious animals. I relish a few quiet moments whenever I'm able to sneak away to visit her and her creatures. Our little miracle, Etôile, nuzzles me with her warm, wet nose and calms my heart like nothing else. The goat has taken to nursing the fawn as though she's her mother, no doubt because of Ravenissa's gentle introduction. Blessedly, Crow is forever nearby.

Helvide is in our quarters whenever possible. She works late into the night in the shed, grinding herbs for her medicines. Many strange illnesses plague the patients in the infirmary. Helvide longs to discover treatments to relieve the endless suffering.

Dear Mabille has been teaching several nuns how to sing to the dying. They've enthusiastically followed her lead.

Sabine has become very thin since we arrived here. The dark circles around her eyes belie her insistence that she is fine. She does her best to fairly determine our duties and to ensure we aren't overworked. However, Sister Marguerite's endless demands for our assistance make Sabine's task, to sort and assign our chores, overwhelming. Lately, Sabine, has been forced to make all manner of excuses for Gertrude's absence to Sister Marguerite. She does her best to calm the nun's suspicions and irritiation.

Sabine is diligent to make certain there's time for us to come together each Sabbath. Often we talk of our longing for the days at Belle Cœur when we spent many an hour seated in our circle, sharing our prayers, stories, and crafts together.

These tender mercies hold us. In this way, our Belle Cœur life lives on here in the immense monastery with its endless, cold maze of hallways, secret passages, and draughty cavernous rooms. Our many duties scatter us about this vast property like a flock of birds tossed here and there in a windstorm.

The Sabbath marks the rhythm of our life together. Beatrice bakes our bread when the day has barely begun. Following our morning prayers, we gather 'round our little hearth as we did at Belle Cœur. We pray for God's blessing and sit together in silence before one by one we share what rests on heart and mind.

Our circle is the time when each of us speaks freely about what she finds life giving and life depleting, with regard to her work and the nature of our sisterhood. Next, we tend to household affairs such as, which of us will help Beatrice to plan and prepare the week's meals, or tidy our quarters. We end our circle as we began, with prayer.

In the midst of endless tasks and demands, there are cherished times that keep our Belle Cœur ways alive. Love, laughter, tears, and beauty find us hour by hour in small moments.

Thankfully, it was my turn this morning to freshen the flowers on our altar. This special act of devotion is a welcomed touch of solace and comfort in the midst of great sadness.

The hanswere remains our way of deciding things. Sadly, since leaving Belle Cœur there has been no time for shared dreamtime, our peramony. However, we've begun to leave small gifts from nature on one another's cots in gratitude for little kindnesses. We call these tiny offerings cescies.

I found a speckled, round, gray stone on my pillow last evening. I'm not sure what kindness I offered, or to whom I offered it. It was comforting to find this *cesci* so unexpectedly as a gesture of love and gratitude. I placed a perfect, gray dove's feather on Ravenissa's pillow the other morning in thanksgiving for the way she cares for our beloved animals.

One of Ravenissa's cats has joined me. He's curled on the bench in the corner. His thick, black fur shimmers in the candlelight. He pauses his preening to stare at me through bright green eyes flecked with amber; they shine like rare jewels. If he were human, no doubt he would be a king, or at least a prince. His purring sounds like prayer.

Oh, how my spirit cries out for the days at Belle Cœur…for the sound of Gertrude happily whistling and hammering in her shed! My tears splash to the page with these words. It's late, and I've pushed the story away long enough. I must turn my mind to face the dreaded task at hand, fortified by the memory of happier days held close to my heart. Where to begin?

I sadly doubt Gertrude will ever wield her hammer again.

Four days ago a one-horse wagon arrived at the main door of the infirmary. Three women delivered their patient. She was cocooned in a bloody blanket. Sabine was in charge of caring for new arrivals that afternoon. The injured woman was our beloved Gertrude. Immediately Sabine sent Mabille to fetch Imene, who was working in the sacristy.

I had just arrived for my chores. Helvide and Beatrice were tending patients nearby. Sister Lunetta ran to us. "Come quickly! One of your sisters has been hurt. *Vite*! Follow me before Sister Marguerite returns."

We followed Sister Lunetta and joined Sabine as the women carried Gertrude to the long table at the west side of the infirmary. The youngest spoke first. Her apron was stained with blood. Her hands were filthy and she smelled of sulfur.

"Your friend pleaded with us to bring her here."

The women lifted her from the cloth stretcher to the table. Gertrude let out a terrible sound, like an animal caught in a trap. Sabine spoke softly to comfort her; then the women unwrapped the blanket.

To our horror, that's when we saw that Gertrude's right arm was gone. Protruding from her shoulder was a bloody stump of bone and flesh. Helvide sobbed and turned away. I couldn't speak. Beatrice sucked for air and grabbed the table.

Sabine turned back again. "*Mon Dieu*!" she said to the women who had brought Gertrude. "How did this happen? Who are you?"

The young woman with the bloody apron replied, "I'm Genevieve; this is Catherine and Audelia."

Audelia told the story. "Your friend here fooled everyone. She was wearing men's clothing when she fell. She'd been working alongside the stonemasons for several days."

Sabine interrupted. "What are you saying? What do you mean they thought she was a man? How did she lose her arm?"

"The men told us she was lifting a stone into place up high…up high on the south wall of the cathedral. The stonemason said your friend…"

"Gertrude. Her name is Gertrude." Sabine said.

"…Gertrude set the stone in place then lost her balance. The scaffolding tipped, and she fell. It was a long drop. Witnesses told us that on the way down, her arm caught between two stones, and her body broke away in an instant and landed in a heap on the ground below. They had to hack her sorry arm to bits to get it out, it was wedged so tight in between those stones." The woman wiped her nose with her sleeve while we stared at Gertrude in disbelief.

Sabine leaned over our wounded sister. "Gertrude, it's Sabine. Gertrude!"

Gertrude's bruised face grimaced with pain, but she didn't respond. There was a deep scrape down the right side of her face. Her right eye was swollen shut and black around the socket. She wore men's clothing stained with blood and urine. Dry blood matted her hair. She stank horribly. Her remaining hand was clenched tight. Sabine gently rubbed Gertrude's fingers. They opened to release a jagged piece of stone that fell to the floor. Sabine retrieved it and put it in her apron pocket.

Again Sabine asked, "No one guessed she was a woman?"

Genevieve answered, "She's big and strong. With her cropped hair and hidden under a man's shirt and work breeches, she looked very manly. Your friend did a good job of fooling them. *Elle est folle, n'est-ce-pas*?"

Beatrice's face was bright red. "*Non*! *Elle n'est pas folle*! Who are you women? We're grateful to you for returning our sister, but I don't like your tone."

"Look, old woman, no need to get angry." One-eyed Audelia approached Beatrice. "You should be thanking us for saving her life. We were on the other side of the cathedral when she fell, caring for another poor soul. Someone fetched us. Said it was real bad and to come quick. I got to her first. Never seen so much blood."

Catherine pushed Audelia aside and poked her finger in Beatrice's chest. "You should be on your knees right now praising God and our skills that your friend here is still breathing." She turned to her companions. "Let's go. We've done what we came to do." The three turned to leave.

Sabine grabbed Catherine's arm. "Oh, we do thank you. *Merci. Merci beaucoup*. We're upset. You can imagine how we're upset, can't you?" She reached inside the neck of her frock and pulled out her pouch. She removed a silver coin and gave it to Genevieve. "Please take this."

Genevieve took the coin and gave it to Audelia. "Hope she lives. We did our best."

Then she smiled a wide, toothless smile and laughed. "But you'd better not get caught wearing men's clothing!"

The women left with their dirty stretcher, and we tended Gertrude's wounds just as Mabille returned with Imene.

Imene didn't speak a word. We stood aside as she seemed to soar across the room to Gertrude. She tenderly kissed the bloody stump where her beloved's arm once was. In a moment Imene's entire body began to shake from head to toe. Beatrice held her tight.

Sister Lunetta went to Sabine. "You must get Gertrude out of here. Take her to your quarters. If Sister Marguerite returns, there will be too many questions. I'll help you move her. Please! We must take her now!"

Imene gathered linen, yarrow, and grapevine from the cupboard. We made a sling from the sheets on the table where Gertrude lay, and together with great effort we carried our broken sister while Sister Lunetta led the way. The angels surely tended us, for our path was made clear all the way back.

Tonight our quarters have become an infirmary. Gertrude is safe from Sister Marguerite's gaze. She is down the hall from my writing room on her cot and in need of constant care. Petronilla's rapture continues, and Marie coughs and burns with fever. We will each take a turn as we tend our sisters day and night. Sleep has never been so rare.

Cibylle has joined me. She's roaming about unable to rest. Her hands and feet are swollen, and I believe her large belly hangs lower than earlier today. She rubs her chest between her breasts and rocks from side to side, moaning softly. I must stop now and put her to bed. Perhaps a lullaby will help her find sleep.

Oh, God, where are you hiding? I pray to You though my faith is sorely tested by so many trials. Protect us from evil! Heal my sisters. Amen.

I return to the page after singing Cibylle to sleep. I went to Gertrude's bedside just now. Imene was near, gently stroking her clean, damp hair. Helvide was busy replacing the tapers.

I whispered in Gertrude's ear, "When you're better you will tell me the story of your great adventure, and I'll write about it."

She opened her left eye ever so slightly and told me, "I saw heaven from up there."

3 April 1259
Le Monastère de la Visite

The cold spring rain drips from the leak in our ceiling. Earlier today the deluge soaked my clothing while I hurried along the muddy path past the cloister garden to the infirmary for my chores. The sun hasn't shone for ten days. Heavy, gray skies reflect my somber mood.

Weariness and still more grief spill from my quill tonight. Is there no end to our suffering? I fear God has abandoned us.

Two days ago in early afternoon dark, foreboding clouds hung low on the horizon, harbingers of the oncoming storm.

"The crows are telling us to find shelter. See how they fly together in one direction, and now see how they turn and fly the other way." Ravenissa and I made our way arm in arm along the path leading to our quarters from the infirmary after our duties. A few moments of conversation, a gentle prelude before the torrent began.

"Goscelin, you must come to the barn to see our fawn. She grows stronger each day. She follows me about as if I'm her mother."

Like carefree girls we stopped to play with the young deer, all the while without our knowing Comtesse and Beatrice searched frantically for Cibylle. She'd been missing all afternoon. She had quietly slipped out the door to make her way through our yard and out the gate leading to the monastery grounds.

Marie, ill with phlegm and fever, took again to her bed three days ago. In her absence we have tried our best to look after Cibylle. The rain began as Beatrice and Comtesse at last discovered Cibylle gathering limbs and branches from the thicket that borders the eastern meadow and monastery gardens.

I made my way to our quarters from the barn only moments before they returned.

Beatrice told the story, clothes dripping and chilled to the bone just before dark. "When we found her, we were thankful no one else was nearby. God's angels must surely have protected her. She might not be so lucky if she wanders away again." She dried Cibylle's hair with a towel and removed her muddy shoes.

"*Elle est folle*!" Comtesse ranted.

Beatrice shouted. "Shhhh, Comtesse!" Then she told us what had happened.

"There she was, our Cibylle, sitting on the ground, filthy dirty, her lap full of twigs and branches. She'd sorted the branches in piles according to size. She'd placed stick upon stick, one by one in a hollowed out burrow in the earth in the shape of a big circle."

Comtesse paced about. "We've known she's mad since she first appeared during the dreadful pilgrimage. It's Petronilla's fault! If she hadn't thought Cibylle was special, surely we'd have left her on the road to Chartres. If it weren't for Petronilla's insistence, we certainly wouldn't risk certain trouble for her. She doesn't even know her own name!"

She shook her wet skirt in front of the fire, removed her cap and veil, and tossed them across the room. In that moment she appeared to be more wild and untamed than Cibylle ever was. Comtesse stomped back and forth wringing her apron. "For all we know, Petronilla is mad as well!"

Marie appeared in the doorway wrapped in a blanket. Her voice was weak.

"Petronilla's not mad, and neither is Cibylle! There's nothing wrong with either of them! Don't speak of our sisters that way! Don't you understand what Cibylle was doing today? She was building her nest!"

A hush fell upon us as Marie put her arms around Cibylle, who sat near the fire with a faraway look in her eyes.

Comtesse laughed. "What do you mean? *Making her nest?* Now you've gone mad as well! She imagines she's a bird, I suppose. Who knows what goes on in that head of hers?"

"Hush, Comtesse! What are you saying, Marie? What's this about a nest?" Beatrice asked.

"All her little shrines, all her gathering and building these past weeks…it's her way of preparing for her child. Her time is near. She's making ready," Marie whispered. She began to cough a deep, wet, rolling cough.

"To bed with you! I'll bring you mullien tea and another blanket. To bed!" Beatrice went to the table to prepare her remedy. Marie bent down and kissed the top of Cibylle's head, and then returned to her cot.

Comtesse continued to pace back and forth, talking to herself. Her tall shadow on the wall appeared to chase after her. "Making ready…making ready to deliver her child…her child…another mad one, no doubt! What will we do when there are two of them to keep hidden and care for?"

Beatrice slammed the kettle on the table. "Stop it, Comtesse! You're hurtful, not helpful. Don't think for a minute that Cibylle doesn't understand what you're saying. Where is your compassion…your charity for your sister?"

"My sister? My sister, you say! Who among you is truly my sister? Where is there compassion or charity for me? I'll tell you where it is..." Again a hush fell upon the room as Comtesse paused before continuing. "I'll tell you where I find mercy and charity and sisterhood!"

"Don't say it!" My warning fell on deaf ears.

"With the nuns!"

With her words Comtesse tore a hole in the fabric of our covenant. She pulled her cape from the hook near the hearth and fled into the stormy night, leaving the door open behind her.

No one moved or spoke for several moments while the wind blew rain into the room. Beatrice closed the door and bolted it. Silence hung in the air like a corpse swinging from a noose.

Down the hall Imene had been sitting bedside with Petronilla. She awakened suddenly and rose up on her cot like Lazarus returning from the dead. "She's coming! She's coming!" Petronilla cried out before she collapsed on the pillow.

Later the same evening after the other sisters had returned from their work, Cibylle's birthing waters gushed and her labor began. She clawed at the door. We struggled to help her understand that for the sake of all, her child must be born inside our quarters, not in the monastery garden...in the nest she had so carefully crafted. Cibylle cried out, and Helvide and Ravenissa pulled her from the door. I moved Cibylle's cot near the hearth for warmth.

Mabille went out into the rain to find a few branches and twigs. She placed the collection of damp sticks near the fire to dry them. Cibylle clapped her hands with joy and stretched out her arms to Mabille, who hurried to embrace her.

"Let's walk a bit, Cibylle. Walking will help. Come now," Imene said while she and Mabille took hold of Cibylle's arms on either side and began to walk her about the room.

Her labor was dreadful. Our sisterhood, with the exception of Marie, who had finally fallen asleep, and Comtesse, who hadn't returned, held vigil through the night. Cibylle screeched and cried out with each pain. Her shouts were so loud it became necessary to muffle her with blankets. We feared someone passing by would hear her and learn the secret we had so carefully hidden these many months.

Imene used all her midwifery skills that night. "If only Gertrude could help. We need her strength. I need her beside me."

Cibylle finally settled onto her cot near the fire. Imene placed cooked fennel and asarum in a linen cloth and applied it to Cibylle's back to ease her suffering. Dried crane's blood was mixed into a bowl of water. Imene gently applied it to Cibylle's winny. Afterwards, Imene raised her from the pillow to study her reflection in the bowl. This helped Imene know her condition more thoroughly. Later Helvide gave Imene a vial of mouse stones taken from her box of XII sacred elixirs, Myrtle's magic.

Imene was delighted. "Oh, wonderful, Sister! Wonderful! Thank you. Mouse stones are exactly what is needed." She placed the very tiny pebbles over Cibylle's navel.

I asked Imene, "Why mouse stones? How are they helpful?"

Imene explained, "When a mouse struggles to give birth, she searches for a place where there's water; then she looks for very small stones. She gathers as many stones as her throat can hold and scurries back to her hole where she spits them out. Then she breathes on the stones to warm them and gets on top of them. This makes the birth happen immediately. Afterwards she kicks the stones away. The stones, if found within the same month as they were discarded by the mouse, can be gathered and used to help a pregnant woman give birth."

I was amazed by Imene's wisdom and Helvide's medicine. "Bless you, Sisters, for the miracles of your sacred knowledge."

Imene vigorously rubbed Cibylle's legs. Hours passed. Every little while we took turns walking Cibylle about the room. Her labor and discomfort grew through the night. When Cibylle's birthing pains became worse, Imene placed her biting bar made of wood wrapped in linen between Cibylle's teeth. Cibylle bit it hard until her strength began to fade.

Mabille sang to calm her without luck. I folded blankets and placed them by the fire to warm them.

As dawn neared, Cibylle grew quiet. Her voice was all but gone from her wailing. She sat on her cot with her legs spread open. Her pains continued, but she hadn't the strength to cry out. Mabille climbed onto the cot and kneeled at her back like a big pillow.

Beatrice rubbed her belly with lavender salve, and Marie came from her sickbed to hold Cibylle's hand. Helvide heated water and prepared the necessary herbal remedies for later.

Imene raised the covers and checked the birth opening, then called out, "Sabine! Open the cupboards and the drawer in our chest; untie the knots on our aprons, and unlock the door! We must help her womb to open. Too many pains have come and gone. I've counted more than twenty. This child needs to be born…NOW!"

Sabine hurried about following Imene's instructions. Two more pains came very close together, and Cibylle, who was lying down now, too weary to respond, barely moved. Imene spread her legs wide, and the dome of the child's head appeared. Light colored hair was visible beneath the glistening, creamy veil that covered the baby's head like a cap.

"When her belly hardens, she must push with all her might," Imene told Beatrice. Beatrice's hand pressed flat upon Cibylle's belly, waiting for the sign. Mabille pulled Cibylle up from under her arms until she was sitting. She straddled her body from behind, cradling the girl into her as if she were the back of a living chair.

"Good, Mabille. It's better if she's reclining rather than flat. Lean her back a bit. There! That's it!" Imene directed.

I went around the cot, stood at Mabille's back, and pressed into her...ready to help if I was needed.

"Push, dear! Push! As if you're the Mother birthing the world! Push!" Beatrice pleaded as she felt Cibylle's belly harden like an unripe melon.

"You must push. Oh, please push hard so your baby can come to us!" Tears ran down Marie's cheeks while Cibylle squeezed her hand.

Cibylle raised her head for a moment. Her gaze fixed on Marie. She gave her best effort. All of us were pushing from somewhere inside us in response to her agony. The baby's head emerged from the womb face-down with a great gush of bright red blood.

Imene was calm. "Push, Cibylle. Push with all your might. I have hold of your baby now. Push!"

Mabille held her up from under her arms and lifted her forward. I leaned into Mabille for support. Beatrice pressed her belly, and Cibylle once again pushed until her face flushed red, then blue.

Imene held the infant's head under the chin and at the back of the neck. She pulled and guided the baby from her mother's womb into life while Beatrice pressed first one side of Cibylle's belly then the other. The shoulders appeared, and in one smooth slip the infant slid forth from her watery cocoon from the realm of spirit into the world of the flesh. The cord between mother and child was tied and severed.

The infant's shimmering, milky white body streaked with blood turned crimson as Imene cleared the birthing waters from her tiny mouth and rubbed her back. She gasped her first breath and let out a long strong cry. For one fleeting moment, laughter and tears filled the room with joy.

"A girl! Cibylle, look you have a beautiful baby girl!" Imene announced.

"Praise God!" Beatrice called out our joy.

"Praise God!" We echoed, as we crossed ourselves.

Imene passed the baby to Beatrice. She swaddled her in a warm blanket; then she turned round to put her into Cibylle's arms.

Cibylle's face was illumined by her wide smile. Later we all agreed in that moment we witnessed a flash of golden light streak across her face, a portent of what was about to happen.

Mabille, still crouched on the cot behind Cibylle, raised her up. The new mother outstretched her arms to eagerly receive her baby. In that very instant, a dark shadow passed over her face, snuffing the light that shone so brightly a moment before. Her smile became an ugly grimace.

"No! Oh, dear God! No! No! No!" Imene was looking at the bedclothes.

An unholy river of crimson blood poured like a flood from our dear sister's loins. Cibylle looked down at what was happening to her with a look of amazement. Her eyes turned to her baby, and she tried once more to reach for her. Sabine quickly put the baby into her arms.

Imene grabbed a blanket and stuffed it into Cibylle's winny. The bloody river continued to flow, and the blanket turned red in the time it takes to draw a breath. All color left Cibylle's face. Her spirit departed her body in one long whisper. Our beloved sister died in Mabille's arms while her infant wailed an orphan's cry.

No one moved except Sabine. She lifted the child from Cibylle's arms.

"She's gone. She's gone. Her baby…we must tend her baby," Sabine whispered.

The sweet scent of roses in full bloom filled the air. It seemed to come from the baby, or perhaps Cibylle. Before I could ask the others about the fragrance, it faded away.

I filled a basin with warm water for the child's first bath. Sabine removed the blanket and gently placed the sleepy infant into the water. The baby began to wail. We gathered 'round her. Sabine said the words.

"I baptize you as a child of God. You are Christ's own and a member of our family. I baptize you in the name of Jesus...You are a beloved child of God...The Holy Ghost's blessing be upon you."

Sabine dipped her finger in lavender oil and made a tiny cross on the baby's little forehead between her close-set eyes. The infant ceased crying.

"Here...we must put a bit of honey on her palate to insure her appetite for the sweetness of life." Beatrice squeezed the baby's perfect, round mouth open to place a dab of golden honey on her tongue with her little finger.

Petronilla suddenly appeared. She looked radiant and well in her long white nightclothes, as she glided towards Cibylle's body, like an apparition floating in a dream. "She's at peace. She's with the angels now," she said softly.

Imene gulped through great, heaving sobs. The precious presence she had worked so hard to care for throughout the night was lifeless. The body appeared to have drowned in a sea of blood. Cibylle's gaze was fixed upward. Sabine crossed herself before reaching down to close her eyes. Mabille slowly untangled herself from Cibylle. Helvide removed the blood-soaked blanket from between Cibylle's legs.

"There was nothing I could do. Hemorrhage is the most unthinkable...There was nothing I could do," Imene whispered through her sobs.

Gertrude entered the room and sat down by Imene. "You mustn't blame yourself. God calt her. Dee angels come for her. Dare's no stoppink dee hour of one's death." Gertrude kissed Imene's cheek.

Beatrice went to Marie, who hadn't moved or made a sound. With Beatrice's touch, Marie's wailing began. She nestled her close. I prayed aloud.

"Merciful, Beloved. Bless her. Open the gates of paradise and welcome our sister, Cibylle. Comfort us in our grief, Beloved, comfort us."

"Comfort us. Amen," all responded.

"Her name is Grace," Petronilla announced. Sabine lifted the infant from the bath, wrapped her in a blanket, and passed her to Petronilla.

"Our little sister of Belle Cœur. We must care for her. She's one of us...but she's not like us. As she grows you will come to understand." Petronilla spoke in riddles.

"What are you saying, Sister? What do you mean, she's not like us?" Sabine asked.

"I can't say more. This is not a night for questions or explanations. Come now. Each of us must give her our blessing."

Around the room little Grace traveled, safe in the crook of Petronilla's arm. One by one we made the sign of Belle Cœur on her tiny forehead, then sealed it with a kiss. Meanwhile, Grace seemed to be blessing each of us with her peaceful presence. When my turn came to offer the blessing, the infant gazed into my eyes with certainty and understanding. I saw wisdom, Holy Wisdom there inside her.

"The Mother's daughter has arrived in the world through Cibylle. She carries the first knowledge, the secrets of Eden." Petronilla spoke slowly, as though she were awakening from a dream.

Questions filled my head and danced on my tongue. Perhaps the others were also curious, but Petronilla had said it was not a time for questions. No one spoke.

Marie's wailing became sobbing. Beatrice patted her gently, then rose and went to Petronilla to give Grace her blessing and her first feeding. "Give her to me," she said as she removed her stained apron, untied the front of her dress, and removed her swollen, leaking breast. She sat down, and Petronilla placed Grace in Beatrice's arms. Gently she jostled her tiny feet. She placed her littlest finger between the infant's plump lips. "Come on now. Grab on."

After several moments of Beatrice's teasing with her finger, the child began to suckle. "Here you are, *ma cherie.* I have what you need." She removed her finger and settled the child against her full breast, using her free hand to guide the brown, wet nipple into Grace's bud of a mouth. After several attempts the baby took hold. "Ahhh. That's it. If only your sweet mother could have done this for you instead of me." Beatrice's tears fell like an anointing on the baby's head.

Sabine was anxious. She paced about. "Bar the door, close the cupboard, and lock the shutters. We must seal Grace in our protection. Pray she's a quiet child so she's not discovered."

In our grief we began to restore order to our surroundings. Gertrude whispered in Imene's ear.

"Come with me, Mabille," Imene said. The two went outside. Soon they returned carrying a beautiful wooden cradle.

"Dis ist mina gift for little Grace. It need a goot polishing." Gertrude smiled.

"She finished building it just before her accident," Imene said as she began to polish the cradle. An angel with wide wings was carved into the wood at the head. The rockers were carved with birds and roses in full bloom.

Soon Helvide and Imene lined the cradle with a warm blanket. Imene tore wide strips of linen, then took the contented infant from Beatrice. She swaddled her tight and laid her in Gertrude's cradle.

All became quiet and still. Grace slept. Others of us cleaned up the remains from the birth, the bloody linens and all. Marie and Mabille cocooned Cibylle's body in a blanket. Only her face was exposed. Her features seemed strangely different, like the figures and faces I'd fashioned from candle wax. Death's gray pallor colored her with emptiness. Her lips were blue. We joined hands and gathered around. Our tears spilled over her.

"We'll put you to rest tonight, dear Cibylle. Your baby is in good care. Don't worry. We'll shield her and care for her. Rest well, our beloved Sister," Sabine whispered through her tears.

Dark circles framed her eyes, and her hand trembled while she stammered our instructions.

"We must go to the infirmary. It's late. Sister Marguerite will be looking for me…for all of us. She knows Marie and Cibylle…I mean, Marie and Petronilla have been ill. She won't expect them. I hope Ravenissa is there; she's supposed to help with the washing this morning. Imene, you must rest. I will make some excuse for you. Beatrice, you are needed by Sister Claudine in the kitchen. Mabille, you come with me. Goscelin, you won't go to the infirmary until tonight. Whom I forgetting?"

"I will stay till midafternoon then I must go to the sacristy," Imene said.

Helvide rocked the cradle gently. "I'll be along soon. I'll care for Grace till Beatrice returns. Please make an excuse for me as well…to Sister Marguerite, Sabine."

"I'll help. I can look after her," I said.

"No, Goscelin, you must record the story of what has happened. Begin now."

"But I fear I'm so tired I won't…" I argued.

"Nonsense! All of us are weary. No excuses, Goscelin. You must write it all down and soon. Who knows how much longer before…" Truly, Sabine was not herself. Her whole body appeared to shiver.

"She's right, Goscelin. You must capture the story," Petronilla instructed.

"All right. I'll begin, but I'm not sure…" My throat tightened, and tears burned my eyes at the sight of Cibylle so cold and pale.

"I am here," Gertrude said. "I vill help tend de baby, and I vill call for help, if I need it. I can still be useful. You go now, Helvide. So no one suspect sumpting."

Beatrice broke pieces of bread for each of us from what remained of the previous day's loaf; muttering a blessing, she doled out breakfast. We ate the bread, but there was no milk, only water from the crock.

Beatrice said, "I'll feign illness later this morning so I may leave the kitchen and return to feed little Grace. Fetch me if she awakens sooner, Goscelin. Stand in the garden outside the kitchen as a signal. I'll keep watch if you should come. May God give us the strength to get through this day."

"Where do we suppose Comtesse has been all night?" I asked.

"Keep the door bolted at all times. Make sure you know who is there before you open it. Go now, Goscelin, stop fretting about Comtesse. You must scribe the story while it's fresh. Off with you!" Sabine snapped as she reached for her cape.

She took hold of the latch then stopped and turned to all of us. We watched as she dropped to her knees. She drew a deep breath, then began to wail and sob without stopping. She twisted her apron and tore her cap and veil from her head.

"It's…too much! Too much! Cibylle…gone… taken from us forever…and now this helpless infant we must care for…the endless demands from Sister

Marguerite. No rest...no beauty...no peace! I can't hold us together any longer. I'm tired of being responsible and brave...God has abandoned us, I fear. Perhaps Comtesse is right."

"What do you mean? What are you saying, Sister?" Beatrice tried to comfort her.

"What if we've gone against God's desires? Our life and our ways...we *are* living outside the Church. Perhaps we're being punished!" Sabine's words struck the room with silence.

We looked 'round at each other; then all eyes fell on Petronilla.

She calmly made her way to Sabine, who was still in a heap on the floor near the door. Her long, white gown revealed the slender shadow of her body through the sheer linen. She squatted down and took Sabine's hands in hers. "Sister, dear Sister, God has not abandoned us, nor have we disobeyed our Creator. We are in God's favor, I assure you. Our purpose and mission are different from the others, but no less important. The prophecy must be fulfilled. Our wisdom, our ways...our sacred life arts must be protected and preserved for those who will follow." Petronilla wiped Sabine's face with her nightclothes.

Sabine sniffed and replied between sobs, "I'm tired. I'm so very tired. Look at her, look at our dear Cibylle so cold and pale. I know in my heart what you say is true, Petronilla, but I don't know if I have the strength to go on." She leaned her head against the door.

"I'll go to the infirmary for you," Mabille said as she reached for her cape. "Let me take care of Sister

Marguerite's demands. I know what to do. You stay here and rest, Sabine. Please let me do this for you."

"No. No. I'll be all right. It's better if I go. I'm the only one who knows what's needed." Sabine tried to stand. She wiped her face with the back of her hand then put her cap and veil in place. Petronilla helped her from the floor.

"I think Mabille has a good idea, Sister. You need to rest," Beatrice said.

"No, it's better this way. My weariness is not the kind that sleep will rid. Only God's peace will refresh me. Perhaps, I'll find God's peace in my work today. I've lost God's peace, and only grace will return it to me."

After Sabine left for the infirmary and everyone had scattered to the various duties, I welcomed the sunlight as the day continued.

Petronilla returned to her bed. Gertrude and Mabille stayed near Grace. I disobeyed Sabine's instructions to begin the story. Instead I helped Imene and Marie prepare Cibylle's body for burial. We removed the blanket and bathed her corpse with rosemary water. We were careful to wash all the dried blood from every limb and orifice. As we went about our final act of love for Cibylle, I pondered the doubts Sabine had spoken during her collapse. I prayed to God that her doubts would not become mine.

When Cibylle was clean, Marie, who couldn't stop crying, anointed her forehead, mouth, chest, and feet with lavender oil. Imene and I followed in turn. Imene offered the prayer through her tears.

"Beloved, we pray Cibylle is welcomed into Your heavenly realm with all the saints and angels. We sing praises for the miracle she delivered, for your mercy, and for eternal life. Amen and amen."

Imene went to the cradle. Very carefully she cut a few hairs from the baby's head with a small knife. It was then that she noticed the heart-shaped blue marking on the scalp behind the infant's left ear.

"Look at this!" Imene pointed to the mark. "In all my years of midwifery, I've never seen a mark like this."

I went to see. It was strange. A perfect little blue heart, as though someone had made an illumination there behind her tiny ear.

Imene placed the snippets of hair in Cibylle's left palm, then carefully folded her stiffening fingers to hold them tight for all eternity. Before we wrapped her body in a linen shroud, we sprinkled rosemary and lady's thistle upon her and kissed her on the lips. Imene folded her arms across her chest.

"Oh, how I shall miss you…" Marie's grief broke open in great, gulping sobs.

We bound Cibylle's body with wide strips of linen, then wrapped it in wider layers of the same. While I wound the linen 'round Cibylle's ankles, I reflected how strange it is that when we die we are swaddled in linen, and the same is true soon after we are born. The light of the world awaits us when we pass through our mothers' wombs into life, and God's light is there when we return to heaven's gate. The light is present at our beginning and our ending.

The sun rose, streaming a golden glow to break the darkness of the past weeks. There was a quality to the light the first morning of Grace's life that caused everything to shimmer, as though dusted with hope.

Late in the morning Grace began to fuss. Within moments Beatrice knocked at the door. She rushed in, removing her cape and her apron, which was soaked with milk from her leaking breasts. She nursed little Grace then returned to her duties. The baby slept while afternoon arrived, and shadows danced upon the floor like playful children. Later Beatrice returned to feed her again.

Imene, Petronilla, Marie, and I carried Cibylle's shrouded body to the long table near the hearth. We surrounded her with candles. Marie took Grace from the cradle and rocked her beside Cibylle's corpse. We prayed over our sister until dusk.

I went to my cot to rest before it was time to go to the infirmary for night duties. Sleep came quickly, and so did a dream. In the dream there was a fire in the middle of town. Many people were shouting and gathering around the fire. There was a terrible smell and thick, black smoke. Men dressed in black stood on a scaffold to one side of the fire. One of them held a cross on a long pole. In the dream I was weeping. When I awoke my tears were real.

Never had I been so tired. The voices of my sisters as they returned one by one throughout the early evening carried down the hall. I stumbled from my bed to join them.

Beatrice returned once again, just in time to feed hungry Grace, who had begun to cry. Sabine arrived soon after, appearing more exhausted than ever. We were silent, except for the baby, who made little squeaks and occasionally let out a bleat like a newborn lamb. We made sure to comfort her quickly, lest someone should pass by our gate to hear her cry.

"I can't believe she's gone from us." Ravenissa had learned of Cibylle's death and the birth of Grace from Sabine while they worked in the infirmary. She cried softly, speaking in a whisper while she stood near Cibylle's body on the table. Later she went to the cradle and gently patted Grace. "Joy and tragedy, in the same moment...in one day's time. It's too much for the heart to hold."

I pulled my cape about me and prepared to walk the muddy trail to the infirmary to begin my night duties. My stomach growled with hunger.

Sabine took hold of my arm as I was leaving. "You must know that our friend, blessed Sister Lunetta, offered us a warning today. She told me she over heard Sister Marguerite in conversation with visiting churchmen this morning. Sister Marguerite told them that two nuns discovered several 'pagan shrines' made of sticks and branches near the woods. She assured the men she will be 'on the look out for the unsaved souls who made such nonsense.' You must be careful, Goscelin. Whatever you do, don't inquire about Comtesse."

Throughout the night, I carried out my duties, free of the disgust and revulsion that usually plagued me. Cibylle's spirit was near when I cleaned maggots from the infected leg of a young man, and emptied the chamber pots of contents too vile to name.

I held Cibylle's memory in my heart like a prayer. She had given us the child marked with the blue heart of Holy Wisdom. Hope and wisdom are our blessing. Hope and wisdom live in the spirit of Belle Cœur.

I made my way back to our quarters some time before dawn. Soon Ravenissa and Helvide returned from their difficult task. They had dug Cibylle's grave by lamplight. The others, I was told, spent the evening sharing their stories of Cibylle and praying 'round her body.

Beatrice sent me to the cellar to fetch ale to warm Ravenissa and Helvide. I lifted the door in the floor under the table where Cibylle lay. The light from my candle wasn't bright enough to scare away the vermin, and for fear of waking Grace I didn't clang warning with the spoon and tin.

The stone stairway was uneven and slippery. The cellar was dank and smelled of earth and the root vegetables stored there. I hurried to collect the jug of ale from the dusty shelf while I heard rats scrambling nearby. Shivers went through me, and I thought of sweet Cibylle's body that would soon be put in the cold, damp ground to become a feast for maggots and worms.

"It's a good place we've chosen, but we'll have to bring her body in the cart," Ravenissa reported when I returned. "It's too far to carry her. We must leave soon while everyone is still before the bells for prayer."

"I'll stay with Grace," Beatrice offered. "In case she grows hungry. I'll join you in prayer…from here." She argued with Marie, who begged to attend prayers at the grave. "I shouldn't let you go. You've been ill for days."

Marie pleaded, "I'll never be with her again. Please, Grand-mere."

Finally Marie won. Beatrice covered Marie's cape with a blanket and tied a scrap of wool around her head for extra warmth.

Petronilla joined us, pale as ever, but she appeared well enough to take part. Comtesse had not been seen or heard from since she had left in the storm the night of Grace's birth.

Several of us placed Cibylle's body on the same cart that had months earlier carried our belongings from Belle Cœur. Ravenissa and Helvide pulled the cart. We dared not use the goat to pull it for fear she would startle or bleat and awaken someone. The rest of us followed along behind just as we had on pilgrimage. I carried only one small lantern lest we be noticed while I fervently prayed for our safety all the way to Cibylle's grave.

Our sister was laid to rest as early spring snow began to fall. We covered her grave with leaves and our prayers.

In among the leaves, I discovered a coquille shell, a marker for pilgrimage, no doubt dropped by a wandering pilgrim long ago. I placed it atop the grave as an amulet for Cibylle's journey to paradise. Mabille whispered her poem before we left Cibylle's spirit to God and her body to the earth.

Cibylle, wan and fair of face,
sweet waif who bore the child Grace,
too soon you leave us,
too soon you go,
your sisters now left to their woe.

What is the secret you embraced?
Now lost to us.
Time does erase.
In your death you hold it close.
Oh, dear sister, share it, spill it!
From the grave send us your truth.
Your hidden holiness reveals
a child who comes to break the seal.

The babe you bore will thrive and grow.
Surely your secret she will show.
Your mystery lives on!
Who begat her?
What man…what boy was he who planted seed
in your womb to bring forth the child Grace?
She now blesses us with light.

Oh, how like Mother Mary, you.
Oh, how this child's birth, like few.
Like Jesus's coming…a mystery.
Perhaps she is He returned again in woman's form
to give the world a song to sing
to open hearts in sweet remembering.

My hand cramps from so much scribing. The north wind blows cold tonight as winter turns to spring.

We are grabbed by grief's icy hand while Cibylle's body rests in the earth beneath the lacy blanket of the year's last snowfall. She is buried with her secrets. May her spirit visit us in our dreams where we might hear the sweet timbre of her voice at last freed from muteness.

I think of Henriette but I no longer reach for her. Oh, how her dear comforting presence would bless me tonight.

29 April 1259
Le Monastère de la Visite

Oh, joy! Oh, blessed reunion! Mabille and I went to Cibylle's grave today just before daybreak. We were careful not to be noticed. We went to put a stone at the place where Cibylle's head rests beneath the earth. As we approached in the faint light of the new day, I stopped in my tracks. There was a beautiful bouquet of dried rosemary and lavender tied with wood-vine placed carefully on the grave and there...resting atop the herbs...was Henriette!!

My heart leapt at the sight of her. I grabbed her up. She appeared clean and fresh, as though she'd been scrubbed while she was away.

"Where have you been? You must have stories to tell me." I wept at the sight of her as I sniffed her for clues of her journey and pressed her to my heart.

"Such a happy discovery, Goscelin! How do you suppose she got here and who left the bouquet?" Mabille asked.

"Perhaps Helvide delivered the herbs, but I can't imagine how Henriette came to be here. Why would she be on Cibylle's grave? Oh, I don't know...or care... how she's appeared like this. I'm just so very happy to have her back again."

I put her in my apron pocket and as much as she has protected me through the years, I now feel as though I am *her* fierce protector.

"I'll never lose you again, I promise, Henriette. We will always stay close to one another. Always!"

I have asked Helvide and the others if they placed the bouquet or surprised me with the return of Henriette. The story astonished them and no one had an answer.

2 May 1259
Le Monastère de la Visite

A month has nearly passed since Cibylle's death and Comtesse's leaving. Strangely, none of us have seen her at all during this time. Surely, she must be enjoying her life with the nuns, but she didn't even say goodbye. I wonder... No, I can't wonder about Comtesse. It hurts too much. I choose to scribe about the blessing of Gertrude's condition.

She is healing well, albeit slowly, without infection. It's still startling to catch sight of her missing arm. She's told us that often she feels a terrible pain, as if her lost arm remains connected to her body. Imene's constant care has surely brought her 'round again. Her wound is red and continues to ooze clear liquid with a faint metallic odor. Imene assures her this is not unusual.

Our brave sister demands to be useful. It's difficult to watch her struggle as she tends the hearth and fills the bucket from the well with one arm. She refuses assistance. Soon after her accident, she assured us she didn't want to be mothered or fussed over. Every day she shouts out in the tongue of her homeland how she must do things for herself. "*Ich muss es selbst tun*!"

Her strength and carpentry skills still burn inside her bones. Knowing Gertrude's determination I'm sure she'll find a way to use her gifts once again. In accordance with Dominions and Graces, fire is her element. She has survived a great calamity, and surely God will reveal new purpose for her wisdom and craft.

In many ways Gertrude's misfortune has taken a greater toll on Imene. She told me two days ago while we tidied the sleeping room, "I'm unable to pray. Mercifully, God spared her life, but I'm so afraid there will be a next time and I might lose her. My heart longs for God's presence, but I feel nothing other than fear."

I shared with her that I, too, had been feeling as if something within my soul had died or been severed, like Gertrude's arm. However, as much as Imene is unable to pray, I find I must

continue my prayers. Surely they will eventually fall on God's ear. I believe the Beloved hears me but is hiding, which means I must seek and pray even more fervently.

The memory of the dreadful night when I was attacked still plagues my mind. One faint scar on my neck remains as an outward reminder. The assault of my spirit will take longer to heal.

Sorrow covers us like a blanket. It's impossible to chase away the gruesome and troubling memories of Cibylle's hemorrhage, Gertrude's tragedy, and my rape. In my thoughts the scenes from the past several months return time and again. Each unexpected and startling appearance of unwelcomed recollection leaves me breathless and shaken.

We always did our best to keep Cibylle hidden when she lived. Now, in death, she is forever safe from those who would mistake her holiness for madness.

Baby Grace is more difficult to hide. Her plaintive, healthy cry is no doubt the lament of the spirit newly arrived to the body. The little one's discomfort causes me to wonder if when the soul is forged with the flesh there is actual pain, until the two fully merge together in time.

Sometimes, to my ear, her forlorn whimpering is her spirit's cry from the loss of her mother. Meanwhile, Ravenissa tends Grace's every need with love and devotion. To our amazement, Ravenissa's breasts filled with milk soon after Grace was born. She is now the infant's soothie, comforter, and guardian. Beatrice sometimes nurses Grace when Ravenissa is tending the animals. But Ravenissa's heart is tied to the baby in a most surprising way... *Ravenissa's way* usually reserved for her animals. Our sisterhood affirmed by hanswere, after Ravenissa requested to be the one responsible for Grace's care and upbringing, that she should serve as her earthly mother.

Whenever I hold Grace, I feel both hopeful and terrified. She is so perfect and so fresh from heaven. Her plump round face and clear deep blue eyes are illuminated by a slight halo of golden hair. Grace is the living promise of new life and new wisdom, while the world around her grow ever darker and more dangerous.

I record in Dominions and Graces:

Grace is air and breath. Her innocence radiates all that is pristine and full of assurance that God is real and present.

Two days ago, in my arid state, I could not have written the words *God is real and present* with conviction. My fearful heart was frozen by my armor of protection. Then last night, I suddenly felt called to tell the sacred story of my vision. In the telling, the armor I had carefully placed in protection of my heart seemed to melt away.

In the evening some of us gathered near the hearth while we folded linen bandages. I looked 'round our small circle at the weary, grief-stained faces of my sisters. Petronilla, pale and terribly thin, meticulously folded each turn of the linen in her lap while she hummed a melancholy tune.

Ravenissa stroked her mouse, then dropped him by his tail into her apron pocket. She sat quietly and began to weave a basket from her nearby pile of twigs and small branches, the remnants from Cibylle's shrines. Bit by bit, as she wove her creation with thin strips of wood vine, the square basket took form.

Two of her cats curled at Ravenissa's feet atop her scuffed and dirty shoes. Their purring complimented Petronilla's melody.

Beatrice's soft, round body rested on the long bench beside Sabine, her bosom heaving up and down like a blacksmith's bellows with each breath. Our beloved cook's hands were raw and red, the same overworked hands that knead prayers into our daily bread.

How will we find the time for you to learn to read, dear Beatrice? I long for you to have your secret heart's desire.

Sabine fumbled with a piece of linen, unfolding and refolding it several times with difficulty. She studied Petronilla's method carefully and copied every motion. I searched my memory to recall when Sabine first exchanged her gentle, happy smile for the constant frown that now lived on her forehead. The wrinkles above her brow made her appear older than thirty years.

Marie sat on the floor near Beatrice's feet. She stared into the flames and rocked to and fro as Cibylle used to do. She often awakes in the night sobbing and crying until one of us comforts her.

Thoughts tumbled in my head as I looked about me. Comtesse. Earlier in the day Sister Lunetta had reported to Imene that Comtesse was safe and with the nuns, but that was all she could say.

The pitiful sight of Marie rocking back and forth made the memory of Cibylle alive with new meaning. I could no longer contain my dread.

"I sense something happened to Cibylle like what happened to me," I blurted out.

"What do you mean?" Petronilla asked.

"Beatrice, remember when I returned home that early morning after he…after I was attacked? Don't you recall how Cibylle helped you tend my wounds? The look in her eyes told me she understood all too clearly what had been done to me." My hands trembled as I talked about that time.

Beatrice stood and patted my shoulder. She doddered to the other side of the table, where her basket of vegetables was waiting, and drew her big knife from her apron pocket. She removed the long, leather sleeve and began to fiercely chop a fat carrot into little rounds.

"Yes, I remember but I saw something different. I don't believe she had suffered an attack, the same as you, Sister. I believe Cibylle was a healer with extraordinary gifts though we never fully realized the truth of who she was. She was wiser than her odd appearance would have us know. Perhaps her strange look was God's way of disguising her gifts. She was a girl who understood…you know…the way of creation… the way all things connect one to another. Oh, how I miss her sweet presence." She stopped chopping and crossed herself.

Marie's voice was still raspy from her illness. She was wrapped in a blanket near the fire. Her rocking ceased, and she spoke in a whisper.

"Her shrines were more than just a game she played. I know for certain they were important because she took so much care when she built them. I don't think anything bad had happened to her. God wanted Cibylle to have Grace. That's how Grace was born. Grace is a miracle. A miracle of Holy Love for the world."

Everyone stopped what they were doing. All eyes gazed at Marie. No one spoke. Beatrice dropped her knife on the table. Petronilla stopped humming, and a wide smile crossed her face. The only movement in the room was the flickering of the fire and the dancing shadows on the walls.

Several moments passed while we took in the full meaning of Marie's proclamation. Her affirmation of Petronilla's announcement, at the moment the baby was given her name, soon after her birth, filled the room with momentary joy.

Soon Grace broke our silence. She bleated out a hearty cry of hunger. Ravenissa went to the cradle, dried her, and put the infant to her breast. Marie left us and returned to her cot, the way an oracle who has completed her oraculation retreats to her cave.

Beatrice sighed when she noticed Ravenissa's contentment as she nursed Grace. "Ahhhh. There's nothing like having a baby at the breast, is there, dear?"

Ravenissa stroked Grace's round, rosy cheek while the little one made sweet, sucking sounds. "I love her. I never dreamed it possible to love a human so much."

Early evening settled in like a welcomed guest. Helvide and Mabille returned from the infirmary bringing the chilly breeze when they came through the door. I added wood to the fire.

Petronilla lit more candles and reflected. "Love is the most potent blessing, Ravenissa. You've fallen in love with little Grace. Oh, how I miss Guy. It's been two years since I last saw him and weeks since he's come to me in my dreams. I haven't a thought of where he might be. It's unclear if he's alive or dead."

Beatrice took handfuls of carrots and potatoes from the heavy board on the table and dropped them into the kettle. She poked the fire with a long stick. "He'll return all right, *ma cherie.* God hears our prayers for his safety."

Again we were silent. Gertrude and Imene joined us from the sleeping room. Imene fetched her jar of lavender oil, grapevine ashes, and wine from the cupboard near where Beatrice was cooking. Gertrude sat at the far end of the table. Imene went to her, kissed her forehead, and then gently unwound the bandages from Gertrude's stump.

Her stump was just that, a stump of gnarled flesh. The tear was not clean. White bone poked through red flesh. It was impossible to imagine how she had survived her terrible fall. My dark curiosity wanted to ask what it had felt like when her arm tore away from her body after being caught between the stones, but I dared not.

I watched Imene cleanse the wound. Her touch was gentle and tender; with one eye on Gertrude's face she watched for the grimace and gnashing of teeth as warning to be even more gentle, more tender. She applied her medicines and then carefully wound clean linens around the stump. When she was finished, she kissed Gertrude's forehead once more before she put away her medicines.

Gertrude smiled. I was witness to healing happening before my eyes. Gertrude's answer to her call to help build the cathedral had come with a price. It had claimed a piece of her. I wonder, was the loss of her arm meant as punishment, or was it a strange honoring for our dear Gertrude? Did the cathedral take away the arm that wielded hammer and chisel to chastise her for doing the work that only men are permitted to do? Or did the great church, like a holy lion, want to savor the flesh of the fine woman who broke the rules to follow God's call to her soul? Perhaps the cathedral reached out to catch her as she fell. Perhaps the cathedral broke her fall and saved her life. Perhaps afterward, all the builders' hacking and scrubbing didn't wash away every remnant of her precious blood and bone caught in those stones. What if a piece of her remains there? Forever caught in the crevices, our Gertrude's flesh might always be a part of Our Lady's earthly shrine.

Unexpectedly, my memory of the first night at the cathedral rushed into my mind and heart. Without warning, I heard a voice inside my head give clear instruction: *Tell your story. It's time, Goscelin. Tell your story.*

Instantly the full recollection of my blessing from Jesus filled my being. My body tingled at the thought of His touch, just as it had that mysterious night. Without hesitation I began to speak, though I felt as if someone were speaking for me.

"I have a story to share tonight, Sisters. I've been carrying it since we first arrived at the cathedral. It's important to share it with you now. May I?"

Their eyes turned toward me, and they smiled while their hands patted their hearts in agreement. I reached into my pocket for Henriette's soft reassuring presence. I held her tightly all through the telling of my story.

I'm not certain exactly how the words came to express my vision, my blessed encounter with Jesus. I only know I began the story with how I had witnessed the cathedral roof open wide. I went on to tell how I'd found myself on a journey that delivered me to the place where I met the shepherd boy. My tears spilled out when I recounted my arrival at the hillside where Jesus was healing the sick. Then I followed the thread to the moment when He touched me and gave me His blessing. When I'd finished, I didn't know how long I'd been speaking. No one responded. I looked around the room at my sisters, who stared at me without expression. I thought I must have been sorely mistaken to tell them.

In the next moment Sabine patted her heart; the others followed.

"Why have you waited so long to share your vision with us, Goscelin?" Sabine asked.

Beatrice wiped her eyes. "Oh, Sister, your story lifts my weary soul tonight. Thank you."

"I had to wait," I explained. "I had to wait to share this until God had fermented the gift within my spirit like fine wine. I was guided to tell you tonight because we…because I…need to remember that Jesus heals all wounds. *He* is our great physician who comforts our grief, mends our brokenness, and restores our flesh."

While I was speaking about Jesus, I suddenly felt inspired to go to Gertrude. My hands reached out to her, and without thought I placed them near her wound and closed my eyes. Heat poured from the center of my hands while in my mind I was back on the hillside while Jesus laid His hands on me. Again, I have no recollection of time, only that eventually my mind cleared and my hands grew cool again. I removed them from Gertrude's body.

She sat quietly with her eyes closed. When she opened them, she smiled and gently rubbed her freshly bandaged wound. "*Danke, Schwester.* I'm tankful for your story. You bring me hope vit your visdom und healing vit your touch." Gertrude stood and hugged me with her strong arm.

"We thank Jesus for the healing, Sister. We are all healers for one another…through Him." I turned to my sisters. "There's more. I must show you something."

On our pilgrimage I had told a story or two about Dominions and Graces, but now it was time to show my sisters a copy of the sacred texts.

I fetched Volume III, *Fire*, from under my cot. This singular manuscript was my subject for the night, chosen simply because it was the first of the four books I reached for. Once again I became the teacher.

We discussed the properties of fire, with its puzzling potential to both purify and destroy. I passed the volume so each sister could see the illumination of the brown dragon breathing long, crimson flames upon the land. Sabine turned the page so they could see my little illumination of a hearth, not unlike ours at Belle Cœur.

"You did this, Sister? How could you keep this hidden from us for so long?" Beatrice asked. "God has surely put a gift in your spirit, dear Goscelin. My, oh my. Such a gift you have."

I thanked them for their compliments, remembering Sabine's teaching to never deny the gifts God puts into us before we're born. Then I read to them.

Fire. The Holy Fire of the Spirit, the spark of the fire of Creation that lives in every soul. Fire, the element that warms, purifies, melds, and transforms lead into gold.

My sisters asked many questions about Brother Paul and my time at the abbey. While I shared what I'd learned and relived my blessing from Jesus, I felt the closed places of my heart begin to open. Not since before the terrifying night in the scriptorium had I felt my soul breathe so deeply. The river within my spirit, the surging flow that connected me to God, had frozen solid with fear from Brother Gilles's violence. Only briefly one night in the infirmary had I been relieved of the *ennui* of my spirit that weighed so heavily. Now, as I remembered Jesus's words and reentered the holy river of God's love, the core of my being began to thaw. The waters of peace and solace flowed once more and I, too, received healing that night.

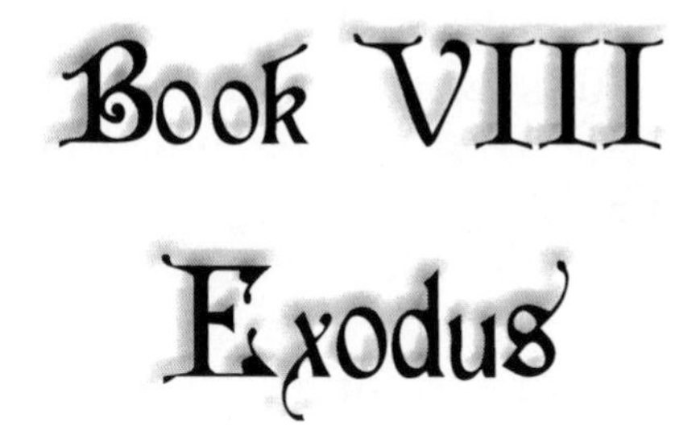

Book VIII
Exodus

3 May 1259
Le Monastère de la Visite

Yesterday's lovely reverie was fleeting. When it was nearly time for supper, to everyone's surprise Comtesse returned.

Sabine's look of dismay when she came through the door spoke for all of us.

Comtesse appeared bedraggled and tired, and I was certain I saw her limp ever so slightly.

"Hello, Sisters."

"Where have you been all this time?" Sabine asked.

"At the monastery, of course." Comtesse hung her cloak on a peg by the door.

"Doing what?"

"Whatever's asked of me...Why are you questioning me this way?"

"Don't you think your behavior is worthy of questions, Sister? You've been away for a month's time without telling us of your whereabouts or your reason for leaving. Now you're back as if nothing is the matter."

"I felt it was time to return, that's all. I told you. There was much for me to do at the monastery. I'm very tired. Please leave me be."

"We need to talk this through, Comtesse. We were all concerned about you."

"Well, no one came looking for me, did they?"

"We asked about you. You're the one who left us, as I recall. You chose to leave."

"Yes, I did and for good reason...Oh, what's the use of it? I'm so very tired. We'll talk later." Her eyes were full of tears.

Sabine and Beatrice exchanged looks.

"Very well. You do look exhausted. But you must explain your absence after dinner. You owe us your story." Sabine left the room, and silence fell over us.

Beatrice set the plates. Helvide filled the kettle. Comtesse muttered to herself and carelessly spilled a pitcher of milk on the table.

Beatrice snapped, "Oh, do be careful! Why are you so nervous? Your hands are shaking. What's the matter with you?"

"Nothing's wrong with me! Why does everyone always think something is wrong with me? I told you I'm tired. Don't you ever feel tired?" Comtesse shouted.

"What's that bruise on your neck?"

"I don't know what you're talking about."

"Never mind, it's getting late. Sisters…come to the table!"

With Beatrice's call to supper came a loud knock on the door.

The voice shouted from outside. "Let me in! It's Sister Marguerite! Let me in now!"

Ravenissa grabbed Grace from her cradle and rushed to my writing room to hide. Helvide shoved the cradle in the corner, out of sight, then opened the door.

"Where is she?!" Sister Marguerite shouted, pushing Helvide aside.

"Who?" Sabine asked.

"The child, of course!" Sister Marguerite's rage flew about the room like a wild bird trapped in a very small cage. "I know she's here. Where have you hidden her?" She shoved her way past us and made haste to the sleeping room. We ran after her.

Sister Marguerite hurried about. She looked behind the cupboard and furnishings. Then Grace began to cry, and the nun turned on her heel and followed the sound down the hallway. Her cloak trailed behind her like an ominous cloud. She pounded on the door of my writing room then tried the latch. There was no lock. She burst in and went straight to the corner in the direction of the cries. There she found Ravenissa huddled with Grace clutched to her chest. The baby continued to bawl while all of us stood by helpless.

Sister Marguerite laughed and shrieked. "Aha! I knew it!"

Ravenissa stammered, "She was abandoned at our doorstep…I'm her soothie…her wet nurse." Her lie dangled about like a worm on a hook. Sister Marguerite didn't take the bait.

We gathered close around Ravenissa and Grace as one protective body. Then we closed in on Sister Marguerite. She was forced to move backwards through the door of the writing room and down the hall. When we arrived at the hearth, she unfurled her wrath.

"That idiot girl you kept hidden away…that hideous creature that you called one of your own died giving birth, didn't she? You want me to believe she ran away. Such lies. She was the child's mother! Do you think I'm a fool? I've been watching you. It's plain as can be. The devil is in that child." Her eyes darted to meet Comtesse's gaze straight on. Comtesse quickly looked around the room at all of us.

"It's clear, you pathetic women have been playing with the devil," Sister Marguerite continued. "The one you called Cibylle—Cibylle, was it?" Again she looked at Comtesse with a questioning glance. "She was mad! Certainly Satan lay with her to conceive this child, who is no doubt evil and mad as well. God have mercy on you!"

Beatrice interrupted. "Oh, good Sister, you're mistaken. Cibylle…"

"Hush! No more lies! The bishop will hear of this. You women have never followed the rules. You cavort naked in the garden, and you disavow God's ways with your levitations and strange potions from your unholy kitchen. You're evil! And I'll make sure you pay dearly for playing with the devil." She turned sharply and left the way she'd entered, leaving the door wide open. When she'd gone a few paces, she called out without turning back, "Comtesse! Come!"

Comtesse never looked up. She grabbed her cloak and ran into the night. No one tried to stop her. Her spirit had already left us long ago.

"What should we do?" Helvide cried. She went to comfort Ravenissa, who was ashen. Beatrice gently took Grace from Ravenissa's arms and began to rock the fussing infant. The child became quiet.

"Who could believe it would come to this? Comtesse is responsible..." Beatrice said.

"Shhhh...Suspicion won't help us, especially now." Petronilla paced back and forth in front of the fire.

The same evening our sisters returned from the day's duties. It was a miracle for the second night that the entire sisterhood, save Comtesse, was together at once. We gathered in our circle near the hearth. Mabille lit the candle in the center. I placed the small round stone Cibylle had given me the night of my attack beside the candle. The warmth of the crackling fire and Grace's little squeaks and chirps were comforting. Beatrice rocked her then laid her in the cradle.

An unfamiliar and tainted presence was with us, like the lingering, sour taste of milk left too long in the sun. I looked across the circle at Ravenissa. Her wide stare shone back to me my own fear and confusion. Despite her discomfort, Gertrude sat upright and spirited with Imene by her side.

Sabine drew a long breath. She reached for the stone, signaling she would speak without interruption. She turned it 'round and 'round in her hand, studying it as if to squeeze some ancient guidance from its core. We were silent.

"It's a tragic day, Sisters." Sabine's voice wavered as she spoke. "We must be very careful not to do anything to bring more suspicion. Sister Marguerite's charges are our demise and doom. Later tonight, you, Goscelin and Mabille, are supposed to work in the infirmary. You must carry on with your duties there as though nothing has happened."

"But what if we see her? Is it safe for us to go?" Mabille asked.

"We mustn't show our fear. If we appear fearful, we'll be seen as guilty. You must go to make it appear as though we believe nothing is wrong. We're on the edge of the abyss, in certain danger for our lives, and still more is threatened. The life of our sisterhood is in peril." She paused and clutched the stone to her heart. "We must carefully make our plan...our plan for escape. Let's talk freely to see what arises."

She returned the stone to the center. "I ask for hanswere. Are we in agreement this is what is called for?"

All patted our hearts in accord. Our attention went to the candle flame in the center, the light of God's wisdom and guidance. We prayed without words, prepared to wait for the answers to arise.

Imene looked around the circle. "What shall we do? Sister Marguerite is going to report us. We have no protection now. There's no one to help us."

Beatrice pressed her palm to her heart. "How could she? I knew it was her! It had to be Comtesse. She betrayed us! She's our Judas as surely as…"

"But how could Comtesse know that Cibylle died? How could she know about Grace? She wasn't here the night when it all happened."

I suddenly remembered something.

"Mabille and I went to Cibylle's grave a few days ago. The day I found Henriette. Remember? I asked all of you if you had left her for me to find, or placed the bouquet of herbs there?"

Everyone nodded.

"None of you knew anything about Henriette or the bouquet."

"Comtesse," Mabille said. "It must have been Comtesse who visited the grave. But how could she know where she was buried?"

"How did she find Henriette? Where did she find her?" I said while my mind took in my revelation.

"Please, Sisters, we can't worry about how or why she knew or didn't know," said Sabine. "What's done is done. We need our wits about us to decide what we must do."

Helvide spoke next. "Sabine is right. It's wasted effort to fret about Comtesse. We need a plan for how we'll escape. I suggest we pray in silence to see what comes to us. There's no time for peramony."

We were silent for only a moment before Petronilla stood and went to the center of the circle.

"Sisters, during my fever I had a vision. The meaning wasn't clear to me until now. I believe it revealed the guidance for what we're to do. Listen carefully." Petronilla stood.

"In the vision, we were each making a small bundle. I understood these to be called *portundae.* That's the name I was given. Each bundle held a particular collection of sacred offerings, our relics."

"Our relics?" Helvide asked.

"Yes. According to the vision we must gather... hmmm. Let me think of how to explain it. All of us have things we use each day, humble possessions necessary for our work or personal needs. Consider how two or more of these things might reflect the sacred wisdom you carry. What objects would you choose to express the story...the *essence* of who you are?"

Her words fell upon us like a spell. She appeared changed. Petronilla's frail spirit had been replaced by new strength I'd never witnessed. The Petronilla in our midst giving instructions stood like a beacon of light in the center of our circle. Her arms outstretched wide, bare feet flat on the floor, she spoke with full authority. She was air, but fire was burning within her.

Imene broke the silence. "I don't understand."

Petronilla made a sweeping motion with her arms while she turned 'round and 'round in the center to speak to all of us. "Sisters, the vision's instruction is that we must create our legacy for the future, for those who will reclaim our stories and wisdom one distant day after our bones have turned to dust."

"But why? What value can our old, worn things possibly hold for others, Petronilla?" Imene asked.

"Just as Goscelin has been scribing our stories in our journal, each of us will *show* her particular story through her sacred objects. The relics we choose to leave behind will someday provide wisdom. It's the *wisdom* within the things that will offer healing for others in a time when they will need what now seems commonplace to us," Petronilla explained.

Marie began to cry. "Are we going to die?" Beatrice hugged her close.

Petronilla responded, "Our lives are in danger, this we know for certain. Only God knows if we will survive. For the moment we must act as if death is coming for us, and so we must create whatever is necessary to fulfill our mission."

Marie's tears increased. "I'm afraid. I don't want to die!"

"Please stop now. Your instructions scare us, Petronilla," Ravenissa said.

Gertrude grumbled, "*Ya. Das ist genug*!"

Sabine chewed her nails. "Don't you see? There's no time! It's certain Sister Marguerite will go straight to the bishop tomorrow—if she hasn't already sent a messenger. There's no doubt they'll come for us."

Helvide's hands trembled in her lap. "So let me understand, Petronilla. We're to spend our precious time, perhaps our last hours on this earth, making bundles? Bundles of what? Am I supposed to gather my herbs and Abbess Hildegard's recipes and put them…where? Am I to believe my *portundae* will one day give hope to people I'll never know? Forgive me, Sister, but this makes no sense to me."

"I'm sorry, Petronilla, this makes no sense to me either." Beatrice held Marie tight and struggled for breath. "If we're in imminent danger, we must flee. And besides why would someone...why would anyone want my old wooden spoon, my pestle, and a pot full of honey? How could these things be of any use, especially if they've been gathering dust while waiting for some 'future time' as you say?"

Petronilla clapped her hands together. "Don't you see? It's not for us to understand how our simple lives, our stories, our everyday belongings and tools will possibly offer wisdom to someone."

She knelt before Helvide and spoke calmly. "I'm not privy...we're not privy to know how others will make meaning of all this. How they will know where to find our relics or what special wisdom our spoons and stones, herbs and feathers hold for the future. I only know my visions don't lie. There is purpose, *holy* purpose, in what we are called to do. Our mission is to simply complete the task the vision revealed. We are not doing this for us, but rather for God and the people our *portundaes, our relics,* will one day serve."

Mabille responded, "So this is a call for an act of faith. That's what you're saying. I can understand following an act of faith. Can we all agree that Petronilla's strange instructions are simply asking us to embrace an act of faith?"

I patted my heart first. It took a few moments, but all agreed.

"So be it. I'll wrap my spoon and honey...like a gift, you said?" Beatrice sighed.

"I'll help you, Grand-mere." Marie sniffed.

"Yes, wrap your relics as you would prepare a sacred gift, *un petit cadeau,*" Petronilla replied. "Make the covering from fur or linen, hide or sackcloth. Prayerfully choose your relics then place them in the center of the covering. Fold the corners inward to make a bundle, and bind it with strips of linen, wool, or thong."

"I'll bind mine with wood-vine. Is that all right?" Helvide asked.

"Yes. Lovely, wood-vine is just right for you, Helvide. Trust that whatever you feel you must include will be right."

I had to ask. "How large or how small?"

"No larger than a small loaf of bread. Make your bundle beautiful. Remember, Sisters, you're preserving your wisdom for the ages. We have no way of knowing how much time will pass before our gifts will be reclaimed."

"When? When must we complete our bundles?" I asked.

"There's little time. We must make them tonight so we can leave before dawn." Sabine answered.

"So soon?!" we all replied.

"Yes, because we must leave immediately!" Sabine removed her cap and veil.

Petronilla continued with her instructions. "Goscelin, you *must* scribe the last of our stories and complete our journal. Also, we need a box or basket for storing our bundles. It must be easy to carry. A kind of reliquary to contain our relics."

Gertrude spoke. "Der ist ein chest in de shed. I bilt it for mein tools. It vill be gutte for dis."

"Thank you, Sister. Imene, will you fetch Gertrude's trunk?"

"Yes. I know where it is."

Sabine twisted her apron. "If we must leave very soon, before dawn, where are we going, Sisters? We must make our plan and time is passing as we sit here talking about all this."

"There's more to our instructions, more to the vision," Petronilla replied. "I couldn't have understood the meaning of all I saw until the time arrived. Now that time is here."

"Tell us. Quickly. Let's hear everything now!" Sabine paced.

"We must work swiftly tonight to complete our portundaes. When all is ready we'll fill the chest with our relics and Goscelin's journal. Then we'll go to the abbey we visited on our pilgrimage, Nôtre Dame des Heures, where the anchoress lives. Remember…it's not far. It's the place that appeared to me in my vision."

"What about the animals? The cats and goats? I can't leave them behind!" Ravenissa said.

"We can't take *anything* with us, Sister, no cart filled with our household belongings, not the goat, not anything. Besides, you'll have Grace to care for. Two by two, we'll share the important chore of carrying our chest filled with our relics. That's all we can manage. I'm sorry. This time we must leave with only our lives and the clothes on our backs."

I had felt frightened by all she had told us, but Petronilla's plan for our exodus made my heart quicken with terror. *We could all be dead tomorrow, or worse, we might be captured!*

"Crow must come!" Ravenissa cried.

"Yes. Yes. Crow, of course...and your mouse, too." Petronilla replied.

"How shall we go?" Sabine asked.

"We'll travel north along the river just at the edge of the woods where we can hide and seek shelter if necessary. The river will lead to the abbey. When we arrive we'll tell the anchoress and the nuns of the vision we've been given. They must be made to understand that they, too, are part of the prophecy. I believe they will vow to keep our relics hidden until the others come to claim them."

Mabille began to sob. "We're running for our lives *again*! It's just like the night when we had to leave Belle Cœur. Is this our lot in life? To always be running and hiding? Is there no peace...no home for us?"

Sabine stopped pacing and went to Mabille. "It's different this time, Sister. This is very different. When we left Belle Cœur, we were completing the prophecy given us by the dying pilgrim. His was a prophecy of protection and guidance." Mabille's tears continued to flow. Sabine went on. "This time when we leave here, we're fulfilling Petronilla's prophecy. Her prophecy portrays our destiny, given to us by God through her vision. Yes, we must leave again...but this time we'll receive the peace of knowing we've fulfilled our mission."

It was past time for supper when we finished our discussion, but there was no time to think about eating. We hurried about. Each sister selected her relics, and now we've gathered around the table to make our bundles. I have brought parchment and ink to our table to capture our story as Petronilla instructed.

It's good to be close to one another. I'm grateful we have a task to complete to keep us from thinking of what may happen to us.

I look 'round the table at my weary sisters, but it's Gertrude I study. She sits beside me. Her steadiness is unshakable as she carefully places her treasures on a rabbit pelt with her only hand. I want *her* courage.

I whisper to her, "How did you do it, Sister…climb so high to work alongside the men? Where did you find the courage?"

"God give it to me."

"But how did you survive the pain? I can't imagine falling so far…"

"God held me," she says, as she sweeps her hand through the air to capture the invisible realm fast in her grip.

I reach for Henriette in my pocket and squeeze her tight.

4 May 1259
Le Monastère de la Visite

The devil is roaming, seeking our ruin and destruction. It will be dawn soon.

In the night Mabille and I went to the infirmary and tried not to look terrified. I scrubbed the waste pots, all the while thinking about our escape. Someone called my name.

"Goscelin! Is Goscelin here?"

Sister Marie-Claire pointed to the door. "One of the brothers is asking for you."

My eyes darted about for Mabille, for someone… anyone…to come to my assistance.

Sister Marie-Claire called out, "Goscelin, don't keep Brother Gilles waiting!"

There was nowhere to hide. How dare he come looking for me!

I went toward the open door. Sister Marie-Claire returned to her duties. He was outside waiting in the drizzle and fog.

"If you have something to say to me, you will have to come closer!" I shouted.

"Come here, girl!" he yelled from where he was standing near the path leading to the woods.

"I will not! If you have something to say to me…"

He stomped toward me. I held tight to the door-frame. He grabbed my arm.

"Let go of me! If you have something to say, then say it and leave me be!" I looked him in the eye. The smell of him made my stomach churn. I imagined how it would feel to kick him in the groin.

"Oh, aren't we full of passion tonight? I saw you cross the yard. I've missed you," he hissed.

I tried to pull away.

"Listen, my little thief, meet me after prayers this noon where the stone path turns to dirt, near the grove." He pointed.

"Never! I know what you want, but you'll *not* have it!" I didn't wait for his response. I began to shake all over, not with fear but with a fierce strength that ran through me. In one swift motion, I pulled away from him and shoved the door tight from inside with a loud slam. My commotion alerted everyone nearby. I waited near the door for him to enter, but he didn't come after me. I reached in my pocket for Henriette. She seemed to leap into my hand.

Thankfully, Mabille and I are again safe in our quarters. All the *portundaes* are ready. My sisters have been hard at work. Tonight, any sudden noise—the rustling branch against the shutters, a cart passing on the stony path outside our yard, Marie's cough—keeps me alert. He's lurking about somewhere. My earlier unfamiliar feeling of rage awakened me, as if I suddenly had hidden powers that I never realized I possessed. I'm aghast at my thoughts of how I could possibly kill him if he attacked me again.

Dawn will arrive soon enough.

They'll be coming for us. Sabine's words echo in my mind.

With each passing hour, the threat of our capture becomes more real. I told my sisters how Brother Gilles came after me at the infirmary tonight. They must know how he prowls about in the dark like a beast in search of helpless prey. We cannot be helpless. We will stay close to one another…very close.

I must record this quickly.

When I returned from the infirmary, I gathered my relics for my *portundae.* A moment ago I took a scrap of linen, spread it on the table, and carefully placed my offerings. I folded the linen corner to corner and tied my gift for the future with a brown woolen cord. After careful thought, I have decided the sacred texts, Dominions and Graces, must remain with me. They cannot be part of my *portundae*. I pray to grow old. I pray to continue to fill the four volumes with my notations, until I recognize and pass them along to the next guardian who will carry on the tradition. Contrary to Petronilla's instructions that we must take nothing with us when we leave, I *will* bring Dominions and Graces, and of course Henriette will travel with me in my pocket.

This is a night of completions, yet so much is left unwritten. At last, after all the months of recording our stories, I have just completed binding our journal in haste. It's now ready to add to the chest with our *portundae*.

I bound the parchment folios into the cover of our manuscript with a simple leather stitch as Brother Paul taught me. At the end of the manuscript, I added one fresh folio to have a place to write my remaining thoughts tonight.

Time is running out. This will be my final record… for the moment.

All is ready, we will leave soon, but we can't leave without our prayers and Sacrament. We gather once more near the fire. Shadows play upon the wall. My fatigue and imagination play tricks on me. I swear I saw Brother Gilles's dark form slithering there.

Baby Grace suckles softly at Ravenissa's breast.

Beatrice pours wine into the sacred cup. She puts bread on the plate and places it on the table.

Helvide fetches the carved statue of Magdalene from the nook near the hearth. Imene unwraps the sackcloth covering our blue placard from Belle Cœur; then she sets the small wooden trunk on the table. It has iron hinges and a heavy metal clasp on the lid. Rope handles on either side make it easy to carry. She removes the pin from the clasp and opens the lid.

I think the chest is a sacred vessel, like the ark, in the story of Noah. Gertrude's trunk awaits its precious cargo and the foretold journey that will ensure the safekeeping of all it will hold.

We are seated round the table. Each sister holds her *portundae.*

There is the musky ether of fear in the air but also the scent of iron and women's blood, the smell of our courage. Usually this kind of gathering is a time when we feel peaceful and still, blanketed in our prayers, but not now. No one dares close her eyes. I feel the prickle of our unrest needle my body the way nettles grab the flesh when walking through the tall summer grass.

The fire burns down to glowing embers. Grace is fast asleep; Ravenissa places her in the cradle then joins us at the table.

Our eyes travel 'round the circle, taking in one another's faces. No more tears fall. We are past the place for tears. Sabine speaks first.

"Beloved Sisters, God has blessed us through the years. We've received countless tender mercies these past months, but we know our life as we've shared it is about, yet again, to change." She lights a candle.

"Tonight our preparations ensure that our relics will be preserved until God deems the proper time for our wisdom to be reclaimed. We must draw strength from our faith even though it is tested in the face of our fears."

Sabine walks around the table, gently touching each sister's head. "God has not abandoned us in our desolation. Our Beloved will not fail us. We don't know what awaits or what we must endure. Be at peace and trust that our work and wisdom will live on no matter what becomes of us." Sabine nods to Gertrude.

Gertrude stands. Her stump is wrapped in clean linen like a *portundae.* The wounded remains of Gertrude's arm are a beautiful relic holding the true meaning of survival.

She places her hand on her bundle on the table. Then she touches the open chest. "Dis chest vas bilt to hold mine tools. Now it has new purpose." She takes a cloth from her apron pocket and gives the metal latch a quick polish.

Petronilla stands and places her hands upon the chest. "Sisters, we must pray for the anchoress and nuns we will soon visit at Nôtre Dame des Heures to receive and protect our offerings until the prophecy is fulfilled. On that blessed day, the women of a future time will arrive at the abbey door to reclaim our relics...to make our wisdom their own." Her arms stretch forward to gather us in. "Place your gifts here for safekeeping for the ages."

Sabine returns to her place. "Remember, Sisters, we responded to the prophecy of the dying pilgrim when we left Belle Cœur. We followed his direction to leave our beloved home and make our pilgrimage to Chartres. On the way we were led by other pilgrims to meet the anchoress and to visit Nôtre Dame des Heures. Now that is the place where our relics will be delivered and we trust will be kept safe. Also, when we arrived at Chartres, let's not forget Sister Lunetta, our angel of mercy. She offered us shelter in trade for the good works we've delivered with our whole hearts."

Sabine continues, "The prophecy of the dying man was the beginning. We had to follow his guidance before we could live into Petronilla's prophecy, the instructions for the completion of our mission. One prophecy fits with the other. God is leading us every step of the way. For those whose faith has been shaken, contemplate how our loving God has guided us to this moment and remember how the Beloved cares for us."

Petronilla takes hold of Sabine's hand. "Yes! The prophecies are intertwined. They become the key that fits an ancient latch, to unlock the gate to Eden. One day those who discover the gifts within our sacred cache will no doubt be inspired by God to reopen that very gate."

Sabine sets about the task at hand. She instructs me to scribe the contents of our bundles. I will do so here, in our newly bound book. Each sister comes forward, names her relics, and presents her *portundae* to Gertrude and Imene to be added to the chest.

As the bundles are brought, one by one, I write each sister's name and assign what my heart speaks about her qualities and particular wisdom. Then I record the contents of each bundle according to the sister's description.

Sabine—counselor. *She is competent and practical. Sabine carries the wisdom of resourcefulness, and an understanding of the importance of order. Her relics are, one remaining golden coin stolen from her uncle. A fragment of yellow ribbon from the dress she wore when she first arrived at Belle Cœur. Her string of counting beads used for Belle Cœur's household accounting and her mother's ring reclaimed from the ashes.*

Petronilla—prophetess. *Mysterious and blessed. Petronilla's mystical wisdom radiates from her gifts of visioning, and prophecy. She offers her relics, her white, knotted prayer cord, a wedding gift from her husband. A coquille shell found on our pilgrimage to Chartres. Her little gazing bowl made of bone.*

Beatrice—soothie and cook. *She is motherly and caring. Beatrice's wisdom provides the blessing of, nurturance, and sustenance. She leaves her small, wooden spoon carved by Gertrude. A little wooden honey pot containing two remaining spoonfuls of honey from Belle Cœur. Her mortar and pestle.*

Marie—helpmate. *Wise and tenderhearted. Marie's wisdom reflects curiosity, and play. Her simple offering is her pouch of sticks and stones.*

Helvide—herbalist. *Calm and confident. Helvide's wisdom combines her understanding of the stars, plants, and mineral kingdom. Her relics are, the vade mecum concertina belonging to Abbess Hildegard. Myrtle's small box of XII sacred elixirs. A tiny glass vessel stopped with red wax, containing rainwater from Belle Cœur. Her golden earring, a gift from Myrtle.*

Ravenissa—healer for God's creatures. *She is quiet and benevolent. Ravenissa's wisdom is born from her interpretation and understanding of animal tongues and nature's rhythms. She leaves her relics that include, a single feather from Crow. Her golden earring given her by Myrtle. A large tooth taken from the doe that died in the forest, an amulet given to her by Goscelin. A perfect hummingbird's egg cupped in a tiny nest.*

Imene—midwife. *Steadfast and intelligent. Imene's wisdom is her knowledge of the function of the human body and midwifery. Her offerings are, herbs of blessed thistle and black cohosh. A little forch tool made from a branch of the willow tree at Belle Cœur. Her biting bar used by Cibylle when she was in labor. A vial of her special serum for healing broken hearts.*

Gertrude—carpenter. *Strong and perseverant. Gertrude's wisdom is her understanding of the value and beauty of the sacred handcrafts. The relics she has chosen are, a wooden mallet and pouch of nails. Her pilgrimage amulet with the sign of Belle Cœur on a leather thong. Her knife used for whittling. A small, jagged stone from Chartres Cathedral found in her hand after her fall.*

Mabille—chanteuse. *Gentle and compassionate. Mabille's wisdom comes from her understanding of the spiritual properties of music and song. She offers, a parchment of musical notes for her favorite Psalm given to her by Sister Lunetta. A tiny wooden flute carved by her brother. A yellow snail shell found in the garden at Belle Cœur the day before our pilgrimage began.*

Cibylle—waif. *Beloved and misunderstood. Cibylle's particular wisdom was rooted in her crafting of sacred shrines and candle making. Her relics were prepared by Marie in memory of Cibylle. A walnut shell, and moss collected from one of Cibylle's shrines. A perfect stork feather that fell at Cibylle's feet. These things are carefully wrapped in her apron.*

"What about Comtesse's relics? Shouldn't she be included," I ask.

Sabine looks 'round the circle. "What do we think, Sisters? Is it right that we should choose something of hers to add to our bundles?"

"We could add the small tapestry she's been stitching, the one of Our Lady, and her needle and wool," I suggest.

"Sisters?" Sabine asks.

I pat my heart first and slowly the others follow. Beatrice is the last to agree.

I quickly gather up Comtesse's stitching, her needle and wool.

Comtesse—needle worker. *Secretive and challenging. Comtesse's understanding of the rewards and dangers of risk taking are her wisdom. Her relics prepared by Goscelin include, a small tapestry, her needle, and wool.*

Imene folds Comtesse's things neatly together to make a bundle; then she tucks them in the chest alongside the others. Cibylle's bundle is moved to the top. Finally Imene nestles the carving of Magdalene inside the pocket of Cibylle's apron.

"Oh! And Grace!" Marie cries out. "Surely she has wisdom to share. We can't leave her out."

Ravenissa names her wisdom. "Grace is the perfect symbol of life itself. I have something of hers that will beome her offering."

She leaves the room and returns carrying a tiny folded square of linen in the palm of her hand. Carefully she unwraps it to reveal what appears to be a small, round, brown, shriveled scab.

Marie frowns. "What is it?"

"It's the remains of her birthing cord that connected her to Cibylle. It's the piece of her that fell away from her belly, ten days ago. It's a true relic, Sisters. We know Grace will grow to be loved and revered by many. This little bit of dried flesh represents her. It's a portent for the womb of Creation, the miracle of life, and the return to Eden."

Again, we pat our hearts.

Ravenissa carefully folds the corners of linen over Grace's relic and places it in Imene's hand. She gently tucks it into the folds of Cibylle's apron for protection.

Grace—the child. *Ancient and new. Grace's sacred gift is seeded in her innocent presence as hope for the future. Prepared by Ravenissa, a remnant from her birthing cord.*

I hand my *portundae* to Imene. She adds my bundle to the chest now full with our wisdom. I assure my sisters I will make my final entry for our journal very soon before we set out. There are still things I must write. I record my own description and the contents of my bundle here.

Goscelin—scribe and teacher. *Diligent and trustworthy. Goscelin's wisdom lives in her understanding of the sacred imagination and storytelling. She leaves behind, a brown goose-feather quill, a gift from her teacher. A glass vessel of ochre stopped with red wax. A round black box containing a queen bee. A small bit of parchment where she scribed,*

"May the one who finds these things discover their meaning and make wise use of them again. Goscelin, Scribe of Belle Cœur."

~

All is accounted for. Gertrude closes the lid, and Imene latches it shut, placing the pin through the iron clasp. At last, she fetches our blue placard from our sleeping room. The sight of our beloved sign from Belle Cœur with its cross enclosed in the circle is both a comfort and a sharp reminder of a time we will surely never know again.

Imene puts the mallet in Gertrude's hand, then she holds the first nail in place as Gertrude fastens the sign to the outer lid of the chest. There are three nails in all.

"It is finished." Petronilla crosses herself, and we follow her lead as the last nail is secured. She prays.

"Merciful God, make us ready for what is to come. Make us brave. Let us not betray or deny You should we suffer torture and death. Amen."

Grace begins to wail. Ravenissa takes her from her cradle and puts her to her breast.

I look around the table at my sisters' faces. Each appears far older than when she first arrived at Le Monastère. Our trials, like so many quills, have scribed countless hardships in the lines and crevices upon our faces. Our bodies are like maps. Each sister's earthly journey is there to behold in the scars, fleshy folds, and darkest hidden places of the heart.

We pray for God's forgiveness for our faults and weaknesses. We pray for Comtesse, and then Petronilla begins our ritual with her familiar invitation.

"Sisters, let us share the story of Jesus when he gathered with his friends at the supper table the night before he died."

Marie. "That evening they enjoyed the meal together. His friends were there, men, women, children, and no doubt people who were thought to be untouchable. Jesus welcomed everyone to the table."

Imene. "After the meal while they were all talking among themselves, Jesus took the bread and held it before them. They became quiet to listen to His words."

Beatrice takes the bread in her hands. "He broke the bread and said, 'This is My body. Whenever you eat it think of Me.'"

Imene lifts the cup. "Then He raised the cup of wine and showed it to them. 'This is My blood. When you drink it, remember Me and all we have shared together.'"

Beatrice breaks the bread into ten small pieces. "Sisters, this is the supper Jesus has given. Come to the feast!" She holds the plate before Marie with the words, "Bread for the journey, Sister." Marie takes a piece of bread and holds it. She passes the plate to Helvide with the same blessing. Helvide takes a piece of bread, and the plate is passed from one to the next around the table.

When everyone has received the bread, we eat it. The cup of wine is passed to each sister with the words, "The cup of compassion."

Beatrice and Petronilla clear away the plate and cup. We are silent. We look at one another with the wide eyes of exhaustion and nerves. My prayers are frayed like a worn apron. I cannot hold a thought. My belly churns with fear no matter how many ways I attempt to turn my heart to pray. The fire grows cold, and the center candle burns out with a gasp. We touch the sign of Belle Cœur to one another's foreheads with the blessing, "Hope and wisdom" as we prepare to leave.

Thunder rumbles in the distance, and the south wind blows under the door. The shutters fly open, and Beatrice hurries about to close them. There's the smell of rain, but no rain comes.

Ravenissa nurses Grace. She has sent Marie to the barn to check on the animals before we leave. I think she finds it too hard to bid them good-bye.

What will become of us? We have endured banishment, illness, injury, death, and finally betrayal. Now once again we are in exile. I'm grateful for the blessing to be traveling in such good and loving company.

I must finish and add this journal to our chest. Surely I will find a way to write more as we journey. I am bone tired, but my senses are peaked. My anger seethes at the monk who stained my already trespassed body with his evil.

You could kill him, the voice whispers inside my head. I stop my ears as if that will make me deaf to my own thoughts. In the corner a spider's web glistens and shimmers. I pay attention as the spider quickly wraps his prey in its silken shroud.

I have never been more alert. I have never felt so fierce. Rage has changed me.

4 May 1259
Before Dawn

I scribe in haste atop our sacred chest to record what has happened, while Ravenissa gathers Grace's things for their journey.

The past hour has born disaster. Brother Gilles surprised Marie when she entered the barn. He pulled her into the hay. Her lantern fell. She broke free... raced back to us.

"He came at me! The barn's on fire! He'll be after me."

Ravenissa puts Grace in her cradle, runs to the barn, calls the animals. Fire rages. Brother Gilles is nowhere in sight. Ravenissa herds the donkey into our yard. Many come to smother the fire. We go out to see. Beatrice, Marie, and Grace stay behind.

Two priests appear with Sister Marguerite and Comtesse while the flames rage.

One priest looks at us. He asks Sister Marguerite, "Are these the women?"

"Yes, these are the ones!"

The barn roof collapses. The priests go to help put out the fire.

Chaos! Sabine, Petronilla, Ravenissa, and I freeze with fear. Moments pass. We return to our quarters to find unholy horror.

Beatrice stands over Brother Gilles. His body, slumps in a bloody pool, his eyes are opened wide and his hands wrap 'round the knife handle stuck in his neck.

Beatrice tells us, "He came at Marie! He was going to..." She points toward the cupboard.

Comtesse steps out. Her hands drip blood. "He had to be stopped."

I ask, "Comtesse...you?! You did this?!"

"I had to stop him. I know what he did to you. What he did to many of us!"

We clutch each other tight.

Grace bawls. Ravenissa fetches her. Beatrice comforts Marie. Sabine and Petronilla are crying. I call out for the others. They are gone.

Sister Lunetta bursts in. "My God! What's happened here?! The churchmen will come! You must hide. Follow me! Now!"

I shout, "Run! Hide! Leave him. Leave him to me!"

Comtesse pleads. "Come with us, Goscelin. You must!"

"Soon. I'll find you. Go! Now!"

We kiss through our tears and she flees with the sisters and Sister Lunetta.

Ravenissa stays behind. Puts Grace in her cradle. Fire blazes beyond the wall.

We drag the corpse into the yard and leave it in the darkest corner near the donkey.

Yes! The Donkey! The donkey will carry Ravenissa, Grace, and our relics to the abbey! I must close this book and place it in the chest. My mission's complete! I'll run to the woods when Ravenissa and Grace are safely on their way. But where are the others?

Epilogue

5 September 1277
Belle Cœur

I dip my quill in ink and pray to continue to scribe the story that began when I was born. Meanwhile my sisters go about their work.

The apples in the orchard are nearly ripe for picking. The honey has been harvested from the hive. Autumn will arrive soon. The elder sisters Gertrude, Imene, and Lunetta care for a new generation of villagers. They arrive at our door in need of our medicines and healing prayers.

Our infirmary is safe haven for pilgrims and those traveling the Holy Road to Vézelay. They have heard of the house with the blue sign, and our sisterhood of Belle Cœur.

What these good travelers and villagers don't know is this…

Far from here, there is an abbey where the anchoress and nuns have vowed to hide a simple wooden chest. A chest full with women's relics, and a precious manuscript, the sacred cache of Belle Cœur. In the abbey's crypt, buried beneath a round stone in the floor, the treasure awaits its reclaiming by women who will arrive long after our sisterhood has become dust.

The hope and wisdom that survives within our treasure came with a price. Many of the early sisters of Belle Cœur lived the darkest chapters of our story. They lost their lives at the stake, in a treacherous time of suspicion and danger.

That time is not yet over. However difficult our struggles, we rely on God's mercy and protection and the love within our community. We also depend on the value of the creation of beauty as a welcomed blessing to our unending prayers. We awake each morning to faithfully carry on the work the Beloved has placed in the tender but fierce heart that is Belle Cœur.

My maman, Ravenissa, and the other sisters passed their knowledge to me when I was very young in preparation for the work that lay before me. Work prophesized by the great visionary of Belle Cœur, Petronilla.

I am called to continue the tradition begun by Goscelin, the first keeper of our stories. She was my beloved teacher, the one who taught me the crafts of scribing and illumination. Before she died of fever, she initiated me in the mysteries of Dominions and Graces. As her predecessor of the ancient knowledge, I pray to embody the wisdom of the sacred texts now in my care. I hope to express the same likeness of passion my teacher shared through her quill.

The gentle breeze carries the scent of rosemary through the open shutters. Portia and Mabille sing softly in the garden. Marie sweeps the threshold. Maman tends her goats in the meadow.

I take worn and tattered Henriette from my apron pocket. I am Grace, the scribe of Belle Cœur, and together we will tell you our story.

Author's Message

There is a sisterhood among women that transcends the boundaries of time and space. This kindred understanding of the feminine life and condition is woven into the fabric of our beings, like an Aubusson tapestry...an intricate weaving that for centuries has endured moth and mildew, flood and flame.

The fibers of women's moment-to-moment experiences are spun from the taproot of ancestral wisdom. We encounter our existence intuitively, through our senses. The threads composing our days are imbued with colors harvested from our dreams and visions. Our souls are our looms, and our prayers are our shuttles that over time create the pattern and texture of our lives.

Ink and Honey is a work of fiction, yet the stories of the sisters of Belle Cœur are universal at their core. They are women's stories of friendship and betrayal, vision and longing, passion and fear.

Within these pages, the sisters of Belle Cœur crafted a collective life, a multicolored tapestry, woven with their hands and hearts, tears and laughter, blood and bones. This book is their reliquary. It is the vessel and container for their story. These pages hold the relics and shards of the lives of ancient members of the eternal archetypal sisterhood of women.

I began writing *Ink and Honey* over twenty years ago. The women of the story spilled the fragments of their medieval life in the French countryside onto the pages of my journal. Their voices and spirits visited me in the early morning hours, when in their day they would have been praying Matins or Lauds.

The sisterhood of Belle Cœur possessed my imagination and revealed how they lived in a time when women's lives were fraught with challenge and danger, as well as moments of transcendent beauty and holy grace. I have come to believe their luminous spiritual and creative gifts and their daily unending sacrifices, although fictional in nature, reflect a part of feminine ancestral *her*itage.

The voices of women have literally been silenced throughout the centuries, but through the stories of the sisters of Belle Cœur, those voices return to call us to remembrance. With our remembering is also a call to action and an invitation to reflect on and honor the stories that create *our* lives today.

Over time I gathered the incandescent bits and pieces of the stories of the sisters of Belle Cœur through my early morning meditations with Goscelin, their scribe. I came to know her companions not only as kindred spirits, but also as creative and spiritual mentors. They informed and inspired my life and led me on an inner pilgrimage to visit and examine the depths of my psyche and soul. They also led me on an outer pilgrimage to attend gatherings and circles of women, and to travel to faraway cathedrals to explore the sacred sites of France.

The collective wisdom of the sisters of Belle Cœur invites the reader to explore life through the lens of the sacred imagination and sacred life-arts. They encourage us to become sacred life artisans as purveyors of beauty and carriers of ancient wisdom, made new for the time we are living in. They moved beyond fear and banded together as independent mystics, to create their own unique spiritual order, not unlike the Beguine movement of their day. These women were outrageous for the time they were living in, and they call us to be holy outrageous.

Writing *Ink and Honey* reacquainted me with my senses. The story found its way from my imagination to the page, often igniting a visceral physical response. In those moments, I felt the rough skin of the women's hands through the tips of my fingers, hands chapped from mopping cold stone floors. My nose filled with the fragrance of the herb garden, rosemary and chive wet with morning dew. I tasted the saltiness of the daily bread as it was shared among the sisters by candlelight after hours of caring for the sick. I heard the women's voices whisper their prayers and sing praises to God during the Divine Office. I saw their faces, one by one. The sisters of Belle Cœur appeared to me like long-lost ancestors emerging from a living scrapbook. I recorded all that I experienced while I gazed through an invisible doorway of time and space into an ancient but hauntingly familiar world.

While I served the scribe, Goscelin, as *her* scribe, it was not unlike a homecoming. Long-lost facets of my being were returned, the way the coat and hat, mittens and scarf are hung on their pegs when the pilgrim crosses the threshold, after her journey. During the writing process I was filled with an intense longing to more tangibly know the women in Goscelin's stories, to somehow step through that illusory portal to fully experience their sacred and simple ways of living. From this place of inner desire, I was inspired to create the online sanctuary and resource center for women, SacredLifeArts.com.

During the twenty-year journey to collect the fragmentary remnants of the lives of the sisters of Belle Cœur, their relics were shown to me. The presentation of their gifts was similar to the way the haunting portrait on a sarcophagus is revealed to the explorer when the dust on the ancient tomb is brushed away. Perhaps Goscelin's stories of her sisterhood, like an archaeologist's discovery, reveal the hidden teachings and beauty within the lives recounted here.

What I have come to understand through my writer's journey and my ministry as a spiritual director is this…

Women are sensing the call to make an interior, soulful, pilgrimage of remembrance to reclaim long-forgotten spiritual and creative wisdom. Inspiration lives in the memory of an ancient time when our grandmothers' grandmothers were healers, and alchemy was their language. The map for this mysterious journey of rediscovery is written on our bones. We carry a ready compass within our imaginations. Our spirits are fueled by God's grace. A spiritual and creative renaissance has begun. A sacred caravan of seekers is setting out to retrieve what is needed for the healing and regeneration of our lives. All the while... the lost key to the gate of Eden lays waiting within the stories of women.

Sibyl Dana Reynolds
December 2012

Glossary

Akasha	The essence of all things in the material world
Aller vite	Go fast
Amulet	An ornament or small piece of jewelry believed to provide protection against evil, disease, or danger
Antiphonarium	A large book containing the antiphons and antiphonal chants sung by cantor, congregation, and choir at Mass
Apiary	A place where bees are kept
Aquilegia	

Canadensis	The red columbine plant
Arret	Stop
Armarius	The director (provisioner) of a monastic scriptorium
Asarum	A plant commonly known as wild ginger
Aubergine	Eggplant (a deep purple color, from the French)
Aves	Refers to Ave Maria, the traditional Hail Mary prayer: *Hail Mary full of grace. The Lord is with thee. Blessed art thou among women, and blessed is the fruit of thy womb, Jesus. Holy Mary, Mother of God, pray for us sinners now and at the hour our death.*
Bâtons et des pierres	Sticks and stones (a Belle Cœur child's game, French)
Beguine	A medieval women's independent spiritual movement
Bleue	Blue
Bloody flux	The former name for dysentery, intestinal inflammation causing diarrhea
Bonne nuit	Good night
Cadeaux de nos cœurs	Gifts from our hearts
Cassocks	A full-length garment worn by certain clergy
Cassoulet	A French dish made with duck, legumes, and sausage

Certainement	Certainly
Cescies	A Belle Cœur term for little unexpected gifts from nature
C'est moi	It's me
Chanteuse	Songstress
Chere amie	Dear Friend
Cherubim	Angelic beings
Compline	End of day prayers (see Divine Office)
Connaisez-vous un herboriste?	Do you know of a herbalist?
Coquille shells	Used as markers/guideposts to mark European pilgrimage routes; a symbol worn by pilgrims
Daimon	An attendant spirit of inspiration
Danke	Thank you
Das ist genug	That's enough
Der Friede Gottes sei mit euch	The peace of God be with you
Distaff	A stick or spindle onto which wool is wound for spinning
Divine Office	A cycle of daily prayers of the canonical hours performed by members of religious orders and the clergy. The cycle of eight canonical hours for the performance of the Divine Office: Matins (three a.m.), Lauds (five a.m.), Prime (six a.m.), Terce (nine a.m.), Sext (twelve noon), Nones (three p.m.), Vespers (six p.m.), and Compline (nine p.m.)

Dovecôte	An enclosure, cage, for housing doves
Elle est folle, n'est-ce-pas?	She's crazy, isn't she?
Ennui	Boredom, dryness of the spirit
Ephahatha	Be opened
Epistolarium	A book of Epistles
Etôile	Star
Forch	A forklike stick used for a variety of tasks (Belle Cœur coined word)
Garth	A square plot of land
Genu	Enough
Gichtbaum	Plant used for medicinal purposes
Hanswere	Belle Cœur's method for democratic voting (coined word)
Herboriste	Herbalist
Humors	Sanguine, choleric, melancholy, phlegmatic
Ich muss es selbst tun	I can do it for myself
Illuminations	The embellishment of manuscript pages with luminous pigmented color
Jemney	A sacred juncture of underground streams (coined word)
Je t'aime, Maman, s-il vous plait, pardonnez-moi	I love you, Mama, please forgive me

Je vous salue, Marie, pleine de grace,	Hail Mary, full of grace,
Le Seigneur est avec vous,	The Lord is with you,
Vous êtes bénie entre toutes les femmes, et Jésus,	Blessed are you among women, and blessed
le fruit de vos entrailles, est béni.	is the fruit of your womb, Jesus.
Kalendarium	Calendar of liturgical year
Kin-dom	Reference to God's Kingdom as an inclusive unified form of kindred spirits
L'Abbaye de Saint Catherine	The Abbey of Saint Catherine
Laines	Linen
Lapis lazuli	Ore used as pigment, deep blue in color
La substance de la vie	The substance of life
Lauds	A time of prayer (see Divine Office)
Lavendula angustifolia	The lavender plant
L'eponge	The sponge
Le labyrinthe	The labyrinth
Le Monastère de la Visite	The Monastery of the Visitation
Le plus certainement	Most certainly

Lepry	Leprosy
Les abeilles	Bees
Les cadeaux de nos cœurs	Gifts from our hearts
Les cauchemars	Nightmares
Les champignons	Mushrooms
Legumes	Vegetables
Les petits cadeaux de Noël	Little Christmas gifts
Les sœurs de la Belle Cœur	The sisters of Belle Cœur
Les sorcières	Witches
Les souvenirs	Mementos to remind one of a person, place, or special occasion
Limbo	The page margins of a manuscript
Ma Cherie	My Dear(est)
Malachite	Copper mineral (vibrant green color)
Matins	A time of prayer (see Divine Office)
Melange	A medley
Memento mori	Reminder of death...of one's mortality
Mon conteur bénie	My blessed storyteller (raconteur)
Mon Dieu!	My God!
Mother-round	Myrtle's name for her pagan prayer beads
Mugwort root	An herb believed to increase the dream life
Naturellement	Naturally, of course

Nos cœuragerie	Goscelin's coined word for the Belle Cœur order/sisterhood
N'est-ce-pas	Aren't you, isn't she, didn't he, etc.
Nones	A time of prayer (See Divine Office)
Novacula	A sharp knife used for cutting parchment
Ochre	Earth pigment (golden yellow or brownish yellow)
Ordinale	A guide to the celebration of the liturgy
Oui! Elle est folle!	Yes! She's crazy!
Oui, le plus certainement, bleue!	Yes, for certain, blue!
Oratory	A place of prayer
Pagan	Country folk or someone holding a different religious belief from mainstream culture
Pain du lait	Bread and milk
Parchment	Animal skin (usually goat or sheep) specially prepared to receive writing with ink
Parchmenter	A person responsible for making parchment
Peramony	A Belle Cœur ritual for dreaming and visioning
Petite Etôile	Little Star

Phitre	A magic potion or charm
Portundae	A sacred bundle containing the relics of a sister of Belle Cœur
Potage du pommes de terre et legumes	Potato vegetable soup
Pour certains c'est qu'elle était un guérisseur	For some she was a healer
Poustinia	A quiet humble place where one goes to pray and be in the presence of God
Prenez garde des abeilles	Beware of the bees
Prime	A time of prayer (see Divine Office)
Protégée	A woman or girl whose welfare and training is provided by an influential teacher
Psalms of Ascent	Title given to specific group of Psalms (120–134)
Quel est vôtre nom?	What is your name?
Quinta essential	The fifth element (essence) after earth, air, fire, and water that expresses the invisible nature of life
Quintessence	The fifth and highest element in nature
Quires	Booklet forms that make up the pages of a manuscript
Regula	Regulation and a specific form/order
Reliquary	A container for holy/sacred relics

Retort	A device made of glass used for alchemical distillation
Réveillon de Noël Mass	Christmas Eve Mass
Rien ne pèse tant un secret du cœur	Nothing weighs like a secret on the heart
Rosa gallica	A species of rose native to central Europe
Sanctorale	Prayers pertaining to the saints' days
Schwester	Sister
Scriptorium	A room for writing particularly illuminated manuscripts (in a monastery)
Seraphim	An angelic being of the highest celestial order
Sext	A time of prayer (see Divine Office)
Shinorage	The reading of the stars and heavens for guidance
Sigils	An image or sign thought to hold magical meaning
S'il vous plaît	Please
Skep	A vessel made of straw for containing bees and their hive
Soothie	Belle Cœur term for wet nurse (coined word)
Squint	A little pass-through window between the anchorage and the sanctuary where the anchoress receives communion

Stachys officinalus	A plant commonly known as bishop's-wort
Talisman	An object believed to have magical powers often used as a symbol of protection or luck
Templar Knights	An order of knights founded in the twelfth century to protect pilgrims during the Second Crusade Terce A time of prayer (see Divine Office)
Toile	Linen
Toile et laines	Linen and wool
Tonnerre	Thunder
Tonsured head	Portion of a monk's head shaved bare at the top
Touchez-le, ma cherie	Touch it, my dear
Un, deux, trois	One, two, three
Un guérisseur	A healer
Un petit cadeau	A little gift
Une sorcière	A witch
Verbena officianallis	A vibrant plant with showy white, red, or purple flowers
Venesection	Obtaining blood from a vein
Vermilion	Vibrant red sulfuric oxide (pigment)
Verdegris	A greenish-blue copper pigment
Verte ou bleue	Green or blue
Vespers	A time of prayer (see Divine Office)

Vigils	A time of prayer (see Divine Office)
Vite	Quickly
Wimple	A cloth worn around the head and under the chin, an underpinning for a veil

Acknowledgements

Gratitude to my beloved sisters of the APC circle for their heartfelt inspiration and support: Christina Baldwin, Kimberly Gilbreath, Ann Linnea, Sarah MacDougall, Harriet Peterson, Pamela Jean Sampel, Linda Secord, Clare Taylor, and Kit Wilson.

I am grateful to my many friends, teachers, and mentors who have lent their listening ears and shared their wisdom on the long journey to the completion of this book. My deep appreciation to Kathleen Adams, Laurie Sandblom, Karen Blessen, Mati Vargas Gibson, Barley Vogel, Victoria Rue and Kathryn Poethig, Nadine Palau, Valerie Rickel, Tricia Kibbe, Trish Thompson, Kathy Williams, Bonnie Bufkin,

Julia Spinetta, Jane Cather, Olivia Doko, Suzanne Thiel, Juanita Cordero, Jane Via, the women and men of Roman Catholic Womenpriests, Jules Hart, Andrew Harvey, Christine Valters Painter, June Boyce Tillman, Susan Barrett Merrill, Patti Barrett, Lawrence Manglitz, Nancy and Dave Phillips, Drew and Gwendolyn Field, Paul and Elizabeth Wrightman, and my dear friends at the Community Church of the Monterey Peninsula, Pam Carroll, Nancy King Monk, Pamela Takigawa, and Sue Williams.

Always and forever gratitude to my husband, Don Reynolds, and my beloved family for your inspiration and support: Jason Reynolds; Amy, Brad, and Haley Richardson; Barbara Carduff; Stacey and Bill Heisler, Alex Carduff, Chris and Elizabeth Carduff, Jim and Joan Hiltabidel, Sharon Gooding, Jill Reynolds and your families; and Sharolyn Richardson.

To my dear friends who have traveled on beyond the veil: Prissy Atherton, Anita Middleton, Susan Stahl, and eternal gratitude to Kedron Bryson, my dear friend, editor and midwife for *Ink and Honey*.

Lastly, I thank the Beloved for inspiring me to tell the story, and for leading me on an awe-inspiring and unforgettable twenty-year journey.

An Invitation from the Author

Please visit www.InkandHoneytheBook.com where you will find the *Ink and Honey* downloadable guide and discussion questions for reading groups and book clubs, as well as, information pertaining to upcoming events, online classes, and workshops.

To learn more about the sacred life-arts, please visit www.SacredLifeArts.com, Sibyl Dana Reynolds' online sanctuary, classroom, and resource center devoted to bringing creative inspiration and spiritual illumination to women.

Made in the USA
San Bernardino, CA
03 December 2013